The Floors

Lucian Poll

Copyright © 2013 by Paul Collin, writing as Lucian Poll

This is a work of fiction. Names, characters, places and incidents are either the product of the author's imagination or are used fictitiously, and any resemblance to actual persons, living or dead is entirely coincidental.

All rights reserved.

ISBN-13: 978-1-490-39301-8

http://lucianpoll.com

This is for anyone with a story to tell.

Write it down and believe.

CRUX CANNIBAL STRIKES AGAIN!

Body parts thrown onto sidewalk in broad daylight

SEATTLE MAIL EXCLUSIVE!

by William D. Summerville, Chief Crime Editor

The hunt for the Crux Cannibal intensified dramatically yesterday afternoon when several gruesome body parts rained onto shocked bystanders.

The incident occurred at approximately 2.20pm outside the Crux Capital building in the Central Financial District, an area of Seattle already nervous of the killer's next move and his apparent motives.

Bones

Witnesses spoke of a hail of long, bloody bones, mostly picked clean, hitting the sidewalk. An elderly man, believed to have been struck by one of the bones, was treated at the scene by paramedics.

Our reporter received unconfirmed reports that the remains were mostly scorched and bore knife marks. Bones that were mysteriously cast onto the same spot two months ago were later confirmed to be human.

No body

Police were quickly called to the scene and stormed the Crux Capital building in an attempt to capture the killer. Using sniffer dogs they worked through each floor but could find no trace of the Crux Cannibal, nor an apparent victim.

The audacity of the killer's latest move has rocked confidence in the Seattle Police Department, and has seen pressure mount on Mayor Dagliani to step up patrols in the Downtown area.

From the front page of The Seattle Mail, Tuesday, 3rd June 1986

The gun turrets in the ceiling juddered into life and trained their red laser sights onto Clive's bony chest. He stopped dead in the T-junction. The soles of his trainers squeaked in protest against the polished metal floor. He squinted and tried to focus.

A striped line of yellow and black ringed the interior of the corridor, unmistakable in the subtle lighting. Beyond the line was clearly a no-go. A short distance ahead was a steel door and, beside it, a single window.

It was the closest thing to an exit he could remember since becoming trapped in this place.

Trapped.

He chewed over the word. It was odd how a lean spell had altered his perspective. For a long time he'd considered himself the King of the Castle. The one chosen to enjoy the shortest odds in this survival of the luckiest. But time always got its man. Over a long enough period everything resolved to nothing. Those favourable odds, it seemed, were salted.

He saw the tall backrest of a black leather chair through the window, tucked neatly beneath whatever table or console lay on the other side. Perhaps someone was there.

'Hello?'

His voice echoed around the corridor.

The lasers continued to pinpoint his heart. He placed a hand in the way and watched as the turrets retargeted a point lower down, perilously close to his testicles. However cloudy his mind had become, at least he still had the sense to know the guns meant business.

'Hello?'

Still nothing.

There were large foreign characters stencilled in red on the walls of the no-go area. Some numerals too. He guessed the backwards Rs made the text Russian.

What was Russian for "hello" again?

'Allo?'

Again, no response.

Fuck it.

He took a few steps toward the line. The turrets smoothly tracked his approach, their barrels spinning faster the closer he came. The corridor filled with a whirring sound, increasing in pitch. The turrets were readying for the kill.

It didn't matter. Better he died on his own terms than to be hunted down like an animal. With no means to defend himself he was a sitting duck. No way would he let his scrawny arse form some bastard's next meal.

He crossed the yellow and black line and kept his eyes on the steel door, only metres ahead. Perhaps if he could get to it and bang his fists against the window then someone...

The sound of gunfire filled the wide corridor. The first bullet caught him in the ribcage. A small explosion made mincemeat of his insides and blinded him with agony. A second bullet shredded his heart.

In that instant a terrible memory flooded his dying mind. He had been bludgeoned by something heavy and red. He felt his knife hand being hacked away. He saw a swarm of flies close in on him and then all was darkness.

*****

The guns spun down. Smoke slid out from their barrels and up into the polished metal ceiling. A couple of spent shells ricocheted around the corridor. Unexploded, they eventually rolled along the floor to a stop.

The man had vanished.

• PART ONE •

THE KILLING FLOORS

Flies lay claim to office block

"We keep killing them but they keep coming back!"

by Rachael Moyne
Environment Correspondent

Businesses occupying the upper floors of one of Reading's premier office buildings, Berkshire Tower, were once again forced to call in pest controllers to deal with another invasion of bluebottles.

Employees of Infoclamp, a computer security firm, were forced to evacuate the fourteenth floor and take another afternoon's leave. Dave Bryte, co-owner, said of the latest disruption, "It's frustrating. Our projects require a lot of on-site work. These disruptions are eating into already-tight deadlines from our big clients."

The flies have repeatedly infiltrated the twelfth and fourteenth floors over the last six weeks. Their repeated appearance has been a source of embarrassment for the building's owners, British Property Securities PLC, who are keen to avoid an imminent investigation

Excerpt from The Reading Evening Herald
Thursday, 19th July 2012

CHAPTER ONE

Clive's house reeked of petrol. The fumes poisoned his tear ducts and made his eyes sting. If only he'd had the foresight to bring some goggles.

He adjusted the swimmer's nose-clip for comfort. One breath of the toxic soup surrounding him and he would surely collapse and die. He checked the gauge on his tank. So long as he didn't panic he had around ten minutes' air remaining. He glanced at his wristwatch and saw it was more like five. Enough time to get what he needed, but little more.

He took in a cold squirt of air and listened to the hiss of his breather.

The oven before him hissed in return, its door wide open, its four hobs urgently belching gas into the kitchen. Someone would come later to disconnect the mains. Another to take away the keys.

Let them try.

His lips curled up around the breather.

A trio of opened jerry cans, filled with petrol, stood in the middle of the kitchen. He had purchased them from a local army surplus store over a number of weeks. The guy never once questioned why anyone would need close to a hundred jerry cans. Neither did his rival.

Another couple of cans littered the hallway alongside the kitchen. The dark blue carpet upon which they stood squelched beneath his Doc Martens as he took to the stairs.

The middle floor sported a box room, a bedroom and a lounge. The top floor had a bathroom, another bedroom and a master bedroom with en-suite. The house was the same as the one next door, and the house next door to that. All three were his, each laced with petrol, each filled with gas.

All of the doors were propped open to let the fumes gather and mingle. As he walked by each room he checked on the jerry cans inside.

A mountain of paper dominated the centre of the lounge. Flecks of red from countless reminders, final demands and other threatening letters lent the pile a sickly chickenpox veneer. Every sheet told its own chapter of his dismal life.

Remortgaging his house to buy three properties off-plan at the height of the housing market had proved to be the biggest fucking mistake he ever made. It seemed a no-brainer at the time, but when he held the keys in his hands he quickly realised he'd bought three houses scarcely larger than rabbit hutches, at vastly inflated prices. "Bijou" was how one estate agent had later described them, as if tiny rooms were somehow a fucking selling point. The builder went bust, the mortgages bit and his savings were quickly wiped out subsidising rents from tenants who seldom stayed put. No-one in their right mind would buy them at the prices he demanded - prices he could ill afford to drop. All available credit cards were quickly maxed, leaving his credit score low enough to be counted on fingers and thumbs. It had been several months since he had a paying tenant in any of the houses.

The last thing he needed was to lose his job.

Not that any of that shit matters any more.

He walked into the lounge. A further four cans of petrol surrounded the pile of paper as if they were worshipping a God. He stepped around them to a large cork pin-board covered with prints of various sizes. The board rested against a scuffed stud wall.

His shrine.

Pictures of the same young woman were pinned to the cork, each taken during the last three years. In most of them the woman had no idea she was being photographed. In all the others she looked furious. Each image had their background meticulously cut away, leaving only her.

Dawn McKenzie.

He knelt by the board. He opened the door to a nearby display case and took a stiletto from the bottom shelf. He ran the fingers of his left hand gently down the collection of photographs.

His was a shrine built initially on lust, a testament of his waking obsession. There were early, now yellowing shots from Dawn's first days at Hardingham Frank, when she sported unnaturally black hair as straight as an arrow and long enough to brush her shoulders. It was a vampy look that she couldn't quite pull off, but it had caught Clive's eye. In a handful of other photographs she had auburn hair, equally unnatural and cut into a disastrous blunt bob. (The photos had been spared the shredder solely because her nipples could be seen poking through her blouse.) But Dawn's current style was little short of knockout. An earthy-brown cross between a pixie cut and a punk-rock bob with dark blonde highlights. Combine that with her mischievous face, her slim, almost boyish build, her amazing tits and her pale skinny legs - well, that made her too damned fuckable. Dangerously so when he factored in Mike, her gorilla of a boyfriend.

Then she cost him his job.

Dawn Lying-Bitch McKenzie.

It took a few short minutes for him to be escorted from the building, but in that time he had figured out a plan. At long last he had found a use for the three shitheaps that were bleeding him dry.

When embarking on a campaign of revenge it often paid to keep any incriminating stuff out of sight. Stuff such as the million and one reminders and final demands. Stuff such as the couple dozen DVDs of violent pornography. Stuff such as his display case and, of course, his shrine of hate.

Each and every photograph on the pin-board saw Dawn's eyes filled in with black ink. For some photos he had pushed map pins into the black holes, making them look like bizarre antennae. In her angrier photos he had pushed brass drawing pins into her eyes. He did the same for a picture where he had caught her by surprise, giving her an eerily comical expression.

The one picture that started all of this, however, the one where she had genuinely come onto him, the photo that still got him hard most mornings in the shower, the one where her eyelids were lowered and her lips pursed almost into a kiss - the one taken from across the office floor. That photograph received the full force of the stiletto blade, right in the middle of her conniving bitch forehead. In her mouth he stuck a large, deep-red coloured drawing pin, making her look like a murdered sex doll.

By the end of the day, it would be the best she could hope for.

He lifted the corkboard onto the heap of papers, pushing down until he heard the DVD cases at its core slipping against one other. He opened the door to the tall display case once more. He took a second to admire the collection he was about to leave behind. In the midsection there stood a beautiful black crossbow, clad in carbon-fibre and accompanied by sleeves of incredibly sharp bolts. There lay on the shelf above a selection of repainted replica handguns and lovingly-restored antique revolvers. On the shelf below lay another stiletto knife, a couple of ornate daggers and a machete supposedly used to murder three women in Suffolk.

The top shelf, however, was reserved for Clive's pride and joy: a pair of parangs - heavy hunting knives with staggeringly sharp blades, eighteen inches long. Chopping, cutting, skinning, they could do the lot.

He glanced at his wristwatch. It was a shade after nine a.m. The lambs would be gathering at Hardingham Frank for another day of fucking people over. His house would have gone up by now, it was scheduled to detonate on the dot of nine. In three minutes this house and its neighbours would follow suit.

You're cutting it fine.

He removed the parangs from the display case and slid them into the sheaths that hung from his belt. Their sturdy plastic handles rattled against his holstered handguns.

Two guns. Two blades. Showtime.

With both hands clamped on the handles of his parangs, Clive barrelled down the stairs and hurdled over the jerry cans. The front door lay ahead and beside it, hanging from a hook, his long black overcoat. Though London was baking in the midst of an Indian summer there was something to be said for the coat's large, useful pockets. He pulled it on and savoured the feel of the cool fabric.

He slipped a hand around one of the guns, unable to resist. He pulled it from the holster, just an inch, enough to feel its pleasing weight. He imagined the looks of his former colleagues immediately before plugging them with hot lead: the way Stevens, the insufferable shit from marketing, would beg for his life, hiding behind his secretary all the while; or how the tireless bell-end Cocaine Dale would laugh his arse off, initially thinking it all a prank; and Barnes, his boss. Sorry, ex-boss. Soon to be ex-living. Clive let the gun slide back in the holster, happy in the knowledge he was about to put that supercilious bastard into the ground.

The first decent day of 2013 came to Clive's mind. What should have been a glorious sunny morning enjoyed by all had somehow descended into accusations of a drink problem, gross misconduct and lewd behaviour from his supposed colleagues and superiors.

By sundown he was as drunk as he was sacked, pissing away what little money he had on him.

And all because of you, Dawn.

He stroked the handle of a parang. He took a long squirt of air.

Oh, you lying little bitch, I'm saving the best for you.

His holdall sat open on the other side of the front door. He glanced over its contents. A pair of submachine guns lay amid a motley collection of ammunition clips. They looked tiny for the money they cost. The last of his money.

Best that he made every bullet count. It was time to move, time to show everyone they couldn't fuck with Clive Brown and expect to get away with it. Nobody would be spared. Security? Fuck 'em. Let them try to stop him.

Oh, please let Mike try.

He reached for the handle of the front door and almost shat himself when the lid of the letterbox rattled open.

'Mr Brown? Bloody Nora!'

The lid slammed shut again. Whoever it was, the man outside was the last thing Clive needed. It felt for a second like someone had replaced his spine with an icy live cable. A fresh layer of sweat oozed from his pores.

He focused on the agenda for the day and cleared all doubt from his mind. He took one last lungful of air, threw the breathing apparatus onto the floor and opened the door.

A man in his mid-thirties stood outside, his fist raised and ready to knock. In his other hand he held a leather-bound folio of papers. The bank's embossed logo gleamed in one of the corners. Clive shoved him to one side and strode along the garden path.

'Mr Brown?' said the man, catching him up. 'Mr Brown, what are you doing?'

'Fuck you.'

'Why have you left the gas on, Mr Brown? That is very irresponsible. We're only doing our job. Now we're going to have to call the fire brigade *and the police* to sort this out.'

Clive dug a large bunch of keys from his overcoat, turned and threw them against the partially open front door. They landed onto the welcome mat with a dull, chinking thud.

'For goodness sake, Mr Brown,' said the man. He dashed back to retrieve the keys.

Clive picked up the pace and hurried towards his car, parked thirty yards ahead. He had no idea whether it was far enough. The contents of his holdall and holsters rattled and clanged much more loudly than he'd hoped. He looked around for witnesses.

Don't pussy out on me now. We're doing this.

Once inside the car he placed the holdall in the passenger seat and looked in the rear view mirror. Bloodshot eyes blinked back at him. They were the last pair of eyes many would see today. That cold icy stare locking on. A look so utterly devoid of mercy.

In the mirror he noticed the man from the bank scampering towards him. The man's expression was of impotent anger.

He was of no concern. Clive turned the key in the ignition and watched as his three shitheaps went up in quick succession.

BANG! BA-BANG!

The flashpoint momentarily blinded him. The windows of each house blew out in a fiery roar. The shockwaves of the explosion rocked the car and kicked in the rear windscreen, scattering glass everywhere. Clive ducked in his seat and checked his cracked wing mirror. His vision cleared quickly. He watched his front doors cartwheel into the cul-de-sac. One of them struck the shredded man from the bank before he could fully settle on the tarmac.

The way the man's head snapped backwards suggested he wouldn't be getting up again.

The explosions continued as each cluster of jerry cans detonated, punching large holes through the walls of each house. Chunks of masonry thudded against the roof of the car and shattered on the road. A few DVD cases clattered into the gutter. Scorched papers fluttered down and settled on the pavement. Thick black smoke poured into the deep blue sky and all around rang with the sound of a hundred and one alarms going off at once.

Clive pulled away and drove to work.

CHAPTER TWO

Dawn replaced the receiver and shuddered.

'Babes.'

She spat the word under her breath and rolled her eyes. Had there ever been a more loathsome term of endearment outside of "bitch"? She fancied not.

She loved Mike to bits, but once he got among his colleagues in security her fiancée would always act like The Big Man. The knowledge that it *was* an act never failed to grate on her. Yes, his machismo had once been a big draw, but only within the context of a throwaway fuck. She hadn't expected to go and fall in love with the big-hearted lunk hiding beneath all those muscles.

'Babes.' She sighed.

For all her good work over the years the guy still had a few too many rough edges. He needed a little extra *conditioning*. And so "babes" became the next thing for her to stamp out before the wedding.

'What was that, sweetheart?'

She knew who had spoken before the man had a chance to open his mouth. It was Joe, one of the admin clerks from the main office behind her desk. She knew almost everyone at Hardingham Frank by their footsteps. It helped her identify those more forgiving of Spider Solitaire.

Joe sidled around the front of her tall desk. He leaned forward slightly, crossing his forearms against the edge and letting the desk take his weight. He had an expectant look on his pale, slightly-sagging face. A strand of black hair came loose from his side parting.

'No,' said Dawn. 'Not you.'

'Not yet?' Joe wiggled his eyebrows up and down in a poor impersonation of Groucho Marx. His dark brown eyes were alive with good humour and crusty bits of sleep.

'Not ever, Joe. Sorry.'

Joe clutched his heart and moaned with expertly overworked melodrama. He spun on his toes and pushed his bottom lip outwards in a show of mock hurt. Once, over Friday drinks, he'd referred to it as his "pet lip", which baffled precisely everybody at the table. Whatever his lip was called it didn't make the guy look any more appealing.

'Oh, light of my life, whatever happened to us?'

'Gee, I don't know, Joe,' said Dawn, playing along. 'Perhaps you knew one joke too many about dead babies.'

'That *still*? Come on, it was one joke!'

'Still one too many, Joe.'

His shoulders slumped and Dawn felt a small pang of guilt. Perhaps it was too low a blow to deal him so early in the day. He'd been rat-arsed when he told the joke, and only blurted it out to compete with the other, more puerile, guys of the firm.

What's grosser than gross? Finding twelve dead babies in a bin.
What's grosser than that? Finding a dead baby in twelve bins.

That bloody machismo thing again.

Dawn watched as Joe straightened up. Despite the jocular front he put up for everybody, there was something not quite right about him, dead baby jokes notwithstanding. His face would sometimes slip when he thought nobody was looking, revealing a sadness in his eyes.

And when someone loses a bit of weight, wouldn't you expect them to look a little *healthier*?

Either way the guy badly needed a girlfriend. Someone to smarten him up a little and make him realise he needn't try so hard to be liked.

'So what happened here?' said Joe, pointing to Dawn's desk. A flat nineteen-inch computer monitor stood at an awkward angle, powered off, with a single kettle lead plugged into the back. Strips of tape held a sheet of clear plastic over the screen.

'My monitor died. Gil brought this one up for me but it needed a different cable.'

Joe examined the rear panel of the monitor.

'Yeah, the DVI's in the detail,' he said.

'What?'

'Hashtag geek-humour,' he said. 'DVI cables. You'd think they'd make them all the same, wouldn't you, but nope!'

'Joe, go and have sex with someone,' said Dawn. 'Please!'

'Well, there's a Friday night ahead of us, Dawn. Anything can happen,' he said. 'Right. I'm off for a slash and a fag. I'll be back in ten.'

'Thanks for the image.'

Joe walked away across the polished concrete floor, unconsciously patting his pockets. Dawn let her eyes drift down the back of his cheap grey suit jacket. For all she saw Joe as a colleague, she had to admit the guy had a nice arse.

Mike had muscles to spare. They were honed, rock-hard and such she could spend hours running her fingers over, but the fact remained her fiancée had an arse you could iron a shirt on. His arse was proof of one of life's truisms. A universal constant that decreed a girl can never quite have it all.

The heavy door to the gents toilets slammed shut. Its echoes rang along the wide elevator lobby and towards Dawn's desk, carrying with it an unexpected chill that caused her skin to prickle. She could sense no breeze, just a momentary coldness. She rubbed her arms and glanced around the corridor. The chill could have come from anywhere, not that she was surprised.

She had long considered the fourteenth floor of 3 Donnington Place to be a sterile affair, epitomised by the lobby she attended day in, day out. It was a charmless place of grey-veined, marble-clad walls and overly-polished concrete floors. There was a huge plate glass window at the opposite end that offered the obligatory dramatic view of London's docklands to the few who could be bothered to walk over to it. Closest to Dawn, around twenty yards ahead, there stood a pair of opposing brass elevator doors that the cleaning staff would buff each week, only for them to attract an inexplicable number of fingerprints come Friday. Beyond the elevators there stood opposing stairwell doors for use in an emergency, or by those with a penchant for hundreds of stairs. A pair of doors further along the right led to separate ladies and gents toilets. A single door opposite those offered a combined kitchen and recreation area.

The whole ensemble was so very Modern London, utterly Big Business and Somewhat Soulless.

The thumping echoes eased, leaving in their wake the tail-end of a strange whisper that slithered along the corridor towards Dawn's desk.

...hhhawwwnnnnneeeeee...

A breathy sound. Almost musical. Taunting her. A call she had not heard for years.

'No way.'

Her eyes darted to each of the doorways in turn, looking for movement - the lift and sigh of a stairwell door, perhaps - but finding none.

There! A small dark shape quickly moved away from the bottom right corner of the large window ahead.

'What the hell?'

The inside of her mouth turned to sandpaper and her heart thumped. She kept her eyes trained on the window while her brain took a few flying guesses.

Something that dropped from above? Or a bird? A pigeon?

She found herself unable to blink.

Would a pigeon bother coming this high up? Where would it land? There are no sills outside.

She froze. The window had her - or more accurately the thing outside the window. She ran the image once more through her mind. It had looked for all the world like a grey distended hand.

Stop looking, damn it!

A faint sound of disorder distracted her. She couldn't tell In which stairwell it came from, but it broke the spell she was under. She took her seat, caught her breath and wished Gil would hurry the hell up.

The familiar hum and buzz of Hardingham Frank's open-plan office helped calm her nerves. The *blip-blip-blips* of desk phones commingled with a gentle undercurrent of Friday morning chitchat, creating a pleasant noise that reassured her she was not alone. Working eight hours a day with one's back to it all made it easy to forget at times. She turned in her chair and examined the imposing partition that hid the rest of the office from view. Around eight feet up from the cold concrete floor "Hardingham Frank" had been set into the plasterboard using thin, silver lettering, alongside it an achingly-corporate and utterly nonsensical logo.

The firm specialised in claiming compensation for mis-sold payment protection insurance. Prior to that, compensation for industrial accidents. As a result Hardingham Frank had garnered an ill reputation among the other tenants of the building. "Another day of raping the poor?" was a common greeting.

The taunts made Mike furious, doubly so when he witnessed them first-hand. The sex they brought out of him, however, was fantastic. Dawn explained afterwards, bathed in sweat, flopped over his broad chest like a smoking-hot ragdoll, that loosening the teeth of a few shithead office workers simply wasn't worth it, or at least not for deputy-heads of security.

The noise in the stairwell rose again, still faint, yet louder than before and more sustained. Some banging too. She wondered what on earth was going on. It sounded like a fight had broken out.

'Good morning, Dawn,' said Mr Wilkes. He walked out from a small office to the left of Dawn's desk carrying a sheaf of large designs. He was a slim, white-haired gentleman who stood over six feet tall and looked good in a waistcoat. Not for the first time that week Dawn found herself wishing he was her dad.

Better him than the one I wound up with.

'It's a lovely day out there,' Mr Wilkes continued.

'All the worse for being stuck in here,' she said, shrugging.

In a floor largely dominated by Hardingham Frank, Wilkes Kneale Sanderson was a relatively small firm of four architects - with the fourth guy presumably a latecomer to the party. Occasionally they would leave open the blinds to their office, offering a peek of their latest project. The small white buildings of the scale models fascinated her, helped in no small part by the dull nature of her job.

An old bugbear briefly surfaced. She got a two-one at university for this? To become an insipid, grinning gatekeeper to a den of sharks?

Two more years, she promised herself. Just another two years and she'd be out of there.

You said that three years ago.

'Are you working on anything interesting?' she said as Mr Wilkes walked away.

The phone on her desk *blipped* and flashed into life, cutting short the architect's reply. She picked up the receiver as she watched Wilkes walk further down the corridor. Surely he wasn't going to take those designs into the toilet with him?

'Hardingham Frank?'

'Dawn!'

It was Barbara from the front desk of the ground floor.

'Dawn, oh, Jesus, Dawn!'

Barbara's voice trembled wildly as she spoke. In the background Dawn heard an almighty commotion. Shouting. Screaming. Crashes and bangs. They all coalesced into an incomprehensible noise above which Dawn struggled to hear what Barbara said next.

'Barbara, what's wrong? What's going on down there?'

'Oh, God, Dawn, it's *Clive*!'

'Clive?'

The man's name turned Dawn's backbone to ice. She could feel her skin contract as claws of the deepest cold dug into her flesh.

'For God's sake, Dawn, run! Get everyone out and *RUN*!' screamed Barbara. 'He shot Mike and he's-'

The elevator doors pinged open and a roar of gunfire drowned out the last of Barbara's words. Deafening peals of fire alarms burst from everywhere and echoed endlessly around the unforgiving interior of the corridor. Dawn dropped the receiver from nerveless fingers, and watched as Mr Wilkes' body was thrown against the opposite elevator by the force of the bullets. The polished brass doors offered little resistance as his twitching, bleeding body slid down to the floor. A second salvo rendered the man still, leaving a dark red pool to grow beneath him.

The body of a second man was thrown from the elevator. It slapped down hard against the polished floor and slid to a halt, leaving a short, bloody snail trail on the concrete. The man had a frozen, open-mouthed look of terror, the horror of his impending death tattooed into every muscle of his face. Then Dawn saw the awful wound. His throat hadn't been so much cut as his neck sliced through to the bone. His short-sleeved shirt bore more red than white. His arms were heavily streaked with blood. In his hands he clasped a cable. It was Gil.

The alarms yielded briefly for an automated announcement.

This is a fire drill. Please evacuate the building via the stairwells and fire escapes. I repeat: this is a test.

THE FLOORS

The awful racket resumed.

Dawn ducked behind her desk, keeping out of sight as best she could. The blinds of the architect's office twitched. Over the incredible sound of the alarms she heard someone nearby shouting to her. Cocaine Dale was in the open doorway to Hardingham Frank's office area. He had a bug-eyed look that suggested he could die of fright any moment as he held out a hand.

'Dawn! Come on, Dawn!' he yelled. His eyes were even wider than usual.

'Dale, it's Clive!' she cried. She reached for him and made a move to stand.

'Clive?' said Dale. 'Shit! Come on, we're using our fire escape.'

She shot a glance back to the blinds of the small office. They no longer moved. The other three architects were obviously still inside. For a horrible moment she found herself caught in two minds: to get the remaining guys out of there, or to leave them to their fate.

'*This is a fire drill. Please evacuate the building via the stairwells and fire escapes. I repeat: this is a test.*'

'Dawn! Move! NOW!'

Too late. In her peripheral vision she witnessed a dark shape emerge from the open jaws of the elevator. A cloaked figure. No, a man in a long black overcoat, a man with both arms outstretched, a man holding twin submachine guns and taking aim. She dived to the floor and heard Clive open fire. She rolled under her desk and saw Cocaine Dale fall through the wide doorway as if he'd been clotheslined. He landed heavily on the floor, unmoving. Splashes of his blood ran down the gleaming white jambs.

The partition exploded in a shower of splinters. She heard terrible screams from the other side as some of the bullets hit home. Clive hollered something in return but she couldn't make out the words above all the noise.

Her fight-or-flight response kicked in. Her ribcage shook against the ferocious pounding of her heart. Time seemed to slow. She heard the sound of each individual bullet fired, barely masked by the drawn-out dirge of the fire alarms. Splinters of wood rained on her ankles with all the grace and urgency of fat snowflakes.

He's come for you, Dawn.

This much was obvious. She recalled the time he waited for her at the supermarket car park. It had been only weeks since she'd had him fired. The vile promise of revenge he'd made formed a deep-seated memory as impossible to erase as her knowledge of how to walk. He'd taken out his smartphone and snapped pictures of her fear, calling her a slag, a slut, a whore all the while.

The guy was a headcase for sure, but she never expected the creepy fucker to shoot up the place! She thought about Derrick Bird and Thomas Hamilton and Michael Ryan and the many lives they took before taking their own. She thought about Columbine and Aurora and Sandy Hook and knew she and everyone in the office behind her were as good as dead.

What the fuck are you still lying here for? Run!

The sound of gunfire abruptly ceded to the harsh alarm bells, teasing her with opportunity, but by then it was too late. A shadow spilled over the concrete floor by Dawn's desk. She saw a pair of Doctor Marten boots and looked up into the barrel of a submachine gun.

'*This is a fire drill. Please evacuate the building via the stairwells and fire escapes. I repeat: this is a test.*'

'In there, *now!*' said Clive. He pointed in the direction of Hardingham Frank's office, but Dawn could look no further than the smouldering firearm in front of her. He jabbed his finger once more. 'MOVE!'

Fight-or-flight be damned. There was no way she could match the speed or force of a bullet. She was a goner, no question. Even if she survived long enough for the police to arrive, the horrible acts Clive had promised to wreak upon her half-naked, ripped body would destroy her from the inside forever more.

She dared to look beyond the gun and saw a pair of grubby jeans heavily stained and streaked with fresh blood. Her chaotic mind swam.

Red wetness dripped from Clive's jeans. Crimson spots developed on the polished floor. Inside the madman's overcoat she caught sight of a long, brown leather sheath and a grey plastic grip jutting from it. Its twin dribbled yet more blood into the lining. Gil's blood. Under Clive's gun arm she caught sight of a holdall, its bottom wet through with gore. She gulped down a rising swell of puke.

'NOW!' screamed Clive. He jabbed the scorching-hot barrel into Dawn's forehead, making her scream.

But still she did not stand. Instead she thought about Mike, her gentle giant with no arse, who called her "Babes", who she was going to marry next month; now the man gunned down by the insane son of a bitch that stood over her. Her muscles twitched as she felt her anger build. Why not be angry? It often came so easy to her. Better to go down fighting than crying on the floor.

She met Clive's eyes with a fuck-you look. Everything about the sociopathic piece of shit made her want to rip out his lungs and push them down his throat. The way he denied his male-pattern baldness was laughable. His bad teeth undermined every insincere smile he worked across his face. Then there was the deathly alcohol breath he tried, badly, to mask with knock-off aftershave from the market. (Perhaps he drank the stuff.) Despite these, and many, many other failings, this loathsome fucktard somehow thought he was God's gift to women.

She tried to stare Clive down but found his eyes strangely different, empty-looking, as if he was running on autopilot. The moment did not last. The man's face twisted up into a ball of fury. Even with the fire alarm echoing around the lobby she heard every syllable of his screamed order.

'I SAID GET IN THERE, YOU FUCKING BITCH!'

He threw one of the submachine guns onto Dawn's desk and grabbed her by the throat. His nails dug into her neck as he drew her up from the floor with near inhuman strength. Before she could respond he threw her into the main office where she landed on Cocaine Dale's body.

Dale's face had been annihilated by Clive's bullets. Entry holes peppered the right side of his face. They had shattered his cheekbone, punctured an eyeball and left a chunky mess around his head like some kind of gory aura. Two wounds punctured his neck like a vampire bite. The arterial spray from them had formed a wet stain on the carpet.

Dawn felt a chill down her spine that worked its way along every nerve ending. The deafening bells hurt her ear drums and her head spun more and more. She coughed hoarsely and felt herself gag. The blood, the death, the madman and what he would do to her - the whole ordeal became too much to bear. With a sudden deep wet belch she vomited onto Dale's ruined face. The smell of his blood mingled horribly with that of her insides and she retched again.

She felt a Doctor Marten boot dig into her side, kicking her from Dale's corpse and onto her back. She gasped for air, gulped it down, trying desperately to equalise her stomach. She shuffled away from the body as best she could but saw two more colleagues hunched over their desks nearby, their flat-screen monitors streaked red.

She looked to the fire escape on the other side of the office and moaned in despair. Thirty or so of her colleagues clawed at each other to get through the door. She saw Barnes, her boss, peel away from the crowd and raise his arms. She couldn't hear a word he said. The man patted his hands down, imploring Clive to drop his weapons.

Clive stepped forward and raised his gun. Dawn saw the bulging, bloody holdall hanging from his shoulder and felt fearful she was staring at a bomb. Then Clive pulled the trigger. He had aimed away from Barnes and into the mass of people trying to escape. They fell one by one, peeling away like bleeding dead petals.

'This is a fire drill. Please evacuate the building via the stairwells and fire escapes. I repeat: this is a test.'

Barnes stormed towards Clive. He screamed obscenities. He had a look of desperate fury on his face.

Clive looked at his machine gun with disgust and threw it to one side. He reached into his coat and pulled out the biggest handgun Dawn had ever seen. The long, brushed metal barrel and black handle looked familiar from the movies, a Desert Eagle perhaps. Whatever it was, the gun made an immense noise and turned Barnes' neck into hamburger meat.

The operations manager spun to the floor in a hideous pirouette, spraying jets of slick red gloop onto the desks and chairs around him. He crashed to the floor and grasped at his neck, trying desperately to contain the wound. The look of outright terror in his eyes soon faded.

Clive fired again and again into the crowd, felling ex-colleagues with neither prejudice nor a second thought. Within a minute nobody stood near the fire escape, and he turned his attention towards Dawn.

She watched the sick bastard leer over her prone body and realised her skirt had ridden up. She tugged down on the hem, but

Clive kicked away her hand. He knelt beside her and slid a hand over her thigh, finding the edge of her stocking.

A fresh wave of revulsion swept over her as she caught him looking between her legs.

How she wanted to kick out at that moment; to smash her heel into that sweaty unshaven face and watch Clive's teeth fly. She moved around to find leverage but felt a sudden force press her head to the floor, a clammy palm planted over her mouth.

Fuck! He's too strong!

She gnashed her teeth against his hand but found no purchase. She dug her nails into the flesh of his wrist. He eventually released her. She made a grab for his sheathed knife.

Something hard smashed into her jaw and knocked her for six. Her vision blurred and doubled. Her brain swirled around in her skull. Her stomach heaved once more. The shock of being pistol-whipped dulled most of the pain but she knew she was in trouble.

Clive holstered his gun and forced her head into the carpet once more. She could smell his disgusting breath and the slimy skin of his cheek against hers. She felt a finger snag against her underwear.

'I think it's high time you lost these, don't you?' he said. He tickled her ear lobe with the tip of his tongue and then laughed.

She grunted and clenched her teeth, the pain in her jaw beginning to take hold. She spotted a mop of black hair over the Clive's shoulder, then the edge of a flat-screen computer monitor.

Joe!

Clive pushed himself back onto his knees, sat up and caught the full force of the monitor as it was smashed into the side of his head. His eyes instantly rolled up in their sockets and he crumpled sideways onto the floor.

Joe threw the monitor hard into Clive's midriff and thrust out a hand to Dawn.

'RUN!'

CHAPTER THREE

Joe hauled Dawn up from the floor and drew her arm over his shoulder. She was still groggy, not quite steady on her feet. Her weight surprised him, a stupid thought to pop into his head at a time like this. He helped her towards the fire escape.

The bodies of fallen colleagues surrounded the partly open door ahead of them. Glistening splashes of red trickled down the paintwork of the walls and coalesced into a wet stain on the carpet. Three survivors struggled to contain their injuries. They inched away from the dead as if fearing their fate was contagious.

One of the survivors, a work experience girl barely into her teens, had managed to prop herself against a desk. She looked to Joe for help, her eyes slick with tears. Her bottom lip quivered. She coughed up a gob of blood into her hand and began to cry.

Barnes lay on the floor between them. He still clutched at his shredded neck. The dramatic stains on the floor made it look as if he had strangled himself with rusty nails. Nearby there rested a small machine gun, discarded on the floor amid a mass of small bullet casings.

Behind them lay Cocaine Dale, with a face of blood and vomit, and a heavily dazed Clive who began to stir.

Clive's hand flopped onto the butt of his holstered pistol.

Shit! Where did that come from? How many guns has he brought here?

'Come on,' said Joe. He shook a little life back into Dawn. 'We need to move.'

'Not the fire escape.' She sounded half-asleep. Joe had to listen hard to her words over the clamour of the bells. 'Use the lift.'

'The elevators are out of action. The fire alarm disabled them.'

This is a fire drill. Please evacuate the building via the stairwells and fire escapes. I repeat: this is a test.'

Clive groaned before the bells cut in again.

'The stairs then,' said Dawn. Her eyes cleared. Her lips pursed into a thin line, as if she was holding something back. Tears. Anger. He wasn't sure. 'Please, Joe, he's shot Mike. I need to see if he is okay.'

It wasn't the worst idea in the world. The fire escape would leave them horribly exposed if Clive chased after them, and there wasn't a chance in hell Joe was going to reach over and grab the holstered gun. Not while the psycho was stirring on the floor. No way. The stairs were an easy win.

'Okay,' he said. 'But we need to leg it, yeah? Two stairs at a time. Slide down the banister if needs be.'

Dawn nodded and he felt some strength returning to her. He turned them both to face the lobby, then glanced over his shoulder. The sobbing work experience girl wiped her shaking hands onto her heavily-stained clothes. Her hands still came away red. The blood that poured unbidden from her mouth terrified her. He saw her cough again, heard her wail over the alarms. Tears welled in his eyes as he mouthed the word "sorry". He looked away, his face hot with shame.

They staggered through the doorway into the lobby and passed by Dawn's desk. She picked up the submachine gun that lay there and waved it under Joe's nose.

'You didn't think to shoot him?' she said.

'I tried, but it's empty.'

He watched Dawn's face darken. He felt her anger build quickly and possess her. She struggled free of his embrace and threw the firearm down the large corridor. It skittered across the polished concrete, clattered into the body of Mr Wilkes and spun into a corner. She leaned heavily against the edge of her desk, breathing hard.

'Are you okay?' said Joe.

Dawn pushed herself away and ran towards the stairwell door without answering him. They ran past the bodies of Gil and Mr Wilkes and slid to a halt by the large black stairwell door.

Three gunshots rang out in quick succession, audible over the bells. Then a fourth shot, and a fifth.

Joe turned to look, expecting to see Clive - but no-one was visible. His heart sank.

That poor girl. Everyone. Dead. This can't be happening.

A shadow moved in the doorway to the main office. Clive's stocky frame shoulder-charged the jamb. He still looked out of it, but was clearly coming round fast. He raised his gun.

Dawn grabbed Joe's arm and dragged him through the open stairwell door. He cried out as the wooden frame near his head burst into splinters. The heavy, black door closed behind them.

The alarm bells rang with intense urgency in the confines of the stairwell, loud enough to hurt his ears. Something immediately struck him about the stairs, something not quite right, something he couldn't put his finger on. There was no time to dwell on it.

Dawn glanced back at him from the landing, and continued down the next flight.

Joe reached out and grabbed her arm before she could go any further. He leaned in close to her ear and shouted over the noise.

'Wait! I've got an idea.'

Dawn didn't look keen. She edged to the next flight of stairs.

Joe pulled her back and pushed open the black door on the landing. The gloom beyond looked like a maintenance floor. He held the door open and pointed inside.

'Let's cut through to the stairwell opposite. We'll throw him off the scent.'

Dawn remained unsure, but then the air pressure in the stairwell dipped, as if a door elsewhere had been opened. Dawn felt it too. Her eyes widened and she mouthed a single word.

'*Clive*!'

Joe waved Dawn through the door and swung in behind her. He pushed hard against the door but it refused to be hurried.

'Come *on*!' He pushed again and again to no avail.

Clive would almost certainly see the door close. So be it. They had to run like hell. He abandoned the door and started after Dawn.

She had stopped in front of a bare breezeblock wall. She had her arms raised in a gesture that said "What the hell?" Spinning on her heels, she looked to Joe with frustrated confusion. She pointed to the wall and yelled something he could not hear.

Joe cupped an ear with his hand and then the alarm bells suddenly cut out.

'*I said where the hell is the other door?*'

Her piercing cry echoed against the unpainted bricks and dusty concrete all around them. The deafening racket of bells and alarms had been replaced with the hissing and huffing of pipes and generators, as if the stairwell door had been heavily soundproofed.

Joe's eyes adjusted to the darkness of the maintenance floor. Pockets of sickly yellow light dotted the solid breezeblock walls of a wide corridor to the right. He pointed to a T-junction at the end and started running.

'Hurry! Up here. The stairs must be around the corner.'

They stopped at the wall and found two plastic plates screwed into the brickwork. They each gave directions: "Biuro / Office" to the left; "Kombinat / Works" to the right. Both corridors, left and right, stretched into dimly lit passages seemingly without end.

'"Office",' said Joe, tapping one of the plates. 'Yeah, that sounds about right. The other stairs must be that way.'

They sped along the corridor, solid walls of breezeblock on both sides. Joe's mind worked on what the hell to do next while his subconscious dealt with a flood of nagging thoughts.

What was it about that stairwell that seemed so odd?
That door took far too long to close. Surely Clive would have seen it?
We'd have heard the fire alarms again if he'd followed us.
Wouldn't we?
Hang on. Why are the bells not ringing on this *floor?*

He spotted a corner ahead that bore right, taking them deeper into the maintenance floor. Dawn slowed to a halt and he followed suit.

'Something's wrong here,' said Dawn, gasping for breath. She looked around, trying to find her bearings.

Joe had a reasonable idea where they stood in relation to the stairwell door but had to concede the layout of the floor was confusing. It brought forth another wave of nagging questions.

Where on earth are the stairs here?
Have they been closed off from this floor for some reason?
Why would anyone close off a perfectly good stairwell?
And how come nobody's ever mentioned it before?
Yeah, fat boy, like you've *ever taken the stairs in this place.*

'No wait,' he said, pointing. 'Look, there's a door up ahead.'

A scuffed grey door was set into to the wall on the left, a sorry specimen. The paint had worn away around the angle of the door handle, and peeled and blistered around the kickboard. Joe tried the door. It opened outwards revealing a storage cupboard filled with mops and buckets, shelves of cleaning fluids and polish and dusters, a pair of stepladders and a large floor polisher in the centre.

'Okay,' he said, closing the door. 'Not a stairwell, then.'

The corner led to a shorter corridor that ended in a mostly black rectangle. Dawn stood facing the darkness ahead, not saying a word.

The buzz of generators and the clanking of pipes rolled out from the darkness, a now familiar sound in the maintenance floor. The music, however, was something new.

'Is that what I think it is?' he asked.

'Chopin,' said Dawn. She glanced over her shoulder, showing off her bruise.

Joe's mouth waggled open but no words came out.

'Don't look at me like that, Joe,' said Dawn. She scowled. 'It's not like I know the name of it or anything.'

She faced the darkness again, still rooted to the dirty concrete floor.

'Any torches in there?' she finally said.

'What, in the cupboard? None that I could see.'

'Shit.'

'Why?'

'I don't like the dark.' She turned and met Joe's eyes to reinforce her point. 'I *really*, really don't.'

'Let's go,' said Joe, nudging her forwards. 'The dark can't hurt us as much as Clive can.'

'Yeah, but what if he's there waiting for us?'

'I didn't hear him come in, did you?'

'No, but-'

'*Avanti*, Dawn. Mush! We need to get out of here. Your eyes will just have to get used to it.'

Dawn nodded with little enthusiasm. She edged along the remainder of the corridor, never once threatening to hurry the hell up.

Joe mulled over the strangeness of the situation. The fact the alarms weren't ringing still bugged him. Had someone simply switched them off at the exact moment the door closed behind him? Too much of a coincidence. Then there was the elusive second stairwell. Could there really be only one on the maintenance floor? It made the layout of the whole floor plain odd. Nothing seemed to match the floor above it. No wonder the climate control in the building had a mind of its own.

Then it struck him what was so unusual about the stairwell.

'Dawn?'

'Sssh!' She flapped a hand, agitated.

'Dawn,' Joe whispered. 'Where *was* everybody?'

'What do you mean?'

'On the stairs just then. Where were they all? The fire alarms were going off and the elevators were out of action. Those stairs should have been mobbed.'

'I don't know,' said Dawn, seeming to tire of the questions. She stopped at the lip of the corridor and looked around.

'Oh,' she said.

'What?'

'I guess this is what they meant by "Office".'

Joe craned his head over Dawn's shoulder to get a better look. The corridor opened out onto a large open space framed by breezeblock walls and two rows of portakabins, angled in a slack L-shape with three cabins in each row. Some of the cabins were lit from the inside, casting a little light onto the floor. Between and beyond the rows of portakabins there lay only darkness and noise. Grubby papers, old and crumpled, littered the open area. Gaudy crisp packets too. So much for the floor being occupied by cleaners.

Three of the cabins stood dark: one in the row directly ahead of Joe and Dawn, and two in the row along the right. The twinkling of a piano continued to play, a little louder now, most likely from one of the dark cabins on the right. The one with the open door.

Joe stepped into the open space and approached one of the portakabins. He peered in through the lit window and found a dismal beat-up swivel-chair behind an equally beat-up desk. Behind those hung a lop-sided noticeboard that sported an oily Pirelli calendar and assorted scribbled notes. A rickety shelf struggled under the weight of assorted bizarre-looking tools and contraptions. Among them there stood a large, yellow, high-power torch.

He opened the door and hopped into the portakabin. He soon returned with the wide-beam torch and a clipboard. He angled the torch over it and looked to Dawn.

'Mind your eyes,' he said, and switched it on. 'Look at these papers.'

'So? They're written in... what? Polish?'

'Looks like it. Don't you think it's a little presumptuous to assume every cleaner here is going to be Polish?'

'I don't care, Joe,' said Dawn. She sighed and hid her eyes. 'I need to find Mike. Please, let's get out of here.'

'Sorry.'

He felt his face flush again with a slight tinge of anger. It wasn't as if he had any reason to hang around. The queasiness squirming inside of him was the result of more than just shock and nerves. He'd forgotten to take his shot of insulin for the morning, like an idiot, and not for the first time. There was no way he'd ever get used to this new lifestyle so suddenly thrust upon him.

He flicked off the flashlight and handed it to Dawn, then threw the clipboard back into the portakabin.

'Let me grab a torch as well and then we'll look for an exit.'

'Okay, but hurry. It won't take Clive long to work out where we are.'

Joe peered through the window of the other lit portakabin but found nothing of use. He tried the handle of the next door along but found it locked. The same result beckoned when he tried two of the other cabins to the right. That left just the one with the open door, pitch black, a radio inside playing Chopin. Joe stepped inside.

The smell of the place aggravated his nose. Disgusting and decayed, it reminded him of rubbish trucks passing by. Something hard knocked against his shin causing him to yelp. Through the smudged window he saw Dawn jump in surprise.

'Sorry!' he said. 'I'm okay. I didn't mean to scare you. Ah, here it is.'

He flicked on the light and Dawn screamed. He screamed too, for the interior walls were awash with dark red blood. The floor of the cabin was a burgundy mess. On the window he saw the smudge had in fact been a gory handprint. It slid down the glass and onto a marked and heavily-stained desk.

But there was no body he could see. Just a lot of scattered papers and blood and an upended chair against which he had knocked his shin. He looked out of the window and saw Dawn turn to run.

'Dawn, wait!'

'Shit, Joe, run! The blood... *He's here!*'

Joe gave chase. He ran from the portakabin and slipped to his knees, the soles of his shoes momentarily robbed of grip. He quickly got back to his feet and hared after Dawn. He saw the faint outline of her white blouse in the darkness ahead, framed on both sides by walls of pipes.

'Wait for me!' he hissed loudly, hoping Clive couldn't hear. It didn't seem to matter, given the clattering noise of Dawn's heels.

He wondered how long Clive had been hiding in the maintenance floor. Surely he'd come from here. The blood in the cabin looked old, a lot older than the bloodshed he'd seen above. Had the sick bastard been building up to this day for some time – had he made a huge mistake, dragging Dawn into Clive's lair?

Dawn slowed as she approached a thick length of silvery air conditioning duct. She looked left and right, unsure of which way to turn. She powered on the torch and pointed the beam to the left. Joe caught up and peered around the corner. In the distance he saw the outline of a black rectangle. Door-shaped.

'You beauty!' he said and gently shook Dawn by the shoulder.

She ran ahead and he heard her sobbing as she neared the door. He couldn't decide whether it was through fear, happiness, relief or whatever. She switched off the torch. She grabbed for the large metal handle and pulled.

Nothing.

She pushed.

Nothing again.

She dropped the torch and pulled at the handle once more, this time with both hands. She squealed with the exertion.

Still nothing.

A horrible sinking feeling infested Joe's stomach as he neared the door. He placed a hand on Dawn's back, hoping to calm her but she peeled away in a fit of angry tears. Putting his other hand on the door to catch his breath, he was surprised at how cold it felt for something made of wood.

Dawn slammed her hands against the door, livid. She kicked it, hard, again and again. Breathing deeply, she fought to regain her composure and picked up the torch, her hands shaking.

Joe saw something on the door despite the poor yellow light, a small hole underneath the large handle. He ducked down to take a better look.

'Ah, see, it's locked. Probably to keep us lot out of the maintenance floor. We just need to find another door. We know at least one of the them is unlocked.'

Dawn reached down and slipped off her shoes. She glanced to Joe, who looked at her as if she was going mad.

'Fine,' she said. 'Let's sneak back to that other door and get out of here. Mike will probably be on the way to the hospital, anyway.'

Joe hoped that was possible. He kept shtum, feeling it better to leave her with some hope.

'You too,' she said, gesturing to Joe's feet.

'What?'

*****

Relatively speaking, the return journey to the first stairwell door was reasonably straightforward, save for the cold concrete floor numbing Joe's feet and sending chills up his bones. Despite his discomfort he held his tongue, knowing Dawn would call him an utter blouse. They soon rediscovered the plastic wall plates of the T-junction and ran down the corridor towards the door and freedom.

But the door would no longer open.

Dawn exploded. She dropped the torch, took a shoe in each hand and smashed them against the door. Her anger quickly led to tears and she crumpled to her knees by the door.

The sinking feeling in the pit of Joe's stomach deepened further still. The other door being locked, that was understandable, but who the hell had locked them in here?

Clive? Could he have had a key? Have we just closed the cage door behind us?

He recalled the state of the portakabin and felt the sweat on his back cool. Maybe Clive had been waiting here for them all along.

'Shit! Come on, Dawn,' he said. 'We need to keep moving. We need to find another door.'

Dawn threw her hands into the air. 'We found the bastard door and now it's locked!'

'Get *up*!' he hissed. 'Seriously, I've an awful feeling Clive's locked us in here with him.'

That did the trick. Dawn gathered her shoes and sprang to her feet. Joe fetched the torch but found its glass broken.

They returned to the T-junction, turning right this time to reach the works area. They made slow cautious progress through a humming maze of pipes. Ducts hissed. Generators buzzed. Machinery whirred. The acrid smell of burnt oil stung their nostrils. The chill of the concrete floor further numbed their feet yet they still refused to pull on their shoes.

Every one of Joe's senses worked overtime. He tried to fathom whether they were alone on the floor and, if not, where Clive could be hiding.

He heard rapid breathing behind him, panicky. He held out his free hand to Dawn without thinking. To his surprise she accepted it without hesitation. He would have taken some pleasure in that were it not for the pain of her fingernails slicing into his skin.

They eventually met with a thick pillar of breezeblock in the middle of the vast maintenance floor. Dripping pipes, thick and thin, ran the length of its sides like railings. Walking the perimeter revealed it to be a wide elevator shaft fronted by a pair of sliding metal doors.

'Oh, great,' said Joe, tapping the door, finding it surprisingly cold to the touch. 'Just to rub salt in the wounds.'

Dawn pressed the call button on the side regardless. She looked to Joe, astonished, when the elevator whirred into life.

'"They disabled the elevators," he said.'

'But they did!' said Joe. 'You heard the announcements yourself. This must be a service elevator, or one not connected to the main lifts.'

The elevator's arrival created rather more noise than was comfortable. The whirring and clanking of engines cut through every other sound around. Joe looked nervously for moving shapes in the darkness between the pipes as his mind again worked overtime.

So who did Clive kill in the portakabin? Was it Clive that did the killing?

Someone, or something, had certainly been slaughtered back there. The inside of the cabin had resembled an abattoir. The lack of a body still gnawed at him. Moving it must have left one hell of a blood trail. His eyes gravitated towards the dirty concrete floor and the dark stains.

'Dawn...'

'Ssssh!'

'The floor, Dawn,' he said. 'Can you feel it?'

'I can't feel a thing.'

She looked down and nearly cut through Joe's hand with her fingernails.

'Fucking hell!'

The floor rumbled and shook without warning, knocking Joe off balance. He saw dread in Dawn's face. There was a loud crack immediately followed by an unnerving crunching sound - concrete rubbing on concrete - over by the portakabins, like an earthquake had suddenly hit the building. Pipes rattled and banged against their supports and a huge hissing noise announced itself nearby. Clouds of vapour rolled out across the floor, impossible to see through. A collection of pipes visibly shook behind them. They looked the next to go.

'What the hell was that?' he said.

'Clive... he had a holdall on him,' said Dawn, releasing Joe's hand. 'I thought... Oh God, it looked like a bomb!'

'Shit!'

The elevator slowed to a halt. The building groaned and vibrated around them.

Joe pulled at the large twin doors and parted them, spilling light onto the concrete and revealing the massive streaks of blood upon which they were standing. He dragged the inner cage door aside. Dawn leapt into the elevator car, leaving small bloody footprints on the otherwise clean metal floor. Joe hopped in and dragged the cage door back in place. He listened to the clattering and hissing and grinding outside, squinting into the impenetrable darkness beyond.

'Joe?'

'Come on, Dawn, get us out of here!' he said without looking back.

'*Joe!*'

He turned. Dawn was pointing to the elevator controls. The bottommost button had a symbol of two opposing triangles, to signify the opening of doors.

Each and every button above it bore the number 13.

A loud bang elsewhere shook the elevator from side to side.

Dawn turned to face Joe. 'Okay, what the fuck is going on?'

CHAPTER FOUR

'Just press something!' said Joe. 'They're probably joke buttons. Push one of the ones near the bottom.'

Joke buttons?

Dawn didn't say anything for fear she would lose her temper again and smack Joe around the head. He was a nice guy but he was seriously starting to get on her nerves, as shot to hell as they were.

The snapping and crashing sounds outside the elevator died a little. The sound of settling masonry faded into a loud hissing of burst pipes.

In the five-by-five grid of buttons the one dead centre was lit - the thirteenth of the "13" buttons in whatever direction she counted. If these *were* fake buttons on the panel, then it seemed the left-most corners were the ones to try. That left a 50:50 choice between top-left and bottom-left. She jabbed bottom left and the elevator car juddered into life.

It began to rise.

'No, no, no!' said Joe. 'Down! We want to go down, not up!'

'I pressed the button to go down!' said Dawn. 'Look! There! Why the fuck would I want to press one that took us up?'

'Okay, sorry!' said Joe. He held up his hands as if fearing a heel across the face. 'I guess the buttons are in reverse. Sorry.'

He leaned over and pressed the top-left button, which then lit up. He returned to his corner of the elevator and looked to the bare-metal ceiling, avoiding eye contact. He clasped his hands shut, then opened them again over and over, rapidly flexing his fingers in a manner that made Dawn's skin crawl.

Grabby hands.

The elevator continued to rise. Outside, in the maintenance floor, the coda of the hissing pipes bore a horribly familiar undertone.

...ehhhhhsssssssss...

She shook her head, refusing to acknowledge the sound. The cold metal floor managed to chill her feet worse than the bloody concrete, but there was no way she was going to put her shoes back on. Not while her feet were covered in someone's blood. Through her stockings she felt stickiness between her toes and tried not to think about it. Instead she gave Joe the dirtiest look that her sore jaw would allow.

'Sorry,' he said again. He stopped the creepy tic, much to her relief.

A deep chill blew in through the interior cage door, colder than any September had a right to be. She instinctively drew her arms over her chest and shivered, her feet feeling even colder now.

A blinding flash of blue-tinged light erupted around the elevator car, followed by a sharp immense noise as if a billion volts of electricity had been discharged nearby. The elevator car shook from side to side. The fluorescent strip light dimmed, flickered off and then plinked back into life again. Dawn felt the fine hairs on her arms prickle.

'Did you hear that?' said Joe, his face smacked with astonishment. He looked out of the elevator, wide-eyed.

'Of course I bloody well heard it!' said Dawn. 'How could I not have heard *that*?'

'Where did it come from?' he said, jamming his nose against the interior door. 'It sounded like God just degaussed his monitor!'

'Oh, shut up, Joe.'

The first glimpse of thick concrete emerged through the interior door, coming down from above, pushing away the darkness. To her surprise the only button illuminated on the control panel was the one pressed by Joe, as if her choice had been cancelled.

The elevator car juddered to a stop. Through the cage she watched a pair of grubby exterior doors part in the middle, pneumatic cylinders smoothly working in tandem. They revealed the relatively peaceful sight of an elevator lobby. A set of polished brass doors stood opposite.

The exterior doors stopped only halfway, like the service elevator was somehow too large for the shaft. The view reminded her of how her widescreen TV back home would show old programmes with black bars down the sides, or at least until she hit a few buttons on the remote.

Home. It suddenly felt so far away.

Time's a-wastin', Dawn.

She jabbed a button in another corner of the panel only to be met with a rude buzzing noise. She jabbed it again. Same result. Joe had a go, pushing another button entirely with equal lack of success.

'I guess we walk then,' he said.

'Fine, whatever,' said Dawn. 'Get the door.'

'Yes, ma'am.'

He slid the cage aside and leaned into the lobby, taking a prolonged look left and right. Too long.

'Mind these doors don't close on you,' said Dawn. It was either that or giving him a kick up the arse with her bloody feet.

'Ah, good point' said Joe, hopping fully into the lobby. He turned to face her. 'This looks a little more like it. The layout's nearly the same as our floor.'

Dawn stepped out onto the cheap nylon carpet. The sea of beige was dull on the eyes but far warmer and much more welcoming than the cold metal floor of the service elevator. She wiggled some life back into her toes and took in her surroundings.

'What happened to the noise? The shaking?' she said. 'The place was falling apart a minute ago, now you can hear a pin drop.'

'Dunno,' he said, moving towards a nearby door. 'What I do know, however, is that I need a Jimmy Riddle.'

'What, again? Jesus, Joe, can't it wait?'

'You try pissing through gunshots and fire alarms and see how far you get!' he said, then calmed. 'Look, you said it yourself, everything seems calmer on this floor. Perhaps it wasn't a bomb that went off. Maybe it was just a boiler blowing up. Made everything seem worse than it actually was. I don't know.'

'But Clive...'

'...isn't here. Listen. Nothing. I'll be back in a minute. If you hear anything come and get me. I'll... er... use a cubicle.'

'Just *go*,' said Dawn. She held up a hand, ready to dole out an almighty slap, but he had already bolted. The door slammed shut, making her wince.

Could Clive have heard that?

Dammit, now I need to go.

She let her eyes follow the left side of the lobby, past both sets of toilets, beyond the still-open elevator door - and a second beside it - and towards a smooth magnolia wall at the far end. She was standing in another T-junction. She fixed on its corners and felt the scratch of a long-repressed fear clawing at her mind. That of the things that once lay beyond corners. Bad things.

Things with grabby hands.

Stop it!

She stepped back once, twice, and felt something cold and hard press into her back. Horizontal. The heel of her right foot struck something solid. She stopped and turned.

A fire door.

She looked back through the lobby-cum-corridor and the T-junction in the distance, then back to the fire door.

Shouldn't this be on the other side of the building?

She pushed down on the metal bar but it wouldn't budge. She dropped her shoes to the floor and tried again with both hands. Nothing. Once more with all her weight, hard enough to lift her feet off the ground. Still nothing. She picked up a shoe, took aim and then thought better of it. The damned fire door seemed little more than a glorified towel rail. She picked up her other shoe and rested against the handle.

Her mind turned to Mike and she felt her insides squirm with worry. Barbara said he'd been shot, but not that he'd been killed. Surely there was some hope to take from that? She looked at her small bloody footprints in the beige carpet amidst those of Joe and wished anything to be by Mike's side. The moment she was away from this ridiculous building she could ring around the hospitals and find where Mike had been admitted.

If only she had her bag, or her phone. The thought to grab them had never crossed her mind, being in such a rush to escape Clive's wrath.

'Fucking Clive!' she hissed. She slammed the sole of her foot into the alleged fire door before fresh tears could arrive. A dull thud rang out, rather than the hollow noise she expected to hear.

The door refused to budge regardless. She checked her temper and steadied her breathing.

The air felt different in this floor. Tasted different too. It left a faint metallic tang at the back of her throat as if a violent thunderstorm had rumbled through the place only moments earlier.

"Kind of familiar." That was how Joe had described the area in which she stood. Clearly the boy had been talking out of his arse. Yes, there were toilet doors to her left, and some other door to her right, but where was the large window offering sweeping views of the Docklands? Someone had replaced it with a drab wall and a broken fire door. And what about the doors to the stairwells? Where were they? There was only another set of elevators standing opposite each other.

Between them there hung a polished brass plaque proudly sporting the number thirteen.

ehhhhhsssssss...

'No,' she whispered, and took a firm hold of the horizontal bar.

The sound came from the far end of the corridor, she was certain of it. From the T-junction. Something cold clawed once more at her mind, trying to find a way in.

Someone was there.

The quiet hum of the floor, the stillness ahead, the expectation, the dread, they each reminded her of a recurring nightmare from long ago.

*****

She would be sitting bolt-upright in bed, with her knees drawn to her chest, her arms wrapped tight around them. Curled into a tight, upright ball.

All the better to stop him getting to you, Dawny Prawn.

The Tickling Man.

The thought of him made her shiver and set her sobbing. She would rock herself gently on the large bed, a bed that felt the size of a prairie, backwards and forwards, forwards and backwards, unable to sit still, nervous energy burning her nerve endings.

Her chocolate brown eyes, wide open, would stare dead-ahead, unblinking, terrified of the open door to her bedroom, the dark landing ahead and the gloomy day-lit bathroom beyond. Terrified because she knew what lay in wait out there in the dark. On the landing. Around the corner.

The Tickling Man.

And it was always the wait that would scare her the most. It fed the slick coiling dread that swirled in the pit of her stomach. It pushed up her heart rate. It made her blood pound and pulse in her ears. Instinct would scream to her, "RUN!" but she could never move, as if she had been stitched to the bed sheets.

The waiting.

The open door.

The dark of the landing.

The bathroom beyond.

The waiting. The waiting. The waiting.

And at the exact moment she reckoned he would not arrive, she would see that of which she was so afraid. Four long, grey fingers would emerge from behind the doorframe, each skinny digit crooked and finished with long, dirty fingernails, yellow and claw-like. Then she would see the sinewy hand from which they dangled. A nervous tic would set all of the fingers going as if playing an invisible piano.

A *grabby* hand.

The hand would snatch hold of the doorframe and then he would emerge in full.

The Tickling Man: a horror of wiry limbs and wiggling long fingers, a broken back and a scarecrow's head ripped through with a sadistic grin. He'd stand in the doorway with the dark landing behind him, as if savouring her fear. Feeding on it. The fingers of his hands would flex and twitch.

Grabby hands.

Dawn would scream for help but only a rasping bark would come, as if someone had slid a razor across her vocal chords as a baby. And then the fiend would charge towards her, long fingers outstretched, eager to dig into her flesh, finding ways into the gaps between her ribs and the tense muscles of her abdomen. The first tickle would be enough to release her limbs and unlock her defences. And then he'd be in, working every possible spot. His horrible scarecrow face would fill her vision, straw leaking from its ripped grin. She would be lost in fits of terrified laughter that starved her of air until she blacked out.

*****

She shook the terrible memories from her head and looked away from the T-junction. She felt a dire need to remain calm lest her mind run away fully with the fairies. The stickiness between her toes was driving her mad, her heart still raced and her bladder was full. She heard the whoosh of a hand drier start up in the gents and realised Joe never had time to wash before helping her escape.

She looked at her hands with some disgust.

Without a second thought she dashed into the ladies toilet.

*****

She ran her hands under the drier, feeling a new woman. Her feet, clean at last, were clad once more in her shoes - though she had to consign her stockings to the restroom bin. She mulled over their next move as the moisture was blasted from her hands.

Okay, so one of the elevators is out of action. There are another three to try. God only knows where those other two came from.

She felt a subtle tremor run through the floor, cutting short her thoughts. A series of loud clunks vied for dominance over the roar of the hand drier. She pulled her hands away and wished the thing would shut the hell up. She couldn't get a fix on where the noise was coming from. The clunking sounds lessened, became more spaced, like an immense radiator nearby was cooling down.

She left the hand drier to its thing and ran into the lobby. She found Joe pacing the beige carpet between the two sets of elevators. He stopped chewing the skin around his thumbnail and met her eyes.

'Did you hear that?' she said.

Joe looked all around him, more than was strictly necessary.

'Yes, Dawn, I heard it. How could I not have heard *that*?'

'Yeah, yeah, funny man,' said Dawn. 'I had the hand drier going full blast, smartarse. What was it?'

'I don't know,' said Joe. 'The banging seemed to come from all round.'

'Shit. So, what, is this thing about to collapse after all?'

He hesitated, then coughed. He rubbed the back of his neck.

'No,' he said. 'I don't think so. Not exactly.'

'What do you mean?'

'Okay, you've got to see this.'

He started from the elevators towards the end of the lobby.

'Yeah, I've played with the fire door already,' she said.

He shook his head and said nothing in return. He instead veered towards the door directly ahead of her, a single door that stood opposite the toilets. He tapped on the small nameplate that had been screwed onto the door at eye-level.

'Read it,' he said, and tapped it again.

Dawn neared the door and examined the Cyrillic script printed on the white slab of vinyl.

КУХНЯ

'I can't,' she said. 'I don't know what it means.'

'I think it means kitchen,' he said, and opened the door. He stood in the doorway. 'It's a bit like the one on our floor, but... well, take a look.'

'What's happened, Joe?'

'Come and see for yourself. You're not going to believe this.'

She relented and walked in through the door. Indeed the kitchen area resembled that of the fourteenth: a large L-shaped floor space with kitchen surfaces and cupboards on the inner wall and lots of large, plate glass windows along the exterior.

But then Dawn saw it. The stunning vista she had expected to see, that of tall buildings, tiny people and the Thames, had gone, swapped for a large number of small, bland buildings that spun off into the distance.

She ran to the nearest window, planted her hands on the thick, cold glass and wailed in disbelief. The city that lay outside was most certainly not London.

CHAPTER FIVE

'This cannot be happening,' said Dawn. She stood in front of the window, her shoulders slumped, her head lowered.

Joe joined her for another look at the city outside. He wished he'd given his socks a little longer beneath the hand drier. Before long he'll have blisters developing on his heels. He rested his forehead against the glass and savoured its coldness against his skin. It helped ease some of the fatigue he felt, though little of his fast-approaching headache.

'I could pinch you,' he said. He looked over to Dawn and flashed his easy smile. 'You know, to prove it isn't a dream.'

'I really wouldn't, Joe,' she said, not meeting his eyes.

'Fair enough.'

He gave up playing morale officer and looked once more onto the street scene far below. Strings of tiny, bland-looking cars slowly worked their way along thin, grey roads, none of which he recognised. The clear blue skies of the morning had been replaced with a uniform grey-white blanket of cloud. Most of the pedestrians wore a coat of some description. What signage he could see sported a mixture of English and Cyrillic script.

His mind continued to pick over the madness of the last, what? Half hour? Hour? He felt a twinge across his belly, something he had felt before, though had not expected to feel for some time yet.

Have we been here longer *than an hour? It doesn't feel like it.*

He thought about the maintenance floor and its strange layout, the hallmarks it bore of a bloodbath, the sounds of collapse and ruin as they escaped. The plastic signs, the papers too, both seemingly in Polish. He wondered how a large service elevator could fit into a shaft seemingly half its size. Then there were the strange noises in the elevator car, the groaning clunks when Dawn was in the bathroom, and the bizarre metallic smell that permeated the air.

Where the hell are we? More to the point, is Clive here?

Images of black, shiny buttons all reading "13" danced and swam when he closed his eyes. The view of a foreign city appeared when he opened them again.

The back of his throat felt rough enough to help strike a match. He sensed weakness in his knees - only for a fleeting moment, but sufficient for him to need correct his balance. Something triggered deep in his subconscious, something that didn't ask questions but made demands instead.

We need to leave, fat boy. Now.

He found Dawn looking at him, concerned.

'Joe? Are you okay?' she said. 'You're pasty as hell. Your eyes are all over the place.'

'Yeah, yeah. I'm fine,' he said, but was unable to summon a smile. 'I'm just a bit queasy, that's all.'

'Ditto,' said Dawn. 'I feel like I'm running on fumes. It's probably shock setting in.'

'Yeah,' he said, peeling away from the window. 'Something like that.'

He walked to the kitchen sink and opened a pair of cupboard doors, but found only empty shelves inside. He met with the same result when he checked all the other cupboards. Had it been too much to ask for a glass in this place? Even a crappy disposable cup would have sufficed.

Defeated, he spun the cold tap and lapped at the water that gurgled from the spout. It was cold and crisp, quite unlike London water. It tasted like the water he enjoyed up North.

Back home.

*****

Dawn turned her attention away from the city outside and watched Joe has he thirstily guzzled water from the cold tap. He stood there hunched over for a long time.

'Where do you think we are, Joe?'

He shut off the tap and straightened up, wincing. The area around his shirt collar was damp with spilled water. He wiped his mouth and shrugged his shoulders.

'Beats me. Eastern Europe, I'm guessing, but don't ask me how.'

A gentle two-tone noise rang out from his pocket, the sound of a text message arriving. Then another. And another. And yet another still. From Joe's expression he had forgotten all about his smartphone. The gentle alerts continued to sound as he plucked the device from his jacket pocket, dropping his packet of cigarettes on the kitchen carpet in the process.

To Dawn it felt as if they had just won the lottery. She walked over to Joe and peered at the small, greasy screen. The icon for the text message app had the number 12 transposed over it. Another two-tone alert nudged it up to 13. Then 14. 15. The name of a foreign mobile phone operator occupied real estate in the title bar of the screen, written in the same style text as the nameplate on the kitchen door. Backwards Rs. The most important thing was the single bar of signal shown in the top right corner. It flickered every couple of seconds, but a thready signal was better than none at all.

She watched Joe thumb through a few screens of bright, glossy icons and launch a mapping app. The screen turned a uniform creamy colour save for a spinning green arrow in the centre. A blue chevron in the title bar indicated they had GPS. The two-tone text message alert continued to sound off in the background.

Joe seemed hypnotised by the empty display. The sadness that sometimes ate him seemed to be doing so again.

'Joe,' she said. She kept the tone of her voice soft and calm. 'Joe, I need to use your phone. Please. Let me try and get hold of Barbara.'

He snapped out of his trance and automatically handed the phone to Dawn. His face brightened, almost his old self again. Almost. 'Sure,' he said. 'Here you are. She'd be away from the building by now, though, surely?'

'I have to try,' she said. 'We need someone to get us out of here, wherever here may be. I also need to know what happened to Mike.'

'Okay, but leave the map running. It'll find us eventually.'

Dawn switched to the phone app and dialled the direct number for the front desk. Eventually she got a connection, albeit over a line better suited to serving pairs of tin cans. The phone rang once, twice, and was picked up.

'Good afternoon. 3 Donnington Place, how can I help?'

The voice was garbled but Dawn caught enough to know who had answered.

'Barbara! Oh, Barbara, thank God! It's me, Dawn, from fourteen.'

Silence.

'Hello? Hello, Barbara? Please say something, it's Dawn!'

'Dawn?' said Barbara, sounding very unsure. For a nervous moment the line broke into noise, and then came back.

'Oh, God, Barbara, it's terrible. Clive pulled out a gun... he killed so many... I think... I think he's still after us!'

'Dawn *McKenzie*?'

Outside the daylight dimmed. The clouds thickened. She felt her insides sink a couple of inches.

'Yes, it's me! How's Mike? Please tell me he's okay.'

'Dawn, where have you been? It's been three-'

The line went dead. A message on the screen read "Call Ended" with casual bluntness. None of the signal bars were filled. After a brief moment the screen went black. She strode back to the plate glass window.

'What happened?' said Joe, following her. 'How are they coping?'

'Hang on. The phone cut out on me. I need to try again.'

She pressed the home button, then sighed and handed the smartphone to Joe.

'PIN please.'

Joe quickly tapped in his security code and unlocked the phone. The map app appeared, a pin icon planted in the middle of a beige expanse. She couldn't read the text but saw Joe's eyebrows raise in surprise. He returned the phone to her.

'*Sofia*?' she said, making it sound more like a screech. 'Bulgaria?'

'Apparently.'

'But that's miles away!' she said. 'I don't think I can take much more of today. Oh, come on!'

The phone had lost its signal again. She held the device ahead of her, scanning the room. She slowly walked the length of the plate glass windows, wishing life into the phone, but with little joy. Hints of a signal would appear but for only a fraction of a second, nowhere near good enough to sustain a call. At least the flow of text messages had stopped. The number 169 lay over the icon for the messaging app.

She ran over Barbara's words while they were still fresh, trying to read her intonation, searching for any clue as to what she could have said next.

"Where have you been? It's been three..."

Three days? Three weeks? She looked at the icon again and considered the large number of the unread text messages. Three months, perhaps?

'Okay, I've got an idea. Let's try the rest of this floor,' she said. 'We must be able to get a signal somewhere around here.'

She made her way back into the lobby without waiting for an answer. She held the phone outstretched, keeping the screen alive with regular finger-presses. She heard Joe collect his cigarettes and call out for her to slow down. As she neared the T-junction ahead she glared at its corners, staring them down, willing nobody to emerge. Not Clive, not some Bulgarian, not anybody.

[Not even meeeeee, Dawwwny Prawwwn?]

Fuck.

She stopped dead and felt a cold sweat develop across her back. There was no doubting the voice now. She glanced over her shoulder, making sure Joe was following, gauging whether he'd also heard her once chief tormentor. Of course he hadn't. Even so she felt a lot safer having someone around. The Tickling Man only ever caught her alone. In her dreams. Maybe this was a dream?

Stop it, Dawn. You're going to drive yourself mad.

'What did Barbara say?'

'Not much,' said Dawn. 'She didn't seem to know who I was at first. Somehow it sounded like we've been away a long time.'

'Really? How long?' His face then lit up with an idea. 'Actually, check the phone. It should have picked up a time signal by now.'

Dawn switched to the calendar app and nearly dropped the phone in shock. Speechless, she flashed the screen to Joe.

'Three years?' he exclaimed. 'We've been missing for three bloody *years*?'

She watched a bead of sweat run from Joe's clammy brow. His skin remained as white as a sheet. His mouth waggled open as per its wont, though that was perhaps understandable. To her surprise she noticed the start of a five o' clock shadow.

'Three years,' she repeated under her breath.

She thought of the times she and Mike had threatened to jilt each other at the altar, usually during a stupid fight over nothing. Of course she'd never meant it, but here she stood in a foreign country, nearly three years after they were supposed to be married. She felt her throat tighten. She imagined Mike's parents winding down the wedding of their only son while he lay wounded in hospital, the bride-to-be missing-feared-dead at the hands of a psycho.

Fucking Clive!

She turned to face the T-junction and strode purposely towards it, eager to get there before her fear could take hold again. She tapped into deep, ancient reserves of anger to help fuel every step. She prepared herself for anyone stupid enough to dare leap out at her. She felt ready to put the fucker through the wall. She made an executive decision to bear left and then held her breath.

She rounded the corner. To her immense relief she saw only the glimpse of an empty open-plan office ahead. A similar sight lay along the right, the edge of the T-junction being some kind of division between the two halves.

'Any signal yet?' said Joe.

'Nothing.' She kept the screen alive on the smartphone and stepped into the office area.

A curved receptionist's desk presented itself, completely bare. Beyond that lay a spartan office floor offering little more than magnolia pillars, cheap nylon carpet and even cheaper-looking ceiling tiles. Power sockets and network points lay hidden beneath panels set into an ocean of beige. A series of five glass-fronted offices ran along the right. She suspected a further five would lie on the other half of the floor.

The surface of the desk stood unblemished and clean of the tiniest mote. The office looked pristine, as if someone had just unwrapped it. Perhaps that explained why nobody had bothered to fix the fire door.

She strode to the nearest plate glass window and resumed her slow careful hunt for a signal. She glanced at the phone's battery life and silently cursed Joe for not charging it more often.

She soon met the corner, turned, and continued along the line of windows. The row of offices formed an island in the middle of the floor, allowing her through to the other side where she found the same layout in reverse and just as sparse. Along the far wall there stood a number of large storage cupboards and a single black door opposite the receptionist's desk.

The largely windowed perimeter of the office floor eventually yielded no better a signal than the kitchen area. She returned the phone to Joe and swore like a stevedore.

*****

'Maybe we should try the kitchen again,' said Joe. 'Can you remember where you were standing when you got a signal?'

Dawn stood, arms folded, surveying the floor like a small slim lighthouse. She shook her head, lost in thought.

He left her to it and unlocked the phone. He found only twenty percent of the battery remaining. He cursed himself for forgetting about the GPS, then disabled it. He couldn't resist opening the messaging app, which had grouped his messages together by sender, the last of each shown.

Mam and Dad: Joe, we know you are still out there somewhere. We will never give up hope. Call home, love. Please. We miss you so much.

Sue: Come on, Joe, give us a sign that you are OK. I'm funding your mobile until you come back. Please call. Mam is worried sick.

Al: Bro, wer R U? Its like U dropped off the planet. Hope U R OK.

Max: Had to let your room go. Sorry. The rent was crippling us. Your sister put your stuff into storage.

079941265...: You are owed £3256 in compensation. Text PPI to-

It felt to Joe as if his Adams Apple had doubled in size. He flicked off the phone and coughed in an attempt to fight back the tears. He waited for Dawn to survey another area of the floor and then quickly dabbed his eyes.

Both he and Dawn had been missing for three years and yet barely a couple of hours had passed since Clive killed half of the office. He felt like the lowest kind of dick for upsetting everyone, especially his mother. It made him think of the one and only time he had made her cry. If only he could raise a signal, call them, tell them all he was okay.

Okay, but just a bit... lost.

He saw Dawn spring into action and head towards the receptionists desk. For a moment it looked like she was about to walk right through it, as if the thing was made of paper, but then she veered away to the left.

'What's up?'

'We're walking out of here,' she said. 'Same plan, different country. Let's hit the stairs.' She hauled open the heavy, black door and slid behind it.

'Wait for me!' said Joe, trotting in her footsteps.

'Come on, Joe,' he heard her call. Her voice echoed in the stairwell. 'We'll get a better signal out in the open.' He heard her shoes clomp on the stairs.

He caught the door just before it closed and headed into the stairwell. The look and feel of the place immediately reminded him of the stairs from his old school. Wide steps of hard-wearing concrete. Knackered-looking handrails. A spine of tall thin windows offered a glimpse of the shitty weather outside. Bleak, in other words. He'd lost count of the number of times the other kids had tried to push him down those stairs.

Hey, it's okay. Fat kids bounce, right?

Rivulets of rainwater raced one other down the thin windows, the weather outside having quickly taken a turn for the worse. A large ovular lightshade in the ceiling bathed everything in weak yellow light. Another black door stood on the opposite side of the landing. A brick wall on the left ran the distance between them, a large, dark yellow thirteen neatly hand-painted onto the surface.

Dawn's footsteps continued to echo around the stairwell. He watched as she emerged on the flight of stairs ahead of him, about to step down onto the very landing on which he stood. She wore the same look of disgusted astonishment he too felt plastered across his face.

The door thunked shut behind him.

'You've got to be fucking kidding me!' she said.

She let slip a pissed-off growl and picked up her feet. She hit the landing running and followed the handrail around. She passed Joe by and clattered down the stairs only to appear once more on the approach to the thirteenth landing.

'Shit!' She slapped her hand down hard on the railing and caught her breath.

A strange sensation of awe and fear gathered in Joe's guts, almost masking the sharp little pains he felt there. He walked over to the handrail and cocked his head over the edge. He saw the top of Dawn's hand repeated again and again in a downwards rectangular spiral, the Droste effect made somehow real. He looked up and watched her hand pull away from the railing in a spectacular infinity shot.

'Sod it,' she said. 'Let's go back to the kitchen.'

She stepped down heavily onto the landing and walked past Joe towards the black door.

He took the opportunity to take another look at the incredible sight above and below him. He weighed up his chances of taking a picture with his smartphone without getting his nuts chewed off for wasting battery life, but immediately cast it aside as another stupid thought.

You're trying to get out of here, fat boy, remember?

Behind him Dawn let slip an exasperated wailing noise and he knew that things had taken another turn for the bizarre. He spun away from the handrail and stepped behind Dawn, who stood propping open the door.

The narrow corridor of a luxury hotel presented itself. Doors ran along both left and right walls, off and away into the distance. It was no longer the empty office floor.

'Okay. I'll say this again, Joe,' said Dawn. She punched the door with the side of her fist. 'Just what the *fuck* is going on here?'

CHAPTER SIX

It felt as if some prankster was playing a cruel trick on them; that a hypnotist would suddenly click their fingers and make reality dissolve into a laughing, cheering audience. Dawn clung to the warming thought of gouging out the eyes of the smug bastard responsible for this latest circle of hell.

A whole new floor - actually, sod that, a whole new *building* lay ahead. Again. It seemed every time she had a grip on the situation something new would come along and broadside her. She thumped the door once more with frustration.

Oh, well done. That'll probably bruise. Keep it together, Dawn, for Mike's sake if not yours. Stay focused!

She imagined him lying in a hospital bed, stuffed with tubes, surrounded by his family. She watched, helpless, ghost-like, as Mike's mother turned and wept into his father's chest. A faceless doctor leaned over to switch off the life support - a doctor with long fingers.

Stop it! He's going to be okay! Focus, *will you? Where are we now?*

She found herself standing in the corner of a luxuriously carpeted L-shape. To her left lay a short corridor clad with windows which then right-angled into another corridor. Hotel doors stretched into the distance on both sides of the corridor directly ahead, broken briefly midway along the left for a lobby area.

'Oh, shit!' she whispered.

Little more than ten yards ahead, surrounded by a mess of dark stains and plastic wrappers, she saw a blackened skull on the carpet. It rested on a pair of charred bones, long and thin. The ensemble sunbathed in a patch of daylight. Opposite, on the right, a door to one of the hotel rooms stood wide open.

'Hello?' called Joe.

'Jesus, Joe!' she hissed, and gave him a filthy look. She felt his hand on her shoulder and before she knew it he had eased past her into the corridor.

'Joe! What are you doing?'

He turned to her, his face serious.

'I don't know about you but I'm starving. Look at all these wrappers. There might be some food in here.'

'Er, yeah, and what about the *bones*?' She thought of the blood-splattered portakabin in the maintenance floor, wherever the hell that now lay. Could this have been the missing body, or at least part of it?

'Yeah, well,' said Joe. 'I'll be careful.'

She watched him edge along the corridor, his back pressed tight to the right-hand side. Despite her reservations she secretly wished he was right about the food. Her stomach growled its approval, so empty she felt it echo inside of her. She recalled how her vomit had mingled with the bloody ruin of Cocaine Dale's face. She cleared her mind and walked into the corridor, releasing the heavy, black stairwell door. It closed behind her revealing a tarnished brass plate on the wall. The number thirteen presented itself once again, this time in tastelessly overworked copperplate.

And so the sick joke continued, it seemed. No click of the fingers for her. No applause. No way out.

Joe reached the frame of the open door and met Dawn's eyes. He gave her the thumbs-up. It was an act of bold stupidity she had seen in way too many crappy movies, usually before some idiot took a carving knife in the neck. She eyeballed the jamb, expecting something to appear, maybe a couple of long fingers tipped with yellow claw-like nails.

Stop it! You're going to talk him up!

[Yesssssss.]

She dragged her gaze from the door. Joe stood psyching himself with deep breaths. He took a quick peek inside the room and pulled away, shoulders against the wall once more. He took a moment to process what he'd seen and dared to look again, a little longer this time. He exhaled loudly.

'It's okay,' he said, letting the door jambs take his weight. 'There's nobody here.'

'Are you sure?'

'It's fine. We're alone. Scout's honour.' He walked into the hotel room.

Dawn picked a path through the empty crisp packets and chocolate bar wrappers, trusting only the carpet she could see. She avoided the near-black stains as best she could. The sinister Jolly Roger monitored her trespassing with accusing eyeless sockets. The charred bones were covered in black bits of burnt gristle and framed by old splashes and streaks of blood against the walls. It seemed to be a marker of some sort, or a warning. She felt like kicking the thing down the corridor, out of sight.

A filthy unmade bed dominated the hotel room. Smears and stains of dark red, brown and yellow infested the once-white linen. A sickly fug of sweat hung in the air. It grew stronger the closer she got to the bed. She caught the scent of urine and backed away. Dirty plastic wrappers and dark stains covered the carpet, too numerous to avoid. The stains were thickest around the open door of the small water closet opposite the bed. The pattern of the linoleum floor was indistinguishable under the brown stains. The porcelain of the toilet bowl and wash basin was orangey-brown with mildew.

Joe stood by the door to the water closet. Daylight from perfect cloudless skies streamed into the room through the windows behind him. He peered into the water closet and pinched his nose.

'I'm guessing we're in the States.'

'Really? Okay, I'll bite. You got that by smelling the bathroom?'

'No, but you could drown an elephant in that toilet,' he said. He sidestepped away and faced the windows, covering his eyes against the strong sunlight. 'Plus I can see a Little Caesar's outside. A bunch of other burger joints too. A really old-school Mackie-Dees.'

She left Joe to drool over fast food outlets and took in more of the hotel room. The future retro decor resembled the set of an old TV movie, as if Columbo would walk in any moment asking about the bones out front. A large wardrobe-dresser set into the wall resembled an accident in a wood panel factory. Someone had carved grooves into the largest of the panels, each a couple inches long: four vertical lines with a diagonal. Groups of five, nearly thirty in number, like a criminal counting down their stretch in prison. What little she could see of the carpet's pattern was a geometric eyesore. A flimsy, glass-topped coffee table stood near the windows, covered in rubbish and grease.

On the bedside table, underneath a grubby T-shirt, she spotted a dull grey slab of plastic. A slab with push-buttons.

'We've got a phone here!' she said, immediately drawing Joe's attention from the window.

She flicked away the T-shirt and picked up the receiver, delighted to hear a tone. A white panel glued onto the base of the phone read: *Dial 0 for Room Service*, and so she did.

'Room service. How can I help you?'

Dawn mouthed the word "American" to Joe, who took a bow.

'Hello!' she blurted. 'Hello, can you hear me?'

'Yes, ma'am, I can hear you. How can I help?'

'Oh my God, you've got to come up here! We're trapped and it looks like something bad has happened.'

She watched as a big smile broke out over Joe's face. Sweet relief. He closed in for a better listen.

'Okay, ma'am, stay calm. What happened?'

'I don't know. There's blood and bones in the corridor. There's blood in this room too.'

'Okay, ma'am, I'm sending up Security. How many of you are there?'

'Two: me and Joe. I'm Dawn.'

'Okay, Dawn. What number room are you calling from?'

She squinted to the open door and saw a small burnt bone jammed underneath it. As if the room didn't have enough hallmarks of death. She fought her revulsion and refocused on the brass plate.

'We're in room thirteen-oh-four.'

There was a sharp tutting noise and a heavy sigh from the concierge. 'Please stop wasting our time.'

The line went dead.

Dawn held out the receiver as if suddenly finding it smeared with dogshit.

'She cut me off!'

'What? Why?'

She looked to the door. The receiver creaked as her grip on it tightened. 'I bet it's because there's no room thirteen-oh-four in this hotel, just like there's no room thirteen-fucking-anything.'

She slammed the receiver into the cradle. It took every ounce of willpower for her not to smash the thing against the wall.

'Well, at least we've got a line to the outside world. Here, let me try.'

Joe plucked the phone from Dawn's grasp and re-dialled room service.

Dawn felt a burning need to sit down but couldn't bear the thought of perching on the edge of the filthy bed. Another whiff of urine tickled her gag reflex. A black, heavily-padded leather recliner stood near the water closet, equally unappealing, covered as it was in old, bloodstained clothes. Atop these there rested what looked like an old military jacket.

'They're not picking up,' said Joe. He redialled and waited. Waited some more. Eventually he cradled the receiver and returned the phone to the bedside table. He shrugged as if it was no big deal, but his eyes betrayed his nonchalance.

'Who were you going to call?'

'*Ghostbusters*!' he said. 'Sorry, I couldn't resist it.'

Dawn smiled politely as Joe's little joke died on its arse.

'No,' he continued, 'I... er... I saw some of the messages on my phone. I just wanted to ring my folks to let them know I'm okay. They're having kittens.'

A swell of heat blossomed in her cheeks. She had never once considered Joe's family and friends in all of this. The poor guy before her was being eaten alive by anxiety just as much as she was. She smiled weakly, a mixture of apology and sympathy.

'So there's no signal on your phone then?'

'Nothing. Not even an operator ID.'

'No Wi-Fi either?'

Joe shook his head. She sighed, hands on her hips.

'Well, I won't be recommending this place on TripAdvisor.'

Joe approached the window and peered outside once more.

'I get the feeling this hotel couldn't care less,' he said. 'Everything out there looks new, but old at the same time. It's like it's 1975 all of a sudden. I keep expecting Kojak to waltz in through that door saying "Who loves ya, baby?".'

Dawn burst into a fit of uncontrollable giggles. Soon Joe too was helpless with laughter, a metric ton of tension released all at once. He gasped for breath and asked why they were laughing, to which Dawn pointed to herself and said "Columbo", thus setting them off again.

Eventually Dawn regained her composure and leaned against the hotel room door. Joe wiped his eyes and felt his sides while he caught his breath, as if he had given himself a stitch. He met her eyes and broke easily into the same supportive smile she had tried.

'I really hope Mike is okay,' he said.

Oh, you bastard! You... you brilliant, brilliant bastard!

She stepped towards Joe and bear-hugged him. She hid her face from his, nuzzling into the lapel of his suit jacket so he could not see her cry. But a single sobbing breath gave her away.

Don't lose it, Dawn. Oh, bloody hell, here we go...

She relaxed and let loose. She tried to talk through her tears about Mike and how worried sick she was about him and what the hell was happening to them today and how shitty she felt for never thinking about Joe and how worried his family would be, but it all came out as a stream of gibberish. She felt a hand awkwardly pat her between the shoulder blades.

Yup. Another one that can't handle a crying woman.

She laughed between sobs and felt the pressure inside of her finally ease. She soon felt ready enough for her usual self to take charge again. She sniffed loudly and found Joe's deodorant beginning to fail.

Okay, that's enough of that.

She wiped a finger under each eye and examined the damage. Yes, splendid, her mascara had run. She never wore much, yet it was still enough to leave a black splodge against the lapel of Joe's suit jacket. She'd let him find that for himself.

'Thanks, Joe,' she said. 'I needed that.'

'Erm, any time.' He rubbed a spot under his ear that probably wasn't itchy. His face could have stopped traffic from twenty yards.

'I didn't notice any food around. You?'

'No, not in here,' he said, heading towards the open door. 'Only wrappers. Maybe we'll find some in the other rooms.'

'Whoa, whoa, whoa, I don't think so,' said Dawn. 'The bones, over there, remember? Let's get out of here before this lunatic comes home.'

'But there's still a ton of rooms to explore.'

'*Avanti*, Magellan!' said Dawn, resisting the urge to slap his arse. 'Mush!'

'Okay, okay, I'm going.'

They headed into the corridor and towards the stairwell door. Joe grabbed hold of the handle and pulled it open.

The yellow glow of artificial light fell onto a harsh concrete landing rimmed by functional metal rod banisters topped with a cheap black plastic-covered handrail. The staircase itself had been fashioned from large slabs of concrete, pieced together like a massive three-dimensional jigsaw. Nobody had bothered to decorate. No dark yellow thirteens on the wall, for example. A complete lack of windows too.

'Hold on a minute,' said Joe, barring the path. 'I just want to try something.'

He let the door close for a moment, then re-opened it.

The stairwell had changed. There was no doubting it. On the other side of the door there lay a landing now covered in grey patterned vinyl. A shining chrome handrail topped thin walls of toughened glass in lieu of banisters. Beyond the stairwell Dawn could see tall window panes, beyond which a glimpse of another building opposite.

Joe closed the stairwell door and opened it once again.

The bland stairwell of an office block appeared. The left half of the wall that faced them had a large number 13 painted in red, while, on the right, rain lashed heavily against smallish window panes.

Joe let the door close and looked to Dawn. She rolled her eyes and sighed.

'So the stairwells change each time we close the door?' she said. 'Great! I mean, this was getting too easy, after all.'

He opened the door once more, this time to a darkened collapsed stairwell. Dawn peered over his shoulder and saw large fragments of concrete jutting from a heavily fractured wall, impossible to negotiate. There were no windows inside. A single wall-mounted light had survived. Joe peered up and down the debris that remained in the shaft.

'Incredible,' he said. 'It really does go on forever, repeated over and over again.'

A chill worked its way through Dawn's bones, prompting her to rub her arms. She recalled how she had made a beeline for the stairs, leaving the door to close between her and Joe. How lucky they were that he had caught it just in time.

'I think we'd better stick together,' she said. 'We don't want one of these doors splitting us up.'

I don't want to be alone.

[You'll never be alone, Dawwwny Prawn. I'll always be waiting for you.]

Oh God, he's coming! The Tickling Man! Staying in the shadows, feeding on her fear, he would surely come for her, fingers outstretched, reaching for her flesh, the touch, the rake of his claws, and then a trip-switch primed by a seemingly endless string of thirteenth floors would flip and she would go stark screaming insane. Perhaps this was indeed a circle of hell, somewhere to live out eternity tormented by one's demons. Clearly they weren't the only ones damned in this place. The clues were everywhere. The bones. The filth. The blood. So much blood.

She took a deep breath and closed her eyes. She tried to focus on something good, something that could give her strength, something to stop her from going batshit crazy, but nothing would come. She was an only child with a dickhead Dad and a dead Mum, and after four years of losing University friends the only thing she had left was a dead-end job and Mike. But now she could no longer think of Mike without her mind conspiring to have him dying in front of her eyes.

At that moment the only nice thing she knew she could rely on, the one person who could help keep The Tickling Man at bay, was the dishevelled and slightly greasy young man standing ahead of her.

'Are you okay?' he said. She must have been staring again.

'Yeah,' she said. 'Just about.'

Joe nodded and let go of the stairwell door, which closed with a soft thud.

The noise echoed, loud and clear, coming from elsewhere in the floor. Dawn felt an icy grip tighten on her heart. Her skin broke out in goosebumps. There was a strangled cry that sounded like "Hello". A man. There were some other words she couldn't quite hear. Something foreign. Slavic? Russian?

From the look on Joe's face she wasn't alone in hearing it, and her heart sank.

Louder now. The noise came from the short daylit corridor to their right and around the corner where anyone, or any*thing*, could be lying in wait.

'Sounds like he needs help,' said Joe.

'Or he could be the guy living in that shitty hellhole back there.'

'I don't think so,' said Joe. 'That's definitely the sound of someone asking for help.' He turned from the door and, to Dawn's horror, he started along the shorter corridor.

'Are we really doing this?' she said. 'We are, aren't we? We're bloody doing this. Jesus, Joe!'

'Relax,' he said. 'The guy might know something about where we are, or what has happened to us.'

'What, and we'd be able to understand a word of it? I got "Hello" and that was it.'

'Let's just take a look. Wow!'

Joe stopped dead, forcing Dawn to walk around him.

The corner revealed another long stretch of hotel room doors, a near mirror image of the other corridor. Halfway towards the lobby, however, on the right-hand side, she saw multiple lengths of rope, each tied around the same single door handle and leading into the surrounding open rooms.

Further banging against the door set the ropes a-shaking with more violence than she would have liked. She could feel every bump raised on her skin as she rubbed her arms.

'Pozhaluysta, pomogi mne!' The man in the room sounded weak. Desperate.

Joe was looking her way. He shrugged his shoulders.

'Bulgarian?' he said, and headed towards the secured door.

'Beats me,' said Dawn. 'I don't really want to find out.'

'Zaberi menya otsyuda!' said the man.

The door handle hammered up and down, taking a chainsaw to Dawn's nerves in the process. The ropes shook with more vigour but the door remained tethered.

Joe approached the door. He pointed to the handle and beckoned for her to see.

'We've got blood here,' he said. 'A lot of it. Different ages too. I think this guy's in serious trouble.'

She sighed and cursed Joe's stubbornness, a side to him she had seldom seen during her time at Hardingham Frank and a little too gung-ho for her liking. And yet, though her conscious self screamed for her to run like hell, deep down she knew he had a point. They couldn't simply leave the guy to rot in the hotel room.

Joe and his bloody-minded compassion would be the death of them, but she knew it was the self same compassion that had seen him smash Clive across the head with a computer monitor when he could have easily snuck away from the gents toilet, safe and unseen.

Dammit, Joe. . .

She dragged her feet to where Joe stood. The man inside the room continued to shout incomprehensibly. The door shook but could not be opened.

Assorted bloodstains decorated the area around the handle of the door. They ran down to patches and streaks of deep burgundy that clotted and congealed on the red, deep-pile carpet. Three lengths of crimson-splattered rope held the lever-style door handle in place to prevent the man from opening the door inwards. Two of the ropes were tethered to beds in the open rooms opposite. She ducked under these and found the other rope similarly secured in the room next door - but here she noted a number of used syringes, rags and empty bottles scattered on the floor. Bloody handprints covered the bed linen, as if someone had used it like a hand towel.

'On sobirayetsya s'yest' menya!' yelled the man inside, and he tugged at the door once more.

She heard a splintering sound and looked towards the rattling handle, then to Joe. He returned her stare, no longer quite so brave. The man in the room perhaps wasn't as weak as they had first imagined.

The air pressure dropped slightly in the corridor. She recalled the same sensation in the stairwell of 3 Donnington Place and knew someone was coming.

The metallic tang of lightning intensified, stinging the back of her nose and throat.

She watched as Joe's hair moved, peeling away from his side parting, standing on end. She checked her gooseflesh and found the fine hairs on her arms similarly bolt-upright, then felt the hair on her head move.

Get out of here, Dawn! Out, out, out! GO!

The heavy thud of the closing stairwell door sounded along the corridor, causing Dawn to choke on her breath. She felt her heart hammering against her ribcage.

The ropes shook. The handle rattled. Loosened.

'Joe?'

A spark of electricity leapt between a pair of distant door handles with a vicious snapping sound. Another spark pinged between the prisoner's door handle and Joe's wristwatch. He cried out in pain, leaping back. He hurried under the ropes to join Dawn.

Inside the hotel room the man squealed, a spark clearly finding him.

'KTO TAM?' Another man's voice boomed in the corridor from around the corner, foreign also.

A lick of electricity met Dawn's engagement ring. The muscles in her arm contracted, stung like hell. It felt like the bones in her hand had been moved and then quickly reset. Every nerve ending felt on fire. When she rubbed her hand she found the white gold noticeably warmer than her body temperature.

Oh, shit, this is bad!

Strings of lightning bolts jumped from door handle to door handle. Another leapt up and struck a light fitting in the ceiling, setting off a chain reaction of flashes and fizzing and electrical pulses that careened around and across the corridor, popping light bulbs and sending down showers of glass and sparks. Darkness came to the corridor, quickly and without mercy.

This is very, very bad! Run! Run away!

The lobby area was still lit. Something to aim for. Beside her she sensed Joe start to run. Someone to follow. Behind her she heard a million volts tear between anything and everything metal. Something to most definitely avoid.

And yet she could not resist a swift look into the electrified chaos, if only to see who was coming for them. She saw in the blue strobe-like flashes a bearded man wearing dark, ragged clothes, possibly an army uniform of some description. He emerged from the corner carrying a weapon, a long blade. A fork of lightning knocked it clean from his hands. He bared his teeth and screamed with pain. The knife landed in the corner, immediately becoming a focal point for the swirling ball of electricity developing in the corridor.

The prisoner howled within the hotel room. Dawn could only imagine the poor man's agony as he was struck repeatedly with fierce lashes of energy.

'Derzhis' ot menya podal'she!' the man in the corridor screamed as he neared the door, his body racked with spasms as the light show in the corridor reached its climax. The plasma ball moved with him. Sparks flew everywhere as bolts of blue light met again and again with the man's head, his belt buckle, the metal buttons of his uniform.

Dawn ran, hoping she had not left it too late, that she was not about to be swallowed by the lightning storm growing behind her.

Joe had almost reached the lobby area. He turned and urged Dawn on, but she could not hear a word. The corridor filled with shrieks from the two men, finding a horrific harmony amidst the intense lightning. It sounded like the universe was about to tear in two.

Dawn met Joe at the corner of the lobby and felt the tension in her skin instantly fade, the hairs on her arms drop. She heard something fall to the ground behind her, then silence. She looked back along the dark stretch of corridor but saw only the faint glow of daylight from around the corner. No lightning. All was still in the darkness.

She stood for a moment and caught her breath.

'What the hell, Joe?'

'I don't know,' he said, looking away into the lobby, absentmindedly flattening his hair. 'They kind of look like codes.'

'What?'

'Over there, on the floor.'

She stepped around Joe and took in the lobby. There were a pair of opposing single elevator doors, each set in an ornate frame, each with bloodstains smeared on their call buttons and on the tarnished doors.

She looked to where Joe had pointed and found brown paint daubed onto the filthy marble-effect floor immediately outside each elevator. A large letter O followed by a number: "O20.1" and, opposite, "O20.2".

CHAPTER SEVEN

Joe pushed the call button nearest him and the door immediately pinged open. Several layers of graffiti vied for dominance inside the elevator. Dark brown stains befouled the floor.

'Oh, lovely,' he said.

He stepped into the car and found the air thick with the stench of stale urine and decay. He staggered back into the lobby where Dawn was covering her mouth and nose.

'No thank you,' he said, and walked to the elevator opposite. 'I think we'll take the other one.'

When the door rolled away, he found the second elevator out of action. Not only had the interior been liberally splattered with old, sticky blood but the car itself had been cleaved in two down the middle. The left half of the elevator had slid a couple of inches down the steep diagonal. How the mirrors inside hadn't shattered he'd never know - there was barely even a crack. Stranger still, the stains of the left half noticeably outnumbered those of the right.

'Joe, I really think we ought to try this one,' said Dawn. She stood by the open door of the first elevator.

'Seriously, Dawn? It stinks like a sewer in there.'

'Use your sleeve or something. We won't be in there for long.'

'Why don't we take the stairs?'

'Because there are a couple of buttons in here with a number four on them.'

'Really?'

Dawn nodded and beckoned him over. This was more like it. At least on the fourth floor they were heading in the right direction - down. Close enough perhaps to find a ledge. Maybe even close enough for someone to see them wave for help.

He drew a hand into the sleeve of his suit jacket and felt a vicious slash of agony course through his abdomen. He cried out, using his sleeve to muffle the pain.

'What's up?'

'Nothing,' he said. 'I'm okay. I think I've pulled a muscle, that's all.'

Liar.

He felt across his belly, gently, fearing even this simple action would see him doubled over in agony. Sprinting away from the lightning show had turned his insides into a coarse sack of electric eels, and the repulsive smell of the first elevator had made him nauseous. He was sure if he threw up that the pain would be immense, as if he too had been sliced in two. A thin film of sweat collected on his forehead.

You're going to have to tell her.

'Okay,' he said. 'But if I chuck up on you it's not my fault.'

'Nice. Get in the elevator, Prince Charming.'

'Yes, ma'am.'

Once inside he found a single small porthole set into the interior door at eye level. The exterior door had nothing of the sort. It seemed they had found another elevator car unsuited to the floors it serviced. Scribbles from a permanent marker covered the glass, but were difficult to read against the darkness beyond. A single exposed fluorescent tube in the roof-space bathed everything with anaemic light.

Someone had whitewashed over the graffiti that once covered the control panel. Handwritten codes were then scrawled above some of the buttons: "Ü218.2", "Ü109.3", "H76.1", "T1.1", "O20.2" - the same "O20.2" painted onto the marble floor outside.

Dawn punched one of the buttons for the fourth floor and the elevator car shook into life. A crackle of static erupted from a cluster of holes set into the control panel.

Breathing.

Smacking sounds of a mouth getting ready to speak.

'Hello, Dawn.'

She leapt away from the control panel and slammed against the wall of the elevator, her face caught somewhere between disgust and outright horror. She breathed hard through the sleeve of her blouse.

'C-Clive?' she said, her voice muffled.

A phlegmy chuckle spilled from the control panel's internal speaker, then a long intake of breath.

'Hmmmmmmm. Yeah, it's me. Long time no hear, bitch. It's been even longer since I heard your tubby arse, Joe. Don't think I've forgotten what you did to me.'

'Me?' said Joe. 'What?'

'Where are you?' said Dawn.

'Oh, you know, some place nearby. Don't worry, though. I know *exactly* where you are. You've stepped in from my floor, haven't you? Well, I hope you said hello to Vlad. He hasn't been entirely himself of late, you see.'

Dawn said nothing as Clive chuckled. She eyeballed the control panel again, as if expecting it to pop open and for the crazy bastard to spring out. The elevator continued to move upwards, taking forever about it.

'Gone quiet on me, eh? Hah! That's a first. Anyway, I couldn't help overhearing you both just now. Fourth floor, yeah? I know the one. Maybe I'll see you there. Maybe you'll see me. Oh, just so you know, I'll be the one blowing a hole through your arse with this little beauty.'

A metallic tapping sound filled the elevator.

Joe looked to the control panel. Two buttons sported the number four, just like Dawn had reported.

How does he know which one we've pressed?

He scanned the corners of the ceiling for anything that resembled a security camera, but found only grime and spray paint.

At long last the elevator car shook against a huge buzzing noise that sounded outside. The fluorescent light flickered above them. A flash of bright light shone through the interior window, as dazzling as a cloudless December sunrise. A hiss of static erupted from the control panel, which then quickly faded into Clive's laughter.

The colour drained quickly from Dawn's face.

'I'm not afraid of you!' she said, but her faltering voice betrayed her.

'Bollocks! I can practically taste your fear from here, Dawn, and I've got to tell you: it tastes really fucking good.'

Dawn pressed herself harder against the wall of the elevator. She breathed rapidly through the fabric of her sleeve.

Joe's mind was alive with questions. He recalled the state of Clive's hotel room: the bones, the litter, the stains, the smell. "Vlad". Whatever had been going on there had taken a lot longer than a single Friday morning. How long had Clive been living there? How had he lived there for so long? Had three years passed for him as well?

He did say "Long time, no hear." Especially from me. What the hell was that all *about?*

'I don't get it,' said Joe. 'That floor was yours? But how?'

'How? How else?' said Clive. 'By force. By taking control. By pulling the trigger on any fucker that stands in my way.' His voice became distorted over the emergency phone's speaker. 'By being the King of the Castle.'

Joe felt a noticeable rise of temperature in the elevator car. A dull roar announced itself outside.

'Whoa! Shit!' said Joe.

The door opened to an inferno that quickly sucked the air from the elevator car. Joe stood, helpless, watching the flames as they roared up from the furniture, from the carpet, from everything in sight. A blast of scalding heat burned his cheeks and singed his eyebrows. His mouth worked like a goldfish, seeking air, any air, as foul as it may have been, but finding none. He looked to Dawn and found her jabbing her finger into the other "4" button, over and over again until the door finally closed.

No air!

The elevator started up.

Joe bobbed open his mouth again.

Still no air! Shit, there's no air in my lungs either!

He looked to the small window of the interior door, praying for a flash of light outside.

There came further metallic tapping from the speaker.

'I said I'm the King of the Castle here, fuckers,' said Clive. 'Do you hear me? This whole fucking *maze* is mine.'

Maze?

The buzzing finally came and the inside of the elevator filled with bright light.

Oh God, my chest! It hurts, it hurts! We're going to suffocate! Shitshitshit!

Joe collapsed to his knees and looked to the interior window, praying for the next floor to arrive sooner.

'Oh, yeah, the air thing,' said Clive. 'I forgot. That'd be my old prep floor. I swear that fire's been going for weeks. Maybe months, now. It's like it's stuck in a loop or something.'

Dawn also fell to her knees. She kept a hand clamped over her mouth as if trying to prevent what little air she had from escaping. Her eyes bulged, unblinking. She looked towards Joe, utter terror carved into her face.

Oh, shit, I'm blacking out! It feels like my lungs are about to implode!

'Anyway, shitheads, I'd love to stay a while and fuck with you some more but I've got to fly,' said Clive. 'I can hear guests coming and you wouldn't want to spoil the surprise welcome I have for them now, would you? Okay, kill you later. Bye!'

After two dull electronic notes the speaker fell silent.

The interior door finally opened, filling the cab with dusty, but oh-so-precious air. Joe lunged towards the new floor, sucking in all the air he could, caring little for the tang of decay and urine all around him, his insides racked with needling agony, his lungs aflame. He saw Dawn crawl out from the elevator and into what sounded like a warzone.

Move it, fat boy.

He scrambled out onto the rubble-strewn, thinly-carpeted floor of the lobby. It was dark outside wherever this particular fourth floor happened to be. Half of the strip light fittings in the lobby were either smashed in or didn't work. A few others flickered non-stop, casting slow strobe lighting over pockets of ruin. Ahead of him the lobby opened out onto a considerable darkened area, which appeared to be a largely-destroyed open plan office.

He found Dawn crouched behind a nearby upright cylindrical bin in the lobby, still gasping for every cubic inch of air her lungs could take. She furiously tried to smooth down her hair but her hands shook too much.

'Dawn? Dawn, talk to me.' Her eyes were wild. 'Clive can't hurt us over the airwaves, okay? We're still getting out of here, you and me, yeah?'

He sensed she was every bit as angry as she was terrified. She looked ready to smack him one.

A volley of gunfire rattled somewhere outside and was met with a swift retaliatory response. Another mortar exploded in the distance.

She continued to bore into him with wild eyes. 'What if we can't get out of here, though, Joe? Huh? What then? You heard him. He called this place a *maze*. What the hell was *that* all about?'

'I don't know,' said Joe. 'I heard it too. It sounded like he's been here for as long as we've been missing. God knows how.'

'We can't just keep going from floor to floor like this,' said Dawn. 'We're going to run into trouble sooner or later. We need a weapon. Both of us.'

'Okay. Sounds like a plan.'

Joe quickly scanned the elevator lobby for anything that could double as a weapon. A large, broken window to his left formed the abrupt end of the lobby. It presented a starless night sky and the left-hand edge of a tall, partially-lit building nearby. Toughened glass from the thick window pane littered the floor in a million tiny fragments. A number of large ceiling tiles rested about the place, each perforated by bullet holes. Next to the elevator a stairwell had collapsed, spilling out large chunks of rubble. The heavy, black door lying nearby had been torn from its hinges. Perfect darkness filled the gaps between the ragged chunks of metal and concrete in the stairwell, like jet black mortar.

'There's nothing much around here,' he said. 'Perhaps there's something better out there in the rest of the floor. We might be okay if we keep our heads down.'

'Okay, let's at least take a look,' said Dawn. 'Just get me away from that fucking elevator.'

They scampered towards a solid white wall directly opposite the broken window and hunkered down beneath a single, ominous-looking bullet hole. The edge of the lobby presented a view of an large, mostly open floor of two halves.

The left side was a burnt wreck of smashed windows, broken furniture and ruined office equipment, of light fittings dislodged from the ceiling, spinning in the breeze, and of small fires flickering on the floor. The sounds of distant gunfire cracked in the night.

The right side of the floor, however, was largely untouched, as if the war outside hadn't reached all the way in. A run of unbroken ceiling lights hung over the entrances to a number of glass-fronted offices, divided in the middle by a length of wall upon which there hung a logo. "CCTV", the second C in red. Some of the glass fronts sported occasional bullet holes.

Joe heard Dawn sighing behind him.

'So much for getting out of here through the fourth floor,' she said. 'It's like World War Three out there.'

'Yeah, and now Clive knows we're here,' said Joe.

He felt Dawn pat him hard on the shoulder.

'Okay, a plan,' she said. 'See if you can find anything useful over there in that mess. I'll tackle the offices. We'll meet over the other side in five minutes and leg it out of here. Deal?'

Joe nodded.

'Don't do anything stupid, Joe,' she said.

Her hand clamped harder onto his shoulder. For once he felt a warmth spreading in his guts instead of pain. He watched as Dawn leapt out from behind him and into the nearest glass-fronted office.

He raised up from his knees and found his bladder swollen.

Great. What a time to need a piss.

Putting the discomfort to the back of his mind he rounded the corner and crept low into the darkness of the floor. He found a photocopier and crouched behind it.

He heard voices from outside. Others close by too, foreign, but unmistakably angry. The yelling mostly came from the floor below, a little from above. He shuffled around the photocopier towards the edge of the floor. The surviving window panes to his immediate left proved too blackened with smoke to see through, particularly given how dark it was outside, and so he homed in on the first shattered window.

You're meant to be looking for a weapon, fat boy.

'I'm only looking,' he said to himself.

Every streetlight had been knocked out or switched off, leaving Joe with scarce patches of moonlight by which to see outside. A short burst of gunfire lit up the small corner of a devastated parking lot, then fell silent. He saw hanzi-style lettering on the nearest street signs. In the distance there were further ideographs on the illuminated fronts of shops and buildings.

China then, or somewhere like it.

Someone shouted from the floor above: 'Quánlì shuyú rénmín!' Machine gun fire rattled into a dark lump that sat in the parking lot, its exact shape masked by the shadows of trees. Bullets pinged and sparked against the metal object, and then tracer bullets, apparently the last of the magazine, hit home like laser beams to reveal the dim outline of a military tank. Joe watched in horror as the turret shook into life and took aim directly into the fourth floor. Gunfire from the parking lot zipped and thumped into the concrete above and below him.

A strangled cry. A bullet had found its target. A man in black civilian clothes dropped from above, the back of his head missing. A woman's voice screamed what could have been the man's name, and Joe heard the sickening sound of the corpse smashing into the asphalt below.

'Shit! Shit! Shit!' said Joe as he scrambled for the safety of the photocopier.

Further volleys of gunfire rattled out in lengthy bursts, the fighters in the building clearly angered by the loss of their fallen colleague. Bullets shattered what little glass remained in the windows as the army outside returned fire. They ricocheted off the dislodged light fittings, swinging them around on their wires. A single bullet thudded into the photocopier, nearly giving Joe a heart attack in the process, and then all was calm.

He eyeballed the wall of offices. He felt his insides twist, the tension against his bladder increase. He counted the bullet holes in the glass fronts, desperately looking for anything new.

Dawn?

He so wanted to call out her name but didn't dare.

The swinging lights flashed across a bent pipe that lay near his feet. A support perhaps for an office partition long since reduced to ash and charred wood. The metal had been sheared off at one end, creating a vicious cutting edge. He reached over and grabbed it, felt its weight.

Yeah, this'll do for now.

'Siwáng de zhèngquán!' yelled a woman from somewhere.

Another fighter: 'Women huì tīngdào!'

Faint clicks of rifles reloading sounded above and below him and then the fighting resumed. Joe looked to the far end of the floor, feeling their five minutes were up, but couldn't see Dawn. A puff of plaster dust erupted beneath the CCTV logo on the far wall, perilously close to the offices on either side. The situation was getting way too dangerous. He had found a weapon of sorts. It would have to do for the time being.

There was a loud boom outside immediately followed by an incredible high-pitched scream as a tank shell roared in through the broken windows and slammed into the offices behind him. The almighty explosion threw him to the floor and rendered him deaf for a moment. A large cloud of dust and debris billowed through the floor. A heavy-looking air con unit crashed down from the ceiling, bringing with it tubes, rubble and a lengthy stretch of silvery duct.

No! Oh, please don't be in there! Please!

'DAWN!'

He struggled to his feet, picked up the bar and ran through the smoke, caring nothing for the firefight outside. He tripped over the air con unit, fell and looked once more around him. A flickering orange glow in the near distance suggested fire.

No no no no! Please be alive!

'DAWN!'

'I'm over here!' A voice through the smoke. 'I'm okay. Where are you?' It sounded as if she was on the other side of the floor, where they had agreed to meet.

'Keep shouting. I'll find you,' said Joe, feeling relief beyond words. He coughed in the smoke that now thickened ahead of him, the last thing his burning lungs and tortured guts needed. He hauled himself over a tangled mountain of destroyed furniture, melted flat-screen monitors and the broken air conditioning unit.

'What the hell was that?' said Dawn. 'It's like we're in Tiananmen Square or something.'

'No, not quite,' said Joe, finally getting clear of the smoke. Much to his surprise Dawn stood ahead of him unhurt and clean of dust and debris. The last few offices remained intact, one with its door open. 'But that was definitely a tank out there.' He offered her the metal bar.

'Thanks. Beats everything I found.' She dropped a marble-effect paperweight with sharp-looking corners. She held out the bar but could barely keep it still. Shock had obviously made puppet strings of her nerves. 'You okay?'

'I think so. No limbs missing.' He held out his hands. 'About as shaken as you, though, by the looks of it.'

He felt a stabbing sensation in his side, making him wince.

Yeah, and the rest.

The floor shuddered as if an aftershock had suddenly gripped the building. A series of huge and familiar clunking noises resonated all round the floor, dominating even the sounds of warfare outside. Fire took a solid hold of the smashed offices behind him and started to spread throughout the floor. The smoke thickened across the ceiling and quickly swallowed the light.

'Head for the emergency exit,' said Dawn. 'Quick, while we can still see it!'

She dashed ahead and hauled open the heavy, black stairwell door. She stepped out onto the landing and held the door for Joe to follow, urging him to hurry.

He hurt near enough everywhere now. Every step he took seemed to halve what energy he had but he forced himself to keep going. When the door closed behind him the clanking and burning and the noise of warfare immediately cut to silence. The smoke that had rolled into the stairwell soon dissipated.

Dawn started down the first couple of steps of the stairwell. Her shoulders sagged. She peered over the handrail, taking in the infinite flights of stairs beneath her, then leaned in deeper.

'You could have told me my hair was still sticking up,' she said, and set about smoothing it down.

'Infinite staircase or handy mirror?' said Joe, smiling to himself. 'You decide.'

He reopened the stairwell door to a completely new floor: a lofty, elongated office, densely furnished, that curved gently to the right into the distance. A bank of tall windows lay along the right-hand side, their blinds bunched high towards the ceilings.

A strong metallic tang immediately grew in the air, the smell of thunderstorms once more. A flash of electricity crackled from some of the metal window frames and flew into a number of light fittings, causing the bulbs to shatter and spark.

'What was that?' Dawn spun around.

Mini-bolts of lightning leapt between chunky old-school computer monitors and danced along the shiny metal poles of the desks. It felt as if a massive build-up of static was about to be unleashed. The smell of raw energy stung Joe's nostrils. He felt his hair reach for the sky again and his blood run cold.

Ahead of him, by the windows, midway along the floor, there stood a woman. She had her back to him, her shoulders slumped.

'What the-?' he said.

The woman stood around five feet six inches tall and had tousled brown hair that sprang out from her scalp in thickets. She wore a once-white blouse and a simple grey skirt, now torn, filthy and covered with stains of red, brown and yellow. The right arm of her blouse had been ripped clean away revealing a bare shoulder and a naked sinewy arm covered in cuts, bruises and pustulent sores. Her legs were just as badly scarred. She looked like she hadn't eaten in a month. A painfully pronounced shoulder blade jutted from her back. She carried in her right arm a foot-long blade, the kind used as a bayonet attachment.

Her left arm had been savagely removed just above the elbow. The badly-cauterised wound looked livid with infection.

Joe stepped into the floor and let go of stairwell door, momentarily forgetting the consequences.

The woman turned and noticed the growing swell of energy behind her, recognised it, feared it. Her face was so hollowed-out as to be barely recognisable. Her scab-encrusted mouth twisted in terror, revealing blackened gums and missing teeth. The sight of her was enough for Joe to collapse to the floor. He found it hard to breathe. He felt like throwing up again.

What stood ahead of him was impossible.

I'm going to die in here.

'Christ, Joe,' said Dawn, emerging from the doorway. 'You nearly shut me in there. Whoa!'

Yet more light fittings burst into showers of sparks as a large plasma ball developed in the middle of the floor. It hovered over the ranks of desks, caressing all things metal nearby with lethal-looking tendrils of energy. It sounded like an electrical substation was about to explode in the room.

And then the haggard woman suddenly vanished, seemingly rubbed out of existence. The electrical storm instantly evaporated into a small series of crackles that then faded into silence.

'Joe?' said Dawn. He felt her hands on his shoulders. 'Joe, are you okay? What happened just now? Who was that?'

Joe kept his eyes fixed on where the young woman once stood.

'I think it was you.'

CHAPTER EIGHT

Dawn released her hands from Joe's shoulders, glared at them, unable to stop them from shaking, as if they were alive with the same electricity that had coursed throughout the floor.

Like Joe she had caught a glimpse of the other woman before she disappeared, and like him she knew exactly who the woman was. Dawn McKenzie: torn, emaciated and racked with disease, an arm hacked away at the elbow.

No! That wasn't me. I'm me!

Another Dawn, then. An older Dawn. A future Dawn, perhaps? *That was someone else! That was Other Dawn, not me. I'm still me.*

She closed her eyes only to find Other Dawn scorched into her retinas. She felt a deep aching sensation spread across her stomach, rattling through her insides. Her limbs trembled as if she hadn't slept for a week. She wondered how long they had been trapped between floors.

How long do I have before... that?

'Joe?'

He looked up to her from his kneeling position, absent-minded, not quite seeing. The cheery face he often put on for everyone had slipped away completely. He seemed lost to the world, as if someone had borrowed his soul and forgotten to give it back. His greasy hair was plastered to his sweating brow. His five o'clock shadow had darkened further. Sweat patches stained the underarms of his suit jacket. Another large patch developed just below his shoulders. He made a wordless noise of acknowledgement.

'Joe, what time is it?'

He slowly drew up his wristwatch, then let slip an angry sigh. Some emotion from him at least.

'I don't know.' He slowly hauled himself up from the floor, grunting and flinching with the effort. 'It's supposed to be one of those radio-controlled watches so I don't have to bother setting it. As you can see it's given up the ghost.'

He flashed her a look at the dial. Indeed all hands pointed resolutely to 12 o'clock.

'Maybe it got fried back in the hotel corridor?' she said.

'Yeah, maybe,' said Joe, unconsciously rubbing his wrist. 'Or maybe it's just as lost as we are.'

She'd never heard him so downcast. She owed the guy her life, the least she could do was gee him up a little. She slid a hand over his shoulders, gently shook him.

'We're not lost,' she said, upbeat, though not believing a word of it herself. 'We're getting out of here, you and me. Together, remember?'

He nodded, so weak as to convey no meaning.

Come on, Joe. Come back to me.
I don't want to be alone.

'This place is just messing with our heads,' she said. She considered telling him about The Tickling Man, then dismissed the idea. 'If we stick together, especially on the stairs, then we'll be fine. I'll superglue our hands together if I have to.'

'It'd be a bit awkward if one of us needs the loo.'

Attaboy, Joe!

She laughed and pinched his cheek.

'Ah, is that a little smile I can see on my hero's face?'

'What?' Though said with incredulity, she noticed the corners of his mouth curl, the faint creases around his eyes deepen.

'Yeah, that's right,' she said, twirling away, the back of her hand against her brow, a display of mock melodrama the like of which the old Joe would have approved. 'My hero!' She made to swoon against a nearby desk, steadied herself and found his eyes. She smiled, surprising herself how easy it came to her.

'Thanks for getting me out of there, Joe.'

Joe's cheeks flushed the colour of tomato soup. He scratched his ear again.

'Any time,' he said eventually. 'Well, seeing as though we've got the floor to ourselves we may as well take a look around. I'll get the bar.'

Dawn looked around the large, banana-shaped office floor: the word "utilitarian" would have been a kindness. Everything was designed, fashioned and positioned in such a way as to get a job done, nothing more. The tall window panes that ran the right-hand side of the floor faced a long, thinly-painted breezeblock wall on the left, unbroken save for two heavy-duty fire doors at either end. To Dawn's surprise the nearest of these doors was unlocked, opening to a similar arrangement on the other side. On either side of the breezeblock wall there stood long ranks of filing cabinets, identical, unlocked and empty.

To the rear of the floor there were three doors: one to the ladies toilets, a second the heavy, black stairwell door from which they had emerged, and a final door to a small, dingy photocopier room. She found the same on the other side of the fire door.

The desks of the floor had been arranged in a regimented fashion. They all faced the same direction in rows of six identical workstations where there was only comfortable room for five. It was as if whoever furnished the floor had to make up for the frivolous waste of space brought about by the architect's high ceilings.

Upon the surfaces of each dreary desk there lay identical chunky, beige keyboards, identical chunky, beige mice and identical chunky, beige monitors, each as deep as they were wide. A similarly artless tower PC lay locked within a dedicated compartment built into the side of each desk. The only deviation came where the ball of lightning had scorched the desk surfaces and equipment.

Who on earth hoped to cram a couple hundred people in here? Surely the clattering keyboards alone would have driven everybody nuts?

At the far end of the floor she saw a single desk facing the others head-on. Perhaps the intended workforce had little choice but to endure their environment.

Beyond the single desk ahead there stood another three doors: one to a room of some description, another to an elevator and another still to the gents toilet.

'Back in a minute,' said Joe, and made haste along the window-lined aisle. 'I just need a wet.'

He placed the metal bar on the single desk. By the time he met the door to the gents toilet he was near enough running. The door creaked then slammed shut behind him, jarring in the silence - the noise echoing back to Dawn.

No whispers this time.

She approached the other side of the floor, occasionally pulling out a random drawer from the filing cabinets, noting the uniform layout of the desks. Christ, even the chairs had been pushed into the same positions. At least the whole place wasn't dark or confined. Nowhere for things to hide and lie in wait.

Don't even think about him, Dawn.

She rapped her knuckles against the surface of a nearby desk hard enough to create a satisfying echo. Something, anything, to break the silence, the anticipation, his invitation. She set her mind on other, more pressing matters to pass the time.

Where were all the electrical surges coming from? Were they a weapon of some kind, or perhaps a deterrent? A means to keep prisoners from wandering or escaping? A way to keep everyone in check?

And what had happened to Other Dawn, vanished before her eyes as if she'd never existed? Other Dawn, who looked like a half-dead cancer patient with leprosy. Other Dawn, the one with a ragged stump for a left arm.

No, she wasn't real. I'm the real Dawn.

Her head burned with questions for which she could find no answers and she hated the feeling. It was like the whole world knew something she didn't and it was agony. But then again, Joe was in the same situation.

Poor guy.

Poor guy? What about Mike?

'You're talking to yourself, Dawn,' she said. 'Stop it.'

She crouched by the elevator door and saw the simple plastic plate screwed into the wall nearby. Thirteen again. She found paint daubed onto the carpet in a similar fashion to that in the hotel lobby, a letter followed by a decimal number: "H132.2". She ran her hand over it, finding the paint long since dry.

Who is doing this?

She heard what sounded like an old starting pistol being fired. The cracking noise came from the gents toilet. She looked to the door and saw flecks of reddish-brown. A couple of dark splashes on the carpet.

Joe! Oh, God, no!

An invisible force shoved her back, causing her to squeal. She fell onto her rump and looked around. The contents of the office were trembling, the lights suspended above her rocking gently. The whole floor was moving. The sound of empty filing cabinets clattering together yielded to the disturbing sound of bricks moving against one another, which in turn gave way to the horribly familiar clanking sound that had so recently stalked them, much louder now and more pronounced against the relative silence. The banging noise echoed around the capacious office floor. It sounded like a deeply unstable shipwreck, huge, raised from the ocean, its twisted metal left to bake in the late morning sun.

Not for the first time it felt to Dawn as if all around her was about to fall to pieces.

A slamming noise caught her attention. The exterior door to the gents toilet squawked open. Joe stepped out, drenched, as if he'd lost a fight with Poseidon. He had an excited look on his face that she was relieved to see. It was like seeing the old Joe again.

'Dawn, you've got to see this!'

That spoiled the moment a little.

'Umm. I'm not sure I do, you know?'

'Come on,' he said, unrepentant. He kept the door open and waved her over.

'Okay,' she said. 'But this better not be what I think it is.'

She stood, taking her time about it, then followed him into the gents toilet, just as slowly. She took the interior door that Joe held for her and gasped.

She found the restroom neatly sliced in two across the middle, separating the four cubicles nearby from the half-dozen urinals further ahead. The entire urinal half of the room had shifted to the right six inches and twisted a couple degrees anticlockwise. The tiles of the walls and floor were slick with water, presumably from the same sudden gush that had drenched Joe. Water continued to gurgle from the ruined pipes.

'Jesus, Joe, I didn't think you needed to go that badly.'

'Yeah, yeah, yeah. But look over there, in the middle.'

He pointed to a reddish-brown splash mark that had long since dried on the floor tiles. An old bloodstain, roughly half the size of a large dinner plate. The bottom half. The stain ended abruptly at the point where the room had split in two, as if it had never existed in the other half.

'Okay, I'll bite, Joe. What happened?'

'I swear to God I was washing my hands, look, smell, see? There was an almighty cracking sound and then pretty much every water pipe in here exploded. The whole room just split in two and twisted how you see it now.'

'So why point out the bloodstain?'

'That was where the cracks started. I watched them spread across the floor, up the walls and meet in the ceiling. Then *we* moved. That tiny half of the room – we moved around it!'

'Yeah, I felt that bit.'

'Okay, then there's this.'

He jumped into the other half of the room, creating a small splash as he landed. He steadied himself and then turned to face her. He waved his hands as if to say "ta-daah!"

'And?'

'I'm off-kilter to you, Dawn, but I'm standing straight on this side. I'm not having to lean over to do this.'

She neared the split in the room. There was a thin layer of water collecting on the floor tiles. The water ran to the edge, yet didn't threaten to spill over into her side of the room. An impossible meniscus. A thin, black crack separated the two halves, as if a sheet of glass had been driven between them.

'Okay, that's new,' she said, then rubbed her arms. 'Colder too. So, what are we looking at here? Two different gravities?'

'I think so. Something along those lines. Mental, isn't it?'

She shrugged, not quite knowing what to make of it. She stepped away from the split in the restroom and watched as the semi-bloodstain wobbled and broke up beneath the thin film of water.

She'd always hated the sight of blood, more so when it was not her own. She recalled a time when Mike sliced through the tip of his thumb while preparing a meal. His blood ran freely all over the chopping board. She had to race for the toilet, retching. They ate takeaway that evening.

Why was it she could no longer think of Mike without him getting hurt? She cursed her masochistic mind. Yeah, and where the hell had The Tickling Man come from? She had grown out of that nightmare the moment she discovered boys.

She kept her eyes on the stain as the water settled over it. Her stomach hurt, but that was all. No dizzy spells. No twinkling lights in her peripheral vision. Perhaps she was hardening against the sight of blood.

But this was old blood. Blood that she had not seen spill from another person. Blood that was just there, going brown.

Cocaine Dale's ruptured face flashed into her mind. His punctured bug eye. The large bloodstain he had left on the carpet, a striking shade of red, wet and warm. She felt her insides squirm like a bag of worms. Her stomach rumbled and cramped. She looked away from the stain.

'Come on, Newton,' she said, approaching the restroom door. She held it open for Joe. 'My feet are soaked thanks to you.'

'Your feet are soaked? *I'm* bloody soaked!'

'Yeah, well, the sooner you stop playing in the water, dear, the quicker you'll dry off. Let's find something else we can use for a weapon.'

She watched Joe flinch as he hopped back into her side of the room. He unconsciously rubbed his belly.

Loss of weight. A seemingly unquenchable thirst. Frequent trips to the toilet. She had seen something like this before.

Once back in the body of the floor Dawn headed straight towards the nearest window for a look outside. She couldn't resist. She had to see whether the building had sustained any structural damage. Entire office floors simply weren't supposed to move like that. The gentle curvature of the building revealed little detail, however, forcing her to walk further along the windows for a better view.

She found nothing unusual. There were no chunks of building jutting out at a funny angle. The floor didn't unnaturally loom over the ground below. There seemed no damage outside whatsoever, just the same gentle curve of tall windows from left to right.

'H132.2,' said Joe.

'Yeah, I saw that just before everything started moving,' said Dawn, returning to the elevator door. 'It's like someone's been trying to number the floors.'

'You don't think they're still trying?'

'Well, the signs aren't good, are they? All we've seen so far is blood,' said Dawn, picking up the metal bar from the single desk nearby. 'Old blood and madness.'

Joe shrugged, then opened the door to the left of the elevator.

'Aha, now this is more like it!' he said and hobbled inside.

Dawn followed to find a small kitchen area dominated by a large black metal box, almost monolithic in stature. Joe leaned against it, his shoulders slumped, his head lowered.

'Shit,' he said, and sighed.

Thin plastic wrappers and broken glass littered the floor around the box, a vending machine. She found the shiny metal coils inside devoid of food.

Joe walked over to the kitchen sink without saying another word. He lapped water from the spout of the cold tap.

Dawn set the metal bar down to rest against the vending machine.

'How long have you been diabetic, Joe?' she asked.

Joe stopped drinking but kept his head near the running tap.

'I was diagnosed a couple of months ago. Type two, they say.'

'Have you told anyone at work?'

'There's not much point now, really.'

'That's not what I meant. You ought to have told someone.' She rubbed a hand between his shoulders and felt a sense of relief when he relaxed a little. 'When was your last shot?'

'I took one last night,' he said. 'A little more than usual if I'm honest. We pigged out watching *Die Hard 4.0*. I felt okay this morning and kind of forgot to top up. I had a few syringes in my drawer, so I thought I'd be okay.' He sighed deeply.

'I'm sorry, Joe.'

'It's my own stupid fault. I wish I'd never dragged us in here.'

'Come on, you weren't to know!' said Dawn, ruffling his hair. 'How are you feeling?'

'Like I'm being stabbed to death,' he said, and grimaced. 'A bit woozy too.'

She slid her arms around Joe's waist and squeezed, just enough to let him know she cared. The fabric of his suit jacket was damp in large patches. Sweat and toilet water, an unappealing combination, but then she could hardly consider herself morning-fresh. Her stomach growled, quickly joined by Joe's, causing them to laugh a little.

The weight of Joe's smartphone brushed against her arm.

'So long as we're able to talk to someone in the real world we have a chance. Is your phone still working?'

'Shit! I forgot all about it,' said Joe, sliding away from her clutches. He reached into his jacket pocket and removed a damp cigarette carton and his smartphone. To his delight the device still worked. He unlocked the phone and passed it to her, then set about trying to light the driest cigarette he had.

The battery life stood at thirteen percent, which brought a snort of derision from Dawn. Another unfunny punch line in a never-ending sick joke. At least she found a signal, weak but stable. She flashed the screen to Joe and watched his face brighten. He waved a hand, encouraging her to dial while he enjoyed his cigarette.

She redialled the front desk of 3 Donnington House. She heard three ascending notes for her trouble and an apology that the number was not recognised.

'Oh, stupid,' she hissed. 'I forgot the hash-four-four.'

She tried again, this time with the correct international dialling code. She looked at the phone in confusion as the number was once again rejected as unrecognised. She swore, sighed and passed the phone back to Joe.

'Can you find out where we are?'

'I'll give it a go,' said Joe. 'There's not much juice left, though.'

He swiped and tapped at the screen a few times. After a moment he tilted the screen towards Dawn. A blunt message read "Server unavailable".

'Figures,' he said, and tapped some more on the phone. 'Ten percent now.'

'Okay, switch it off. We'll only use it if we find a floor that looks like it's somewhere in England.'

'Okay,' said Joe. 'Though it might not come back on when the battery is this low.'

She walked to the cold tap and took in some water, before checking the state of her clothes. Her skirt was grubby in places that gave her pause to think where the dirt had come from. Her blouse was clammy from hugging Joe and still carried some of his stink, but she didn't mind. She could smell her own body odour too, so knew her deodorant was failing. She felt her skin chafe beneath the wings of her bra. She regretted not wearing something a little less severe. The distorted reflections in the chrome spout did little to disguise her bedraggled look. She sighed and flattened more rogue tufts of hair.

'Oh, wow!' said Joe from the corner of the room. He stood with his head inside a tall thin cupboard set into the wall.

'What is it?'

He waved her over. She turned off the cold tap and heard a fine high-pitched whine from within the cupboard. She peered inside and saw a rack of elongated boxes. They were each laden with cables, mostly grey, some red. A matrix of tiny lights lit up in unison across all of the boxes, twice every couple of seconds.

'Contact!' said Joe.

CHAPTER NINE

The bearded man in the filthy soldier's uniform screamed as he ran through the hotel corridor and towards Clive. His eyes were wild, though fear alone seemed the man's true driving emotion. Clive could smell it on him. The soldier eyed Clive's right hip with each step, clearly gunning for the parang that hung there. He was a survivor, and an excellent one at that. You only had to look at him. Wiry as fuck with all four limbs intact. His battle cry may have yielded results in the past, but then he had never crossed horns with the King of the Castle.

Come and get me, motherfucker.

The soldier lunged to the right but Clive had already guarded the parang's handle with his right hand. Clive dropped his shoulder and positioned himself ready to use the other man's momentum and send him flying. He didn't anticipate the soldier smashing an arm across his face.

Clive fell against the door opposite his hotel room, scattering his skull and crossbones.

The soldier careered into the side of the corridor, a little beyond the open door, and rolled awkwardly onto his back.

Clive didn't hesitate. He twisted round, crouched and placed his left knee down as if ready for the starting pistol.

The soldier rolled again, now onto his belly, getting to his feet.

Clive sprang towards him and focused all his weight onto the soldier's back, crushing him into the carpet.

Wiry as fuck the man may have been but he was stronger than he looked. Very much alive and kicking, at least for the time being.

Clive drove the soldier's face into the rancid carpet before he had a chance to wriggle free. He fetched out the parang with his right hand and smashed the handle into the base of the other man's skull a half-dozen times.

The soldier fought on, albeit noticeably dazed. He bucked and wriggled in an attempt to throw Clive from his back.

Fuck's sake. This is getting nowhere.

He dropped the parang behind him and grabbed clumps of hair in both hands. He pulled hard on the other man's scalp and banged his head into the carpet another half-dozen times.

Still the soldier fought back, albeit more through autopilot than any conscious form of self-defence.

Clive released a clump of hair and used his spare fist to rabbit-punch the soldier in the back of the head.

Eventually the other man lay still. Clive checked for a pulse. The man was still alive.

Excellent.

He re-sheathed his knife and strode through the open door to the hotel room. He pulled open one of the elongated panels of the wardrobe. Inside lay a collection of odds and sods gathered from other floors: some rags and a heap of rope filched from a rare maintenance floor; a half-dozen bottles of chloroform retrieved from some hapless bullet magnet.

He took a bottle of chloroform and a grubby rag from the wardrobe, then closed the door and looked at the marks he had gouged into the wood. A hundred and eighteen sleeps had passed since he had commandeered the hotel room, whatever a sleep was worth in here. It didn't matter. After such a long time being trapped in this hellhole it was clear he had been cast into this place to die. If only he knew by whom and where. It sure as hell wasn't at Her Majesty's pleasure. Over time it became obvious that each day in this fucked-up maze was a simple case of seeing how long he could survive.

The fella in the corridor ought to keep me going for a while.

He took the bottle and rag into the corridor and set them down beside the soldier, then rolled him onto his back and straddled him. He waited for the man to make a move, his hand primed over the handle of his hunting knife, ready to slice through the soldier's neck if needs be. The man remained unconscious. Clive soaked the rag with chloroform and held it over the soldier's mouth and nose. He counted the rise and fall of the man's chest until satisfied he was under. He tucked the small bottle and rag into his pocket, stood over the prone man and grabbed him from under his armpits.

Let's see if this works.

He dragged the soldier up towards the elevator lobby, crossed to the other corridor and back towards a room midways, one he had successfully managed to unlock without using brute force.

He hauled the soldier into the room and propped him against the footboard of the king-size bed. Within five minutes he had the man naked. He tossed the soldier's uniform and undergarments onto the mattress. Four long lengths of rope led from the wooden slats of the footboard. Clive tied the soldier's left wrist tight against the bed, and then the right, making a sitting Jesus Christ pose of him. He relaxed a little, knowing that the other man now stood little chance of breaking free.

The soldier moaned. The rate of his ragged breathing changed.

Clive quickly worked the other man's legs wide apart, as if inviting the world to kick him in the balls. He then secured the soldier's ankles with the two remaining ropes from the footboard. It wasn't great, but it would do until he could knock the guy unconscious again.

'Chto...' slurred the soldier. One of his eyes opened and looked around the room as if unable to focus on any one thing. He then met Clive's cold, semi-vacant stare.

'Morning, sunshine,' said Clive.

He slapped the soldier across the face hard enough to leave a red handprint.

'Nyet!' yelled the other man. 'Nyet ty!'

He struggled against his bindings as life slowly crept back into his limbs. He looked down, suddenly realising he was sitting naked on the floor.

'Shut the fuck up,' spat Clive.

He punched the soldier hard in the face. The other man sagged immediately. Clive retrieved a belt from the pile of clothes strewn across on the bed.

'Pozhaluysta! Ne nado!' moaned the soldier. Blood trickled from his mouth.

'Yeah, whatever,' said Clive, kneeling in front of him.

He slapped the other man about the face, this time with the leather belt. 'Do any of you fuckers speak English in this shithole?'

Not any more, Clive, old son. There's only you now.

The man said nothing.

Clive reached to his right and pulled the sole remaining parang from its sheath. It made a satisfying *shinggg*. He held the vicious-looking blade to the eyes of the soldier, nicking the bridge of the man's nose and drawing blood.

'This, Vlad, old son, is what is known as a parang,' said Clive. 'That's eighteen inches of "fuck you", to you.'

He let the blade rest, digging into the soldier's nose, letting him see the old bloodstains that still clung to the cold lethal metal.

The soldier's breathing deepened, quickened.

'Look at the workmanship. You Ruskie fucks would kill for a knife like this. The middle, here, is meant for chopping. It gets sharper towards the tip for skinning. Here, let me show you.'

Clive quickly slid the blade across the bridge of the soldier's nose. The other man screamed and pulled his head away to avoid the blade, letting it slice into his cheek perilously close to his left eye.

'Clumsy bastard,' said Clive. He drew away the parang and slapped the flat of the blade hard against the man's cheek, cutting him again.

Satisfied he'd sufficiently fucked with the soldier's mind Clive set the huge blade down directly in front of the man's shrivelled genitals. He sized up where to begin. The soldier was painfully thin, so thin as to make Clive wonder how he had been able to struggle beneath him.

The soldier's lily-white skin had broken and ruptured in several places with vile purple sores, and was heavily bloodstained from his straggly beard down to the hairs on his shrunken pigeon chest. The guy obviously didn't mind shovelling his meat down raw, the fucking dirty animal.

There were a couple of badly drawn tattoos on the stringy bicep of the man's left arm. They could have been from the guy's army days in Russia or wherever the fuck he was from, but to Clive they may as well have been dotted lines on a butcher's wall chart.

Decision made. With only one arm the man would really struggle to get free of his bindings.

He uncoiled the leather belt and looped it around the soldier's upper arm, just under the armpit. He pulled it tight until the man cried out, then held it in place until he was sure the arm was dead.

The soldier howled in agony. He looked to his lifeless arm with utter dread.

Clive shoved the end of the belt into the soldier's mouth and forced the man's jaw shut.

Tears formed in the man's eyes. A bubble of snot grew and burst onto his greasy bloodstained beard.

'I know you'll understand this bit, you Russian fuck,' hissed Clive into the soldier's ear. 'I'd strongly recommend you keep the pressure up on that arm of yours otherwise you'll bleed to death, and I wouldn't want that.'

He gently slapped the soldier's cheek, a small perverse act of encouragement, then fetched the heavy hunting knife from between the man's legs.

From between gritted teeth the soldier yelled for all he was able, anything that could help see him through the horror to come.

The stench of fresh piss filled Clive's nostrils. He shuffled away from the growing wet patch that grew out from beneath the other man's balls. He ran the sharp tip of the parang across the skin of the soldier's forearm, just enough to break the skin below the elbow and help him aim.

The soldier bit harder on the belt and looked away, tightening the grip on his arm even further. He blew snot from out of his nose and spat from the gaps in his teeth as he screamed some incomprehensible mantra.

Clive took hold of the man's bicep and raised the parang high above his head.

The door to the hotel room lifted and settled again against the frame. Then a dull thud, most likely the stairwell door closing.

Company! Excellent.

He lowered the large hunting knife and pulled the leather belt from the other man's mouth, giving him free rein to holler down the hotel.

The soldier duly obliged.

'Eto lovushka!' he cried. 'Pozhaluysta, pomogi mne!'

Clive let him wail. All the better to honey his trap. He grabbed the soldier's pants and used them to prop open the door, cramming the fabric underneath. The door held, but only just. He could see it creep forward, eager to shut again.

'On yavlyayetsya u dverey! Pozhaluysta, pomogi mne!' yelled the solider towards the open door.

Clive held his hand out to the man, palm up, then flipped his fingers upwards.

Come on, Vlad, sing for me.

He switched the parang to his right hand and flattened himself against the wall by the doorframe, waiting to see who had paid him a visit.

When he saw the impossibly thin woman emerge in the doorway he nearly dropped his knife. She stood around five feet six inches with greasy brown hair that had long outgrown a feather bob haircut and now stuck out in matted clumps. Her grubby, ragged blouse hung off her skinny shoulders. Her neck looked thin enough to snap, like a chopstick. Her cheekbones jutted from her face. Her deep-sunk and dark-ringed eyes caught his. For a moment the woman seemed just as confused as Clive.

Dawn Fucking McKenzie. But that's impossible! I killed you. I ate you!

The shock of seeing her again nearly proved to be his undoing. She whipped out a long bayonet blade from her left side and immediately thrust it towards his ribs. He dodged out of the way, but felt her blade cut deep into his forearm.

Where the fuck did that come from?

The last time he saw her – the time he finally fucking murdered her – she had lost an arm to someone, making it a cinch to put her down. And yet here she was, hacking away at him as if nothing had happened.

She pulled the blade away and slashed it across his chest, ripping a hole in his shirt, further wounding him. Murder filled her eyes, as if she suddenly realised exactly who she was fighting.

'You FUCK!' she screamed and lashed out again.

Clive instinctively flicked out the flat of his parang and met Dawn's bayonet blade in mid-swipe, creating a loud, flat clang. Before she could react he smashed her across the jaw with his other fist.

She staggered backwards towards the naked man trussed to the foot of the bed.

He kicked hard against her blade hand and knocked the weapon from her grasp, sending it spinning into the corner of the room.

Dawn swung around and clawed at Clive's face with a handful of broken fingernails. The ragged edges dug into the skin of his cheek, narrowly missing his eyes. He caught her by the wrist and spun her around. He then grabbed the back of Dawn's neck in one hand and viciously slammed her into the hard wood panels of the wardrobe ahead. He caught her before she could fall and then threw her onto her back. She lay in the piss-ridden area between the soldier's legs. He threw his large hunting knife onto the bed, then pounced on top of her, straddled her, and pushed her down by her bony shoulders.

'Nyet! Nyet!' wailed the soldier, seeing his chance of escape vanishing quickly between his legs. He began crying a jumble of over-pronounced consonants.

'Shut the fuck up, Vlad, I'm busy here!'

Dawn's eyes shone with pure hatred. She shrieked incomprehensible invective laced with the foulest language. She spat into his face and tried to thrust a knee into his balls.

Clive felt an old fury bubble up within him. This uppity bitch had come back to haunt him, a new arm and everything, and she somehow thought she could put him down? Clive? The fucking King of the Castle?

Dawn hocked up another ball of spit, pulled her head up to launch it, but Clive brought down his forehead hard onto the bridge of her nose, snapping her head back into the gaudy, piss-soaked carpet with a heavy thud. Blood streamed from her broken nose and ran down her laugh-lines. Her eyes rolled upwards.

Clive released a shoulder, then forced her head over to one side. He placed his mouth over her ear, took a deep breath and screamed: 'Yeah! Not so lively now are you, bitch?'

Dawn howled and spat blood onto the naked leg of the soldier, who continued to scream for help, for mercy, for whatever reason.

Once-hazy memories became clear in Clive's mind. He remembered the Christmas party years ago when Dawn blew him a kiss across the crowded office floor, how she denied it afterwards, even when presented with the picture on his smartphone. He recalled how she started fucking one of the gorilla security guards just to spite him, how he'd ached for her, and how she'd teased him with her body ever since.

Clive ran his free hand over the outside of Dawn's thigh. Even though he felt hair and lesions and scars across the surface of her skin, and despite the evident wasting of her muscles, she still had the power to get him rock-hard in an instant.

Dawn groaned, coming to. She weakly slapped Clive across the face.

Clive brought his mouth to her ear again, licked it: 'Yeah, moan for me. That's right.'

As quick as lightning, Dawn twisted her head round and clamped what teeth she had remaining hard into the flesh of Clive's earlobe. She bucked and thrashed beneath him, hammering blows wherever she could land them.

A fuckstorm of white-hot agony corkscrewed along his nerves and dug deep into his brain. As Dawn struggled on he could feel the skin of his ear lobe give way. Warm blood ran into the hairs of his greasy beard and down his neck.

The pain brought him more memories, scenes of teasing and betrayal. He remembered how Dawn's dark nipples would often stiffen whenever he stopped by her desk to chat, pushing out from her perfect tits. He remembered how she would often blush when she caught him looking, and tell him to jog on when he told her how badly he wanted her. She wanted to fuck him, that much was obvious, and why not? He had a dick like a baby's arm and a taste for the good life. She could have lived like a queen.

Eventually.

But then she had to go and lie: making sure they were all alone in the photocopying room before screaming the place down, crying rape, saying he had groped her.

You lying little bitch.

The same lying little bitch that dropped the charges days after he got the sack.

The self same lying little bitch, now back from the dead, the same Dawn Fucking McKenzie that was trying to chew away his ear.

Clive took a deep breath and hauled himself away from her mouth, feeling the flesh of his ear lobe tear, peeling a strip of flesh an inch or so long from his neck. He watched the small chunk of skin wiggle in Dawn's bleeding, gap-toothed mouth. Her anger seemed tinged with an edge of satisfaction.

Clive's peripheral vision darkened at the edges, much like they had done every time he lost his temper. He quickly moved his other hand from Dawn's shoulder and clamped it hard onto her windpipe, no longer caring whether he crushed it. He balled his free hand into a fist and brought it down into Dawn's right temple as hard as he could. Her flailing arms immediately dropped down to her sides, but Clive kept going. He pounded his fist into her face for as long as his hand could withstand the pain, then grabbed her heavily-beaten head by her ears. He brought it up and smacked it down hard into the soggy carpet with a squelch, again and again until the darkness no longer clouded his vision.

Exhausted, gasping for breath, he lay hunched over Dawn and examined his handiwork. Her face had swollen in places where her body could still manage it, but otherwise it oozed deep red blood. Her right eye had completely closed over. Her left eye stared at nothing in particular, quite still. He had succeeded in destroying Dawn's jaw in several places, giving her a slack expression he found morbidly comical.

She was dead.

He clamped a hand to his torn ear and examined the damage. His palm came away slick with fresh blood. The salty grit pitted into the skin of his hands bit into the open wound. He growled with the agony it caused him.

'Fuck it!' he said. 'What are you looking at, Vlad?'

The soldier had fallen silent, nobody left for whom to call. He stared, unblinking, into Clive's eyes. His arm twitched, some life creeping in through the tourniquet.

Clive looked at Dawn's broken face.

Oh, well done, fuckerknuckles, you've gone and killed her again.

Again? What do you mean "again"? How could I have killed her again? *You're going soft in the head, old son.*

He ran a hand down her chest and found her braless. He continued across her belly, then poked her here and there. Though skinny, there was still enough meat on her corpse to keep him going for a while. Hell, by using the four mini-bars lugged into the hotel room he may even stretch her out for a fortnight.

'You're a lucky fucker, Vlad.'

CHAPTER TEN

'What do you mean "contact"?' said Dawn.

Joe pointed to the thin horizontal boxes in the rack. Their lights blinked twice in unison.

'These are network switches,' he said. 'They're like relay stations for data. These bad boys connect to all those computers out there.'

'Okay, that explains the bazillion grey cables. What about the red ones?'

'My guess is they link the switches to a more centralised part of the network.'

'And the blinking lights?'

'Data passing through a particular cable. Those for the grey cables are the switch talking to the computers out there. You can ignore those. I'm more interested in the ones for the red cables. There, see? That means something is talking to the switch.'

'Contact.'

'Exactly! It's like there's something in the outside world polling this floor for a response, a super-switch if you will. Maybe one with a couple of servers attached.'

'And you know all of this how exactly?'

'I haven't always been a rapist of the poor, Dawn. Us geeks paid a heavy price when the credit crunch hit.'

'Well, my international man of mystery, best you go say "Hello" to the world.'

Joe closed the cupboard door and felt a deep harsh pain in his abdomen, as if he'd ripped a muscle in two. He gasped out loud and nearly soiled himself. He leaned against the door handle and took in shallow breaths, fearing the stabbing sensation would return.

'I think you might have to give me a push,' he said.

He felt Dawn's hand slide over his back and focused on it, letting her touch comfort him. She held him gently by the side while he placed a hand on her shoulder.

'I'll try, Joe, but you're a bit bigger than me,' she said.

'Are you calling me fat?' He let out a gasping laugh, then instantly regretted it.

'You used to be,' she said, guiding them through the kitchen door. 'In a way I wish you still were.'

She helped him into the seat of the nearest workstation. He caught a lungful of his own body odour has he settled. Christ, he needed a bath. To peel off his clothes, to jump into a tub of hot foamy water and to just lie there, as still as the dead, letting the sweat, stink and dirt lift off him. Heavenly.

A sudden wave of nausea quickly put paid to such thoughts, a stark reminder of his grave situation. His eyelids begged to close. It felt as if his body was shutting down bit by bit.

Dawn bent down and switched on the tower PC. The interior fans whirred into life and a green power light appeared on the casing. Joe turned on the chunky monitor. It buzzed into life, a familiar sound in miniature. Assorted white text skittered down the jet black screen. He swung the monitor left and right on its stand but couldn't push it any further back. The screen felt uncomfortably close.

How old school is this?

The white-on-black text flickered away and in its place appeared a loading screen for Windows 95.

Okay, very *old school.*

Dawn clapped her hands onto Joe's shoulders.

'Ouch! Thanks a bunch.'

'Shush,' she said, her eyes fixed on the kitchen door, lost in thought. Her bottom lip twitched. She met his eyes, then stepped around into the aisle. 'See what you can find on the computer, Joe. I've just had an idea.'

The kitchen door banged shut behind her.

The loading screen gave way to a uniform background of light teal. A grey and blue login window appeared, upon which sat two text boxes and a lot of Cyrillic script he didn't understand. The text boxes were almost certainly for a username and password. Joe pushed "Esc" on the keyboard and grinned as the login window disappeared, shortly replaced by a desktop and some icons.

Heh. Good old Windows 95.

The locale looked Bulgarian or Russian or something similar. It didn't matter. He knew the underlying text commands would be the same whatever the language. Indeed, much of the screen furniture already seemed familiar. Start menu. Taskbar. Recycle Bin. He double-clicked on the clock in the corner.

8:27am. 7th Jyn 1997.

A second wave of nausea had him doubled over the arm of the chair. He wished the damned thing had casters. The slightest movement sent his brain swilling around the bottom of his skull like day-old lager cut with battery acid. He looked to the gents toilet but doubted he had the strength to make it. The pain was as bad as he'd ever known it, even immediately before his diagnosis. The time he blacked out. He gulped down hard and took deep breaths. Anything to clear his head. He didn't want Dawn to come back to a pile of vomit.

His stomach gurgled for a full ten seconds. His insides settled a little. Feeling marginally more human he pushed himself back into the seat and moved the keyboard closer. He rubbed clear his blurry vision and opened a command prompt window. A blinking cursor awaited his instructions.

'Okay computer,' he said, wiping his brow. 'Let's get to know each other a little better, shall we?'

He typed *ipconfig* and pushed the Enter key.

Dawn burst from the kitchen door. She ran past Joe and continued along the aisle of filing cabinets.

'Keep going!' she yelled, her voice echoing.

'Will do. Ow!' Shouting did him few favours.

He returned to the information he had requested. His computer seemed part of a large private network, capable of seeing just over a thousand neighbouring computers. No internet gateway had been specified, but then how much of an internet would there have been to surf mid-1997?

Hardly any if you took away the porn.

Nevertheless he fired up the web browser. After ten seconds a splash screen finally appeared.

'Version three!' he said. 'This thing belongs in a museum.'

He waited for the program to fully load. The computer's hard disk clunked and clattered like a crazed jazz drummer, echoing noisily in the desk enclosure. The noise grew distant, muffled.

'Whoa, shit!'

His vision blurred, then doubled outright, then cleared again. He stopped himself from nodding off.

This is bad. I don't want to fall sleep. I might never wake up again.

He heard Dawn crash out from the photocopying room at the far end of the floor.

'Hold on, Joe! I'm just going to try through here.'

He heard the fire door slam shut, and had an awful feeling he was being watched.

He twisted around, gasping at the pain it caused him. He found row after row of desks and chairs and the tops of fat computer monitors. They stretched into the distance, bending in line with the curvature of the floor, scorched in the middle.

All around him was still. The only sounds he heard were those from next door. Slamming doors. The dull clomping of Dawn's shoes through the walls.

'Just my imagination,' he said.

He faced the keyboard and monitor once more, suffering the pain of a hundred rusty razor blades under his skin.

I need to close my eyes. Just for a moment.

'Oh, no you don't,' he said, rubbing some life into them.

He refocused as best he could. The address bar of the web browser contained the text "about:blank", a completely empty homepage. It suggested a lack of corporate intranet for him to tap into. He took a punt regardless. He entered "http://intranet" into the address bar. No joy.

What's Russian for "intranet"?

'Probably not *intranetski*,' he said.

He returned to the command line window and examined the *ipconfig* results.

He spotted an IPv6 network address, a complex new-fangled string of letters and numbers. Hardly anybody used IPv6 addresses, though, even in 2013. How the hell was a Windows 95 PC from 1997 using them?

He leaned over and touched the top of the computer, glared at it. An anachronism made somehow real.

'Who the hell *are* you guys?' he said.

He punched in *ipconfig /all* to pull up more comprehensive information about his network connection. He scrolled through the results and found the address of the DHCP server, the bit of kit that had issued his computer its IP addresses. He typed the address into the browser, prefixing it with "http://". Another punt. His finger dithered over the Enter key.

Then his head hit the keyboard with a crunch.

*****

He looked over the black plastic handrail of the stairwell, down into a rectangular spiral without end. He saw innumerable flights of stairs in impossible detail. They seemed to move, to pulse almost, creating a tunnel effect.

Calling him.

He focused on the back of his head, visible beneath him, repeated into infinity. Large. Too large. His black hair was greasy and loosely held in a side parting. He saw the beginnings of a bald spot near his crown. He moved his head to the side hoping for a better look-see, saw the same action replicated below a thousand times over.

He called out to himself but there was no noise, as if he stood in a vacuum.

I can breathe.

He felt something warm and wet splash against the back of his neck. He caught sight of a few drops of red as they fell endlessly down the middle of the stairwell. He rubbed at the moisture, found more red on his hand.

He turned his head slowly round a hundred and eighty degrees, like an owl, like something from *The Exorcist*. How, he didn't know.

He couldn't see the back of his head and this made him sad. A thousand dead faces looked down on him, each peering out over the handrail, one floor after another, up and up and up. Their eyes were half-closed, their mouths slack, all colour drained from their skin.

His dead face, copied and pasted to the edge of the universe and beyond.

I don't want to see this.

A shower of warm red rain splashed his cheeks.

He saw something falling down the middle of the stairwell, high, so high above him. Something big. He watched it strike one of his heads, causing it to explode like a bloody water balloon.

The red rain came quickly, falling far quicker than the tumbling thing.

He heard Dawn speak from somewhere, unseen.

So, what are we looking at here? Two different gravities?

He watched his dead faces mouth something he couldn't hear. Expressionless. He read their blue lips. His lips.

I think so. Something along those lines. Mental, isn't it?

Another of his heads exploded, struck by the tumbling thing, sending a fresh shower of blood down onto his face.

It's getting closer.

He focused on the tumbling thing, found some detail at last. He saw the naked torso of a heavy-set man falling over and over, smashing against the handrails and into Joe's heads, bursting them. The torso was headless and without limbs. Huge long knives had been driven out through the bloody stumps, like a grotesque starfish.

And still it tumbled, drenching Joe with showers of his blood.

Oh my God.

Tumbling. Only two floors away.

It's coming.

TUMBLING.

Coming for me.

Impact.

*****

He jolted awake. Dawn jumped in shock. She sat at the next workstation along from him. She leaned over, stroked the hair away from his brow and smiled, the best thing he had seen for what felt like years.

'It lives!' she said. 'Welcome back.'

'Hi,' he said, a cottonmouth croak.

He raked the inside of his mouth with his tongue, seeking moisture, finding nothing but a funny tang. His heart felt ready to burst from his chest. At least his aches and pains had eased a little.

A red plastic case lay open nearby, smallish, its contents strewn over Dawn's desk. A torn slender box. A used syringe. An antiseptic wipe.

'How are you feeling?' she said, and stroked his hair once more.

'Ill, but better, thanks. Where did you find those?'

'In the kitchen next door,' said Dawn. 'I just had a feeling there'd be a first aid kit somewhere, what with all the office equipment here. I guess I lucked out. At least we know some of these floors aren't completely empty.'

Joe nodded. 'Thanks again.'

'Don't worry about it,' she said. 'Let's call it one apiece.'

'Deal.' He slowly straightened up in the chair, found his suit jacket over the back. He eyed the detritus on Dawn's desk. 'I hate needles. It was the first thing I thought about when the doctor diagnosed me. The sooner they create a pill for this stuff the better.'

'Well, there were only two syringes,' she said, holding up the remaining box. She swapped it for a small blister strip of glucose tablets, two missing, one left. That explained the taste in his mouth. 'These too. I snaffled one. Sorry, but I was famished. Still am. I did get you this to make up for it, though.'

'Oh, you beauty!' said Joe, taking a glass of water from her. He swilled it round his mouth, trying to kick start his salivary glands. He swallowed and guzzled the rest in large, breathy gulps, then wiped a few trickles from his mouth.

'Bloody hell, I've got the start of a beard here,' he said. 'How long was I out?'

'I don't know. Not long,' she said. 'Long enough to have me worried sick, I know that much. I only really relaxed when you started snoring.' She looked to the computer monitor. A series of lines and curves bounced around a black screen. 'So did you find anything?'

'Not much, I'm afraid,' he said. 'Only that these things seem to have flux capacitors installed.'

'Hashtag geek humour?'

'Yeah, kind of,' he said. 'Someone has gone to a lot of trouble to future-proof these ancient PCs. This one's also got a second network card for some reason. Maybe they all have.'

He caught Dawn trying to stifle a yawn. She gave up and made a meal of it. She stretched out her arms, arched her back. He watched her, hypnotised. He swallowed. The back of his throat ached.

'Sorry,' she said. 'I'm dead on my feet. Well, dead on my arse to be precise.' She shuffled the blister back and spare syringe towards Joe. 'You'd better have these.'

'Why?'

'You've had a nap,' she said. She leaned forwards and placed her forearms across the desk, making a pillow. 'It's only right that I have one too. Give me a shout in an hour.'

'I'll wake you at twelve, shall I?' He flashed her his watch.

'You're a funny man, Joe,' she said.

Within minutes she was snoring.

*****

A thin strip of newfound sunshine slowly claimed territory over the cheap, green carpet. Joe sat gazing from the windows, allowing the sun to creep over him. He felt it dry him and was happy for its warmth. He sat midway along the aisle in the middle of a huge, gentle curve, as if the entire building had once been part of a giant, ring-shaped edifice. He saw above him the fourteenth and fifteenth floors, below him the twelfth and so on. Seamless. He let his eyes fall onto the world far below. Tiny cars traipsed along an unbroken stretch of road in the distance, occasionally peeling away to enter the semicircular drive beneath him. Beyond the road lay a park, or perhaps the edge of a forest. Either way there were a lot of tall pine trees.

His insides still hurt from the insulin withdrawal, but at least he no longer felt woozy. His fear of the future, however, remained intact. He knew that his life now depended on finding first aid kits that catered for diabetics, and that not every kit would have what he needed. He looked at the slim, unbroken carton in his hands and considered whether he was looking at his last ever shot of insulin.

Then there was the small problem of finding something to eat. He felt for the remaining glucose tablet in his pocket. Patted it.

This place sure makes a fella hungry. This impossible place.

He continued to fit assorted pieces of the puzzle together in his mind while Dawn snored in the background, but it was as if the pieces were all from different jigsaws.

Both he and Dawn had been cast into a bunch of missing floors stitched together with elevators and random never-ending stairwells. But why? Why this place? *Where* this place? And where the hell did Clive get to? Why didn't he follow them into the maintenance floor?

He recalled the heavy stairwell door and how it had so nearly separated him from Dawn.

So Clive must have stepped into another floor. A different part of the maze.

A maze of dead floors, somehow hidden from the world, an impossible catacomb of the damned. He pondered its extent. How many buildings across the world had at least one missing floor? Hundreds? Thousands? Tens of thousands? How many stairwells and elevators did each of those buildings house? 3 Donnington Place had two of each, but he knew some buildings had masses of them, like the ones in Canary Wharf.

Hundreds of thousands?

He considered the floor in Sofia, three years hence; the floor in America, a lifetime behind; the floor in China from who knew when, and the floor in which he sat, from 1997. All different points in time. Floors numbering in the tens of thousands, elevators and stairwells numbering in the hundreds of thousands, and points in time numbering... what?

In the millions? A million million? A million times infinity?

He felt his bowels move.

Surely not.

We're going to die in here.

He looked away from the windows and into the office floor. Death coated every tangible square inch around him. The whole hellish place felt barren. The only signs of life here were the hallmarks of death: burning floors, collapsed stairwells, and portals into conflict and destruction; the grime of decay, the stench of piss, and nearly always the blood. Blood that had seeped into the fabric of most every floor they had stepped into. Blood that seemed able to tear rooms and gravity itself in half.

His thoughts of blood led him to the work experience girl and the terrified look in her eyes as she hacked another gob of her life into her hands. She'd had so much ahead of her, only to be snuffed out by a lunatic.

A lunatic who seemed surprised to hear Joe's voice.

He looked once more at the boxed syringe in his hands.

CHAPTER ELEVEN

'Wake up, Dawn,' said Joe, shaking her. He sounded excited. She saw the metal bar in his other hand. 'We've got company.'

Shit!

She sat bolt upright, light-headed, as if she'd left her brain on the desk. She grabbed something nearby, anything that could double as a weapon. She frantically scanned the corners of the office floor for movement, then across the rows of desks behind her.

'Where?' she said. She eased her grip on the chunky beige keyboard.

'Outside,' said Joe, walking away. He pointed to the other end of the office. 'Can you see the cables?'

She followed the curvature of the floor. The windows bunched closer together the further ahead she looked. She shook her head and saw him beckon.

She sighed. 'That was never an hour.'

She hauled herself into the aisle. She found a chair pulled to the windows, empty. Upon its seat lay a torn cardboard box, long and thin. A used syringe beside it.

Looks like we need to move.

'How's the patient?' she said.

'Getting there. I still hate needles, though.'

Once past the chair she noticed the cables ahead, two pairs of two, thick and black with oil. They stood erect quivering in mid-air like aerials, neatly cut away level with the top of the twelfth floor.

She looked up and saw the other ends severed at the bottom of the fourteenth.

'Okay, that's impressive.'

'Ah, you missed the best bit,' said Joe. 'Sorry.'

Her eyes followed the cables downwards to find a middle-aged man in blue overalls. The man busied himself cleaning the windows of the twelfth floor. He stood in a cradle with waist-high metal walls, a foaming bucket nearby. He seemed engrossed in his work but happy. He shook some excess suds from his wiper, picked his spot and attacked the windows once more.

'How long's he been out there?'

'About half an hour, maybe,' said Joe. 'I left it a while before I woke you.'

'Really?' she said, a little harsher than she'd intended. 'Sorry, that came out wrong. Thanks for the lie-in.'

Joe shrugged. 'Anyway, the real reason I gave you a shake was so I didn't startle you with this. Cover your ears.'

He swung the jagged metal bar behind him and brought it down hard against the glass, eliciting a sharp clang that *thummed* and echoed around the floor. He did it twice more.

'It's working, Joe! He's looking.'

Joe had peeled away from the window, his face twisted. He sucked air loudly through clenched teeth. He dropped the bar on the floor and clutched his belly.

'I'm okay,' he said, gasping. 'It'll pass.'

'For crying out loud, Joe, you're going to do yourself a mischief.' She placed an arm over his shoulders and steered him towards the empty chair. 'Is the insulin having no effect?'

'No, it's doing some good,' he said. 'I think I just overdid the heroics. I'll be okay.'

That bloody machismo thing again.

'Well, you just leave the heroics to me, old man. You have yourself a nice sit down.'

'Thanks. Here, who are you calling an old man?'

'You, you old fart. Don't worry, the lady can take it from here, thank you.'

'Fine. I'll sit here and suck on my sweeties then.' He broke out the last glucose tablet and popped it into his mouth, grinning. 'I'm only thirty.'

THE FLOORS

Dawn picked up the metal bar and turned her attention to the window cleaner below. The man continued to gawp blindly into the building. He craned his head upwards, turning left and right, trying to get a fix on where the noise had come from. The moment soon passed. He shrugged and picked up a squeegee.

'Oh, no you don't,' said Dawn.

She whacked the bar into the window, hard, close to the scratch marks Joe had made. Another sharp *thumming* noise resounded, satisfyingly loud. The shockwaves rode up the bar, jarring her wrist.

'Jesus, that hurts!' she said. She shook the pain from her hand. 'Couldn't you have found one with a handle?'

'Sorry, they were fresh out,' he smiled.

A little more of the old Joe coming back. Good.

The man in the cradle looked towards her once more but was still unable to find her. He sheltered his eyes from the sun that bounced off his gleaming windows. He squinted to get a better look. A smile flickered across his lips. He waved his wiper, a gesture that suggested he'd grown aware of the joke, as if to say "Yeah, yeah, very funny, guys."

'No!' yelled Dawn, upping her efforts. She battered the window with a quick succession of blows. 'We're in here! Help us! Please!'

The man waved goodbye to the window above him and manoeuvred the cradle lower to continue his job.

Dawn slumped against the cold, unyielding glass and slid to her knees, exhausted. She had managed to add more scratches to the window pane but the thing showed no sign of breaking, not even the tiniest crack. She had sustained more damage to the metal bar than the pane of glass. It lay on the cheap nylon carpet beside her, showing a distinct bend in the middle.

She looked at Joe, still sitting in his chair. He made a face that said "never mind".

'Give him a while, warrior woman. He'll be back up here again.'

His face changed. He twisted around and looked to the ceiling, then to the desks, and finally, it seemed, to the chairs tucked in beneath them.

'What is it?'

'Keep whacking those windows when he passes by. See if you can get his attention again,' said Joe. 'I've got an idea.'

*****

'Can you see him yet?' said Joe.

'Yep,' said Dawn, looking up. She eased herself away from the cold glass. 'I can see the bottom of the cradle.'

She readjusted herself in Joe's suit jacket, trying not to breathe in too much of its unique bouquet. She patted the inside pocket and found it reassuringly empty. She looked to the desk in which she had stashed Joe's phone, then glanced at him. She shook her head.

'You're mad, by the way, Joe,' she said. 'I just thought I'd tell you that.'

'You won't be saying that if this works,' he said, looking down on her from above.

'If this works, Joe, I'll make you my chief bridesmaid.'

She watched as the guy struggled to maintain his balance. He stood atop a stack of office chairs placed on a desk four rows from the front. Progressively smaller stacks of chairs stood nearby, his stepping stones.

His face showed intense concentration. He even went so far as to stick out a tongue. A crafty wink let her know he was making a show of it all, but a swift counterbalancing move on his makeshift plinth saw him wince terribly.

He had refused Dawn's offers to take his place up there, insisting he was the only one qualified for what needed to be done. For once she had no comeback. He had a good six inches on her and a longer reach thanks to his gangly monkey arms.

She watched as he plucked a crumpled packet of cigarettes from his shirt pocket. He placed his five surviving cigarettes into his mouth. He threw the packet onto the floor and retrieved a cheap plastic lighter from another pocket. Lighting each cigarette in turn, he clamped them between his forefinger and middle finger, took in a lungful of smoke and blew it up in the air.

He lost his balance.

'Joe!'

'It's okay,' said Joe. 'Whoa! I'm okay. Whoo! Wow. It's just the nicotine rush.'

'Christ, Joe, that was close,' she said. 'Watch yourself up there. Please.'

Don't leave me alone in here.

'Yes, mum.'

He regained his composure and brought the cigarettes to his mouth again. He drew in a puff and immediately blew the smoke towards a disc-shaped detector stuck to the ceiling. The red LED that punctured its base continued to blink impassively. He thrust his cigarette hand upwards and held it there like a sweaty Statue of Liberty.

Dawn returned her attention to the window, keen to witness what was about to happen. She had seen it once already and found the sight one of the most bizarre, disgusting and captivating spectacles she had ever seen, despite all that had gone before.

The cradle kicked into life and began to lower. Its bottom then disappeared, revealing a man and his equipment floating in midair above her. The metal floor immediately reappeared a full storey below. Within seconds there was half a bucket full to the brim with motionless brown water. A yellow plastic tube stood off-centre, exactly level with the murky liquid. The handle of the wiper. There stood nearby a pair of dismembered feet, cut off just above the boots with hoops of thick blue fabric floating around the outside. The toe of the right boot tapped impatiently against the metal floor.

Above her Dawn could see the man and his cradle being drawn into nothingness, disappearing inch by inch only to then reappear at her feet. She stood transfixed by the incredible CAT scan being acted out in front of her, astonished that she felt so unaffected by the sight. No light-headedness. No nausea.

No blood. Just... just... wow!

She watched as the window cleaner was reassembled at her feet, layer by layer. The fatty skin and muscle that surrounded his entrails and vital organs. The rings of his pale blue veins and red arteries. The man's spinal column, his ribs. The discoloration of his lungs, the movement of his heart. His jaw, his teeth, his eyes, his brain. And then the man was complete, his bald spot gleaming in the sun.

He sloshed his wiper around the bucket of brown sudless water as if nothing had happened, trying to work up a lather as best he could. He glanced up, into the window, as if expecting to catch someone there. He maintained an expectant look on his face, like a beagle awaiting a dog treat.

Dawn whacked the bottom of the window with the jagged metal bar. It struck a couple of feet above the window cleaner's head. Anything to keep the guy interested. Her arms hurt like buggery. She gave up on the metal pole and proceeded to toe-poke the bottom of the window.

The man reached behind him and pulled out a substantial walkie-talkie. He listened intently, then spat some words into the receiver. He watched the windows with suspicion while he listened to the response.

'Man, I think these are the best damn ciggies I've smoked in years,' said Joe.

Dawn looked back towards Joe and the cigarettes he held aloft. She watched the smoke as it commingled then faded into the air, seemingly into nothingness, achingly close to the blinking eye of the smoke detector. He took another lungful of smoke and blew it upwards.

'Keep it up, Joe,' she said, and switched her attention to the man outside. She considered one last attack on the window but had little energy left in her arms. She needed to recharge.

The window cleaner continued to look in her general direction. He shook his head, twisted his face in a bemused smirk and reattached the walkie-talkie to his belt. He picked up his wiper and slapped what suds he could onto the top of the window below.

The sun escaped behind a cloud, casting a momentary gloom onto the outside world.

Surely he can see me now?

Instead the man took his squeegee and laid a few deft strokes against the glass. He threw it into the half-empty bucket and stepped to the controls of the cradle.

'Shit, Joe, he's about to go!' she said.

The electricity supply suddenly cut out, extinguishing the lights and killing Joe's computer. The harsh peals of fire bells rang out across the floor. Freezing cold water urgently cascaded from the serrated sprinkler heads, extinguishing Joe's cigarettes and very nearly the man himself. The shock of the cold water saw him tumble from his pedestal of chairs and clatter awkwardly onto the desk below.

'Joe!'

The desk held under his weight, but he lay still in the icy rain.

'Joe, are you alright?'

She clenched hard on the metal pole and glanced down towards the window cleaner. The man looked in her general direction once more, but obviously couldn't see her. He heard the alarms, however. He reached eagerly for the control panel and set the cradle in motion, rapidly disappearing downwards.

'Shit!' said Dawn. 'He's going, Joe!'

What are you doing, you stupid cow? Joe's hurt!

'Fuck.'

She looked to Joe and dropped the pole. He hadn't moved, but she could see he was still breathing. She held shut the suit jacket and turned to fully face the freezing cold downpour.

He stirred, just a little. To her great relief, he gave her the thumbs-up.

*****

Joe looked out from the office window, oblivious to the water that fell relentlessly onto his head and ran down his shoulders and back. He barely noticed the rivulets racing down the inside of the glass, nor the pain he was in. Subconsciously he knew his back now hurt every bit as much as his front, but it didn't register inside. The coldness of the water, the helplessness of the situation, the empty aircraft hangar that had been his life up to that point; whether it was one of these, all of them or more, it left him feeling numb and hollowed out. And so he simply looked onto the scene of organised chaos ensuing outside.

The forecourt of the building was a sea of blue and red flashing lights as vehicles from every available emergency service vied for space. Men and women in assorted uniforms milled around in a confused and disorganised manner. Others in dull civilian clothes gathered on the fringes, presumably having been evacuated from the other floors of the building. Those real, tangible floors that allowed their occupants to flee in an emergency.

Not like this hellhole.

Dawn was right. The place was a sick joke.

A growing nauseous dread usurped fully any last curious fascination he had remaining.

We're going to die in here.

The fire alarms finally cut out and the freezing rain stopped. He watched as one by one the emergency vehicles extinguished their flashing lights and peeled away onto the main road. Angry gesturing between some men had broken out, one a fire officer, the other a man in a suit. No doubt they were rowing over the false alarm.

There had been no conflagration. Just a general "Holy shit, everyone! There's a fire!" kind of alarm triggered by sensors on a non-existent floor.

The air hit the cold water that hung in his clothes and clung to his skin, making him shiver. It started in his shoulders as a twitch but he was shortly quivering all over.

He heard a scraping noise behind him - Dawn coming out from under one of the desks most likely. He didn't look. He genuinely didn't care if it happened to be some bloodthirsty piece of shit coming to slit his throat.

He felt a hand on his shoulder.

CHAPTER TWELVE

The last fire engine on the forecourt chugged into life, reversed, swung around and rolled onto the stretch of road, leaving behind a brace of police cars, their lights no longer flashing. An ominous-looking charcoal sedan with blacked-out windows stood parked between the police cars. A pair of middle-aged men in civilian clothes gestured towards the building and seemed to beseech the officials for leniency. Obviously there had been a fault in the fire alarms.

Obviously.

The workers had long since been shepherded into the building to continue their daily grind. The tops of the black cables outside quivered. The window cleaner had continued where he'd left off.

As the situation continued to wind down outside, Dawn found herself thinking about Mike and how every step had taken her further away from him, regardless of the direction. Her very first steps in this place had taken her three years away from her fiancée.

Three whole years.

She tried to remember an old boyfriend, an unrequited love from her university days, but could only remember the major details, enough for her to recognise him in the street. Was that what was to become of Mike, or, indeed, of her: a bunch of hazy memories and a catalogue of good and bad points?

She rubbed her thumb and middle finger around her engagement ring. She would have swapped it in a heartbeat for a cheap tacky locket containing Mike's photograph. Had someone offered her a three-course meal she would have given the deal some serious thought.

And then there was Joe, the former self-declared morale officer of Hardingham Frank. He had barely moved since the sprinklers cut out, opting instead to stare gormlessly onto the forecourt where the three remaining cars finally rolled out onto the main road. His shivering had subsided leaving a shaken and broken man in its wake.

'Joe?' she said, and turned to face him. The carpet squelched under her soles. He didn't respond. 'Joe? Sweetheart? Light of my life?'

His unfocused eyes finally sharpened and the barest glimpse of a smile tugged at his cheeks. Dawn rubbed a hand between his shoulders. The fabric of his shirt clung to his back in large wet wrinkles.

She continued: 'I think it's time we moved on. You tried - and it was an awesome plan, Joe - but we need to find more medicine for you. Maybe a hand drier too. Something to sit under for half an hour.'

Joe nodded, albeit weakly. His broke his totemic stance and slowly hobbled away from the window, his whole body flinching with each step.

'Oh, hell,' said Dawn. 'You really took a fall back there. Are you okay?'

'Yeah,' said Joe, though Dawn had to listen up close to hear him. 'I'll walk it off.'

'My hero.'

'My warrior woman.'

Dawn looked at the bent tube of metal in her hand and laughed.

'Yeah, I really gave those windows what for, didn't I?'

She took a blister pack of painkillers that bobbed around the first aid kit. She popped a couple open for Joe and stuffed the rest into the suit jacket alongside his smartphone. They started towards the elevator door, but then Dawn tapped Joe lightly on the shoulder.

'Hang on, Joe,' she said. 'Let's take the stairs. We can flick through umpteen floors in the time it takes the elevator to do its thing. We'll stop at the next furnished floor and look around for another first aid kit.'

Joe nodded. 'Sounds like a plan.'

She held Joe as he hobbled along the aisle and towards the heavy, black stairwell door. Dawn grabbed the cold metal handle and pulled. She dragged the door open, stepping backwards and letting Joe go through first. He looked directly through the doorway.

'Wow!'

Dawn swung around for a look.

Through the doorway there lay a large open space bordered by a long horseshoe-shaped gallery. She could see a couple of storeys above and below, each edged with a smooth white wall topped with highly polished handrails of brass. Directly ahead of her a line of escalators zigzagged downwards. Behind the white walls there stood tall impressive glass fascias. Offices, or maybe shop fronts. Each of the storeys gleamed in the dim artificial light.

The same could not be said of the phantom floor that intersected them. Their floor, the thirteenth. Here the paintwork of the outer gallery wall had visibly yellowed, and the brass handrails had tarnished. The frontages of each unit seemed different. The dirty panes of glass were smaller, and sectioned by thin wooden frames, rather than offering a dramatic all-glass fascia. It was as if the rest of the building had been renovated and moved on, leaving the thirteenth floor behind to fester and rot. It looked like a seam of limestone within a slab of chalk, or a diseased vein running through otherwise healthy tissue. Pieces of random rubbish littered the floor of the gallery. A crisp packet here, the occasional drinks carton there, maybe dropped from the floors above. At least there were no splatters of dried blood to worry about.

She helped Joe out onto the gallery, letting the heavy stairwell door close behind them. They leaned against the yellowing wall and took in the splendour of the atrium.

The open space was huge. The horseshoe galleries resembled a bell sliced down the middle, when taken as a whole. The white walls that bordered each floor made the atrium look like the inside of a ribcage, lending the central elevator shafts a spinal quality. The entire area lay protected from the elements behind an extraordinary shield of glass, steel and huge concrete supports. It was dark outside. The glass reflected snatches of the atrium, casting false light against anything not already lit, such as the gallery of the thirteenth.

Inside the atrium most everything was deathly quiet. No people milled around the other floors, the hour outside either too late or too early. The all-glass fronts remained dark. A gentle hum underscored the scene, emanating from the massive air conditioning units high above. A slight breeze wafted around the atrium.

'Nice,' said Joe. 'I wish our building was as posh as this.'

Dawn thought back to a business campus that Mr Wilkes had worked on some months before. She'd admired its centrepiece from beyond the blinds: a sail-shaped building with a large glass front. Perhaps it housed an atrium such as this. She laughed inside. Maybe she was standing in the finished article. It wouldn't have surprised her. A fitting punchline to an increasingly sick joke.

'I guess it's a business centre of some description,' she said.

'An area like this must see a lot of people in the daytime,' said Joe. 'We could stick around until sunrise and see what happens.'

Dawn shook her head. 'That might take hours, Joe, and knowing our luck it'll be Good Friday out there. We need to get you well again before we do anything like that. Oh, hello?'

She held her tongue. A man in a light tan shirt had stepped into the large lobby area far below. He wore matching slacks and a black tie. He strode across the polished marble floor, twirling a small black object in his hands.

'Is that a gun?' said Dawn.

'Shush!' said Joe. He even drew his finger to his lips.

'What do you mean shush? He's our ticket out of here! *Hey! You down there! Up here!*'

The security guard continued along his path, oblivious to her calling. She looked over the handrail to get a better view of the lobby. Directly beneath her she found another two guards. They both sat behind a thick marble desk banked with screens.

'*HELLO?*' she yelled, hearing her voice echo around the atrium.

The security guard changed direction and headed for his colleagues, with whom he struck up a conversation.

'Okay, let me have a go,' said Joe.

He placed his thumb and index finger into his mouth and blew perhaps the loudest whistle Dawn had ever heard, loud enough to tickle her ear drums, and certainly loud enough to make her jump, even though she was expecting it.

There was no response from below.

Dawn took a tighter grip of the metal pole and whacked it against the tarnished brass handrail, creating a sharp clanging noise and a deeply satisfying echo.

Joe pointed to the marble desk far below. 'That did the trick!' he said.

All three security guards looked in their general direction. Two of them to the centre of the lobby.

'Who's up there?' said the fatter of the two, his hand resting on his holster.

'Come on out of there,' said the other, who held his gun in both hands, primed to aim and fire. 'Now!'

'Help us! Please!' called Dawn. 'We're trapped up here!'

She surveyed the gallery of the thirteenth floor for exits. The ambient light faded just beyond the central elevator doors, eventually turning the colonnade opposite into a grey blurry stripe. The phantom floor became a poorer imitation of its cousins the more she looked. The zigzag of escalators down the opposite side of the atrium stopped directly above and resumed immediately below the thirteenth, as if the floor had been rudely jammed in between them. The black stairwell door behind her had been haphazardly slapped onto a wall between two business units. The number thirteen had been spray-painted next to the door, rather than elegantly stencilled onto a plaque.

The floor looked *unfinished*.

The guards in the lobby continued to survey the sides of the atrium. The fatter guard pulled a torch from his belt, switched it on and dragged the beam slowly along one of the lower floors.

'For God's sake,' said Dawn. 'Nowhere near close.'

She took a tighter grip on the metal pole and beat it against the handrail once more.

The torch beam leapt suddenly, grazing the twelfth. It darted left and right.

'We know you're up there,' called out the burly security guard.

'Then come up here and find us!' yelled Dawn. She swung the metal bar hard against the handrail once more.

Whack!

'Just don't use the escalators.'

Whack!

'Because the escalators don't reach this floor.'

Whack!
'Because that's not now this sick fucking joke works, is it?'
Whack!
'IS IT?'
Her shoulders slumped, her arms too weak to continue. She caught a glimpse of Joe staring at her.
'I'm losing it, aren't I?'
He wiggled the flat of a hand from side to side. 'Ish,' he said. He turned and started limping along the gallery.
'Where are you going?'
'I'm going to take a look at the elevator over there. See if there's another one of those codes around somewhere.'
Dawn looked down into the lobby. The security guards had split up, taking opposite sides of the atrium. She leaned further over the handrail and found an escalator for the twelfth directly beneath her, as suspected. She stamped her feet on the ground, cursing it, hoping she could somehow break through the floor. She kicked an empty soda carton into the wall, crushing it, then sighed.
'Feel better for that?' said Joe, looking back.
'No,' said Dawn, catching him up. She tapped the metal bar along the handrail like a bored child. 'I can't see how a bunch of handwritten codes are going to help us.'
'It depends if we can figure out what they mean,' said Joe. 'I've been thinking about those numbers. Maybe the higher the number, the closer we can get to whoever is coding these floors.'
'But Joe, look at all the blood we've seen. Most of it looked old. Whoever was marking these floors, there's a good chance they've been killed.'
'Then we ought to continue their work,' said Joe. 'Maybe we can help the next victim that falls into this trap. Code a few floors of our own before we die in here.'
'Jesus, Joe, have some hope, please!' She stopped tapping the bar. 'Look, we can't do much of anything in here until we've gotten you fighting fit again. That means insulin. That means food. I say we avoid all the coded floors. If we do that there's a better chance of finding one that hasn't been raided.'
Joe stopped by the elevator doors, lost in thought. He eventually nodded.
'Fair enough.'

There were no handwritten codes to be found near the elevator doors. Joe shrugged and pushed the call button set into the wall.

'We may as well take a look inside,' he said.

But no elevator arrived. Instead the doors rolled aside to reveal a rectangle of utterly incorruptible darkness, as if they had met the edge of the universe.

Joe pushed his hand against the doorway to keep the elevator from closing. His mouth waggled open. He seemed entranced by the obsidian nothingness outside.

Dawn approached the doorway. She poked the metal bar through, trying to gauge some kind of depth, but then felt the thing pulled from her grasp. She watched as the bar quickly disappeared into the night without a sound.

She pulled away her hand, looking at it accusingly.

'Holy shit!'

'Well, what happened there then?' said Joe.

'Something just yanked it out of my hand,' said Dawn. 'I just felt it go, like it was attracted to a magnet.' Her shoulders dropped. She balled her fists, felt her fingernails dig into the flesh of her palms. 'Why is this happening to us, Joe? The second we get a foothold, just a little ray of hope, then something comes along and fucks us over. Someone's playing games with us, I swear, and I've had enough of it.'

She grabbed the handrail and screamed to the world.

'You hear me? I've had e-fucking-nough of it!'

'You better come out, fella,' said one of the security guards. 'We're coming to get you.'

'Oh, fuck off!' said Dawn.

She grabbed a carton from the gallery floor and felt a couple mouthfuls of coffee swill around the bottom. She pressed down on the lid and launched it over the side. She watched as the carton plummeted downwards, picking up speed until it eventually clattered and burst against the polished marble floor of the lobby.

The two security guards poked their heads out from their respective floors to investigate. The solitary guard at the desk looked up to them.

'Okay,' said Dawn. 'That I did not expect.'

'Are you thinking what I'm thinking?' said Joe, a welcome smile flickering across his lips.

'Yeah. I think we've got a way out of here.'

CHAPTER FOURTEEN

The heavy, black door opened onto the combined nightmares of M. C. Escher and Francisco Goya.

The empty capacious office floor that lay ahead had been split, sheared and twisted in so many places it baffled Joe how it all remained in one piece. The main body of the floor resembled an archipelago of concrete islands fused together by a turbulent sea of metal rods. Some islands were topped with blue carpet. Others were covered with broken glass, crushed tiles and mangled light fittings from a perfectly dark ceiling. Around half of the islands had blackened and burnt surfaces, making the floor resemble a massive malformed chess board.

The corners of the room were badly fragmented, so curled up and twisted it was impossible to discern the ceiling from the floor. They each resembled the insides of meat grinders fashioned from chunks of concrete and metal rods. Broken sunlight spilled into the office space from a hundred different angles. The thick supports dotted around the floor had been split and wrought in so many directions they'd be contenders to win the Turner prize. Even the air looked fragmented, as if viewing a collage of photographs of the floor ahead.

A cool breeze ran through the destroyed office space, seemingly from the open front and sides, as if most of the window panes had burst. Joe heard multiple sirens through the impossibly fractured floor. The sounds came in from all angles but each sounded close by. Under the kerfuffle he sensed a similar noise to that in the atrium, only here a gentle buzzing rather than a hum.

A large island lay in the centre of the archipelago, relatively unaffected by the surrounding chaos. Within the island there stood a thick central elevator shaft outside of which, painted onto the floor, Joe noticed another code. The letters and numbers were elongated, and too fragmented for him to see properly.

He stepped out onto the floor.

'Joe?' said Dawn.

There lay on the edge of the central island a fuzzy black mass that had melted into a large dark smudge on the carpet, a smudge flecked with white. Its skin seemed alive, almost liquid, but Joe's eyes rested solely on the long blade that jutted out from its body. From a distance the blade looked familiar, but it also looked deadly and therefore exactly what they needed.

He stepped further into the floor.

'Christ, Joe!' said Dawn.

'What?' he said.

'It's like you've stepped through a broken mirror or something.'

Joe turned and found the same true of her. He saw three noticeable splits in the air that cut up his view of the open doorway. A further split neatly bisected a fire extinguisher hanging by the door.

'Well, I've not come apart,' he said. 'I'm guessing it's safe. It's weird though. It's like I want to fall over in three different directions at once.'

'Let's open onto another floor,' said Dawn. 'We need to keep looking for rope. Anything to help us down. There's nothing here.'

'Well, there's that bloody long knife over there,' said Joe. 'We could definitely use that. Hold the door open and I'll be back as quick as I can.'

'Joe, no!'

'I'm already on my way. I told you I'd walk it off,' he said. 'Besides, it's my turn to go. I'll have a weapon soon enough, so I won't be in danger for long.'

He reached the halfway point between the door and the central island when he heard Dawn finally relent with a quiet 'Okay.' He looked back and saw the image of her in the doorway break up into more thin triangles and rectangles, as if viewing her through the purest crystal.

Of course he had lied about his condition. The painkillers were doing their best but he had seriously jarred his back, and the less said about his guts the better. He slowed his pace, feeling confident that Dawn wouldn't notice. He hobbled towards the area outside the central elevator where the smell of spoiled meat filled his mouth and nostrils.

The buzzing grew louder as he neared the black mass. He immediately realised the shimmering skin was in fact a thick carpet of flies. A couple landed on his arms, on his face and in his ears. He batted them away as best he could.

He stepped foot onto the central island. A large swarm of flies fled together, leaving behind a maggot-covered hand. There was no skin to speak of. Three of the fingers bore little flesh on the bones. Both legs of the corpse had been hacked away. The left leg was missing up to and including the knee. The right leg had been severed halfway along the thighbone, ending in a jagged and blackened point. The bloated heap of rotting flesh in between its legs showed that the cadaver had once been a man. The bones of his left arm were intact and stained with blood and decay. The right arm was simply not there. The same was true of the man's head. The victim's entrails were missing.

Thick buzzing noises came in from all around him, so loud and intense. They dominated everything, even the sirens outside, as a succession of massive bluebottles thrummed against his ears. He needed to get to the blade as a matter of urgency. He staggered through the swarm of black static towards the man's body.

The long blade had been thrust into whatever meat remained on the corpse's chest. Joe tugged on the handle, inadvertently raising the carcass in the process. He felt his guts shift. The blade had dug into the bone. He placed his left foot into the soft maggot-riddled flesh of the ribcage and pulled harder, finally releasing the blade.

He staggered away from the corpse and looked around to find his bearings in this hall of broken mirrors.

The blackened area of the carpet was the result of rotting flesh and the remains of a fire close by. The elevator doors near the body were heavily stained and layered with various ages of blood. The sight reminded him of the elevator in the hotel floor. In front of the elevator doors, beneath black streaky stains and splashes, someone had written a code in large letters and numbers. It read: "Ü312.1".

A U with two dots suggested whoever numbered the floors didn't speak a lick of English.

So what? Move it, fat boy!

His insides were agony. Someone had replaced his nervous system with one capable only of delivering pain. He dashed for an open window area that lay ahead for some respite.

A stiff breeze blew against his skin and chilled his wet clothes.

'Did you get it?' yelled Dawn from across the floor.

Joe turned and found he could scarcely see the stairwell door through the corrupted space between them. Her voice came to him in waves.

'Yes,' he called back. 'I just need some fresh air. I'll be back in a second.'

As he returned to face the glassless windows he took in the maws of the corner space, around ten yards to his left. It looked like a frozen vortex of black and yellow and blue and dark red; of fragmented sunlight and metal and concrete and glass.

And a pair of eyes.

'What the-'

Joe stepped back from the window. It was like looking at the corner of the room through an insane kaleidoscope. Sunlight shone out from the vortex in all directions like a laser show.

Outside the wailing sirens cut out abruptly. Above the distant hum of the flies and the wafting breeze he heard men with loudhailers commanding people to step back. Policemen, presumably. Ahead he could only see a mess of cut-up windows from the skyscraper opposite.

He reached for a support, six inches thick and bisected diagonally across the middle. He tested its strength. To his amazement the support held firm as if it had never been broken. He held onto the support and dared to look down.

The building in which he stood was one of four large skyscrapers that occupied the quadrants of a crossing below. The accent of the policeman suggested they were somewhere in the United States. A large number of people had gathered between and around a cluster of emergency vehicles. Their emergency lights continued to flash. Many of the people on the ground were looking up in his direction. He was about to call out to them when he saw a body in the clearing.

A number of police officers pushed the crowd back. They cleared a perimeter around the lifeless woman. She lay half on the road and half on the sidewalk, smashed. A thick channel of blood ran along the gutter and into a storm drain. Paramedics swarmed around the body, but it was obvious there was nothing they could do but scrape her from the ground. A couple of detectives muscled their way into the clearing. They headed towards a number of people sitting at the back of an ambulance, most likely eyewitnesses.

'Get back!' yelled an officer through his loudhailer. He struggled to make himself heard above the growing cacophony of shouting and honking car horns. 'I repeat, get back! Give us some room here!'

A camera flash went off in the crowd, and then another as reporters and photographers arrived at the scene.

'The bitch jumped before I could get to her.'

The slurred voice seemed to come from fifty different directions, all from Joe's left, all from the impossible swirl of space in the corner of the floor. The voice sounded horribly familiar. Joe felt his heart rate double and his throat constrict. A renewed chill cut through to his bones, contrasting the flames that licked across his belly. He fought for breath. He turned his head and saw something move in the vortex, its fragmented form circling around the kaleidoscope, an incomprehensible mess that came together piece by piece. It became the shape of a man. The shape of a man holding a massive hunting knife. A running man with madness in his eyes.

Fuck!

'JOE!' screamed Dawn.

He pushed himself away from the support.

Clive sprang into full view from the twisted vortex.

The two men circled each other for a moment, each holding their respective blades.

With his long greasy beard and black straggly hair Clive looked as if he'd been trapped in the maze for months, maybe even years. His beard hung from the undersides of his gaunt overly-pronounced cheekbones. He grinned, revealing four rotten teeth in his mouth, and the broken, blackened nubs of the rest. He wore a patterned shirt, torn in several places and splattered with vile splodges of brown and red. A bib of dark blood stained the front of his shirt. The sleeves were rolled up, revealing dangerously thin forearms covered in scabs, sores and scars. His jeans were marked and shredded and looked to be three sizes too big. None of these things he had worn when he shot up the floor of Hardingham Frank. Only the heavy, black boots looked familiar.

But the eyes were unmistakably Clive. They stared at him without blinking.

In the background Joe heard the stairwell door slam shut and his heart sank.

'Long time, no see,' said Clive, chuckling.

'Speak for your-'

But that was all Joe managed to say. Clive leapt towards him and Joe knew straight away something had gone very badly wrong. The pain he had suffered up to that point paled in comparison with the searing, white-hot agony he felt as Clive buried the tip of his hunting knife deep into the side of his belly and then dragged the blade across Joe's abdomen to free it.

Joe crumpled to the floor and desperately tried to stem the hot flow of blood from the enormous gash. He held his hand to the deep wound in his belly. Every touch unleashed waves of unrelenting agony across his overworked nerves. He placed his forearm over the length of the gash. He looked up. Clive was preparing to strike again.

I'm going to fucking die in here!

'NO!' screamed Dawn.

CHAPTER FIFTEEN

Dawn hauled the fire extinguisher from the wall and took off into the floor. She raced towards her fallen friend and the filthy creature who stood between them. The fragmented air began to clear. The fractures in the floor soon evened out. She upped her speed and started swinging the heavy metal cylinder up and around.

'NO!' she screamed, and saw the beast turn.

She smashed the fire extinguisher clean across the side of the man's face, sending him crashing into the fucked-up floor.

She glanced to Joe. His midriff was slick with blood that pooled beneath him. He'd propped himself up with one arm, using the other to cover a serious wound. He took in short gasping breaths, as if afraid to expand his lungs any further. He looked like he had seen a ghost.

Dawn returned her attention to the other man and the massive knife that lay near him, the handle of which she had seen before.

She caught a glimpse of the other man's face as he struggled to gather himself from the floor. His eyes were all over the place, but she had seen enough to know it was Clive.

No fucking way.

She and Joe had been lost for perhaps a couple of days, but Clive had somehow been trapped here for an eternity, deteriorating into some cannibalistic parody of Robinson Crusoe.

He tried to speak but it came out as nonsense: 'Eb... ab... Duh...'

But then he found the handle of the large hunting knife.

In that instant Dawn remembered everything she despised about the evil, withered fucker before her. His constant ogling. Every sexist comment he ever made. The arrogance he wore like bad cologne and the disdain he had for everyone in the world bar himself. The groping in the photocopying room and the accusations she was a slut, a slag, a whore.

The shooting and the shooting and the shooting and the shooting.

The threats he made in the supermarket car park and the fears he was following her home every night. The taunts he made about her fiancée and how he was going to kill him.

The shooting and the shooting and the shooting and the shooting!

How he killed Mr Wilkes. How he slaughtered Gil. What he had just done to poor old Joe.

But most of all she remembered Barbara's trembling voice on the phone, seconds before the fucker came and destroyed her life and those of so many others.

'He's shot Mike.'

She snapped. She swung the fire extinguisher around her shoulders and behind her head and slammed its body down as hard as she could onto Clive's brow. He dropped to the floor like a sack of shit and the knife fell from his hand. She brought up the fire extinguisher again and smashed the bottom of it into his skull. A sickening crack sounded as the front of his face caved in, and then he was still.

Dawn dropped the fire extinguisher onto the floor and felt close to fainting. Her heart pounded hard against her ribcage, fuelled by little more than adrenaline and outright hatred. As her conscious self resumed control she took in what she had done.

Fresh blood trickled from a deep gash gouged into Clive's brow. There was no way a human head was supposed to look like that.

Joe gasped and cried out in pain, catching Dawn's attention. His forearm was proving no match for the wound he tried to contain. The bottom of his shirt was soaked through, a vivid shade of red that glistened in the broken daylight. He leaked precious blood onto the floor. His breathing drew shorter, sharper, close to hyperventilation. He had the pallor of a zombie. He looked panicky and afraid.

Dawn's anger dissolved into nausea. But this was no time to succumb to her phobias and failings. She needed to get Joe to safety somehow. She had to keep trying the stairwell doors until... until...

Until what? We find a fucking hospital? In this place?

'Got to try something,' she whispered.

She removed Joe's suit jacket and knelt beside him. She eased his forearm away and retched the moment she saw the deep gash in his abdominal wall and the unstoppable flow of blood that ran from the wound. She swallowed hard, knowing too well she had nothing left to puke.

'Press your jacket hard onto the wound, Joe,' she said. 'Do you think you can stand?'

Joe's shoulder shook, which set the rest of his body going. Dawn sincerely hoped it was due to the strain of propping up his weight on one arm, but it looked for all the world as if the poor guy was going into shock.

'I don't know,' he said between shallow breaths. 'It hurts. F-f-fucking Clive!'

'I need you to try, Joe.' She rounded behind him and grabbed under his armpit. 'We need to find a safe floor and see how badly you've been hurt.'

'I-I'm af-fraid!' he sobbed.

The way he said it broke Dawn's heart into a million pieces.

'I know, Joe,' she said. 'But your insides aren't going to fall out, okay? That only happens in horror movies, yeah? It's bullshit. The body just doesn't work like that. But I need you to clamp that jacket onto your belly to stem the bleeding. I need you to stand up. Can you do that for me?'

Please believe me, Joe.
I'm so sorry.
Don't leave me alone in here.

He nodded and took as deep a breath as he dared. He cursed and screamed every second as he staggered to his feet. By the end of the ordeal he was crying helplessly.

The rawness of Joe's pain had her bordering on tears but she had to be strong for him. She had to be his warrior-woman, as stupid as that sounded.

Once he regained his balance she found he no longer leaned so heavily against her, suggesting he somehow had strength enough to stand on his own two feet.

'Okay, Joe, you're doing brilliantly,' she said. 'I'm just going to get this blade of yours and we're out of here, right?'

Joe nodded, unable to speak through his sobbing.

Dawn quickly retrieved the bayonet blade from the alarmingly large pool of fresh blood in which it rested, then returned to help Joe walk.

She ignored the central elevator shaft and slowly guided Joe towards the black stairwell door. She knew it lay ahead, somewhere beyond all the cut-up layers of space. Each step they took proved precarious. As they crossed the jagged islands of the floor she found the gravity dictated upon her often differed from that dictated upon Joe. He pulled on her, instinctively, and she steadied him. If she pulled on him, accidentally, he cried out in agony.

Each step took them deeper into a chaotic swarm of flies, flies that sensed fresh meat in which to lay their eggs. They amassed on Joe, Dawn's blade useless against them.

She looked at the bayonet attachment and felt a distinct unease spread from her cramping stomach, as if someone had walked over her grave. She had seen the blade before. It was the same blade Other Dawn had wielded before she vanished.

The knife had disappeared too, and now here it is.

She recalled once more how Other Dawn had staggered away in fear. How she only had one arm. How she seemed so thin and diseased. Thin and diseased like Clive, but *not* Clive. Some Other Clive she had just killed.

'Duuuhhhh...'

She felt the sweat on her back cool and the skin of her arms instantly tighten. She knew she could not keep the bayonet blade. Other Dawn had been a portent, a warning of some kind that she was on the wrong path.

'Duuuuuuhhhhhhnnnn.... Duuuhhhnnnuuh...'

The deeply slurred voice chilled her blood. The sick fucker was coming back to life again just to spite her. She stopped and looked over her shoulder. Flies homed in on her face. She saw Other Clive stirring, fragmented on the floor. Joe moaned. At least he could stand. Just.

She took a firmer grasp of the bayonet blade.

'Joe, keep going as best you can and keep these fucking flies away,' she said. 'I need to do something. I'll be back as quick as I can.'

She released Joe and ran towards Other Clive. She found him trying to get to his knees, an incredible feat for a man with his head smashed in. His one remaining eye caught hers, dulled, as if he was working on instinct alone. Instinct enough, however, to take hold of the large hunting knife once again.

'Don't you fucking dare!'

She smashed the bayonet blade into Clive's wrist, cutting deep into the flesh, drawing blood instantly. The blade jarred against his arm bone, enough for him to release the knife. It clattered against a tangle of metal rods, resting over a pitch-black gap between two chunks of concrete. She threw the bayonet blade into the vortex in the corner of the floor.

Good luck to anyone finding it in there.

She watched as fragments of the blade appeared and disappeared in and around the vortex, before finally settling wherever the hell it landed.

Dawn picked up the hunting knife and examined her new find. The flat of the knife had once enjoyed a brushed metal finish, but now looked old and heavily stained. The blade was chipped and rusting in places, though still looked exceedingly sharp, particularly nearer the guard. Thin red letters were etched into the length of the short, grey plastic handle.

PARANG.

Fuck only knew what it meant.

'Djuhh...Duuuuhhhnnnnn...' murmured Clive. He looked with some confusion at the deep cut sustained above his wrist and the blood that now poured from it onto his knee.

Dawn looked towards the elevator shaft, the pile of burnt wood and the festering heap of meat and bones nearby.

Glancing around the broken twisted floor, she recalled the split in the gents toilet that Joe had witnessed. She had no idea why it happened, but knew it involved a bloodstain. And there were an awful lot of splits on this floor: splits behind splits beyond splits beneath splits.

This floor, therefore, had been an abattoir. A killing floor.

She grabbed the hand that Clive still held outstretched. She tugged hard to straighten it up at the elbow. She lifted the parang high above her head and brought it down hard. It sliced into the flesh of Clive's forearm, its lethal momentum cutting through the bones and passing straight through. She felt his hand come away. A squirt of hot arterial blood splashed against her knee and ran down her shin.

And she didn't care. Not one fucking iota. She felt nothing for the braindead piece of shit that knelt before her.

She watched Clive instinctively cover his gushing wound with his one remaining hand. His slurred voice changed, reached a higher register, an expression of pain perhaps. She threw the severed hand into his lap.

'Here,' she sneered. 'Have that if you're so fucking hungry.'

To Dawn's disgust he did just that. He stuck his bleeding stump into the leg of his filthy, too-big jeans, picked up the hand from his lap and immediately tore at the ragged flesh with whatever black teeth he had left. Flies upon flies descended on him, covered his skin and landed on his severed hand. He chewed on flesh and flies alike.

She left the doomed bastard to his fate and dashed towards the fragmented image of Joe in the distance. She found him crawling on the floor.

'Joe?' she said, her voice tinged with fear. 'Joe, talk to me.'

'Help me, Dawn,' he said. 'P-please!' The poor guy sounded weak, defeated against the incessant buzzing of his ghastly tormentors.

A wave of shame and regret swept over her. She had spent far too long getting the hunting knife from Clive, leaving a badly wounded man, her friend and a better friend than she realised, leaving him to struggle on alone. It was obvious he could no longer walk or stand unaided, and she doubted she could get him back on his feet again even if she tried.

Ahead she saw the black mass of the stairwell door, haloed with slivers of obsidian. At least they were close. She threw the heavy knife towards the door and picked Joe up by his armpits. He was damned heavy.

'Joe, sweetheart, love of my life,' she said, the words choking up at the back of her throat. Hot tears welled in her eyes and immediately attracted more flies. 'Please, Joe, I need you to help me drag you to the door. Push up your arse if you can and walk with me.'

To her astonishment he did. With the heavily stained suit jacket resting on his opened guts he put all of his remaining strength into his back and into his legs. Her friend's spirit amazed her and within minutes they had reached the stairwell door.

She picked up the parang and yanked open the door. She threw the knife onto the landing and stopped the door from closing with her backside. She leaned down, helped Joe through the doorway and at long last let the fucked-up madness of the killing floor disappear behind her.

The moment the door sealed she pushed it open again, scaring the hell out of a bespectacled man sitting beyond. He quickly gathered himself and nervously waved a pistol in their direction.

'Ne gyertek sőt még a távolabbi!' he yelled, and briefly glanced behind as if looking for support. 'Segítség!'

'Don't just fucking sit there!' screamed Dawn. 'Help us!'

CHAPTER SIXTEEN

Two more figures emerged from the gloom beyond, a man and a woman.

The tall man wore a stiff, crumpled shirt and trousers held up with braces. His hair was black, lank and greasy. His black beard bushed around the jowls, suggesting his face had sunk. His eyes shone with intelligence, hawk-like.

The woman stood shoulder-high to the man. She wore her blonde hair in a loose ponytail, helped in place with grips, also in need of a wash. Her wrinkled cotton blouse favoured function over style. The hem of her dark green woollen skirt hung well below her knees. A slim black leather belt wrinkled the waist. She wore black shoes with flat soles. She would have once been attractive except that her eyes were too far apart.

All three of them were desperately thin.

The tall man rested a hand on the shoulder of his colleague with the pistol in order to calm him, perhaps to reassure him. He looked towards the other woman.

'Menj vissza, Ajtay Anya,' he said in soft, but commanding tones. 'Minden rendben less.'

The woman shook her head and said something equally incomprehensible.

Fuck it. I can't wait for this.

Dawn threw the hunting knife onto the carpeted floor ahead and gestured towards it with her open palms.

'Look,' she said. 'See? We're not armed, now let us through!'

She didn't wait for a response. She dragged Joe through the doorway.

The man with the pistol said something in a raised voice, seemingly in protest.

'I don't care,' said Dawn without looking towards them. 'We're coming in! I need help for my friend. He's badly hurt.'

The stairwell door knocked against Joe's legs and slowly closed. A pair of fluorescent strip lights above them bathed the immediate area with pale light. The gloom beyond suggested it was dark outside. Only a handful of other lights were switched on. Perhaps they were the only surviving bulbs.

Dawn lay Joe on the ground, then knelt over him and smoothed the greasy hair from his brow. He shivered uncontrollably beneath a layer of cool sweat. The unimaginable pain he suffered drew down the corners of his mouth. His eyes conveyed a look of terror that Dawn would take with her to the grave.

To her left she saw the tall, thin man once more pat the bespectacled man on the shoulder. He said something else she didn't understand. The bespectacled man returned the pistol to a leather holster hanging from his belt. Three further people gathered in the murk to see what was happening.

Dawn removed the heavily-bloodstained jacket from Joe's midriff. She dared to look at the damage wrought upon him. She saw the worst through a ragged tear across Joe's once-white shirt. She felt her head spin once more. She desperately resisted the urge to faint.

His chest rose and sank with quick, shallow breaths. Too quick. All the while his belly continued to bleed and bleed and bleed.

She looked over to Joe's face and saw in his terror that he was crying, and only then did she surrender fully to her sorrow. She sat back onto her heels, placed a bloody hand to her face and for a moment let it all pour out of her: the violence; the familiar faces destroyed by gunfire; her lack of knowledge about Mike's condition; their entrapment within a sick never-ending joke, and now, to top it all, having to watch the constant companion of her most recent days bleed to death in front of her. She shook uncontrollably with each wave of grief that struck her. She didn't bother to wipe the hot tears than ran freely down her cheeks and into her laugh lines. She knelt, crumpled like a broken toy.

'I'm sorry,' said Joe, as faint as a gentle breeze in the trees. He tried to raise his head from the ground but couldn't manage more than an inch.

Dawn tried to collect herself but found her feelings too raw to touch. She knelt over Joe and pressed her forehead into his clammy brow. She stroked his cheek. 'No, don't be,' she said and was quickly overcome once more.

'It's all my f-fault,' said Joe. 'You were right.'

'No, Joe,' was all Dawn could manage. She sniffed loudly and rubbed her hand harder against his face.

'Did you kill h-him?'

Dawn nodded against Joe's brow and saw the corners of his mouth twitch up into some semblance of a smile.

'My warrior woman.'

Dawn reached her mouth close to his and cupped his face.

'My hero' she said, falteringly, and kissed him, but he was gone.

She cradled his head next to hers and cried the clouds from the skies.

*****

'Don't touch me!' spat Dawn. She placed a protective hand over Joe's body. She looked back to see the blonde girl retract her outstretched hand. To her surprise she too had tears in her eyes.

'Sorry,' said the girl, and placed her hands in her lap.

Sorry?

The tall, thin man crouched down beside the girl. He addressed Dawn in a hushed, mournful voice.

'Nagyon sajnáljuk.'

'He says we are sorry,' said the girl in a thick Eastern European accent.

'You speak English?'

'A little,' she said. 'Enough.'

She then spoke to the tall, thin man, presumably to translate her exchange with Dawn. The man's hawk-like eyes bore into the girl, intense with thought. He asked her a question, sounding curious, and the girl gave a lengthy reply.

Dawn returned her attention to Joe's lifeless body. His eyes were closed, his lips set as if he had died anticipating her kiss. She stroked his cheek and found he was already cooling.

A medley of emotions vied for dominance within her: sorrow, hurt, anger, even guilt for grieving over Joe when Mike could also be dead. She tried to sweep such thoughts from her mind but they refused to leave, preferring to fester in her conscience.

She took Joe's jacket. Her heart skipped a beat when she saw how stained it had become. There were seldom few grey patches remaining, the fabric of the suit was now heavily infused with Joe's cooling blood. She watched the suit jacket drip onto the carpet. A cold droplet splashed onto her knee and trickled to the floor. She noticed just how covered in gore she too had become. She again tried to focus on something other than blood and death.

She dug Joe's smartphone from the jacket pocket and realised she couldn't remember his PIN. It didn't matter. When she powered on the phone the screen briefly displayed a "battery empty" graphic and switched itself off again.

'What is that?' said the girl.

'Nothing,' said Dawn, handing her the phone. 'Not any more.'

The girl looked at the device with profound bafflement. She slid her fingers over the greasy glass surface.

Surely you've seen a mobile phone before?

'Who are you?' said Dawn.

The girl looked up and met her eyes.

'Ajtay Anya,' said the girl, pronouncing it "aye-tay". She smiled briefly, politely. 'You would call me Anya.'

'No,' said Dawn, seeing yet more haggard people gather in the gloomy distance. 'I mean who are you? All of you.'

'We are all lost,' said the girl.

'Okay, fine, whatever,' said Dawn. 'I've got no time for bullshit riddles right now, thanks.'

And yet she hesitated. Her rational mind took hold of the reins. The folk on the floor were a little odd-looking, but at least they were some way normal. They hadn't attacked her. They hadn't chased her. They hadn't vanished before her eyes. And she'd found someone who finally spoke a little English.

Maybe I can get some information, or, even better, some food.

She looked harder at the new arrivals that gathered nearby. They, like all the others, were terribly thin. Perhaps they had all been forced to ration what little supplies they possessed. Maybe it was they who had found the vending machine and smashed it open for its contents. Maybe they were down to their last couple of chocolate bars.

The skinny onlookers gathered in front of four storage rooms ahead. The rooms formed an island dead-centre of a large open office floor. Dawn found herself facing the right-most storage room. To her right there hung a series of wet-looking sheets, each suspended from a washing-line that stretched from one side of the floor to the other and propped up twice along the way. The sheets hid the extent of the floor beyond. To her immediate left there were three open elevator doors and another door to a stairwell, similarly guarded. All of the elevators had old chunky computer monitors jammed in the doors to prevent them from closing. A symphony of complaint droned quietly from the elevator cars, but not loud enough to annoy. She heard murmuring in the near distance to her left. A faint smell of sweat and body odour hung in the air. Another smell too. One she couldn't immediately place.

The tall, thin man stood straight with some effort, his knees cracking. He said something Dawn couldn't understand. She looked to the girl for guidance but found her focused on what the man was saying. Eventually she caught Dawn's eyes.

'He says your friend cannot stay there,' said the girl, a little too blunt for Dawn's taste.

Dawn's initial reaction was to fight, as had so often been the case over the years. Few people got to tell her exactly what to do. But then what could she do? Joe was dead, murdered, and as much as it pained her there was precious little she could do for him now.

She couldn't even offer him a decent burial.

She considered the elevator door of the atrium, and the perfectly black void beyond. He could dissolve into the night, almost like a cremation. It was the best she could manage for him.

But the atrium had been lost to the randomness of the stairwell doors.

Fucking Clive.

At least he was dead, and by her hands too, even if he did look... older. Thinner. Weaker.

The tall, thin man stepped over Joe's corpse and took hold of an armpit. The bespectacled man took the other and they lifted. Joe's head hung back and swung loose between his shoulders as they turned him on the spot.

'Leave him alone!' said Dawn. She placed a hand on Joe's chest to stop them.

Can't you give him a moment?

To do what, though? Why would they want to keep a dead body on their floor, their home?

But it felt wrong to disturb Joe's remains so soon.

The girl, Anya, sensed Dawn's distress. She started to apologise on behalf of her friends.

The tall, thin man looked to Anya and spoke. 'Mondd neki!' he emphasised at the end of it all.

Anya looked at Dawn and then averted her eyes almost immediately.

'He says we are sorry,' she said.

The two men dragged Joe's body towards the line of soggy sheets. Dawn quickly got to her feet and followed them, unable to take her eyes from the slash in Joe's belly. They drew aside one of the sheets and carried on through. The area ahead housed a row of individual offices, but the light was too poor to see any detail. The funny smell strengthened beyond the sheets. It began to stain the back of her throat.

The blonde girl, Anya, tagged behind, and put a hand on Dawn's shoulder to pull her back.

Dawn shrugged her hand away with a grunt.

The thin man said something to Anya, his tone sterner than before.

Dawn turned back to find Anya averting her eyes again.

'What are not telling me?' she said. 'Tell me exactly what he is saying. Now!'

But still Anya could not meet her eyes.

Someone had opened a door to one of the offices, a room filled with machines that whirred and hummed.

'He says we are sorry,' said Anya.

'What *else* is he saying?'

She heard a switch being pressed. She turned and saw the lights of the open office flicker into life. The room contained a wall of fridges and freezers of varying shapes and sizes, with mini-bars from hotel rooms stacked on top.

She heard the inhabitants of the floor gather behind and around her, and felt an awful sensation as if she was in the middle of a pincer movement. Somewhere behind the skinny army, near the stairwell door, there lay the hunting knife. She knew she had made a terrible mistake.

The lights of another office to the right flicked on. Inside there stood the bespectacled man and a large white formica-topped table, cut with grooves. There was an electric knife on the table.

Dawn's eyes dropped to Joe's corpse. It lay outside this second office. The carpet around the bespectacled man's feet was noticeably pinker than the rest of the floor. The wallpaper too.

'He says,' said Anya, her voice wavering. 'He says we are sorry but we must eat.'

Dawn caught sight of the office guillotine that lay beneath the white table, a hefty slab of blue plastic with an enormous curved blade attached to one corner. The blade, like the floor and the wallpaper, carried an ominous reddish stain.

The tall, thin man drew the guillotine out from the table and placed it solemnly beside the electric knife. He lifted the huge curved blade.

'No!' cried Dawn. 'No, you can't!'

Hands grabbed her arms, more locked around her waist. She tried to force her way forward, but someone held her ankles. She tumbled to the floor.

'You can't do this!' she screamed. 'Leave him alone! You can't fucking eat him!'

She felt the weight of a half-dozen people push her to the floor, stymieing her attempts to wriggle free. She looked over to Joe's body ahead, helpless to prevent what was happening. The two men grabbed the body by the armpits and dragged it into the pink-tinged office.

'You fuckers!' she yelled. 'You heartless motherfuckers, leave him alone!'

The tall, thin man looked back to Dawn. At that moment they were perhaps the saddest eyes she had ever seen. He bowed his head, made a sign of the cross and closed the door.

'Mi vagyunk sajnáljuk,' said one of the women pushing down on her back. She sounded close to tears.

Another, a man, repeated the words, and another.

'We are sorry,' said Anya. 'But we are so hungry.'

Dawn fixed onto the large window next to the closed door. The venetian blinds had been drawn but she could still see vague shadows from within the room.

'Let me *go*!' hollered Dawn, her voice becoming hoarse.

'Please, we must eat,' said Anya, and she began to weep.

'Mi vagyunk sajnáljuk.'

Dawn heard the harsh scraping sound of the guillotine being brought down hard against snapping bones, and then her brain gave up. As she passed out all she heard were the mantra-like apologies of her captors and the whining, cutting sound of the electric knife working on Joe's body.

• **PART TWO** •

ANTHROPOPHAGY
IN EXTREMIS

SIGN OF THE TIMES
STARPHONE RECORDS' FAMOUS STREET SIGN HARBORS A FEW FINAL SURPRISES

by Tobias Zyrybowski, ★★★★★★★★★★★★★★★★★★★★★★★★★★★★
L.A. Chronicle's No. 1 Entertainment Reporter

THE FINAL CHAPTER closed on Starphone Records' story yesterday when its famous street sign was removed by the building's new owners.

The sign had been a prominent feature of Vine St since 1959, but had fallen into disrepair after Starphone Records filed for bankruptcy in 1992.

During the removal of the street sign workmen discovered a master copy of Hellsbayne's then-infamous second album *Hell To Pay*, long-believed to have been lost following an explosive dispute between the band and the record label. The compact disc would no longer play in a conventional player. An old weather-beaten notebook was also found lodged behind the sign. The pages inside were ruined, but there was a single word faintly visible on the cover: "SOS".

It was a chilling reminder of Starphone Records' dramatic decline in the late 1980's following a string of high-profile contract disputes with big-name rock bands and a disastrous change of direction in 1990 towards rap and hip hop.

Excerpt from the LA Chronicle
Friday, September 23rd 1992

CHAPTER SEVENTEEN

Dawn stirred. She emerged from a sleep so deep it was like being hauled from a pit of quicksand inch by sucking inch.

Silence dominated her surroundings, as if she had been the first to wake on Christmas morning. A red tinge to her eyelids suggested she lay in strong daylight. She kept them closed.

She felt sluggish, like she'd slept for decades. Sluggish and sore. Her muscles ached and trembled with every move she made, as if they had atrophied in her sleep. Someone had stolen her stomach and left a dense ball of cramp in its place. She no longer felt hunger, only twisting pain.

She rubbed the crusty bits of sleep from her eyes and then dared to open them. The sun bore into her, bright and startling. She squinted, trying to get her eyes to adjust.

She caught the fuzzy outline of a thin-limbed man sitting opposite her. He knelt with his fingers pressed up together, as if making a church roof.

She closed her eyes again, finding them as sore as her limbs. The inside of her mouth was the texture of rough wallpaper. She pushed the palm of her hand onto perhaps the hardest mattress in the world, but she could not raise herself from the bed. She was still dog tired.

What on earth possessed me to sleep here? Where am I?
Oh, my God. Joe! They took Joe!

She heard something rustling nearby. Something dry, something that didn't sound like clothes.

The man kneeling opposite her then spoke.

[Hmmmmm. It's high time you lost those panties, Dawny Prawn!]

Her eyelids sprung open like a pair of roller-blinds.

The thin-limbed man ahead of her had a broken back and long fingers tipped with claw-like nails. His fingers twitched restlessly.

Grabby hands.

'No!' It came as a whisper.

She lifted her arms to defend herself and found them as heavy as wrecking balls. She screamed for help, a hoarse rasp, but by then it was too late.

The Tickling Man leapt on top of her, straddling her, forcing her back onto the hard mattress. He dug his cruel claws into her bruised flesh, finding her ribs with ease. He worked every muscle, every sinew he could find and beneath him Dawn wriggled and giggled and gasped for air.

Please, somebody help me! He's suffocating me! I can't scream!

She felt his long, probing fingers poke through her ribcage and burst her lungs like balloons. She cowered at the hideous sight that loomed above her.

The scarecrow head of The Tickling Man had changed, replaced by the gormless smashed-in face of Other Clive. His ruptured eye dropped and hung uselessly from its socket. It jiggled as he worked her with his fingers. She felt the eye touch the tip of her nose, still moist.

No air! No air.

She gagged and gulped to no avail. She opened her mouth wide enough for her lips to tear, but she could draw no air in.

Her ribcage gave way with a nasty crunching sound, crushed like a ball of waste paper.

She knew then she would soon be dead.

*****

Dawn woke bolt upright with a long, terrified scream that echoed around the office floor. The tall, thin man and Anya noticeably jumped. Anya placed her hand to her chest to help steady her nerves. The man held out both hands and gestured for Dawn to relax.

They both knelt close by, tending a bedside vigil for her. Behind them a number of people woke from their slumber, no more than a dozen and mostly women. They each slept in single beds beneath grubby duvets. The woken propped themselves upon thin arms, curious to find what all the fuss was about. When they saw Dawn they immediately looked away.

Dawn found she too lay in a single bed and felt uncomfortably warm within it. She kicked away the dirty duvet, hauled herself into a sitting position and rubbed some life into her face.

At least they didn't undress me.

She heard a loud sniff. A sob.

In a corner to the left, beside a door to the gents, another woman sat on the floor. She wore a long nightdress and held her knees to her chest, rocking in a way that unsettled Dawn. She had red bags under her eyes as if she had been crying for a long time. She bit furiously at her fingernails and the skin around them. She looked old for her years, but then so did everyone. Her large, wet eyes bore into Dawn.

Dawn broke free of the woman's stare and looked over her shoulder. There were a series of six large individual offices close behind her bed. They spanned the entire width of the floor. From there a number of tall windows dominated the walls along both sides. The blinds of some were fully open, pouring strong sunshine onto the grey-brown carpet, releasing a musty odour akin to an old woman's scullery.

The floor then narrowed a little beyond the arrangement of single beds. The island of storage rooms ahead bisected a lobby of elevator doors and stairwells, an area much larger than she remembered. A male guard sat near each stairwell door, four in all.

She caught sight of the discoloured sheets beyond the lobby. A spindly middle-aged man walked out from behind the island and dampened the sheets with a spray gun. The sight of those sheets screwed her stomach into an even tighter ball.

I'm so sorry, Joe.

She couldn't give him a decent burial. She couldn't even preserve the guy's dignity. She heard once more the appalling noises that came from beyond those sheets as they harvested his cooling corpse.

She looked to Anya, but the girl struggled to meet her eyes.

She then looked to the thin man with the thick, jowly beard. He did not look away, nor did he try to disguise his shame. He spoke softly and then bowed his head.

'Please understand,' said Anya. 'That we had to do what we did.'

'He was my friend,' said Dawn.

'I know,' said Anya. 'We are sorry.'

'What are you going to do to me?'

Anya seemed genuinely taken aback by the question. She translated for the thin man. He looked to Dawn and shook his head.

'Nothing,' said Anya. Her eyes brightened. 'You are hungry. Your belly keeps growling.'

To Dawn's horror Anya fetched a plate of meat from the gap between her and the thin man. She held it out, an offering. The scraps of meat were small and bitty and wholly unappetising.

'Oh, God no,' said Dawn, pushing the plate away. 'How could you?'

'Sorry, no. This is not your friend,' said Anya. 'This is what we had left before you came.'

The meat looked horrible all the same, and yet her stomach grumbled long and loud at the sight of it. She felt a deep shame burn across her cheeks and a flash of pain in her guts.

'But it's still human,' said Dawn.

'Yes,' said Anya, matter-of-factly.

Dawn looked away from the plate and found the woman in the corner still staring at her. She had stopped eating the ends of her fingers and simply sat, knees still pressed to her chest, with her arms wrapped around her shins. She rocked backwards and forwards slightly and began to cry again. She shook her head as if begging Dawn not to touch the meat.

Anya set the plate down by Dawn's bare feet, but Dawn immediately pushed it away.

'No,' said Dawn. 'Just... no.'

As she sat back again she caught sight of her clothes. The stains. Sweat. Dirt. Clive's blood. Joe's blood. Her skin itched everywhere, more so under her hair. She felt savage rawness in several places beneath her underwear.

The woman in the corner held her face in her hands and shook as she wept. Another woman from a nearby bed got up and walked to her. She too wore a nightdress. She looked to be five or six months pregnant, an incredible sight. The woman's paunch was at complete odds to her otherwise frighteningly thin frame. She knelt by the weeping woman with some effort. She slid a hand across her shoulder and drew her into an awkward hug.

Dawn looked away from the scene and towards the opposite side of the floor where there stood a door to the ladies toilets. She tugged at the front of her filthy blouse.

'I need to freshen up.'

*****

The water ran hot within twenty seconds. Dawn looked to the sink and wished it was a hundred times bigger. She pulled up on a metal knob that stood between the hot and cold taps. A rubber-rimmed metal stopper dropped into the plughole. She let the sink fill and tried the soap dispenser nearby. Empty. She tried the dispensers by the other sinks and found they too were spent. The crusty soap residue that clung around the spout of each dispenser suggested they had been empty for some time.

She turned off the hot water and thrust her blouse into the steaming sink. She would have to lift whatever she could of the stains with hot water and brute force alone.

She set another sink to fill with hot water and took off her bra. It felt good to finally get some air onto her skin, but the feeling didn't last for long. In the line of mirrors above the sinks she caught sight of the marks on and around her chest and belly. She lifted up her left arm and cupped her breast away for a look at the damage. She found patches of angry red flesh where the garment had chafed hardest. It was the same story under her other armpit, red marks the size of large postage stamps.

Wait a minute.

She cupped both her breasts and observed how they filled her hands.

'No way.'

Either her hands had grown a little or her boobs had started to shrink.

What the hell is going on here?

She was ravenous, yes, but it couldn't have been *that* long since she'd last eaten. Surely it took more than a few days before people started to waste away, even if there wasn't much to them to begin with.

She picked up the bra and held it over a small overflowing bin next to the row of sinks. She had never liked the thing. It always felt too restrictive. Mike had loved it, of course, saying it gave her knockout tits, but it was damn near cutting her to pieces.

And Mike isn't here.

She swallowed hard and dropped the bra onto the overfull bin., then stopped the hot water tap of the second sink.

The yellow light from above each mirror did little to lessen the large streaky bloodstains on the front of her skirt. She had picked a very bad day to wear grey. She undid the zip and slid the skirt over her hips and down her legs. She looked in the mirror and examined a strip of relatively clean skin between the top of her knickers and a pinky-red tide mark across her belly. She rubbed a thumb over the stain, smudging it slightly.

She placed the skirt in the second sink.

Crap. I hope the hand drier works.

She stepped over and waved a hand beneath it, felt it whoosh into life. At least she wouldn't have to walk around the place in a pair of damp knickers.

She rolled her underwear down her legs and threw them into the sink to soak along with her blouse, and stood naked in front of the mirror.

A familiar sense of self-loathing descended upon her, even now. She ignored the good points Mike had always loved, especially now they were shrinking, and looked straight towards her hips. She would never attain the wasp-like look she had craved since puberty. If she lost any more weight then what hips she had would soon vanish along with her tits and she'd look more like a boy than a woman of twenty-four.

'Jesus, look at you,' she said to the mirror. She plunged her hands into the hot water, letting the heat sting her skin. She took her wet hands away and rubbed at the bloodstains on her belly, then her arms and legs.

The interior door moved slightly on its hinges.

Shit! Someone's coming!

She immediately hid what she could with the arms God gave her. She scanned the restroom for potential weapons but found none save only for the toilet brushes in the cubicles.

She suddenly felt very, very vulnerable.

'Shit! Shit! Shit!' she hissed under her breath.

Anya stepped through the interior door with a bundle under her right arm.

'Hello?' she said as she entered, then, upon seeing Dawn, 'Ah, hello.'

'Jesus, Anya, do you mind?' said Dawn, still covering herself.

'I brought you clothes,' said Anya, unabashed. She stepped towards the washbasins and placed the bundle into an empty sink. 'Some soap too.'

Dawn twisted her body around, still protecting her modesty.

'Yes, okay, thank you!' said Dawn. 'I'll take it from here.'

Anya drew closer, uncomfortably so, and looked Dawn in the eyes.

'Please,' she said. 'You must let me come with you.'

'Whoa, whoa, whoa, wait a minute. What happened to the whole Russian spy accent?'

'I will explain later, but I must leave this place.'

'Then go, I'm not stopping you,' said Dawn. 'Do it.'

'I cannot leave on my own!' said Anya. 'Please! I can help you.'

She grabbed hold of Dawn's bicep, but Dawn shrugged her hand away.

'Help me? *Help me?* You and your oh-so-fucking-sorry cronies had me pinned me down,' hissed Dawn. 'You go and desecrate poor old Joe's corpse before he's even gone cold and now you want to tag along and help me? Eff... you... see... kay... off. Now!'

She stomped over to the sinks to continue washing, caring nothing now for her nudity. In the mirror she saw Anya mournfully look her way and then walk to the interior door with her head down. She left the room without saying another word.

'Unbelievable,' said Dawn to the mirror, and angrily rubbed the fabric of her knickers together in the hot water.

She glanced over towards the bundle of clothes that Anya had dumped into the sink. To the girl's credit they looked moderately clean and a whole lot drier than her current clothes, even if she had dragged them out from the nineteen-forties.

She reached for the thin sliver of soap and worked up a small lather. She mulled over Anya's sudden change of accent while she cleaned herself. She pondered how best to make her escape.

Perhaps she could use Anya's little secret to her advantage.

*****

The door to the ladies toilet briskly swung aside and out stepped Dawn, feeling a lot cleaner but still craving a hot bath. She walked barefoot over the grey-brown carpet and toward the shoes neatly arranged beside her bed.

She took a moment to take in the bizarre little civilisation she had stumbled upon, this most skewed simulacrum of the life they'd all left behind. Even in these extremes there were certain standards the long-lost men and women strove to maintain. It made the extent to which they had all dehumanised themselves so much more disturbing.

Then there was the downright creepy arrangement of single beds that dominated the floor space, more beds than there were people and some long-undisturbed. The crying woman lay in one, facing away from Dawn and breathing heavily. The pregnant lady lay asleep in another.

Anya sat on one of the beds and applauded Dawn's new look with a big smile on her face. A big, fake smile to match her big, fake accent.

Dawn felt somewhat less enthusiastic about the outfit. The dark brown skirt looked terrible. The material felt like a cross between a tarpaulin and a dog's blanket. She had to wear a belt to keep the thing from falling down over what hips she had. The stiff, cream blouse was at least two sizes too big and more resembled a man's shirt, but at least it was cotton and allowed her skin to breathe.

Anya had dressed her like some kind of big sister. No wonder she was so happy.

Dawn sat on the bed and slipped on her shoes. She vowed a change of clothes upon the very next wardrobe she found. There had to be one around somewhere.

Why? What's to say you aren't wearing a dead woman's clothes?

She glanced at the empty single beds.

'Nikola has something for you,' said Anya, once again adopting a thick Eastern Europe accent.

'I don't care,' said Dawn. 'Just let me get out of this nuthouse.'

Anya's smile flickered away. She looked a little nervous. Dawn noticed some of the others eye the girl with suspicion, as if nobody had known she could speak another language.

'I have something too,' said Anya, maintaining her facade. 'Something that will help you.'

She stood from the bed, straightened her clothes and walked away, eventually disappearing into the central island of rooms ahead.

The tall, thin man with the jowly beard, presumably Nikola, then immediately strode out from a room on the opposite side, like a scene from some French farce. He carried the large hunting knife that Dawn had taken from Clive in both hands. The blade was swaddled in something dark that she could not readily see.

The bespectacled man had resumed guard duty. He sat by the nearest stairwell door on the right. As Nikola passed him by the man spoke angry words and gesticulated in Dawn's direction.

Nikola returned a volley of equally harsh words. He too pointed towards Dawn and then over to the line of wet sheets. The bespectacled man stopped talking and sulkily resumed his position.

Dawn felt her hackles rise. It seemed all was not well this morning in the cannibal commune.

She scanned the lobby for exits. Each of the elevator doors on both sides remained jammed open with computer monitors. Escaping through them would be time-consuming and risky. That left the four stairwell doors, no less tricky. She'd need to somehow overpower a guard and hope to get the door closed between them.

She stretched her arms and legs, testing them. They ached and trembled with fatigue.

It'd be a lot easier if I had that knife.
Didn't Anya say Nikola had something for me?

She looked closer at the hunting knife he held by his side.

Yeah, and didn't Nikola also point to those wet sheets just then? Don't forget what lies behind them.

Nikola stopped amidst the beds and looked around. He called out for Anya by her surname like some kind of headmaster. He shrugged and shook his head in mild annoyance. He continued toward Dawn until he stood only a couple of feet away. He tried to smile but it looked hopelessly awkward. He began to speak but trailed off halfway through. He sighed and stopped talking.

The knife he held seemed agonisingly close. It dangled by his side. One good lunge and Dawn would grab it and be off.

Nikola held out the parang to her with both hands.

'Okay,' said Dawn. 'What's going on?'

The man tried the smile again, failed. His eyes were too haunted to convey anything other than profound regret and a lifetime's sadness. He offered her the knife with a little more urgency.

He had placed the blade in a leather sheath which, bizarrely, seemed tailor-made for the job. She took the knife from him for a closer inspection. The word PARANG had been stitched into the leather on both sides in the exact same style of lettering as that used on the blade's handle. A smaller chunk of leather hung from the sheath by a large metal ring. A number of small buckles from it allowed the sheath to hang from a belt.

She slid the parang a couple of inches from the sheath, felt a slight snag along the way. The blunt areas of the blade seemed to catch against the furred lining.

'Um. Thanks?' said Dawn.

Okay, this is a big one-oh on the what-the-fuck-o-meter right here.

The bespectacled man shifted in his seat. His anger had risen once more. He launched another salvo of strong words towards Nikola, who visibly rankled against them.

Nikola turned and gave his colleague both barrels in return. He walked towards him like a maddened parent. He flapped his arms about and pointed once more towards the sheets.

Okay, this looks promising.

She followed close behind Nikola, more to get near the stairwell door than anything else.

The bespectacled man motioned to Dawn as he ranted and then most definitely pointed towards the creepy arrangement of beds behind her. It seemed he meant for her to stay.

The others resting nearby woke from their slumber to see what was going on.

The fiery exchange continued between the two men, escalating to such a degree that the bespectacled man pulled out his pistol. He seemed surprised he had done so at first, but soon waggled the pistol between Dawn and Nikola like he meant business.

She looked to the other guards for a reaction. The one at the other end of the lobby remained seated, as if content to see how the impromptu power struggle panned out. Near him she saw Anya peer around the corner of the island. She seemed shocked at the drama unfolding.

The bespectacled man stood up from the chair. He waved the gun at Nikola as if claiming him for his prisoner.

'Jár,' he said.

Dawn kept Anya in the corner of her eye. The girl had tiptoed midway along the lobby towards them. She held what looked like an old school satchel of a kind that went out of fashion somewhere around the Triassic period. She had a hand inside of it.

I hope there's a machine gun in there or something.

'Jár!' said the man with the gun. He sounded like he would shoot before saying it a third time.

THE FLOORS

A sharp clattering resounded in the lobby, the noise of something hard dropping against the plastic shell of a fat computer monitor. Something had fallen out of Anya's bag. Dawn saw a look of someone fearing almost certain death in her eyes.

The man with the gun took the briefest of glimpses, but that was all the invitation Nikola needed. He leapt forward and grabbed the man's gun hand. The two men whirled around, carried by Nikola's momentum into a strange dance of death. They smacked against the stairwell door, cursing each other all the while.

Dawn sidestepped around the tussle, happy to leave them to it, though annoyed they blocked the easy way out.

She heard scuffles and excited noises from those gathering behind her but she paid them no heed. She leapt for the nearest elevator and pushed the call button to re-open the door. She stepped inside and kicked away the computer monitor.

There was a muffled gunshot in the lobby that made her jump. There were screams, more excited noises, the sounds of movement, but she resisted the temptation to look.

Screw them. Screw them all.

Screw their fake humility, their broken honour and their lost dignity. Let them all wither and die for what they did to Joe. It was time to leave.

She examined the control panel of the elevator and the neat handwritten codes above each of the buttons, another grid of thirteens.

She pushed a button at random and let the interior door roll shut.

Anya burst in and stumbled to the floor. The door closed behind her and the elevator jerked into life.

CHAPTER EIGHTEEN

'What the hell are you doing?' said Dawn. She tugged the parang part of the way from its sheath, a threat of what to expect. 'Get out of here, now!'

'I cannot go back,' said Anya, looking up from the floor. 'Nikola is dead.'

The strap of the satchel slipped from Anya's shoulder, dropping the bag onto the vinyl floor with a dull chinking thud. Inside there were a number of hardback notebooks and several marker pens of various sizes and colours. A couple of slim silvery things hid amongst them.

Dawn sensed danger. The girl could easily spring up and pounce. She stepped back and met the elevator wall. She withdrew the rest of the blade and let the sheath fall to the floor. She grasped the handle with both hands and held out the knife, ready to defend herself.

Anya glanced to the control panel and its single lit button. She shook her head, a little irritated. She paid Dawn little attention and rummaged in her satchel with a pensive look on her face. She dug out a notepad and started thumbing through the pages.

'No, no,' she said. 'Not that one.'

'What do you mean, "not that one"?'

An enormous buzzing sound filled the elevator car before Anya could respond. The warm lights in the ceiling dimmed for a second as the whole compartment rocked gently from side to side. The rocking then developed into a shudder whose violence grew quickly. Before long it was as if the whole elevator had been placed on a platform of live pneumatic drills. Through the walls there came fantastic noises of crashing and crunching and the agonised squeal of metal on metal. It sounded like they were falling down a mountain.

'Yes,' said Anya above all the racket. She held open her notebook with one hand and used the other to steady herself. Then, without a shred of irony, she said: 'Yes, this floor is no good.'

The elevator finally juddered to a halt. The interior door whirred aside, revealing a partially open exterior door, burnt and buckled. Darkness lay beyond the door, though thankfully not the total void witnessed in the atrium. At least here Dawn could see the charred carpet of the floor. Someone had chalked a code against the burnt mess, matching the code written above the lit button. A bitter smell of ash and embers wafted into the elevator car and stung her nostrils.

She examined the upside-down pages of Anya's notebook. There were rows and columns of abstruse codes written in assorted colours. Groups of codes had been ringed together as if discovered in a wordsearch puzzle, the groups then linked to others via long meandering lines. Sometimes the lines ran off the page. Sometimes they led to single codes such as the one beneath Anya's finger. All of the codes comprised capital letters and decimal numbers.

Dawn had found Joe's mapmaker.

'This is all your doing, then? These codes?' said Dawn. She nodded to the control panel of the elevator, but the girl's attention was elsewhere.

The knife dipped suddenly in her hands.

Shit, this thing's heavy!

She felt the muscles in her arms tremble, lactic acid burning into her forearms. The tip of the blade began to shake. She prayed Anya didn't notice her weakened state.

But the other girl's attention was fixed on her notebook. She traced a line that ran to a circled number on the edge of the page. Then she leaned over and pushed a button on the control panel.

'Steady!' said Dawn, waving the blade from side to side. 'No sudden moves!'

The interior door of the elevator closed behind Anya.

'Sorry,' she said. 'This floor smells bad. We need to move to a new one.' She looked up from her notebook, suddenly possessed by a new line of thought. She frowned and put her head to one side as if she was trying to remember something. 'What is your name?'

The question caught Dawn by surprise. She ran through the last however many hours in her mind and indeed Anya had never once asked for her name. Nobody had. Perhaps their food was a little easier to digest when they didn't have names.

'My name is Dawn McKenzie. The guy you ate, his name was Joe Bradley. Remember that when you go back for seconds.'

The tip of the parang now wobbled noticeably from side to side. Dawn found herself sizing up the girl on the floor. Anya was painfully thin, that much was obvious, but the girl had recently eaten while Dawn had not. If Anya called her bluff... well, that didn't bear thinking about. She kept the blade outstretched, the backs of her arms now throbbing.

'We cannot go back, Dawn,' said Anya. She focused once more on her notebook. 'We need to move on before this elevator is called.'

The girl thumbed through more pages of her notebook. Having found the page she wanted, she ran her finger along a line parallel to the left-hand margin and down to a ringed series of codes written near the bottom. She reached over and pushed a different button on the control panel, slowly and deliberately so as not to alarm Dawn. The elevator then set about shaking itself free of the malformed shaft.

Dawn released a hand from the knife and gripped the handrail for balance. She felt gravity immediately pull the heavy blade down to her side, the triceps of her arm unable to take the strain.

A big buzz sounded all around, the lights in the ceiling dimmed and they were away again. The elevator soon slowed, its approach to the new floor mercifully smoother this time.

Dawn took the knife in both hands again and considered the girl with the coolest body language she could muster.

She must know by now I can barely lift this thing.

But Anya simply collected her satchel from the floor. She looped the strap over her shoulder and slowly stood, keeping the bag flat against her side.

The interior door whirred aside, this time revealing a marble floor, ornate but grubby with desire lines. Directly opposite in the lobby there stood an outrageously ostentatious elevator of painted gold, more fitting of a pharaoh's tomb than a high-rise building. Ahead of it, scrawled on the floor, there lay another code, upside-down and squashed by perspective. A further code, O211.3, had been written onto the marble surface outside their elevator. The letters and numbers were jagged, having been written a number of times with thick permanent marker.

Anya stepped out into the floor and beckoned for Dawn to follow.

'Please,' she said. 'We must move to another elevator.'

'Why?' said Dawn. She picked up the sheath from the floor and attempted to place the parang inside. 'I'm not going anywhere with you.'

'If you do not move from the elevator then the others can still call it back to their floor.'

'Good,' said Dawn. 'Maybe I can get a little payback for Joe.'

What, and literally bring a knife to a gunfight?

The parang slid into the sheath at the third attempt.

'No!' said Anya. She stood in the elevator lobby and pressed her hands together as if in prayer. 'Please, Dawn, I have seen what this place does to people.'

The doors began to roll along. Dawn looked through the narrowing gap to Anya.

I don't want to be alone.

She gritted her teeth, determined to show the girl no emotion.

Anya bore the look of someone who suddenly realised they had made a big and potentially lethal mistake.

'Dawn, please! I have seen you before,' Anya cried. She added, as the door almost closed: 'That is why I changed you!'

'What?' Dawn slammed her palm into the buttons and watched the doors slide open again. She met Anya's eyes with her best steely stare. 'What do you mean "you changed me"?' She did not move from the elevator car.

'Your clothes,' said Anya. 'You were wearing your old clothes when I saw you last. Weeks, months ago maybe. Grey skirt. White blouse. Lots of blood. You looked...' She tried to find the right words to say.

'I looked like shit with an arm missing? Yeah, I know.'

Anya's eyes widened. 'Then you have seen the future? An older you? You have seen the sparks and the lightning? That does not need to happen. Do you see? If we move to another floor quickly we can break the connection to your old clothes. I will have changed you!'

What the hell are you talking about, girl?

Dawn's head swam with a hundred other questions. Two things, however, were clear, and they both related to the girl. First, Anya had been instrumental in mapping many of the floors - one only had to look at her various notebooks to see that. Second, and of much greater importance, the girl knew how the place worked, otherwise how would she have created her map?

The desire to discover more smouldered deep in Dawn's mind. Anya was a huge unknown quantity, but Dawn knew she would follow her at least until such time she had what she needed.

It all boiled down to a matter of trust.

'Look, I'm not going anywhere with you until I know what I'm dealing with,' said Dawn. She kept her voice slow and steady. 'I want to know something personal about you. I want to know where all this English has suddenly come from.'

Anya's eyes locked onto Dawn's. It took a second for the girl to respond.

'I know a number of languages,' said Anya. 'It is not uncommon. I am Magyar, Hungarian to you, but I am fluent in German. My French is good too, and I know enough Russian.'

'Yeah, but why did your friends not know you could speak English until recently?'

'I am not a Soviet spy!' said Anya. She spat on the floor.

Hmm. Sounds like I hit a raw nerve back there in the bathroom.

'Okay, so you say, but there's a lot more to you than you're letting on,' said Dawn. 'Out with it or I'll hit one of these buttons and go.'

The elevator door trundled across the threshold once more.

'I am an informer,' said Anya, just as the door closed.

Now we're getting somewhere.

Dawn pressed a button on the control panel to reopen the door. She tried to keep the smile from her face. 'Keep going.'

'I am an informer, not a spy,' said Anya. She looked away and shrugged. 'That is, I *was* an informer before becoming trapped in this place. I often wrote reports of Soviet activity within Budapest to an American agent.' She locked eyes with Dawn. 'But I am not a spy. I have *always* been Magyar, and always shall be. I am *not* a traitor.'

'Wait a minute,' said Dawn. 'The Russians are in Hungary? Since when?'

Anya sighed and broke eye contact. 'Please, Dawn, you must trust me! We need to move from the elevator. I will tell you more when we have reached a safe place, I promise.'

Well, I can't stay here all day. Besides, this door's getting on my tits.

Dawn felt a cold sensation trickle down her spine as she recalled the nightmare she recently suffered on the Magyar's floor; of how her childhood tormentor was returning to haunt her. Then, despite what Anya had said about changing her, the haggard sight of Other Dawn sprung to mind: afraid, diseased, rake-thin. *Alone.*

Dawn prevented the elevator door from fully closing once more, then stepped over the threshold and into the lobby. She took a firmer hold on the sheathed parang and nodded in Anya's direction.

'Be sure that you do.'

Anya broke into small, excited applause. A wide smile grew across her face, revealing a number of gaps in her yellowing teeth.

'Thank you!' said the girl. 'Please, we must go.'

Dawn turned her attention away from Anya's chilling smile and glanced around the vaulted lobby. She found three pharaoh's elevators lining each of the walls left and right. At either end of the lobby there stood a huge open doorway, each lined with painted gold and leading to a wide corridor beyond. Outside each elevator door she noticed the codes ran in sequence: O211.1, O211.2 and O211.3 along the left, and O211.4, O211.5 and O211.6 along the right.

'Okay, I think I'm getting the hang of this now,' said Dawn. 'So these numbers after the decimal points are just ways of telling the elevators apart. Am I right?'

Anya smiled and nodded. 'Yes, and this was the two hundred and eleventh hotel floor we found.'

'So where does the O come from?'

'O means "Hotel". It is the same in your language and mine.'

'Yeah, but why not use an H?'

'We already used H for Hivatal.'

'Right,' said Dawn. 'Of course. Stupid of me to ask.'

'We need to move,' said Anya.

She fished out a smaller notebook from her satchel. Each handwritten page within comprised a heading and then long sequences of codes underneath. She thumbed a few pages further ahead and settled her index finger midway through one such sequence. It rested on a familiar-looking code: O211.5 (11). She then walked to the ornate door of O211.5 and pressed the call button. The door slid aside and she stepped into the jaws of the elevator. A pair of flies buzzed out into the lobby, surprising her. She leaned in for a look inside.

Dawn stepped closer to the elevator only to be stopped by Anya's hand.

'No, not this one,' said the girl. She stepped back into the lobby and allowed the doors to close.

The smell from the elevator was enough for Dawn not to argue.

'So what then? We call for another elevator?' she said. She walked to the next door along, that of O211.4.

'Yes,' said Anya. She pushed the call button again, keeping her finger in place.

'But isn't that just going to call the same...'

She heard a familiar old buzzing noise, large but somewhat muted through the walls. After a moment the door slid aside once more. Cheesy muzak floated out from within, an awful jazz rendition of *Frosty The Snowman*. Mercifully the elevator soon closed and the girl pushed the call button once more.

'I don't believe it,' said Dawn. 'We knew that the floors changed every time the doors closed, but we never thought to try the elevators as well.'

'The trick is to hold the button in,' said Anya. 'If you tap the button then the door just opens. If you hold it in, however, then it calls another elevator.'

She flashed Dawn a page of her notebook. The header read "Fedélzet 13". The girl held her index finger near the end of a long sequence of codes, pointing to O211.5 (11).

'Eleven elevators come to this door,' she said. 'We want the one that will take us here.' She inched the tip of her finger along to the next code.

'This subway map of yours won't get us onto the DLR by any chance, would it?'

'The what?'

'Never mind.'

She examined the open notebook while Anya called another elevator. Over half the codes had empty parentheses next to them - a sign that Anya's work, apparently so long in the making, was still in its infancy. Then, of course, there were all the floors that the girl hadn't yet mapped. How many of those lay in wait out there? Hundreds? Thousands? Hundreds of thousands? The more she considered it the more she felt hope being chipped away.

'Yes, this is the one,' said Anya. She beckoned Dawn in through the open door.

Dawn hesitated. She swapped the sheathed parang into her other hand, the very act of holding it sapping her strength with each passing minute. 'You seem a little keen to head somewhere in particular. Where are we going?'

Anya popped her head through the door and smiled. 'Somewhere beautiful.'

CHAPTER NINETEEN

The elevator opened not onto a thing of beauty but onto an emaciated woman choking and convulsing on a cold marble floor. The woman kicked out her bare feet as she tried desperately to contain the blood that escaped her long, thin neck. She jammed her palm against the wound, pressing hard into her rock-solid tendons, but to no avail. Her blood dripped and splashed and pooled beneath her head, more than could be soaked up by her long, black hair. It splattered and spilled from her mouth as she gurgled and shook. It covered the filthy torn nightdress she wore.

'Marika!' screamed Anya.

She leapt from the elevator and into the small, poorly-lit lobby. She dropped the satchel with a clatter and knelt by the stricken woman. She tried to help but the other woman, Marika, fought away the attention.

Dawn locked onto Marika's terror-stricken eyes and instantly placed her on the bizarre floor of contrite cannibals. The last time Dawn saw those eyes they were red and swollen with grief and despair. They were the same eyes that begged Dawn not to eat the meat Anya and Nikola had offered her. Those eyes now widened before her, recognising her, their irises fully dilated, but then, just as quickly, they softened and rolled upwards under heavy eyelids.

Dawn stepped from the jaws of the elevator and into the lobby.

Marika lay motionless beneath her on the harsh, heavily-marked floor. A crimson aura continued to grow around her head, her cooling blood seeking new territory before it dried.

Anya closed first Marika's eyes and then her own. A single tear ran down the girl's cheek as she bowed her head and whispered something. The Lord's Prayer, or perhaps a prayer for the dead. Either way Dawn couldn't understand a word and left her to it.

She had just witnessed the death throes of a woman she'd left behind only moments earlier. But here Marika lay covered in bruises, scratches and grime, killed by a single stab wound to the neck. Her hair seemed longer than before and bore the beginnings of a grey streak.

Tragic? Yes. Odd? Definitely. But, more importantly, where is her killer?

Dawn slid the parang out from its sheath and held it in her right hand, letting the heavy metal blade hang by her side. She prayed for the strength to use it. She kept hold of the sheath in her other hand.

'Anya!' whispered Dawn. 'Anya, we don't have time for this!'

Anya tilted her head to one side in acknowledgement, but also as if to say "give me a minute". She continued murmuring.

'Shit.'

Dawn scanned the immediate area for movement. Compared to the large foyer of the pharaohs, the lobby here felt like the inside of a shoebox. A pair of halogen spots in the ceiling cast twin pyramids of light onto Anya and Marika, but afforded little illumination to the rest of the floor. Dark circles in the ceiling tiles suggested all the other bulbs had blown.

She found an ugly wall of rough, red bricks to the left. A black fire escape door stood with a bent metal bar across the middle. A cylindrical bin rested nearby. The dent in its base suggested someone had tried to use it on the door. Proof, if such was needed, that the fire escapes may as well have been painted onto the walls like cartoon tunnels. Perhaps on some floors they were. The scene reminded her of the atrium; of how *unfinished* some of the floors appeared to be.

To her right, the marble floor ended at a dark brown strip of carpet. Corridors of night ran away left and right. She ran her eyes over their corners and observed how quickly they dissolved upwards into the darkness.

The corners of the walls.

The darkness beyond a perfect place for bad people to hide.

She felt her ribs ache and a familiar dread develop.

Don't think about him. Not now! Speak of the devil...

[Yessssss!]
'Anya! We're moving. Now!'

'Okay,' said Anya. She made a sign of the cross and muttered some more words, grabbing her satchel.

Dawn stepped around Marika's body and made for the call button opposite. She felt her eyes unconsciously drawn to the bloody floor and the small dark slit in the woman's famine-thin neck. The back of Dawn's throat tightened. She felt her mouth flood with saliva, a sure sign she was about to retch. Twinkling lights appeared in the corners of her vision. She looked away and focused hard on the call button, desperately seeking means of distraction from the butchered woman at her feet.

'How many elevators come to this door?' said Dawn.

'Just the one,' said Anya.

The butchered woman's cooling blood inched closer and closer to Dawn. She poked the tip of the sheath into the call button.

Hang on a minute.

'Isn't that going to make us easier to find?'

The door slid open.

'Ne mozdulj! NE MOZDULJ!'

In the jaws of the elevator stood another painfully thin woman, similarly dressed in a filthy gown. She held the same kind of pistol once brandished by the bespectacled man in her trembling right hand. In her left hand was a long blade, the first four inches slick with fresh blood.

The sight of the blade sent a shiver up Dawn's spine.

It was the same blade that Joe had given his life trying to retrieve. The same blade Other Dawn carried before vanishing in a veil of lightning. The very same bayonet attachment Dawn had thrown into the twisted corner of Other Clive's killing floor. Here it was, back to haunt her.

The woman looked familiar, irrespective of the raw-looking scar that ran down her cheek. The woman had once comforted Marika as she sat distraught in the corner of Anya's floor. Marika's carer had become her murderer. The deeply sunken features of the woman's long face now carried a steely edge. Her eyes were set cruel, as if madness had taken her, but also carried a tinge of fear.

Her paunch had disappeared.

'Ő az enyém, Ajtay Anya,' said the woman. She flicked the long blade between Anya and the corpse of Marika. It sounded like a warning.

Anya replied but Dawn could not understand what she was saying. It seemed as if the girl was trying to calm the situation.

With the woman's attention elsewhere Dawn took a firmer grip on the parang and sized up her options. The woman still had the gun trained in her direction, but the barrel inched slowly away as she talked. The bayonet blade was less of a threat. The woman seemed content to use the thing for pointing.

Yeah, but she can easily use it to save herself a bullet.
That's assuming the gun's even loaded, of course.

The elevator door pinged and began to close, distracting the woman. She shuffled to her right, towards Anya, and refocused the gun on Dawn. She gestured with the bayonet for Anya to step around Marika's corpse. The woman kept the body between her and Anya as the girl joined Dawn near the elevator. She jabbed the bayonet blade towards the door from which she had come.

'Go,' she said, and fixed them both with a chilling stare.

Anya said nothing. She hit the call button. The elevator door slid open instantly and both she and Dawn entered.

The woman slowly knelt by the body. She placed the bayonet blade across Marika's prominent ribcage. She kept the gun trained their way. As the door slid shut again the woman called out.

'Mi a jó abban a térkép most?'

The woman spat on the floor and then the brushed metal door closed fully.

*****

'What was that all about?' said Dawn.

Anya gently pressed a button on the control panel of the elevator, almost without thinking, as if muscle memory had briefly taken over. Her oddly-spaced eyes seemed to look down onto two different spots on the floor. Her shoulders sank as she leaned against the relatively clean interior of the car. She waited for the inevitable mighty buzz to quieten before answering.

'She thought we were going to take Marika from her,' she said with her eyes still lowered. 'I said we just wanted to pass through.'

'She was going to eat her?'

Anya nodded grimly.

'What did she say at the end?'

THE FLOORS

'She asked what good is my map now that everyone is dead.' She looked to Dawn, her spirit wounded. 'She recognised you. She called you a grenade thrown into our floor, destroying us all.'

'What a drama queen,' said Dawn. She saw how her throwaway line did little to improve Anya's mood. 'Sorry. That was a bit harsh.'

A soft ping announced their arrival onto another floor. The elevator door rolled aside to what, incredibly, sounded like the hushed roar of the ocean. Dawn heard the unmistakable call of a nearby seagull. The outside air flooded into the elevator and filled her nostrils. It was unbelievably fresh, clean and harboured just the slightest bite of salt.

'What on earth is this?' said Dawn, bowled over by the sudden change of scenery.

Anya finally managed a small smile.

'As I promised,' she said. 'Something beautiful.'

There was a large sign ahead of the doors, screwed into a stunningly blue wall.

DECK 13.

*****

A few gentle swirls of cloud sailed by peacefully overhead. A number of inquisitive seagulls glided elegantly on the air currents, keeping pace with the ship with minimal effort. The baby-blue sky made for a calm ocean of vivid cerulean, stretching unhindered to the horizon on all sides, a wondrous tapestry of calm.

Dawn stood astern of the ship with Anya, taking in the sights, the sounds, the air, the change of pace. She clamped a hand onto the guardrail, though not before swapping the increasingly heavy hunting knife to her other hand. She peered over the railing, looking for the place where the bottom of the ship met the ocean, far, far below in a wake of chaotic foam.

She hadn't been on a cruise ship before, but never imagined they could be as big as this. They looked huge on the TV adverts, certainly, but here it felt as if they were sailing the oceans on a floating skyscraper.

A strong midday sun hung in the sky and yet the scene aboard the ship was one of peace and quiet. There seemed not a soul on board, no guests, no crew, not only on this deck but all of the others too. It felt like they had stepped onto a modern-day Mary Celeste.

And yet despite the cawing of the seagulls and the sounds of the waves beneath her, Dawn could still hear the same faint humming noise that had underscored every floor she had seen thus far. She could still taste the coppery tang of electricity, salty now with the sea air.

Deck thirteen, she told herself, was somehow just as fake as all the other floors.

She looked onto the water and remembered how the drinks carton had fallen down through the atrium, before eventually clattering onto the ground. It was tempting to dive overboard, but she knew she was way too high up. The impact would kill her just as surely as jumping onto concrete.

And even if by some miracle she survived who would be around on the Mary Celeste to see her fall other than Anya? To whom could she raise the alarm? No. She needed to find a floor like the atrium to stand any chance of getting out of this place. She'd also need to carry a bunch of knotted sheets at all times, as if escaping from Colditz.

I've barely got the strength to carry this damn knife, for crying out loud.

She turned from the handrail and took in more of the scenery. A stack of deckchairs stood beneath the short overhang of deck fourteen, secured with blue and red sailing rope as if anyone in their right mind would actually holiday here. The rope would have been useful had it been twice as long and made of fishing wire.

She looked to Anya, who stared off into the distance, lost to the world. Her plain face twitched and flinched as she considered the ocean ahead. It seemed she was running through both sides of some internal dialogue.

At least I'm not the only one who does that.
Perhaps she's thinking about how good Joe tasted.
Maybe.

She took advantage of the excellent light to finally attach the parang's sheath to her belt. She shook the lactic acid from her tired muscles and admired her handiwork. She rested her palm against the handle of the parang and then slid the knife out a couple of inches. She did this a few times until she was satisfied with the action.

Anya continued to chunter inwardly, so lost in thought that Dawn could creep up behind her, slap the back of her head and watch her eyeballs pop out into the sea. She remembered a comic strip along those lines, one from long ago in a magazine filled with swearing and crudely drawn nudity. She hadn't a clue what it half of it meant, but found that one comic strip hilarious. But then her dad found the magazine in her room. He smacked her all round the house for reading it, and kept the thing for himself.

Christ, which part of my shitty childhood did that *come from?*
You're talking to yourself again.

'How long have you been lost here, Anya?'

Anya's head moved slightly, an acknowledgement. Her eyes still stared into the horizon.

'I do not know,' said Anya. 'At least six months, I think.'

'Six months!'

'Maybe. I do not know for sure. Time is broken in here. It is difficult to keep a record.'

'Huh. Tell me about it. We stepped in here and found we'd been missing for three years. To us it felt like an hour.' She joined Anya in staring at the same nothing. 'Three bloody years. We only found out because Joe's phone went mad with messages. He had one from his mum and dad. They were worried sick about him.'

Anya's shoulders tensed and she bowed her head. She gasped and finally spoke.

'I am really sorry, Dawn. We all were. Please, you must believe me.' She turned her head to Dawn. Her eyes were rimmed with tears. 'You have no idea what we have been through.'

CHAPTER TWENTY

You are not like us. You are English, yes, but you do not speak or act like I had expected. You use ugly words like The King of the Castle. You carry a small screen of metal and glass, saying it is a telephone. You act surprised when I say the Soviets occupy my homeland.

We are obviously from different times.

My name is Ajtay Anya. Being English you would call me Anya, my given name, while my fellow Magyars would call me Ajtay, the name of my family. I think I am twenty years old, but I could be twenty-one now. I have lost track of time since we became lost in this place. We all have.

The people you saw earlier are *my* people; my neighbours from a tall building we all shared in Pest. The last I remember before all of this was a night of great joy and fear and terror, with each emotion running one after the other.

Change was in the air, and had been coming for some time. We Magyars had had enough of our Soviet keepers, their idiot ideas and rules, and the threats of torture and death they used to enforce them. The puppet-master Stalin was dead, his great Plan in tatters, his followers and successors clueless. And yet the free world did not seem to care, certainly not for a country such as ours. The information we had leaked about the Soviets was being ignored.

And so, sensing weakness in our supposed masters, we alone took to the streets in defiance them.

Nikola, God rest his soul, lived on the floor below me and had long tried to gather others brave to his cause. He often spoke of subverting and weakening and mocking and, with hope, destroying the Soviet rule over our lands. 'Revolution is upon us, friends!' he would always say, even when someone had only daubed a slogan on a shop window. But this time he was right. Revolution had come at last! This was his moment and he quickly amassed a small army of supporters, of which I was one. I felt proud to help, more so for a neighbour. My heart leapt and swelled in my chest as he spoke of change.

Elsewhere in Pest, even up in Buda, we were thousands strong, much stronger than we had dared hope only months before. We even had the courage to pull down Stalin's statue! Such actions would have had us killed in the past, but we did not care. We were giddy with newfound power, and we liked it.

Eventually we gathered outside Radio Budapest and demanded a voice that could be heard all over. Our people needed to hear that our time had come. The world needed to hear how the Soviets were killing our country. But they tried to trick us. They gave us a voice, but made sure nobody could hear it. We spoke of our oppression but the radios did not carry our cries. Their stupid trick angered us all. We tried to storm the building but the police fired at us.

Then the fighting began. Machine guns and ammunition were seized from our enemies and our streets became a warzone, although one where we knew all of the alleys and shortcuts. The Soviet tanks that came and rolled through our streets could not move as well as we could. We would emerge from the darkness, pick off a few soldiers and disappear before their turrets could turn and fire. The Soviets who fought us stood little chance. Other soldiers would simply stand by, caring as little for their orders as they did for us. We knew then that we were right, and that we would win our battle for freedom.

Nikola and his small army took arms, fell back and protected the streets around our building. The men would not give me a gun, though. Not even Nikola. He wanted the women to take care of the wounded.

My pride faded quickly that night.

It did not take long to drive the Soviets from our land, such was our anger, but we were amazed at how quickly we had brought

THE FLOORS

about change. We were so happy! The Soviets had raped our lands, our industry and our women for years since the War, and we now had a chance to rebuild our lives.

None of us expected what happened next.

We woke one night shortly afterwards to the sound of gunfire and exploding shells. The Soviets had returned, and in far larger numbers. They had come to take back Budapest and to crush our resistance. From so high up I watched from my window as the tanks rolled down a neighbouring street and fired shells into our shops and offices. A mass of soldiers ran alongside the tanks with rifles in their hands, bayonets attached. They entered buildings at random. Despite the cold November air I opened my window and could hear screaming amidst the explosions.

There was chaos outside my apartment door. Many of my neighbours had gathered in the corridor and stairwell. We were all confused and scared. I was not the only one to have seen the soldiers enter the buildings around us. Nikola tried to calm us all and rally support, but few of his men lived in the same building as us. Most that did gathered their weapons and quickly made makeshift Molotov cocktails from whatever bottles of vodka we could find, then they raced down the stairwell to fight for our lives.

Marika emerged from a door two down from mine. I had not seen her for days, not since the revolution had ended. The older men and women of the building often looked upon her with disgust for having laid with a Soviet soldier, when we all knew that she had been raped. When word escaped that she had sought to end her pregnancy she became a pariah. Even now her neighbours shunned her, leaning out of her way for fear that she would brush against their clothes and stain them with her sin. She walked towards me, the only friend she had in the building, weeping with terror. I remember how her dress rested over her growing belly, more noticeable on a slim girl than someone like me. The baby would have been due in perhaps five months, maybe four.

The stairwell was open all the way down to the bottom of the building and we could hear terrible fighting from the lobby: bursts of gunfire, agonised screaming from those hit with bullets, and then a sound that chilled us all.

It was the sound of glass breaking. Not a window pane, but a Molotov that had broken inside the building. There must have been more than one because the flames took hold incredibly quickly. Thick black smoke and the sound of gunfire rose up rapidly through the floors. We heard shouts, both Magyar and Russian. Nikola ordered his men to fall back to the upper floors.

I knew instantly what Nikola was thinking. Mine was the top floor, the twelfth. The stairs that led up from my floor would take us to a flat roof and a metal ladder that ran down the side of the building.

What we did not expect to find was another floor.

*****

'You were chased into this place?' said Dawn.

Anya nodded.

'That happened to me too. Me and Joe. We became trapped in here when a madman shot up our office. We tried to escape to the floor below and found this maintenance area. Well, you can probably guess the rest.'

The coincidence was not lost on Anya. Dawn could see that she was processing this new information. Her lips moved slightly but she did not say anything.

'You mentioned "The King Of The Castle",' Dawn continued. 'I've heard that name before. That was the guy who chased us in here. His name's Clive. He's hardly king material.'

'He is a bad man,' said Anya. 'He is like a spider lying in wait. Many of us have crossed paths with him since we became trapped. I am lucky. His bullets have never found me. Others were not so fortunate. Each time we met he would boast of his dominance as I fled. He would shout after me, saying he was the King of the Castle. I think he says that to everyone.'

'Jesus, what a dick,' said Dawn. 'Thank God he's dead.'

'Dead?' Anya met Dawn's eyes for the first time in what seemed like hours. 'You saw his body? Did you kill him?'

'I think so,' said Dawn. 'I can't imagine he'd have lasted much longer after what I did to him, anyway. He was in a state to start with, like he'd somehow been starving for years. But then he attacked Joe. He slashed the poor guy across the belly with this knife and I kind of lost it. Well, you know what happened next. Poor Joe.

'Fucking Clive. I hope he rots in hell.

'He was the piece of shit that made my life a nightmare. He used to work near Joe's desk, but would make up any excuse to walk past mine. He would always boast about what he would do to me, sexually, when nobody was in earshot. Him and his so-called ten inch dick. He would lean down into my face, close enough for me to choke on his alcohol breath. He would wash with aftershave on a morning to try and cover it up but everyone knew he was a pisshead.

'It got to a point where he would try to feel me up when nobody was looking, and then laugh it off in front of the other men when I told him to stop.

'He got the boot when I complained to my boss, Barnes. He was one of the ones that got shot. Barnes tried to smooth things over with me, anything to keep the matter quiet. He was desperate to brush the whole thing under the carpet. I guess I lost my head for a moment. I hadn't been in a position of power like that before. I never told Mike, my fiancé, about what happened. I just took their money and said it was a bonus.

'I haven't told anyone that before. I guess it doesn't matter now.

'The harassment didn't stop when Clive was sacked. I knew he was following me around, but I never saw him when I looked. He was there, though. He would sometimes appear out of the blue, in a car park somewhere, and threaten to fuck me over, making sure it was the last thing Mike would see before I bled out.

'When I got the police involved the harassment stopped. They couldn't prove anything, but at least I had my life back. I thought that was the end, but, of course, I was wrong.

'Clive came back to work, armed to the teeth, and tried to kill everyone he saw. He shot Mike...'

Dawn felt tears run down her cheeks. She felt her throat spasm as she tried to continue.

'I don't know if Mike is alive or dead,' she said, and then she buried her face into cupped hands.

'I am sorry,' said Anya. 'You will see your Mike again, I am certain. We will find a way out of here. You are not long lost in this place. Am I right?'

Dawn nodded, unable to speak.

Anya placed a hand on Dawn's shoulder and looked out to sea once more.

'Then you will benefit all the more from my story, and perhaps, in turn, so may I.'

*****

I held open the door and counted thirty-five of us into the new floor. When Nikola and his surviving men ran through, clutching their pistols and rifles and coughing heavily with smoke, I shut the door behind them. We were amazed to hear the noise outside stop so suddenly. I even tried to open the door again to see if the outside world still existed, but I found it had stuck fast. I pulled on the metal handle as hard as I could but the door would not budge.

Nikola ordered me to leave the door alone. He said that the Soviets were coming up the stairs and that we had to find another means of escape. So we looked around this new, hidden floor.

The walls were bare and the ground was dirty. The light was poor and there were pipes everywhere. 'A floor between floors.' That was how Imre, an elderly neighbour, had described it. His son worked up on the girders as they rebuilt the cities after the War. He said floors like these were used to hide the ugly parts of buildings: pipes, ducts, storage cupboards and so on.

But what good was such a floor when none of the doors opened? All we could find was a large elevator. Few felt confident in its use — not when we considered the fire still raging outside - but we knew it was our only way of escape. The elevator was a tight fit but we managed to squeeze everyone inside. That was when I noticed all of the buttons had the number thirteen on them.

I see you nodding, so the same must have happened to you.

As you can guess, the elevator took us to a floor in another building entirely, in the daytime even though only minutes had passed. The floor was large and filled with desks and chairs and television screens with keyboards and odd, mouse-like things with buttons that clicked when you pressed them. We later found they were typewriters of some sort but we could never really figure them out.

What interested us most were the odd-looking telephones that sat on all of the desks. There were no dials to be seen, only buttons and screens that sometimes displayed the numbers you were pressing, but they seemed to be little more than crude musical instruments. No matter what buttons we pressed the telephones would only play notes instead of connecting to an operator. Why would someone go to the expense of buying so many telephones only for them to play terrible music? We suspected someone was playing a trick on us.

I see you are nodding again. You have seen these?

We did not find much else on the floor, certainly nothing of any use, and so we decided to move on. Though we felt safe somehow from the fire and the soldiers we still had to find a way out. As you can see we had little success.

We decided the easiest way to escape was to simply walk down the stairs and out of whatever building we had stumbled into, but we quickly found the stairs were also there to trick us. I stepped down a flight only to be greeted by my companions walking out from the door I had only just left, as if top and bottom had somehow been stitched together.

That first time on the stairs we lost somebody. The old man, Imre. We were gathering once more on the floor, but the stairwell door closed on Imre before he could stop it. When we noticed he was no longer with us we feared that the old man had fallen in the stairwell. We opened the door but found that the stairs had completely changed. We called out for him but of course he was gone.

We knew then that we had to stick together and that this place was more dangerous than we first thought. We did not trust the elevators as they were often too small for us all to fit inside. The stairwells were therefore the main way we commuted between the floors. We made sure to keep the doors open for each other.

It was hopeless, though. For hours we walked through floor after floor with no end in sight, and, more alarming, no food to be found. We discovered a couple of apartment buildings but their kitchen cupboards were always empty.

I remember our first night in the maze, as sure as it was yesterday. We had found a floor where it was night outside and the others used the darkness to help them sleep. I could not rest and so I had a look around. The floor had four elevators and I opened the doors of each of them. They all looked different inside, which I thought was odd. When I jabbed their call buttons the doors would open as expected, but when I held my finger in for a moment I was amazed to find an brand new elevator appear. I did this six times before the original elevator returned.

I was fascinated. I called the elevator again and again and found the same sequence of cars appear behind the doors. I looked back, hoping to find Nikola awake, if only to tell somebody what I had found, but they were all asleep. I decided to return to the elevator for an experiment.

I jumped inside and pushed the button at the top-left hand corner of the control panel, something that I'd easily remember given that all the buttons were the same. I stepped out onto a floor bathed in bright sunshine from a low sun. I let the elevator doors close behind me, then poked at the call button to open them again. I then pressed each button of the elevator in turn until I found the floor I had left. I was delighted and relieved to find everyone, still asleep, after seven attempts. I made a mental note of the buttons I had pressed and repeated the exercise.

I realised that it was possible to map the floors.

*****

'But why?' said Dawn. 'What's the point?'

'The process of elimination, I believe it is called,' said Anya. 'Or at least that was my first idea. If we found a floor that we had seen before then we knew we could ignore it and look at the floors that were connected to it. Also, if we found something useful on a floor, something we could not easily carry, then we could at least find it again.'

'So what happened? Looking around I'm guessing people liked the idea.'

'No,' said Anya. 'Somebody died and changed everything.'

*****

When I told Nikola the next morning about what I had found he was pleased with my discovery, but saw little value in mapping the floors. He, like everyone else, was keen to leave as quickly as possible. 'We have to escape while we can still walk,' was how he put it. During the night, perhaps while I was playing with the elevator, he had a different idea. If the floors and stairwells were going to change each time the doors closed then we would simply stop them from closing. We immediately looked for things that we could jam under the doors wherever we went.

Deep down, I was jealous of Nikola's idea. It was so much simpler than mine, and yet I still liked my idea more. It felt worthwhile, useful somehow. I began to think of how such a map would work. I cast my mind through the different types of floor we had found, and how they could be numbered to tell them apart. I observed how the floors often had different numbers of elevators, some as many as eight, and factored that into my plan.

As the others looked for food and supplies and things to jam under the doors, I looked for things to help me write: notebooks, pens, pencils. I found a worker's toolbag to hold them all before finding this. Some floors had cans of paint. I thought they would be an excellent way of marking the outside of each elevator. I carried some cans with me but my arms quickly tired. Nikola warned me that I was wasting valuable energy but I did not care. The map was taking shape in my head.

But then, when I thought I had a hold of how the maze worked, we found a floor that turned our world upside down.

Some of the floors we had seen up until that point looked like the builders had thrown away their tools halfway through the job. There were doors that were actually part of the wall. We found gaps where staircases should have been. Sometimes we even found a door that led to nothing but darkness.

To us, this one particular floor looked like a placeholder, as if it was something the builders would get to eventually. The inside of the floor was coated with thick, smooth wallpaper. It even covered the floor, windows and the ceiling. The papered windows glowed dimly all around us but the light inside the room was poor. We cast torch beams around the room and found a large number thirteen painted onto the floor, as if it could have been any other number. The only thing contained in the room... it was strange. It was a large microphone. Huge, the size of a small bus. It just sat there doing nothing with a thick cable curling up out the back and into a hole in the ceiling. We heard a low, booming noise all around the room. It sounded like laughter, as if God himself had found our plight humorous.

But there was no God here. Only a room designed to test our faith. A trick floor in a cruel maze that had been made by man and man alone. Nikola was disgusted and outraged. We all were. We felt watched. Ridiculed. How dare they laugh at the mice they had trapped in their maze? But they underestimated us. We were not mice. We would fight them, as surely as we had fought off our Soviet keepers. We moved on, driven with a renewed purpose. We were determined to cut a path through their maze, like explorers in the jungle. We would pass through every single floor they threw at us. We would keep going until there were no more floors to find. We knew there would be an end somewhere. We knew that this maze could not go on forever. At the end of the maze we would find the way out, and then Heaven help those who laughed at us.

We stormed through the next couple of floors at double pace, our blood rising as surely as our voices, but then one of the old women yelled for us to stop. Her husband, Fredek, had fallen to the back of the group and now stood clutching his chest. He gasped and moaned for a moment and then collapsed onto the floor. We hurried around him but there was little we could do. He died stuttering some last words to his wife, his sentence half-finished. Our anger faded quickly.

Fredek's death presented a problem. He needed a proper burial. We could not leave his body lying there and yet he could not come with us either. That would have been much too ghoulish. And of course we could not stay because then we would never find a way out.

It hurt us immensely but we chose to leave Fredek's body where he had fallen. His wife chose to remain with him rather than to continue with us. She was heartbroken. She had lost everything in the space of two days.

The only one of us who did not grieve for them was Marika.

We continued to cut a path through the floors for some time, but then Gregor ordered Nikola and everybody to stop. I remember we were surprised at his outburst because we thought Nikola was in command, so quickly we had looked for new leaders. What Gregor said next was outrageous, but, if we were honest, he only put a voice to what was starting to fill our minds. He said that we had not found any food on our path, and the only food we had was lying dead on the floor a distance back.

He was quickly talked down, some even called him a demon, but I could see in the eyes of the others that Gregor's idea had taken root.

We found Imre's corpse on the very next floor. It looked like someone had removed the muscles from his arms and legs and then left him to rot. The look of tormented agony on his face suggested he was alive at the time. It was a cruel thing to put before us so soon after Gregor's idea. It was further proof that someone, somewhere, was surely tormenting us.

We moved on, but, of course, we eventually gave in to our hunger, so great a hold it had on us. The frail could barely move because they were too weak. Marika looked ill and deeply worried. We sent a party back through our path in order to retrieve Fredek's body. They returned much too soon with dire news: someone had deliberately closed one of the doors behind us. People began to accuse others of betrayal and arguments broke out.

Then someone screamed in agony and dropped to the floor. We were horrified to see a soldier behind him. He must have followed us! The soldier unstuck the bayonet and swung his rifle around to keep us away. He looked as if he had been stuck in the maze for a year. He spoke less in Russian and more in grunts. He had a wild look in his eyes. His mind had turned to sludge.

Gregor felled the soldier with a single bullet in the brain.

Within an hour we had two bodies to eat.

*****

'Was it easy?' said Dawn. 'The first time, I mean.'

'Yes,' said Anya. She did not look Dawn in the eyes, preferring instead to keep watch on the ocean. 'The first mouthful was easy. The second was harder.'

'This is what I'm going to have to do to survive, isn't it?'

Anya nodded, but still stared out to sea. 'There is very little food left now other than ourselves.'

Dawn looked to the deck. 'I don't think I can do it.'

'Then you will die,' said Anya.

*****

Nobody wanted to eat the meat – we hated everything about it, and still do, believe me! – but we knew we had to eat our dead in order to carry on living. Not everybody agreed. Some left our group in disgust, eight in total. They took to an elevator and vanished into the maze.

The rest of us decided we could no longer continue walking through the floors. We were struggling to find ways of jamming the doors open - I even had to sacrifice many of my pens - and we needed to preserve the meat lying dead before us. We based ourselves in the last apartment floor we passed through. We forced the doors and found luck finally with us, for each of the apartments was furnished. We had six refrigerators in which to store food.

Because we had rooted ourselves to a single floor we decided to follow my plan. We began mapping the floors connected to our elevator, and outwards still until we either found food or our freedom. We took turns to hunt for new floors and whatever they contained. I gave the hunter a marker pen and a list of the current floor counts: how many office floors we had found, for example. This would be the next number to use in the code. The hunter marked the button in the control panel, then the area outside of the elevator, and then look for food and supplies. When they returned to me I logged their findings in my map.

That was when we noticed something very strange and very dangerous about this place. More and more we saw the men and women of the splinter group out of step with ourselves, like a needle jumping around on a scratched gramopho...

Shush! Quiet! I hear voices.

CHAPTER TWENTY-ONE

Anya slipped the strap of the satchel over her arm and kept her hand flat against the bag to keep it shut. She shuffled her feet further apart, ready to run.

Dawn kept her hand firmly on the handle of the parang as she watched two men emerge onto the sunlit deck. The older of the two, a grizzled man in his late fifties to early sixties, waved in their direction with little conviction, as if he was surprised to see them there. The younger man, tall and slim with jet-black hair and a long face, held a gruesome collection of charred and bloody body parts in his arms. His clothes were heavily bloodstained, more so than the old man's.

From twenty yards Dawn could see shreds of gristle clinging to the joints of the blackened bones. The seagulls continued to keep pace with the ship, but came no closer, as if they hadn't yet noticed the scraps of food the man held.

The younger man glanced towards Anya, by way of Dawn. He then turned and looked out to the sea. He shook his head, keeping an internal monologue.

'See how he cannot bear for us to watch,' said Anya. 'He was one who left us, saying we were animals.'

'And the other guy?'

'Radek Milos. We thought we lost him to the maze shortly after we began creating the map. He is a stupid old goat. I gave him his pen and floor counts but he never came back. Some of us saw him wandering the maze a few times afterwards, but the old fool was always too scared or too mad to return to us. It was because of him that I had a gap in my numbers.'

'What?' said Dawn. 'Jesus, Anya, get some perspective.'

She observed the two men some more. The older man, Milos, rounded the other and slapped him gently on the arm. They were too far away for Dawn to hear what they were saying - not that she would have understood.

'Do you think they're a threat?'

'They are carrying bones,' said Anya, utterly deadpan. 'From now on everyone we meet will be dangerous.'

'What about you?'

Anya kept silent for a moment longer than Dawn felt comfortable with.

'Nikola is dead and that puts us all in danger. He was the one that kept most of us together and gave us belief in what we had to do. But Gregor has killed him. I watched Nikola's head burst, and then everyone ran. Some fled to the stairs. Others jumped into an elevator, like me. Now we are all scattered across the floors. Because of this we will meet each other out of order. An older me could meet a younger Gregor, and the other way around. Most of the time we will both be mad with hunger.'

An icicle of unease slithered down Dawn's spine. Anya had dodged her question and she didn't like it. She kept the girl in her peripheral vision and looked towards the men. The younger of the two stepped towards the railings and threw the bones he carried overboard. Dawn waited, counted the seconds, but heard no gentle splashes from below; a chilling reminder of how far they were from the surface of the water. The sight of the bones made her think of Joe. She saw in her mind a horrific glimpse of his bloody carcass picked clean of easy meat. She felt her throat tighten. Nausea faded to sadness.

'What happened to Joe? His body, I mean.'

'He is still on our floor,' said Anya. 'You woke not long before we finished... before we gathered our plates. Had Gregor not been so stupid we would have also cast your friend's body into the sea.'

'Huh. Easy to say that now.'

'It is the truth,' said Anya. 'It is the safest thing to do.'

'Why?' said Dawn. 'Shit, they're coming this way.'

The man called Milos waved again, this time with more feeling, but was unable to maintain eye contact. Instead it appeared Dawn's hunting knife had caught his attention.

Dawn had every intention of letting the two men see it.

'Stay back,' she growled, and took a firmer grip on the handle. 'Anya, tell them to fuck off.'

'Maradjon ott!'

Dawn drew the chipped blade from its sheath but felt it catch in the lining. She looked up, fearing the worst, but was relieved to see the two men continuing their slow approach. She yanked harder and the knife came free.

Shit, this thing's too heavy!

She found the muscles in her arms ached as badly as her stomach. It was as if someone was switching them off one by one. Every part of her craved sustenance. She felt her legs buckle as the momentum of the heavy hunting knife shifted her off-balance. She cursed herself for carrying the weapon around for so long when she should have fixed it to her belt. She had wasted energy that she could ill-afford to lose. The knife continued to have a life of its own. It wobbled dangerously in her grasp.

Jesus, I'm going to lop a leg off at this rate.

And still the two men approached, now just ten yards away.

'Give me the knife,' said Anya. 'You must trust me!'

'No.'

There was no way she was giving up the only weapon they had. She grabbed the handle of the parang with both hands and steadied the blade. She stepped back and felt the guardrail press against her backside. She glanced around, horrified to find herself surrounded by practised cannibals with only a suicidal drop into the ocean for a means to escape.

'Marray-dyon ott!' she yelled at the two men. 'I fucking mean it!'

The two men finally got the message and stopped five yards away. The man called Milos gestured that he meant her no harm. His eyes were still fixed on the knife. Dawn felt the eyes of the other man all over her body. Her flesh broke out in goosebumps.

'I want to know everything they say, Anya. You too. Ask them what they want.'

'You should give me the knife, Dawn. Please!'

'No way! Ask them what they want. Do it!'

Anya burbled something to the old man. He motioned to the sky and the sea and the ship while he burbled back. Dawn noticed his clothes were too big for him, like hers.

'He says they were just passing through. He thought we might like to team up together. With him and Farkas.'

Dawn shook her head. 'No chance.'

The old man burbled some more. It gave Dawn an opportunity to look directly at the younger man, Farkas. The way he leered at her made her feel like a stripper. She tried to stare him down. Farkas only thrust out his chin in response. He kept his eyes fixed on Dawn's and refused to blink, as if initiating a staring contest. He looked about as scared as a wolf in a field of sheep.

'He says if we come together we stand a better chance of survival. It would be like old times again.'

'For you lot, maybe. I haven't been here long enough for "old times". The answer is still no, and tell him to stop looking at my knife like that.'

As Anya and the old man talked, Dawn looked once more at Farkas. The young man smirked and pushed his thumbs into his trouser pockets. He wasn't as scrawny as his companion. Though slim, Farkas still filled his clothes, and now that Dawn thought about it he didn't look as long-lost in the maze as Milos. That, coupled with the fact he had probably eaten recently, meant only one thing in Dawn's mind. Right now this guy was a hell of a lot stronger than she was.

'He says they have food. Normal food.'

'Bollocks. Why did we just see them dump a load of bones into the sea?'

Anya replied without translating the question. 'Because you keep whatever food keeps and eat the food that perishes.'

The younger man took a step forward and Dawn exploded.

'Get back over there, you fucking piece of shit! Now! Move, before I fucking murder you! Do it!'

The violence of her words stopped Farkas in his tracks, but he refused to step back. He plucked his thumbs out from his pockets and let his arms hang by his sides like a gunslinger. He continued to run his eyes up and down Dawn's body.

Dawn realised Farkas wasn't getting a hard-on for her. The bastard was sizing her up. She felt a rush of cold spread through her veins, chilling her heart. Her arms started to tremble.

THE FLOORS

The man called Milos stepped forwards and tapped Farkas on the arm. He mumbled something that Anya struggled to hear, or chose not to translate. It sounded like he was trying to diffuse the situation, but then he looked directly at Dawn.

'You too, old man,' said Dawn. 'Don't think I don't know what you're both up to. Get back, now!'

Anya translated and the old man showed her his palms again. But like Farkas, he stood his ground.

'Anya, we're going to have to run for it,' said Dawn, as boldly as she could manage, playing the odds that neither man would understand what she was saying. 'What are our chances?'

'Poor,' said Anya. 'You need to give me the knife, Dawn. I'm stronger than you.'

'No!'

Shit! My arms!

And then she realised exactly what Milos and Farkas were doing. They were biding their time, watching her arms weaken, patiently letting the minutes pass by as her strength ebbed away. She watched, helpless, as the parang dropped six inches. She gasped when she found she no longer had the strength to heave it upwards again.

'Kapd el, Farkas,' said Milos to the younger man, almost as if releasing a bloodhound.

And with that the younger man pounced on Dawn with frightening speed.

She tried to swing the heavy blade into Farkas but he slapped the parang from out of her hands. The knife rattled and skidded across the deck and away behind him. It stopped inches short of the guardrail and spun on its hilt.

Farkas grabbed Dawn by the throat and squeezed hard. He grinned. His yellow teeth were pitted with flecks of trapped flesh.

Dawn tried to fight back but her arms weren't long enough. Her hands batted uselessly against Farkas' shoulders. She then tried to prise away his chokehold but found her hands were too weak. The muscles of her arms stung as if they had atrophied in vinegar. Instead she used the next best thing in her arsenal. She dug her fingernails deep into the flesh of Farkas' hands and forced a knee as hard as she could into his balls.

She hadn't fully connected but it was enough for the man to release his grip. Before she could take advantage, however, she felt a hand slide under her armpit and another grab firmly on her other arm. The world spun round and then *BANG!*

Her back slammed into the hardwood deck, instantly knocking the air from her lungs.

As she fought once more for breath she saw Anya, upside down. The girl was screaming something Dawn couldn't understand and Farkas loomed into view. He straddled Dawn and placed the bridge of his right hand onto her throat. He then began to squeeze the life from her. She flashed out a hand, hoping to gouge out his eyes, but found her arms were still too short. She watched Farkas gesture to the old man with his free hand, telling him to get the knife. He brought his hand back down onto Dawn's right breast and squeezed hard.

The back of Dawn's tongue scraped against the top of her windpipe and felt like sandpaper. The gagging sensation, coupled with a lack of air, sent fresh pulses of fire across her lungs. She could feel her life fading and the corners of her vision darken. Her arms flopped to the deck, totally spent.

Farkas brayed with harsh laughter. He called over to the old man, demanded his attention, and Dawn felt his hand grope her once more.

She wanted to pull the fucker's eyes out and stamp on them.

She saw a flash of Anya over Farkas' shoulder. The vile leer on his face changed to a look of confusion, then hideous comprehension and straight on into outright terror. He released his grip on Dawn's throat, slapped a hand to the deck and reached around to his back. When he brought his hand around again it was sopping with blood.

Dawn watched the droplets stain the off-white cotton of her blouse. For once the sight of the stuff felt *good*.

Farkas whimpered, as if caught between a shriek and a cry. Anya thrust a flat heel into his shoulder and pushed him over onto the deck. He reached around to his back once more, saw yet more of his fresh blood and then opted to shriek.

Dawn coughed and fought for breath. The back of her throat rasped like a rusty saw. It still felt like Farkas was choking her. She coughed again, hard enough to nearly make herself sick. She laid her head back and spotted Anya nearby, confronting Milos.

The old man had gotten his hands on the parang and held the long blade out towards Anya. He seemed afraid, like he was trying to fend off the girl, but at the same time he yielded little ground. He was clearly trying to play Anya, but Dawn could not warn her. She could only croak and even that felt like swallowing broken glass.

Anya held something in her hand, small and shiny.

The old man babbled something to Anya. He sounded like he was begging for something. Forgiveness, his life perhaps, or simply to be allowed to flee.

'Lies,' Dawn whispered and fell into another coughing fit.

Anya spoke three words and the old man made his move. He swung the heavy blade around with one arm, meeting his other hand above his head. With both hands firmly on the handle he brought the knife down hard, fully intent on splitting Anya in two.

But Anya was too quick for him. The weight of the hunting knife made it easy to see what the old man was planning. She sidestepped and, seeing him desperately adjust the path of the blade towards her legs, jumped back and away from its path.

The tip of the blade bit deep into the hardwood deck and jarred Milos' wrists. He released the handle and left the parang juddering in the crosswinds.

Anya was on him, her arm pulled back, readying to strike. Dawn now saw what the girl held in her hand. Three inches of steel jutted from her thumb and forefinger: a scalpel, its neck slick with fresh blood, its blade wiped clean. A flash of sunlight glinted across the lethal cutting edge an instant before Anya plunged the blade deep into the old man's throat. She released the handle and stepped back, happy to leave the thing jutting out just above his Adam's apple.

The old man's blood ran freely in pulses from around the barrel of the scalpel. It ran in twin rivers down his bristly, scrotum-skin neck. A soaking wet gurgle erupted from his throat and splattered more blood from his mouth, covering his chin with gruesome crimson streaks. A red slimy tongue poked out from his gaping mouth as if making a bid for freedom. His eyes bulged in their sockets in full realisation of what Anya had done. He frantically tried to find the scalpel but his hand knocked the handle. It sent him on a coughing fit that shredded the insides of his throat. He pulled out the scalpel and dropped it onto the deck. His blood poured and squirted unhindered from his neck wound, splashing on the hardwood beneath him. Thick, red gobs of gore dribbled down his chin and hung down to the floor in bloody strings.

Farkas continued to shriek beside Dawn, only more so now he saw what Anya had done to his colleague. He frantically wiped his hand against his back and each time it came back red and bloody, sending him into further hysterics.

Dawn felt some strength return to her body, as if her coughing fits had loosened a pocket of energy somewhere deep inside of her. She slid up onto her backside and propped herself up by her arms. She drew up her right foot, let it linger in the air and allowed the stiff fabric of her skirt to slip back over her thigh. With Farkas' attention inevitably caught, she then thrust the heel of her shoe into his face, once, twice, and a third time, laying him out cold. She looked back to the scene of carnage behind her.

Anya stepped towards the parang and pulled back on the handle. She worked the knife backwards and forwards, and finally wrenched it free from the hardwood floor. She held the flat of the blade across her palm and looked over her shoulder.

Dawn met her eyes. Barely ten minutes earlier, during the girl's story, she had seen every horror of Anya's recent past haunt those too-far-apart eyes. Now they were sharp, eagle-like and wholly possessed of an innate survival instinct.

'I want to leave,' said Dawn. Again it came out like a rasping noise. She coughed and felt around her throat. Still raw.

'You must eat,' said Anya, as sharp as her scalpel. 'You are not strong enough to walk.'

'Just give me a minute,' said Dawn. 'I'll be okay.'

Anya sighed. 'Check Farkas' pockets.'

'What for?'

'Matches. Cigarette lighters. Papers too that might tell us where their floor is. We might find something there. But mainly we want anything that can make a fire.'

A queasy feeling spread across Dawn's stomach that mixed ill with her starvation pains. After witnessing the horror of Clive's killing floor it became obvious what Anya was thinking.

'No, please.'

Anya slapped the flat of the blade against her palm.

Milos was still crouched behind the girl, kneeling, head down, blood leaking from his throat and mouth, his knuckles set into the deck like a sprinter mortally wounded before the start of a race. He coughed out more blood and gurgled.

Anya slapped the blade once more.

'You know what you must do here to survive,' she said, her mouth set stern.

'I can't-'

'You must,' said Anya. She gripped the parang with both hands. 'And you will.'

Anya swung the long, heavy blade around, up and over her head, and used its momentum to bring down the chopping edge hard and fast, slicing deep into the back of Milos' neck, nearly decapitating him.

Whatever blood remained in the old man's arteries gushed out from all angles as he finally crumpled to the floor. The parang jutted out from both sides of his neck like Frankenstein bolts. His body twitched a couple of times and finally lay still.

And then, with an almighty cracking sound, the ship, the ocean and the sky split in two.

CHAPTER TWENTY-TWO

It started somewhere amidships, announcing itself through a cacophony of tortured steel and cracking wood. The whole world shook violently across all six axes, an easy six point five on the Richter scale. The quake woke Farkas from his stupor and set him screaming again.

Dawn sat on the deck and tried to absorb the worst of the violence. Through the guard rail she saw a distinct line develop out from the ship and race towards the horizon, subtly cutting through the waves. The same line ran through to the other side of the ship and into the distance. She followed the line up from the horizon and into the sky. Sure enough she saw a cloud gracefully glide across a fine crack in the baby-blue beyond.

The shaking continued and knocked Anya onto her backside. She looked nervously beyond Dawn towards the satchel she had dropped.

Dawn turned and found the bag bouncing around perilously close to the railing. Notebooks and countless marker pens spilled across the hardwood deck. A second scalpel bounced out of the bag, its blade embedded in a piece of cork.

There was a sudden sense of motion. An immense sight seized Dawn's attention as the entire front half of the cruise ship tilted up ten degrees and twisted slowly to the left. Not just the ship but half the ocean along with it, as if folded along a crease.

She looked port, then starboard. On both sides the waters lapped neatly along the fault line she had seen develop, as if the ocean came up against an invisible wall separating two parallel universes, the impossible meniscus she's seen earlier writ large. In the gaps of the ship where things no longer quite met she saw nothing but unadulterated darkness, like someone had cut slivers from a photograph and placed the picture against a jet-black background.

The ship's horns blasted out a cry of pain that rattled Dawn's teeth. When the noise subsided she once more heard the terrible clanking sound that had followed her ever since she stepped foot into the maze. It was louder than ever before. Each massive bang cut through her ear drums and pierced deep into her nervous system, sending out shockwaves that nearly stopped her heart. Thankfully, as before, the noise gradually petered out as the whole world settled into its new configuration. The seagulls continued to glide on the air currents. They cawed to each other as if nothing had happened.

For a moment Dawn sat on the deck and simply gawped at the sight ahead of her. Both she and Anya were rendered speechless. She scrunched her eyelids shut until she saw patterns of light dance across the backs of her eyes. When she opened them again there was no doubt about it. The whole world had been split in two across the middle of the ship in exactly the same way as Joe's restroom, and yet the ship remained afloat. Indeed its two halves continued their respective paths across the ocean, taking the huge rift in reality with it, raking a sliver of nothingness through the waters as if they weren't there.

It was an image Dawn knew she would never forget. It was splendorous, beautiful even, but it underlined her dire need to find a way out of the floors.

'I want to go,' she said, staggering to her feet.

Anya turned to face Dawn, disappointment written across her face.

'Don't look at me like that, Anya. I want to leave now. This place is falling to pieces.'

'Fine,' said Anya. She looked like she wanted to say more, but said, 'Check Farkas' pockets. We are still going to need fire, if not here then someplace else.'

'Excuse me? Didn't you see the massive fuck-off rip in the world that just appeared? It's right there in front of you in case you missed it. And it's happening all over the place, Anya. Wherever we are, it looks like it's collapsing.'

'It is not collapsing,' said Anya. 'It is dividing.' She stood and brushed her hands down her clothes, then walked to her scattered belongings.

Dawn looked over to her hunting knife, still deeply embedded in Milos' neck. She gulped down the queasy feeling that blossomed in her cramping stomach.

'Segítsen nekem,' said Farkas. He sounded weak. He reached out a bloody hand, first to Anya as she passed him by, and then to Dawn. 'Segítsen nekem, kérlek! Sajnálom.'

'He is asking us to help him,' said Anya, gathering her things. 'He says he is sorry for what he did.'

Dawn looked down into Farkas' pleading eyes and enjoyed the tears she saw in them. Without saying a word, she smashed her foot hard into his jaw, laying him out cold once more. The momentum stole her balance and she collapsed to the floor beside him. Pain racked through her body, sapping her strength. The hurt dulled to an ache that possessed her bones. She looked behind Farkas, amazed that so much blood could come from one man.

'You are wasting your energy,' said Anya. 'It is a foolish thing to do if you are refusing to eat.'

'I needed him unconscious so I can check his pockets,' said Dawn. 'I got the impression you weren't going to help me.'

Anya glanced over and let a small smirk curl her lip. 'I think Farkas had even less strength in him than you.'

Dawn sneered in response, then rolled Farkas forward. She shuffled around until she could work her hand into his trouser pocket. It ran deeper than she thought and so she readjusted herself. She found something warm and solid at the bottom of the pocket.

'So the whole world cracks in two and you're not at all bothered by it?'

'It was not the whole world, Dawn, it was just this floor. This ship is not so different from any other floor we have seen. It is just more open to the outside world. It allows us to throw our dead into the sea before their bones rot and spread disease.'

Anya's words immediately brought back painful memories of Joe. She pulled the warm object from Farkas' pocket, anything to take her mind from the horror. In her hand she held a brass petrol lighter, its lustre long since tarnished. She popped open the lid and tried the wheel. She saw sparks but no flame until her third attempt. She swung the lid shut again with a flick of the wrist so as not to waste any more fuel.

'Okay, but it still doesn't explain what the hell is going on here.'

'Truthfully, I am not sure,' said Anya, shouldering her satchel. 'We saw it first on our apartment floor, the one I was telling you about. One of the eight who abandoned us returned much later in his time than ours. He had been driven mad with hunger and saw us an easy meal. Gregor and Nikola stood guard at the time and killed him with little difficulty, making an easy meal for ourselves instead. A few weeks later our floor suddenly broke in two. We were terrified and immediately gathered our things to evacuate the floor. Gregor returned from his mapping duties, dragging a man's body from the elevator behind him like some caveman hunter. The body was that of the man we had already killed and eaten, only younger-looking.'

'So... Milos?'

'Most probably he was supposed to die on this ship further along his time.'

'Jesus, I can feel my head spinning.'

'Yes. You must eat,' said Anya, stepping beside Dawn. 'I have said this already.'

'Shut up and help me turn this piece of shit over.'

They rolled Farkas onto his back but found nothing of consequence in his other trouser pocket, just a wallet containing a photograph of a plain-looking woman and some useless bank notes. Anya helped Dawn to her feet and stashed the petrol lighter in her satchel. They headed to Milos' corpse.

The old man's eyes were still bulging out from their sockets, staring at nothing. His head tilted much further forward than was natural, such was the severity of his neck wound. The blade of the parang sat deep into his flesh. Though the sight of his ruined body disgusted her, Dawn could not take her eyes away for long. She would try but then a ghoulish fascination would quickly draw back her attention. She felt weak at the knees and stumbled.

'I see you do not like the sight of blood. Of death?' said Anya, helping Dawn steady herself.

'I'm getting used to it,' said Dawn. 'It's hard to avoid it in this place.'

'Okay,' said Anya. 'Sit down and regain your strength. You might want to look away.'

'Jesus, Anya, really?'

'You must stop looking at him as a human body and start seeing it as food. You will regret passing by this opportunity. And stop blaspheming.'

'Anya, this place is falling to bits. We need to find a way out now, not play butcher.'

'Before we escape we need to survive. Help me take off his trousers.'

They rolled Milos onto his back, dislodging the parang in the process. His head flopped back into roughly the place it should have been, not that it made his body any easier to look at. His mouth was set in a terrible upside-down smile, teeth apart, a bloody tongue poking out between them. His dead eyes looked up to the clouds and the seagulls.

Anya unbuckled the old man's belt, unbuttoned his fly and eased down his trousers. He wore no underwear and his groin reeked of urine. A marker pen slipped from a pocket and rolled into a groove in the hardwood deck. Dawn removed the man's shoes and dragged his trousers towards her while Anya slid the hunting knife out from under his head. She wiped both sides of the blade against his shirt, removing the gore.

Dawn dug her hands into the pockets and tried her best to not inhale the smell from the trousers. She pulled out a leather-bound handle with a slit down one side, a flick-knife. There was also a ballpoint pen and a folded-up piece of paper, frayed and wrinkled around the corners.

She watched Anya smooth a hand over the old man's thigh and down to the kneecap, upon which the girl took a firm grasp. Dawn knew what was coming next and dared herself to watch. Being told she may want to look away was like being slapped across the face, like she had been challenged to a duel. And so she followed the path of the blade as Anya scraped it across the surface of the hardwood deck, thrust it vertically into the air and then let gravity take over. The front part of the blade, the chopping part, bit through a couple of inches of flesh at the top of Milos' thigh with a dull thud. Blood trickled out from the wound and down both sides of the deep cut. This action Anya repeated, each time letting gravity do the work, conserving energy, being smart, and each time Dawn forced herself to watch.

After half a dozen whacks, Dawn's stomach had had enough. She leaned over to vomit but nothing would come. Her stomach dry-heaved, which sent pain shooting across her belly, which in turn set her arm and leg muscles complaining in sympathy. She retched again, belching only air from her stomach, squeezing tears from her eyes. Eventually she felt a thick bitter gob of bile slide out from her mouth and onto the deck. She coughed, spat out the saliva that flooded her mouth and then emptied her nostrils like a footballer.

She looked back to Anya through tear-filled eyes and found the girl staring at her, shocked at her unladylike behaviour. She held the handle of the huge bloody hunting knife, resting at a forty-five degree angle deep into Milos' leg.

'I'm getting better,' said Dawn, and retched again.

Anya used her scalpel to slice down the length of the old man's inner thigh, once to cut through the skin, twice to gain purchase into the lean muscle beneath and third time to make the cut more pronounced.

'I told you it would be best to look away,' said Anya while she worked. 'You are wasting your strength being sick.'

Dawn nodded and kept her line of sight away from the scenes of butchery nearby. She looked out onto the fractured sea and watched how the horizon of the left half stood noticeably higher than that of the right. It made her wonder how much higher it would be all the way over there. A hundred metres? A mile? Maybe even nothing at all? She pictured herself sitting at the invisible gate of a huge canal lock that defied the laws of pretty much every science thrown at it.

While the image was certainly arresting it did nothing to smother the sounds from behind her. The cutting, the chopping and, most alarming of all, Anya's humming. Dawn sincerely hoped it was simply the girl's coping mechanism at work. She glanced back and met her eyes. In her peripheral vision she saw Anya had fully removed the skin from Milos' thigh. She was astonished to see how succulent the meat looked. It glistened in the sun, red and raw, like a huge cut of the butcher's leanest steak, stretched from groin to kneecap.

Anya's eyebrows arched upwards. 'What is it?'

'You're humming,' said Dawn. 'That's fucked up.'

'I could whistle?' said Anya. She then smiled, revealing a number of missing teeth that made her look even more sinister. 'Whistling is cheerier.'

'Seriously, no,' said Dawn, looking away again. 'Just... no.'

Anya kept on humming.

'What are you doing this for, anyway? It's not as if you have anything to keep the meat in.'

The very fact that she had referred to Milos as meat shocked Dawn, but she could not readily think of a better word. That brief glance at the old man's exposed thigh muscle, though sickening and wrong, still looked appetising. Her stomach cramped, far beyond rumbling now. She did not know if her body was punishing her or applauding her for her inhuman thoughts.

'I have flexible bags rolled up in my satchel,' said Anya. 'Two of them, joined together. We will use one to take what we can carry. When we find an oven, or a fire floor, we will cook the meat to make it last longer.'

Anya pulled out a thin roll of bin liners from her satchel and placed it in the groove of the hardwood deck. She then placed a knee on top to protect them from the crosswinds and began work on skinning Milos' slim, taut calf muscle.

Something gnawed at the back of Dawn's mind. She felt her sanity bobbing and swaying in a barrel heading speedily towards a massive waterfall, but, despite that, a few questions still bubbled to the surface.

First, Anya's missing teeth suggested scurvy or something else related to malnutrition. Milos and Farkas' teeth, while yellow, bent and crooked, were intact.

And second...

'What happened to Marika?' said Dawn, still looking towards the sea. 'Before your friend with the gun went crazy.'

Anya stopped harvesting Milos' meat.

'Gregor was never a friend of mine,' she spat. 'Never!'

Dawn heard the rustling of a plastic bag and the thud of wet chunks being thrust inside.

'Okay, whatever, but the question still stands. What happened to Marika?'

'Not here,' said Anya. 'Please?'

'I want to know. The meat that you and Nikola offered me...'

'Dawn, please, no!'

'Was it Marika's child?'

'Yes!' cried Anya.

Dawn heard the parang clatter to the deck. She looked over her shoulder to see what had happened. She saw Anya still kneeling, her blouse and skirt splattered with Milos' blood, a look of utter distress pulling her face in all directions. She kept her gory hands held up and away from her face, though it was clear that she wanted to hide herself from the world.

CHAPTER TWENTY-THREE

Marika lost the baby.

She lost the baby and we... we argued over its... over his tiny body.

Oh, God, forgive us!

Gregor... he saw the baby the same as he saw the elderly and weak... the ones that died.

He took it... took him away and... and...

We could not eat him. Not with Marika there. Not ever.

Oh, God, Marika!

I hated Nikola when he agreed with Gregor and not me. Especially after we... after we...

I... I never told him I was late.

How could I? Gregor had poisoned his mind. He saw women the same way he saw Marika, as vessels, and... and Nikola agreed!

Oh, God, I am so sorry!

*****

Anya stared glassily at the remains of Milos, his blood drying on her shaking hands. It took time for her urgent tears to subside, leaving her empty, defeated and short of breath.

'That was when we all went to Hell.'

CHAPTER TWENTY-FOUR

Dawn knelt behind Anya and gently hugged her. She could think of little else to do. She felt for one horrible moment that the girl had snapped. In picking away another nugget of truth from Anya it felt to Dawn like she had lost something precious.

She hugged a little harder and felt Anya tense. The girl was skinny to the eye, but quite how thin she had become was astonishing. It was as if she had been sculpted from papier-mâché and wire coat hangers. She found it baffling how the girl could be stronger than her, but none of that mattered now.

As incredible as it sounded, Anya was pregnant. The girl's desire to leave the cannibal commune suddenly make sense.

'How are you feeling?'

'Ill,' said Anya. 'Sad also.'

'I'm not surprised,' said Dawn. She rubbed the sides of Anya's arms a couple of times. It was a token gesture of reassurance but one that seemed to soften her up a little. 'How long have you known?'

'I am not sure,' said Anya. She subconsciously placed a hand on her belly. 'Time is so broken here, but the baby is starting to show now.'

'That means we really need to move,' said Dawn. She gently slapped Anya's arms and stood up. 'No pissing about. We need to cross off more floors and add them to your map. We won't get anywhere staying in places we already know about. We need to find a way out of here quickly, yeah? You and me, because this place is broken and it's falling apart; because I'm starving and I've got a fiancée I'm worried sick about, and because you're pregnant and all of your mates are now running amok in here. Have I missed anything?'

Dawn didn't wait for an answer, her pep talk was done. She picked up the parang from the deck and wiped the blade on the dead man's chest in the same way Anya had done. She then slid the knife into the sheath. It went in without a hitch this time, as if the blade had been oiled with blood. She then made a beeline for the man's shoes.

Behind her Anya stood and said something immediately stolen by the crosswinds. It could have been something about Joe, but she didn't want to think about the poor guy. More to the point, she didn't want to think about how she was going to break the news to his family. She tried to drive such thoughts out of her mind.

There'll be time to grieve later.

She had placed the folded-up piece of paper underneath Milos' shoes to stop it from blowing away. She retrieved it and looked back towards Anya.

'I'll tell you what I want right now, though,' she said, gesturing with the paper in her hand. 'Pockets! Big, deep pockets. I've got nowhere to stash things in this skirt, plus it makes me feel like a toilet roll cover. I'm calling shotgun on the next pair of jeans we find. And a bag.'

Anya held out the remaining bin liner, still rolled up. It immediately bent double in the wind.

'No,' said Dawn. 'But nice try.'

She stood with her back to the wind and gently prised open the folds of paper, revealing what looked like a map. While Anya's map was an esoteric mishmash of lines, circles and mysterious codes spread across umpteen notebooks, Milos' map was small, limited in scope and contained words in the bottom left hand corner which Dawn did not understand, but knew to be a key of some kind. She recognised one of the words.

'What's a "Hivatal"?'

'It means "office",' said Anya. She collected her bag of meat and twisted it into a bundle to make it easier to carry. 'One that contains furniture. In my map I used the letter "H". We found a lot of those when exploring. Sometimes inside we would find a machine filled with chocolate, but never often enough.'

'Okay, he's got "Hotel" here. That seems obvious enough. What about this one, yew-res? The U's got some dots above it.'

'That means "empty". Üres. We pronounce it "oo-resh". We saw a lot of empty floors also. Huh. It seems Milos stole my ideas for his own. Perhaps he was not as stupid as I thought.'

While most of the words were handwritten in one corner of the page, there was a single prominent word, top right. Someone had even ringed it.

'Here's one for you. Cor-has?'

Anya's face changed. She looked momentarily confused and strode over towards Dawn.

'Kor-haaz?' she said. 'Kórház?'

'Yeah, he's written it here, look. Kor-haaz. It's got a red cross written next to it.'

Anya gasped and took hold of the paper map. She looked up to Dawn and, for the first time in what felt like years, she smiled.

'A kórház is a hospital.'

*****

'No, not that one,' called Anya.

Dawn stopped by the elevator. She turned to find the girl engrossed in Milos' map, paying little attention to where she walked, heading, as she was, towards a wall.

'Why not?' said Dawn. 'How do you know?'

'That is the one we used. It only leads to one floor, yes? The floor we left.' Anya paused and looked up from the map. Her face darkened briefly, as if she had caught a vision of what also lay there. 'Has the elevator been kept open?'

'No, it's shut.'

'We will find another somewhere on this ship. One that has been jammed open, I am sure of it. Holding the elevators open would let Milos and Farkas return to their floor.'

'Wait, what? I thought you said these elevators always went to the same floors. Why would keeping the doors open have any effect? Couldn't they have just followed their map again?'

'Yes,' said Anya. 'But, at the same time, no. They would return to the right place, yes, but if Milos and Farkas did not keep the elevators from moving away they would risk coming back at a different time. Do you see? No? I will explain along the way.'

On the other side of the ship they found another elevator. A metal bar jutted out from a vertical chink of soft orange light visible beyond the brushed metal door. The bar had been sheared off at one end, similar to the one she had lost at the atrium. Telltale drops of blood had fallen onto the decking just outside the elevator doors, splattering over the weathered handwritten code still faintly visible in the wooden surface.

'Yes, yes, this is the one,' said Anya. She seemed happy again, engaged, as if this new information had reignited a waning passion. 'Look out for another elevator jammed open on the next floor, then another, and then we will find their floor. An elevator from there goes straight to the hospital.'

But Anya's words went in one ear and straight out the other, lost to Dawn's disquieted mind. Though the girl had only just bared her soul, Dawn could not bring herself to trust her.

Don't forget what she and her friends did to Joe.
But then she did save my life back there.
Yes, and why did she do that, do you reckon?

Dawn found herself staring at the black bin liner stuffed into Anya's satchel.

'Could you grab that?' said Anya, breaking the spell.

'Um. Yeah, sure.'

Dawn held onto the metal bar while Anya pressed the call button. The door slid aside, revealing a knee-high pile of bones on a feculent linoleum floor.

'Holy shit!' said Dawn. She nearly fell overboard in shock.

A pair of meaty skulls rested side-on atop a scorched ribcage. The bones bore knife marks and other signs of feasting. Beneath these lay a hip bone with some vertebrae still attached. The spine had been crudely hacked in two, the remainder still attached to the ribcage. A neat melange of longer bones from the arms and legs of unfortunate prey propped up the macabre display. The entire hideous mound was slathered with fat bluebottles. The whole elevator car reeked of rotten meat and hummed with the sound of flies.

'We must have stopped them from finishing the job,' said Anya. 'We need to get throw those bones into the sea before the flies spread. Please, will you help me?'

Dawn looked Anya straight in the eye.

'No. Fucking. Way.'

*****

The elevator pinged open onto a smallish office floor, completely empty save for two thick concrete supports. It was a simple design that placed all of the office space to the front and sides of the building, leaving all the ancillary stuff to the rear, such as storage, recreation areas, toilets, stairwells and, centrally, two sets of elevators.

From the left of these Dawn ran out onto the floor screaming and flapping her arms. She scratched at her hair and brushed wildly at her blouse and skirt, hell-bent on squashing any overly-inquisitive flies that had hitched a ride.

'Get them off me!' she shrieked. 'I have had it up to here with flies!'

'Calm down,' said Anya. 'How many times must I tell you to save your strength? Look, the flies are mostly gone now the elevator has closed.'

'I can't believe you made me do that!' said Dawn. 'And why was I the one that had to pick up the skulls?' She unconsciously wiped her hands on her skirt.

'It is something you are going to have to get used to.'

Dawn could only reply by letting out one final strangled cry. She scratched once more at her scalp and shook her head hard enough to make herself dizzy. She then stood still, arms at her side, and caught her breath, suddenly very aware that she was acting more than a little insane.

'Aha!' said Anya, her attention focused elsewhere. With the sheared metal bar in one hand she swung it around and pointed it towards the doors of the other elevator. 'Look. Do you see? There is another metal bar jamming open the elevator. They are like breadcrumbs.'

Upon hearing those words an icy sensation flooded across Dawn's nerve-endings. It felt as if a spider had sunk its fangs into her flesh. She could feel its venom working its way through her bloodstream. She felt the back of her neck but knew there would be nothing there other than grime and sweat. It had only taken the simplest of thoughts, brought on by Anya's simple words, to chill her bones. Breadcrumbs. Following them tended to lead to one of two places: a way out of the woods or A Very Bad Place.

Despite the horror she had endured and the carnage Anya left behind, deck thirteen was most definitely a way out, but only for those unfazed by outlandish odds of survival, or for those who could not take the madness any more. So if the fairy tales were to be believed, then that, of course, meant they were heading to A Very Bad Place. She felt butterflies develop in her stomach, six-inches wide and made of stainless-steel.

'This might be a better time to explain what I was saying before,' said Anya. 'So we have the elevator we came from over there on the left. If I tap the call button on the side the doors will open. We could return to the ship now and it would be exactly how we left it.'

'Not with all those flies in there we're not,' said Dawn, rubbing the back of her neck again. She joined Anya between the pair of elevators. Once there she noted the thick bloody streaks that joined the two sets of doors across the cheap vinyl floor. The blood partially obscured a pair of codes that had been written onto the vinyl floor in foot-high letters using permanent marker. The codes had started to fade, like the one on deck thirteen.

'However, if I push the call button, and hold it in, we will get a different elevator, like I was telling you before. But if I do that I will break the connection we had to the ship. When the elevator we want comes around again then, yes, we can go back to deck thirteen, but time there will probably have jumped. Sometimes forwards, sometimes backwards.'

'And that's why we are meeting people out of order? Is that how I managed to see...' She didn't want to voice its name, that future her, Other Dawn, in case her words made her real. 'Another me?'

'I think so,' said Anya. 'It is my best theory, but there are parts of this place that still confuse me.'

'Yeah, well, we're not here to study this place, Anya,' said Dawn. She approached the other elevator. 'In fact we don't want to be here at all, if you remember. I can tell you one thing I've figured out over the last however many days. If we sit still then we die. Come on, we need to keep moving.'

*****

To Dawn's instant disgust there were more flies when the elevator door slid aside, though thankfully not as many as before.

Anya placed the two metal bars she had accrued against the corner of the elevator car. She unfolded Milos' map. Her eyes danced over the paper for a moment and she pressed one of the buttons on the control panel to set the elevator in motion. The gentle shaking dislodged the hardiest of the flies. She dug around her satchel and fetched out a notebook, a permanent marker and an ordinary ballpoint pen.

'Now what are you doing?' said Dawn, leaning against a rare clean patch of elevator.

'Look at the controls. See how only a few of the buttons have got my codes written nearby? The one that is lit has no code, so I need to write this down.'

'Okay, but do it quickly.'

Dawn relaxed, letting more of her diminishing weight rest against the wall of the elevator to give her leg muscles a rest.

*****

The respite was all too brief. The interior doors opened again. With no mirrors in the elevator Dawn had little idea what lay in wait. Her only immediate clue was a nondescript slice of smooth beige wall outside the open door. Her body didn't want to move despite her brain's commands, and so for a moment she relied on her senses to fathom where they had landed. The floor beyond was possessed of a uniform humming noise, instantly noticeable and much more pronounced than the hum heard on all the other floors. An overpowering stench of decay immediately flooded the elevator. Finally there was the look of horror and awe on Anya's face as she took in the scene ahead of her.

Dawn felt the back of her neck again. This was going to be bad.

With great reluctance she pushed her body away from the wall and took in what lay beyond.

CHAPTER TWENTY-FIVE

Ahead there was a lengthy corridor from an apartment block, though it required a second glance to see it as such, so corrupt the passageway had become. Like deck thirteen, and like Joe's restroom before it, the narrow corridor had been sliced and segmented, only here in several places. The corridor twisted and buckled into the darkened distance like scenery from *The Cabinet of Dr Caligari*, as if Dawn had viewed the corridor through several chunks of broken glass.

The place instantly reminded her of Clive's killing floor. She felt the fine hairs on her arms immediately stand on end.

The further she peered into the corridor, the more alive the crooked floor became with maggots. What she had first taken to be darkness ahead then *moved* across the broken walls and ceiling; a thick, oily mass that shimmered, swirled and buzzed. A solid body of bluebottles, each as big as the end of her thumbs.

'Oh, God, no,' said Dawn.

And deep in the corruption, hiding in the shadows, forever itching to step out when she was most afeard, she felt the horrid presence of a figure that had haunted most of her childhood. She heard a voice hiss musically, menacingly, through the swarthy humming horror ahead.

[Yesssss, Dawny Prawn! I'm over heeee-ere. Come to meeeee!]
I'm going mad. I swear to God.
[Heh-heh-heh. I can taste your fear from here.]

'What? Whoa, no way,' she said. 'Not here. There's got to be another way through.'

'I cannot see one on their map,' said Anya.

Dawn rested her head against the cold metal interior of the elevator car and weighed up their options. It was obvious that Milos and Farkas had valued something in the hospital otherwise they wouldn't have singled it out on their map and based themselves nearby. But the path to it could hardly have been any more repulsive. She could already feel the flies on her body. Her skin itched all over at the thought.

The doors began to close. Anya laid down one of the metal bars across the threshold, jamming the door. The awful humming of the flies continued through the slit. A handful found their way inside, landing immediately on the drying blood, feasting upon it.

Meanwhile Anya rested notebook after notebook against the wall, scribbling in each with ballpoint pens of varying colours. She took out a thin black marker pen from her satchel and wrote a code, "L287.1", against the lit button of the control panel.

Dawn looked to Anya's handiwork and shrugged her shoulders.

'The "L" stands for "Lakosztály",' said Anya. 'It means "apartment".'

'You know what's through there, don't you?' said Dawn, caring little for Anya's cartography skills.

'Yes. Lots of flies.'

'No, not flies. You know exactly what I mean.'

'Maggots?'

'No, I mean I can feel something wrong here. This is a bad place.'

'Yes, this floor has seen much death, but we will be quick. I need to write my code on the carpet outside but after that we can run through the corridor.'

'That isn't what I meant. Look, Milos and Farkas go over to deck thirteen to get rid of a load of bones, yeah?'

Anya nodded but said nothing. She dug around her satchel and swapped marker pens, opting for a chunkier one.

'So who's looking after the place while they're away?'

'Do you mean who is guarding their floor? Nobody,' said Anya. '. . . probably. When you are in a group you tend to stay in a group. At least we did until we started to build my map, but then we were extra careful. We too used breadcrumbs. We all remembered what happened to poor Imre all those months ago.'

The mention of Imre brought with it a fleeting memory of how close one of the stairwells door had come to separating her from Joe, a useless thought now. Her shoulders tensed. Her disquieted mind immediately took her to the dreadful moment she saw Clive emerge – no, assemble! – to mortally wound Joe across the belly.

An easy kill on Clive's killing floor.

A killing floor like the one that lay outside.

Maybe one of the cracks in reality out there belongs to Joe.

She felt her hand go numb. She looked down and found it white, tendons raised, doing its utmost to crush the parang's handle. It took a surprising degree of effort to relax her grip, as if rigor mortis had set in without first waiting for her to die.

Anya opened the elevator doors and then quickly knelt over the threshold, out of Dawn's line of vision. The girl worked at speed, quick enough to be standing again before the doors closed.

In the meantime, dozens more inquisitive flies had found their way into the elevator. They landed on anything resembling food or places to lay their eggs. They landed on the bloody floor, the bloody handrail. One landed on the inside of Dawn's knee. She felt it crawl over her skin.

'Okay!' she said, battering her skirt. 'Okay, we'll run for it. Do it now. Just get me away from these fucking flies!'

With a nod Anya secured her satchel, grabbed the sheared metal pole from the corner of the elevator and looked Dawn in the eyes. She nodded again.

Ready.

She reached for the control panel of the elevator, inching towards the button that would reopen the door. With grim inevitability she started to count down.

'Three...'

Flies.

'Two...'

Maggots.

'One...'

Tickling Man.

Fuck.

'GO!'

The doors slid open. Anya leapt out through a frenzied pointillism of black and green and blue. The flies had caught the scent of something new. They flooded into the elevator car as Dawn tried to escape. Their soft, furry bodies bounced off her face, her neck, her arms, her legs. A couple landed on her lips and stayed there. She swiped them away as she tried to pick up her speed.

But her legs immediately tired. She had only gone five yards. She could see Anya ahead. The girl pulled away into the dark distance. Her body fragmented in the broken realities. Dawn tried to ignore her morbiferous assailants. She had to focus on getting to the end of the corridor, wherever that was. All she had to do was pick up her feet and run, but now they felt as heavy as moonboots.

By the time she reached the first crook in the corridor, the first split in reality, the choking cloud of flies had found her. They sought out her lips and her eyes. They buzzed and rustled in her ears as they tried to crawl inside. They bounced off her neck and into her blouse. They flew up her skirt and tickled her thighs and calves. She batted and swatted and shrieked and flailed but with little success. There were simply too many to fight away.

So intent was she on killing every fly around her that a sudden shift of gravity knocked her off-balance and off-course. She staggered forward and bounced off a locked door, crushing flies into the fabric of her blouse and releasing yet more into the corridor. She pinballed her way through as best she could but each shift of gravity and every change of camber in the floor sapped her energy until, finally, she stumbled and collapsed.

She landed hard on the carpet of the corridor and saw nothing beyond the end of her nose save for a dense, writhing mass of maggots. She looked up and saw they were all around her. The entire carpet was alive. She could barely see the fibres, only fat, off-white larvae shuffling around looking for food. They were all around her and, of course, underneath her. She could feel them working their way in through the gaps in her blouse. She felt their cool dancing bodies beneath her arms and her hands. They stroked the sides of her naked shins.

She shrieked and tried to lift herself up but the strength had vanished from her arms.

To her left she found an open door to one of the apartments. A split in reality cut straight through into the room beyond, a room

THE FLOORS

that had experienced a maggot eruption. A body-shaped mound of squirming maggots lay on the floor of the room. What little of the body she could see resembled raw, rotting meat. It was impossible to determine whether the body was that of a man or a woman.

'Anya!' she yelled. 'Anya, help me!'

But then the body-shaped mound of maggots moved in the corner of her eye. She locked onto the cadaver and was instantly paralysed by what she saw. The great carpet of maggots had partially subsided to reveal the overlarge head of a scarecrow with angry, black slits for eyes and an evil, ragged mouth stuffed with dry, itchy straw. Its shoulders moved next, casting more maggots onto the surrounding carpet to join their cousins. And then it lashed out an arm, casting a repulsive shower of hungry, white larvae into the air. A rotting, half-eaten hand hung from the end of the arm, bones visible in places along its foot-long fingers.

[Yessssss... there you are.]

And suddenly Dawn was eight years old again, stitched to the floor, unable to move, incapable of screaming, and filled with sickening dread of what was to come. Once again she felt abandoned to her fate. Her mother would be working from stupid o' clock in the morning at the cafe. Her father would be too drunk to help, lying semi-conscious on the sofa. And so now, like then, she would have to endure what was coming on her own.

The fingers of The Tickling Man's hand suddenly snapped outwards and grabbed at the air, his reach somehow getting as far as the doorway. The hand then slammed down onto the carpet, grinding maggots into the fibres, and then he started to lift his gangling body from the floor.

Dawn tried to scream but no sound came. The air she forced from her lungs merely passed through her windpipe unhindered and then out from her mouth in a rasping hiss.

The darkness ahead intensified as the flies found her. They landed on every visible part of her, coating her as surely as they covered the walls and the maggots the floors.

She felt herself mad. The floors had snapped her mind. Hadn't they? That was the only way The Tickling Man could be here, rising up from the carpet of maggots, up from the dead, coming to finish her off. But if she was going mad she was not laughing about it. Wasn't that a sure sign of madness? Trussed up in a straight-jacket, pissing oneself laughing all the way to the funny farm? She didn't know, but being pinned down in a corridor, covered in flies, lying on a bed of maggots, and with a childhood nightmare now standing over her, reaching for her, all she knew at that point was that the situation was not at all fucking funny.

And that was when she found her voice again.

'ANYA!' she screamed for as long as the flies would allow.

She spat out the few that had flown into her mouth. She tried to lift herself from the floor. With a monumental effort she pushed up her hips and dragged her knees inwards so that she now crouched. She looked over to the doorway, almost daring The Tickling Man to still be there, but she knew he would be gone. Instead the body-shaped maggot mound glistened, its skin dancing in the daylight afforded by the curtainless window above it.

The flies continued to crawl over her clothes, her skin and into her hair. She found the strength she needed to prop up her arms so that she could at least crawl through the rest of the corridor.

'ANYA!'

In the dark, fractured distance she saw movement. Slivers of white and blue and red danced like a kaleidoscope and assembled themselves as Anya bounded back through the corridor.

'Dawn! What happened?'

'Get me off of this fucking floor!' She choked and spat out the soggy bodies of more flies.

Anya circled around and helped her up into a standing position. They inched their way through the remainder of the corridor, ignoring as best they could the remaining open doors that each spewed crawling white life onto the carpets from the hellish apartments therein. The flies hounded them every step of the way, trying to find purchase onto anywhere warm and inviting, but Dawn and Anya had taken to breathing through their sleeves and batting away any flies that tried to land near their eyes.

Eventually they passed through the last split in the corridor and Dawn saw the faint outlines of doors ahead through the chaotic black static of flies. As the scene grew clearer Dawn found the elevator jammed open with a metal bar. The satchel and another metal bar lay nearby. It was the one that Anya had dropped to come back for her.

Underneath it she saw the code "L287.2" written upside down in permanent marker.

*****

The doors slid shut, locking Dawn into the elevator with Anya and a couple dozen flies. Dawn immediately pulled her blouse out from her skirt and tried to shake the crushed flies and maggots that still clung to her body.

'You wrote down that fucking code before helping me?' she said, intending for every word to puncture Anya's eardrums. 'Thanks a fucking bunch, you selfish bitch!'

'I am sorry,' said Anya. 'It did not take me very long.'

'Don't even fucking speak to me!'

She felt a couple of maggots crawling around the insides of her shoes. She would have to deal with them later. She swatted away attack waves of flies as Anya decided where the elevator needed to go next.

The flies buzzed.

The elevator buzzed.

The two women did not speak.

A soft ping sounded and then the doors opened onto Milos and Farkas' floor.

CHAPTER TWENTY-SIX

Dawn looked round the open-plan office ahead, which was an oasis of calm compared to the corridor of death that had preceded it. The floor, from a small office block, lay blissfully unbroken and clean of bloodstains. The area was eerily tidy, as if the terrible deeds undertaken by Milos and Farkas had been the exclusive domain of the killing floor.

The men had consigned the desks, chairs and office equipment to the perimeter, leaving a clearing in the middle. A refrigerator and a freezer gently hummed together in the far left corner. A small table on the right played host to a microwave oven and a slow cooker. A chunky ghetto blaster sat on top of a fat television set dead ahead. A wire coat hanger hung from the back of the television in lieu of an aerial. A number of comfortable-looking executive chairs stood about the place, one near an upturned milk crate, a makeshift pouffe. Towards the rear a blood-red sunset leaked through generous blinded windows, casting warm, orange hues across the floor. She thought it resembled a large studio flat, or perhaps the beginnings of a hoarding obsession.

A door-less storage room to the left offered a tantalising glimpse of clothes, as if the men had enjoyed a large walk-in wardrobe. The other doors, left and right, were intact and closed.

The wooden partitions that once separated the office furniture had mostly been cleared away to the edges. A few, however, were arranged in three of the four corners as a means to section off sleeping areas.

'Well-' said Anya, but Dawn cut her off by tapping on her shoulder with her index finger. She placed it to her lips and angrily pointed towards each of the sleeping areas.

'You see?' she whispered. 'Look at the beds. What did I tell you? One... two... *three* people!'

'You did not have to jab me so hard.'

'Shush!'

Dawn studied the area for signs of movement. The large jumble of furniture around the outside created a number of excellent hiding places, more so in the fading sunlight. She leaned in closer and listened for any telltale sounds: the creak of wooden furniture, the rustle of clothing, the easily-forgotten sounds of breathing.

Nothing.

She looked to the open storage room. Inside she would find a pair of jeans, she was certain of it. She could already feel the rough fabric on her legs. Hard-wearing jeans that could fend off armies of interested flies and curious maggots. All she had to do was go in there and find them.

But then something moved in the doorway. Something horribly familiar. She watched as four long, bony fingers slowly emerged from the edge of the doorframe, each tipped with yellow, claw-like fingernails. The fingers locked in place against the jamb, one by one, with the theatrical grace of a stage magician. The inhuman hand tightened its grip.

[Iiiinnnn heee-ere, Dawwwny Prawwwn.]

Oh, no you don't.

She removed the parang from its sheath and let its heavy weight swing by her side.

'I think we are alone here,' said Anya. She turned to Dawn. 'What is so funny?'

Dawn hadn't realised her sneering laughter had reached her lips.

'Nothing. Don't worry about it.'

Anya nodded slowly and kept her eyes on Dawn.

She thinks I've gone mad. She's not the only one. I can feel my mind slipping away. I am being haunted again.

But why did it have to be him *that came back? The Tickling Man. Why couldn't it have been Mum?*

I'd have happily gone mad then.

She watched as the grey hand released its grip. The slim, foot-long fingers then slowly and silently slid behind the door jamb and out of sight. She felt a small sense of triumph swell in her chest. Could it be that she was breaking free of her fears? Perhaps she wasn't going batshit crazy after all. Perhaps. It was a small victory against her demons, but a victory nonetheless.

I've got your number now.

'I think you're right. There's nobody here,' said Dawn, her normal confident self creeping back. 'Either way, keep your eyes peeled.' She pointed to the second elevator behind them both. 'Shout for me when you think you've got the right elevator. I'll be in that room over there.'

Anya said nothing. She turned to face the elevator and popped open her satchel. She dug around for her notebooks and pens.

'Okay, look...' Dawn sighed and let her shoulders drop. 'Look, I'm sorry I shouted at you. I guess all those flies and maggots really freaked me out back there. I thought you'd left me behind, like Imre. I'm glad you came back.'

Her words sounded as genuine as a politician's promise. She'd long hated apologising, even as a child. It had never been the admission of guilt that troubled her, but the acknowledgement that she had been wrong. She looked to Anya and fixed her with a weak smile. She needed the girl on-side, at least for the time being.

'Okay.' Anya left it at that.

The spotlights in the ceiling dimmed. A large, muffled buzzing noise sounded from below the second elevator. Dawn felt a slight tremor carry up her legs. Nearby furniture creaked and cracked. The whirring noise of an approaching elevator sounded through the door.

'Shit!' said Dawn. 'Hide!'

*****

The elevator door slid open and a scruffy-looking man stepped onto the floor. He wore a grubby soldier's uniform. In his left hand he clutched a white plastic bag half-filled with small elongated boxes. In the same hand he held a long bayonet blade.

His right arm was missing.

He had pinned the cuff of the empty sleeve to the shoulder of his jacket. His trousers were holed at the knees and stained faintly around the crotch. He wore relatively new black trainers with flashes of white down the sides.

The elevator door closed behind him. He looked out onto the floor with his one good eye. A brown, makeshift bandana-cum-eyepatch kept his long greasy hair out from his eyes. He slowly surveyed the clusters of office furniture that bordered most of the floor. He scratched at his thick, black beard. Nothing seemed out of place and yet something simply wasn't right.

'Farkas?' he said, not needing to shout. His deep voice growled like an old motorbike engine.

He looked to both elevators behind him. The doors of each were fully closed. He returned his attention to the open-plan floor.

'Milos?'

No response.

He took in a lungful of air and found a faint lingering odour. Something that did not belong to either man. Something new.

He dropped the plastic bag on the floor and kept a tight hold of the bayonet blade.

*****

Hiding by the jamb of the open storage room, Dawn sensed *him* behind her. Not the new arrival. He – if it was indeed a he, she hadn't dared to look – still stood somewhere in the clearing. No, she knew exactly who lurked behind her. She could smell his straw. She could hear his raspy breathing. She could sense its grabby hands hanging loose from spindly arms, long fingers dangling over her head, claw-like fingernails tickling her greasy hair.

What the fuck *was I thinking?*

It had seemed a natural place to hide when the elevator buzzed into life. After breaking free from her dreamlike paralysis and then wrenching herself from the maggot-infested floor she reckoned her phobias were finally dissolving into what, deep down, she knew them to be all along: silly little fears of small consequence. In life she tended to enjoy confrontation, but only when she knew she could get away with it. This had felt like one of those times.

But once she crossed the threshold and escaped into the storage room her bravado instantly evaporated. The endorphins that helped carry along her exhausted body had since fermented into raw adrenaline that now coursed through her twitching, shaking muscles.

And her silly little fears spread out across her mind like ink spots, made manifest in the monster she knew to be behind her. She hadn't overcome The Tickling Man at all, just like how she hadn't fully conquered her squeamishness, just like she hadn't quite defeated her fear of the dark.

But some piece of the jigsaw had fallen into place. She now understood the foundations upon which her demons lay. That sense of the known unknown lingering in the darkness, choosing never to reveal itself fully, ever biding its time; the ever-mounting anxiety she would feel at the potential menace it represented; the poisonous knowledge that the unknown could reveal itself at any point it chose, and then flood in to take her. She understood her tormentor, but could not shake her fear of him. Perhaps, perversely, this was for the best. A dull mind in this place was a dead mind.

The Tickling Man did not speak, nor did he hiss. In fact she could no longer hear his raspy breathing. Perhaps he too was hiding from the new arrival.

Silence ruled in the clearing outside. The last thing she had heard was a plastic bag dropping on the floor with a hollow sound. Since then, nothing, not even a footstep.

She held the parang uselessly at her side. She had pulled the blade from its sheath but barely had the strength left in her arms to use it. The weight of it made her hand ache. So much for bravado. She leaned softly against the wall, the doorframe to her right. She switched the parang to her left hand.

The storage room was empty and dark. The Tickling Man had vanished. She squirmed. The crushed, rolled-up body of a dead maggot had worked its way under the sole of her foot.

'Jesus!'

A flash of dark brown swung into view from the doorway. With what little strength she had remaining she hauled up the parang and stabbed it hard into the intruder, horrified to find nothing there but stiff, brown fabric. Her momentum caused her to stumble into the doorway where she saw a one-armed man in a stained white T-shirt, braces and filthy combat pants. His right arm had been removed, leaving a badly scarred fin that twitched uselessly. In his remaining hand he held the bayonet blade to the side of Dawn's neck. She kept hold of the parang and sank to her knees.

'Ah-ah,' he said. It sounded like a warning.

She looked up to the soldier, then to the blade he held, and then finally met the man's one good eye. He looked on Dawn as if she'd fallen out from a diseased dog's arse. He opened his lips to speak.

'Ah-ah,' said Anya.

The girl placed her scalpel against the man's neck and grabbed a handful of greasy hair. She pulled back his head and tightened her grip on his scalp.

'Bros' nozh, tovarishch,' she sneered. 'Seychas!'

Anya dug the blade in a little further when the soldier refused to pull away. A trickle of blood escaped from beneath the scalpel.

'Seychas!' she snarled.

The bayonet blade hit the floor with a dull clang. Dawn grabbed it and felt a familiar unease take hold. The blade looked a hell of a lot like the one Marika's killer had carried, the one Dawn had tried to lose - and yet here it was again, turning up like a bad penny.

There's got to be more than one of these, surely? Hmm. I'll get rid of you one way or another.

'Get out of there, Dawn,' said Anya. She eased the one-armed man out into the clearing and towards one of the executive chairs.

Dawn slid the parang back into its sheath and used the bayonet blade to help her stand. She hoped to bend it out of shape, something to render it null and void, but the blade held firm. Perhaps she could throw it into the next pitch-black sliver of nothingness she came across. Now there was an idea.

'Sidet,' said Anya.

Once the soldier had sat in the chair she inched away, keeping the scalpel out at arm's length all the while. The man looked impassively at both her and the knife. He dabbed at the small nick in his neck.

'Gde oni?'

'What's he saying?'

'He is asking where his friends are,' said Anya, still focused on the soldier. 'My bag is over there. You will need to carry it for me.'

Dawn found the satchel in the footwell of a nearby desk. The bag was heavier than advertised but she still managed to sling it over her shoulder, covering the sheathed parang. She slid the bayonet blade into the bag, handle-first. She heard a gentle rustle from the bin liner stuffed inside, which instantly reminded her of its grisly contents. She tried not to think about it as she returned to Anya.

'Gde oni?' repeated the soldier, impatience sewn through his gritty voice.

'Open the bag. The black bag.'

'What? Oh, God, no.'

'Open the bag, Dawn! Open the bag and reach inside.'

It occurred to Dawn that the only person in the room wielding a knife at the moment was one both willing and exceptionally capable in its use. She also happened to be the person who still felt sore about Dawn's little rant.

'Okay! Okay, I'll do it. Aw, bloody hell!'

She held one end of the black bin liner and let it roll down to the floor with a sickening slap. She slid a hand into the thin plastic folds and grimaced when she felt the cold moist insides. Deeper and deeper into the bag she reached until the tips of her fingers slid against the cool, slimy meat therein. She took a deep breath and grabbed hold of the first chunk she could lay her hands on. When she drew her hand from the bin liner she found the bottom half of her sleeve splattered red.

Anya grabbed the meat with her free hand and threw it into the soldier's lap.

'Milos.'

The soldier did not flinch. He showed no sign of fear, revulsion or any noticeable emotion. He simply looked down at the food that lay in his lap. It was around twice the size of his remaining hand, red and succulent. He sat back in the chair and, to Dawn's surprise, he shrugged.

'C'est la vie,' he said. 'C'est la guerre.'

There seemed nothing left of the man, as if all sense of humanity had been stripped away, leaving the soldier to function on instinct alone. A mere ant in human form.

'Keep watching him,' said Anya. 'I will fetch the elevator.'

CHAPTER TWENTY-SEVEN

The elevator rocked gently from side to side as it pulled away, setting a collection of sheared metal bars clinking together musically in the corner. Dawn shielded her eyes from the blast of light that broke through the small windows of the interior doors. The familiar buzzing sound of old rattled around the inside of the elevator, and then, in the space of a heartbeat, was gone again. The light quickly faded outside to perfect black and the elevator made its approach to a new floor.

It occurred to Dawn that she had shielded her eyes with her bloody hand.

Great. War paint. Just what I need.

She let her arm flop down. She was spent. The confrontation with the soldier had sapped her reserves once again. She was no longer running on fumes. Instead it felt like she was devouring herself from the inside. Her stomach was a tight Gordian knot that would never again accept food. She hurt almost everywhere. She wondered if this was how Joe had felt before he died. She sagged against the brushed metal wall opposite the control panel and pitched guesses at how long it had been since her last meal, the one she'd lost over Cocaine Dale. Too long.

The elevator came to a stop and the door rumbled open, revealing a narrow corridor from an apartment floor.

'Doesn't look like a hospital to me,' said Dawn.

Anya ignored her and studied the control panel, flummoxed by it and yet spellbound. She took one of the metal poles and placed it over the elevator's threshold.

The elevator door slid across and met the bar with a crunching sound, eventually giving up before retracting for another attempt. And another. And another still. A pre-recorded voice politely asked whoever it was to clear the doorway.

Dawn let her eyes rest upon the control panel. She stood slumped against the wall, resisting the demands of her heavy eyelids as best she could.

A pin-sharp and relatively clean touchscreen glowed in soothing pastel colours. Even the door alert icon that suddenly appeared in the corner of the display pulsed in pleasing shades of red. A page of buttons populated the remainder of the screen, eight of which contained the number thirteen in an achingly upmarket font.

Anya pressed her index finger against the bottom of the screen. One of the buttons, a right-facing arrow, instantly lit up. The girl watched, transfixed, as the screen filled with another page of thirteens.

'I take it you haven't seen an elevator like this one,' said Dawn.

'Not one with a television inside, no. Certainly not one you can touch.' She opened up the frayed piece of paper and held it into the light of the overhead spots. She placed her finger on some small writing to the left of "Kórház". 'I wondered why their map had a page reference here.'

Dawn looked down to the fragile piece of paper. Her head rolled forward, as heavy as a medicine ball. She spotted the numerals nine and one close together.

'Page one, button six,' she said with mock nonchalance, a flying guess, and let her head drop back. 'Stick with me, girl, and you'll learn things.'

'Nagyokos,' said Anya, a sneer.

'What was that?'

'It means someone who is wise.'

Yeah, I bet it does.

The girl crouched by her satchel and pulled a thin marker pen from it. She returned to the control panel, uncapped the pen and hesitated at the glowing screen.

'But there are no buttons to write on,' she said.

She let slip a short, astonished chuckle. Her face was as if she had just stumbled upon a doorway to Narnia. Even now the girl could find new and surprising things here, which, for Dawn, raised two troubling questions.

Just how big a place are we looking at?
And, more to the point, does Anya actually want to leave?

A large mirror dominated the wall to Dawn's immediate left, opposite the door. She winced at the tired, ridiculous hag gawping back at her, war paint and all. Dark bags had developed under her eyes. Her cheekbones seemed more pronounced. Her hair spiked outwards in random tufts as if she'd recently taken to licking stun guns. Her shirt-like blouse lay untucked around the waist of her too-big skirt. Stark red stains peppered the starchy fabric of the blouse, complemented with creamy-yellow splodges of maggot juice.

'Jesus, I actually feel how I look.'

Anya began writing on the mirror, saying nothing, lost in thought. Behind her the elevator door continued to crunch shut and roll open with tiresome regularity.

The smell of solvent wafted up Dawn's nostrils as the girl worked. She had always liked the smell of marker pens despite all the warnings. There was something sweet and pleasant in the odour, until the headaches kicked in.

Anya eventually capped the marker pen and returned her attention to the touchscreen. She hovered a fingertip over the left-arrow button, then changed her mind and pressed right instead. The screen refreshed and presented a new collection of buttons. She pressed again.

'Seven. Eight. Ah, page one. Goodness, this elevator must serve sixty-four floors!'

'Fascinating,' said Dawn.

A scintilla of truth lay in her sarcasm. Before her stood someone who, by the end of her first day trapped in the maze, had discovered the secret of its elevators, and, soon after, established a provable means of exploring its floors; someone who had not only grasped the idea of a touchscreen user interface but then factored it into her way of doing things before drawing her next breath; someone who spoke a number of languages, to the complete surprise of her fellow countrymen. It was as if the girl could nail anything at the first time of asking.

Dawn felt a taut violin string of jealousy ping in the recesses of her mind. She considered herself to be reasonably clever, but she always had to work damn hard for it. Nothing ever came easy.

But then there was the cold, brutal side of the girl. What Dawn had considered at first to be an inability in Anya to see much beyond herself, a mild autism perhaps, had seemingly developed into a mind that could slaughter another human being, feast on their flesh and be totally at ease. Perhaps that was why Anya was so keen to tag along. It might have had nothing to do with helping Dawn, toughening her for the ordeal ahead and destroying her taboos.

Maybe she sees me as a future snack. A steaming ham with two legs, like in the cartoons. Or am I going crazy and none of this shit is real? I'm seeing bogeymen, for God's sake.

You're not mad, you're just overthinking again. Brainpower costs energy, remember that.

'Button six,' chirped Anya.

She dabbed the screen. Button six pulsed green in tandem with the door alert icon. The girl retrieved the metal bar from the threshold and allowed the doors to close. The elevator shook into life once more.

As the flashing light outside faded and the buzzing sound eased Dawn realised she was still holding onto the soldier's plastic bag. She drew it up to her chest and peeled apart the handles. Inside she saw a collection of elongated boxes, each covered with Cyrillic script that made no sense. She picked out a box for closer scrutiny and found the anglicised name of the product in smaller letters.

Glucozeal.

'Yes!'

For a moment she too had found Narnia.

*****

The door slid away, revealing a spacious open area, curiously oval in shape, with a low false ceiling and a prairie of hard-wearing vinyl beneath it. A wide corridor straight ahead stretched into the distance, stopped only by a pair of large double doors that suggested more corridor to come. A large "XIII" had been stencilled onto a nearby wall in a strikingly modern font unbecoming of hospitals. A series of enormous scorch marks scarred the surfaces from top to bottom. A number of the overhead strip lights had blown.

Anya stepped from the elevator and cautiously looked around. She held the bayonet blade in one hand and a metal bar in the other.

Dawn followed close behind. She bagged the box of Glucozeal and sucked on one of the tablets. She turned on the threshold and looked to the code Anya had neatly written on the mirror: "R1.1", the first "R" of her map. While "K", for Kórház would have been a better letter fit, the girl had already used "K" to signify maintenance floors. The word she used sounded like "Carbon-tar-tash", which conjured bizarre thoughts of jet-black facial hair.

Anya turned and placed a metal bar onto the threshold, then staggered back and gasped.

'Dawn,' said Anya, pointing to the elevator. 'Look at this!'

When Dawn turned to see for herself she found the elevator wasn't wide enough to fill the shaft it occupied. There were six-inch vertical strips of utter darkness both left and right. Dawn peered into the gap on the left-hand side. She found the exterior of the elevator clad in thick gold foil, not at all like the hinges and levers and cables she expected to see. The exterior of the elevator looked, for want of a better word, *alien* - but also familiar. It reminded her a little of a satellite she had seen at the Science Museum.

'What the hell is this place, Anya?'

She stepped aside, allowing the girl a look.

'Oh! Beautiful,' she said. She reached out as far as she dared but couldn't quite reach where the gold foil started. 'I wonder if all of the elevators are as rich as this one.'

'I wouldn't reach in too far if I was you.'

Dawn rolled the Glucozeal tablet to the other side of her mouth. She willed for it to return some strength to her muscles. She watched as Anya eased her skinny frame from the gap and stepped back into the floor. She caught sight of the bayonet blade, still jutting out from the satchel, and wished it gone.

She has more knives than you, and you can barely lift the one you've got.

Dawn found her hand around the parang handle again. She took a firmer hold and tugged. The blade slid an inch from the sheath before catching, but the effort still made everything hurt.

Give it time. Get your strength back.

Anya knelt opposite the jammed elevator and fished a thick black marker pen from her bag. She drew in large letters an upside-down "R1.1" onto the vinyl floor.

Dawn took in their surroundings and slurped on the remains of the raspberry-flavoured tablet. The large, open space of the lobby offered no view of the outside world, which struck her as odd. The walls were of white matt plastic, scorch marks, elevators and doors, but there was nary a window to be seen. Stranger still, the lobby had way too many elevators, five of them, all in a row, the one marked "R1.1" in the middle. A further two wide corridors spilled away to the left and right of the lobby, each soon interrupted by swing doors.

Above the lip of each corridor there hung a cascade of signs; white Cyrillic text and numerals on a dark blue background, with arrows for directions. The numerals seemed to be bed numbers: to the left of the elevators, one through thirty-six; to the right, sixty-four to one hundred; ahead, thirty-seven to sixty-three, plus something else one to four. After that she was lost.

'Do you understand any of these signs?'

Anya looked up and around her for a couple of seconds. 'They are Russian,' she said. 'Some of the letters look different though. They have been changed slightly.'

'Okay, but can you still read them? I guess the numbers are for beds or something.'

The girl looked to the left of the elevators.

'That one says "sorting", or something similar. "Emergency" too.'

She turned to the corridor opposite the elevators. Dawn peered at the sign.

'The one over there looks like "intensive care". Above, it says "surgery rooms" one to four.'

Finally she turned her body around to see the corridors on the right. Her eyebrows rose slightly as she scanned the text. She hummed with interest.

'Go on,' said Dawn.

'I think that one says "pharmacy".'

*****

Dawn approached the swing doors of the corridor to the right of the elevators, the corridor that would lead to the hospital's pharmacy. The doors automatically opened outwards. Reflections of light flashed across a semicircle of glass inset in each door.

She surveyed the wide corridor beyond. It stretched out another twenty yards before it met another set of swing doors. Along the left there were four brushed metal doors with windows. None of the doors had handles, only small, black screens set nearby into the wall.

A number of strip lights in the low ceiling had blown. A single light flickered above the next set of swing doors. The light tinked off and then tonked back on again. She found scorch marks in the corridor, though not as pronounced as the ones in the lobby. A smooth, white wall ran along the right side of the corridor, broken by another elevator and heavy, black stairwell doors on either side.

'You're not going to believe this,' said Dawn. 'There's another bloody elevator through here.'

'We need more things to jam open these doors,' said Anya. She sat on the floor of the lobby, scribbling into her notebooks. 'This will be an excellent floor to make our home.'

The strip light flickered again and tinked off, catching Dawn's attention. She glared at the relative darkness cloaked over the swing doors ahead. She felt herself being drawn into the semicircles of glass set into the doors, finding an odd shadow there that unsettled her. The light tonked on again after what seemed like a week.

Four long, bony fingers slid away from the window and out of sight.

She tried the handle of the parang again, glad to find some strength returning.

'What is it?' said Anya, catching her up.

'Nothing,' said Dawn. 'It's just my imagination getting the better of me.'

Though The Tickling Man still had his claws dug into her mind, it was clear that his grip on her was loosening. A shift of power had taken place the moment she hauled herself free from the broken corridor of maggots. His gas-leak words carried little threat for her now. Perhaps she had stolen his voice the same way he had often stolen hers.

Why are you still here?

'Dawn?'

'Sorry. My mind wanders sometimes.'

They stepped deeper into the corridor, past the brushed metal doors and their dead screens. Dawn peered inside the last of the doors. The room beyond was spacious and pristine with four beds, unlike any hospital bed she had seen. They resembled flat shelves that had been raised up from the floor. They jutted out from the wall and looked uncomfortable. Beside each bed there stood a large, white, oblong box, featureless save for a visible split in the middle and a strip of unlit panels and buttons across the top. Like the lobby there were no windows in the room.

The swing doors whirred apart into the next segment of the corridor, a carbon copy of the first save for a single scorch mark that arced across the ceiling and down the white wall. The faltering strip light above them flickered and tinked off. Dawn watched the yellow claws of long, bony fingers scrape the glass of the swing doors ahead. They slid once more out of sight. Again she heard no voice, no call, no taunting. He was just *there*, lurking.

What are *you?*

'Another elevator,' said Anya. 'I wonder why so many.'

The strip light above tonked back into life.

'Yeah, me too. I'm starting to wonder whether this floor is from a real hospital after all.'

'I assume you have not seen one like this?' said Anya.

'Sarcasm, all of a sudden?' said Dawn. She stopped and looked over at the girl, unable to contain the wry smile that tickled the corners of her mouth. 'This English of yours is getting better and better, I see.'

'We Magyars have sarcasm too,' said Anya, walking ahead. 'I think ours would be more subtle than yours, however.'

'And why would that be?' said Dawn, catching up.

'Subversion carries a high price in my country,' said Anya. 'You are taken away and tortured by the police. You are made to confess crimes you did not commit. Sometimes you do not come back at all.'

'So, not exactly the best place to speak a bunch of languages then?' said Dawn.

Anya shook her head. 'Speaking another language is not uncommon in my country, but I felt safer restricting myself to my mother tongue and what little Russian I knew. Anything more and such information could find its way into Soviet hands. Who knows what would have happened then. I could have been tortured, or vanished, or both. No, as I had only moved into the apartment block a year previously, it was best for me to blend in and not to raise suspicion.'

'So when your friends found out you could speak English back there...'

'I no longer blended in,' said Anya. 'It made me feel like a target.'

The swing doors ahead opened onto the final segment of the corridor, longer this time but with the same features as before, including yet another elevator. At the very end of the corridor was a single door that had been forced open. A small screen near the door had been smashed in. A circuit board and several wires spilled out from the hole. Footmarks on the floor suggested the room ahead had been a popular haunt.

'When was all of this? Sorry, I'll put it another way. What year was it when you were chased into this place?'

'Nineteen fifty-six. I know it was early November, but I can no longer remember the date. You?'

'Twenty thirteen,' said Dawn. 'Sadly we still don't have flying cars.'

'And yet so much has changed. I see it in the way you walk. I hear it in the things you say,' said Anya. 'You were surprised before to learn of the Soviet occupation of my country. Does that mean we are free in twenty thirteen? Did we win our fight?'

'Yeah, I guess. Well, eventually, anyway. Russia kind of imploded just after I was born.'

'It took so long?'

Dawn shrugged. 'I guess.'

Anya fell silent, consumed by her thoughts as they took their final steps towards the pharmacy. Dawn decided to leave her to it.

The lights inside the storage area flickered on as they neared the door. To Dawn's surprise the room inside was huge, easily as big as the three segments of corridor that preceded it, and maybe the same again wide, and all throughout were medical storage units and shelves stacked high with supplies and obscure-looking equipment.

What she found on the first rack of shelves felt like a heavy punch to her guts.

'Son of a bitch.'

CHAPTER TWENTY-EIGHT

Dawn took one of the small boxes from the middle shelf. The text on the box was Russian, like the packaging of most everything around her. As with her packets of Glucozeal, however, she found an English translation across the bottom.

Insulin.

She pulled more boxes from the shelves and found a dizzying array of the stuff, arranged by how long they lasted. Some were only intended as a quick top-up, lasting only a couple of hours. Others lasted all day. Every delivery method looked to have been catered for. There were insulin syringes, pumps and pens, and even inhalators, patches and pills.

The sooner they create a pill for this stuff the better.

She replaced the boxes, stood back and looked once more at the shelves.

There wasn't a single box missing.

'You are crying,' said Anya, half-asked, half-stated.

As if to prove the girl's point a warm tear spilled down Dawn's cheek and dangled from her chin. She let it drop into her collar.

'I'm so sorry, Joe,' she said softly, and turned away.

The shelves nearby sported an equally diverse range of energy tablets and vitamin supplements. Though they had been raided several times the shelves still offered more potions and pills than Dawn could ever hope to carry.

She popped another raspberry-flavoured tablet into her mouth from the Glucozeal dispenser. She felt sparks of life return to her aching limbs at long last, welcome evidence that her stomach still worked. She took a box of multivitamins from one of the shelves and shook it. A pleasing rattling sound filled the room. She lost count of the times she had used pill bottles like primitive maracas. Her mum always seemed to have thousands of them on her dresser and in the bathroom cabinet.

'I wondered why those guys still had their teeth but some of yours were missing,' said Dawn. She tossed the box to Anya. 'Mystery solved, or at least I hope so. Either way you're going to need some of those. Meat alone isn't going to cut it now you are eating for two.'

'At least now I know where my scalpels came from. Ah! I see just the thing we need!'

'What is it? A cold water tap?' said Dawn, shaking another bottle of vitamin pills. 'Please let it be a cold water tap.'

Anya approached a trio of large refrigerators along the left-hand wall. She fished the bin liner from her satchel and opened one of the doors.

'Eew,' she said. 'I think someone had the same idea before me.'

'Seriously, I don't want to know,' said Dawn. She removed the bottle of vitamins from its packaging and dropped it into her carrier bag. 'Just find me a glass of water or something.'

Anya deposited the black bag inside a different fridge, closed the door and then wandered away to explore.

Dawn continued filling her carrier bag with bottles of vitamins, leaving their collapsed boxes on the shelves. She wondered whether she could survive in the maze on pills and tablets alone. Perhaps not in the long term, otherwise Milos and company would have done the same, but anything that delayed the inevitable was welcome. She flooded her mouth with saliva and gulped down a couple of multivitamins, accidentally taking the remains of the glucose tablet with them. She popped another Glucozeal in her mouth to replace it and felt a little more alive.

Next on her shopping list were painkillers. Nothing as severe as morphine, but something a bit stronger than off-the-shelf paracetamol. Anything that could take the edge off her cramping guts and aching muscles.

'I'm not seeing much here that can help us block the elevator doors,' said Dawn.

'No,' said Anya from across the room. 'There is nothing here either.'

'Any painkillers?'

'No. There is penicillin?'

'I'll pass, thanks.'

Her mind ticked over as she walked the along the shelves. They had discovered eight elevators on this floor through exploring a single corridor and a lobby. Why on earth would a hospital need to be so well connected? It was as if the place was some kind of hub, like Amsterdam airport, a stepping stone to somewhere else. If Anya genuinely planned to resume her map from here, they could die of old age before getting around to mapping the final elevator.

She walked to the end of the room and rounded the corner. The edges of supply cabinets and high-reaching shelves shrank into the distance, reminding her of a DIY megastore. There were even signs above the aisles, albeit covered in gobbledegook and odd characters and backwards Rs and Ns. She looked along each aisle as she walked by and scanned the shelves. There were bathfuls of saline packs and several hundred mummies-worth of bandages. There were apparatuses of assorted sizes and curious function. There were shrink-wrapped packets of fabric gowns and enough boxes of disposable gloves to satisfy even the most ardent rubber-fetishist.

She didn't catch sight of The Tickling Man in any of the aisles. This would have been the ideal place for him to lurk; plenty of things to hide behind; plenty of opportunities to mess with her head. Perhaps she really had him licked.

She found a large, elongated medicine cabinet opposite some of the aisles, windowed with dark glass. The doors of the cabinet were all locked. A few of the windows were cracked but had held against their attackers. Most likely this was where the really powerful drugs were kept.

As she neared the completion of her tour she found shelves stocked high with painkillers of varying strengths. She slid a few boxes into her bag and hoped for English instructions inside. She soon found herself back at the insulin supply, where Anya stood waiting for her.

The girl's eyes were locked onto the broken door to the pharmacy. Her lips twitched. She was working something in her mind.

'When Milos never returned from his task we thought he was lost to the floors, like poor Imre,' said the girl. 'I think he did not come back because he found this place. I think he abandoned us.'

'As you said, perhaps he wasn't as dumb as he looked. Wouldn't you have done the same thing?'

'Not back then,' said Anya. 'But now I would, yes. I think. It does not matter. I feel let down. Betrayed. It makes his death more...' She glanced over to Dawn. Her pensive look transformed into a warm smile with the unnerving skill of an overly-bronzed shop assistant, albeit one with gaps in their teeth. 'You are looking better.'

'Yup,' said Dawn. She slid the parang from its sheath and waved it around a little. 'Anyone comes at me now will get this stuck in their neck.'

'Be sure of it.'

That means you too, Anya.

Dawn set down her plastic bag of goodies and returned the blade to its sheath.

'Did you find anything we can use?' said Anya.

'Not really,' said Dawn. 'Most of the bulky stuff looks too useful or expensive to go and squash in an elevator door.' She slurped noisily on yet another Glucozeal, working up enough saliva to down a painkiller. 'I've been thinking what our next move ought to be, though,' she continued. 'I know somewhere we're bound to get metal bars and the like, and the more elevators we have to get there the better.'

I've beaten one demon today, why not another?
You're mad, Dawn. You've finally cracked.

*****

Reconnaissance of the remaining corridors yielded another three elevators along the way to triage, and a further two towards the operating theatres.

The doors of one such operating theatre whirred aside, returning Dawn and Anya to the corridor. The temptation to look inside had proven too much for them to resist.

Dawn turned in the doorway for one last look into the large, white room. The windows of the viewing gallery formed a halo of black mirrors the ceiling. An array of expensive-looking machines clung to the walls as if to keep the theatre tidy. Directly above the uncomfortable-looking bed, in place of portable lights, there hung an imposing surgeon's workstation. Along its flanks were a series of small screens, all switched off. Its assorted metal arms were tucked in underneath. The whole thing looked vicious. She pitied anyone unfortunate enough to need an operation beneath it.

'I like the plan,' said Anya. 'When you mentioned coming here through a maintenance floor, I wondered whether this was more than a coincidence.'

Dawn stepped from the doorway, allowing the doors to close.

'Go on.'

'What if the maintenance floors were the way in? Could they be the edges of the maze? If so, could they then be the way we get out again?'

The first set of doors in the corridor swung aside automatically. A further pair lay ahead, leading to the oval-shaped lobby.

'Yeah, but all the stairwell doors were locked on my floor, the same as yours. The elevator seemed the only way out.'

'But the doors must open some of the time,' said Anya. 'Otherwise we would not be here.'

'Fair point. I guess it's worth a try while we're there. Where do you want to begin?'

'The lobby,' said Anya. She winced and shuffled her satchel round as if something was jabbing her. 'We can call five elevators at once until we get something maintenance-looking.'

'Yeah, well we don't want your soldier friend coming back. You take the left two and I'll take the right. Leave the one in the middle jammed.'

'Okay... ouch!'

Anya stopped and lifted the flap of her satchel. She pulled out the bayonet attachment for a better look inside, holding the ridged flat of the blade between finger and thumb. A bright spark lashed out from the knife and up into the air, making her jump. She dropped the knife, sending it clattering against the vinyl floor. It slid to a stop and erupted into a fountain of sparks.

Dawn felt the skin on her arms prickle and her itchy scalp tighten. She watched the loose tresses from Anya's ponytail stand out like antennae. The metallic threat of thunderstorms flooded her nostrils and she instantly knew they were in trouble.

The swing doors ahead crackled with energy. Tiny white sparks leapt between the metal push panels, eager to find fresh hosts. A lethal yet delicate lightshow played across the hinges and opening mechanisms, and the doors parted.

The elevator lobby was alive with scalding tendrils of electricity, each emanating from a small ball of light hanging in midair. The brilliant-white bursts of energy snaked their way across the floor, searching for a means of escape, eventually zapping up towards the strip lights and sending sparks down into the lobby. A menacing crackling sound spilled through the corridor.

Beyond the stormy chaos there was a man wearing a soldier's uniform and a brown bandana-cum-eyepatch. He stood some feet behind a long bayonet blade that also rested and sparked onto the floor. He wore the same confused expression as that slapped across Anya's face.

'Shit!' said Dawn, struggling to make herself heard. 'There must have been another way here that wasn't on their map.'

'No,' Anya yelled. 'He is younger. Look at his arm!'

The sleeve of the soldier's uniform was pinned to the shoulder, though here the man clearly had more remaining of his arm above the elbow than before. He attempted to fetch the long blade from the floor but quickly pulled away. He shook his hand as if the metal had been white hot.

'Step away from the knife!' said Dawn.

She frantically waved for the man to move, which attracted a small spark from the bayonet blade nearest her. She jumped back and swore in shock, then felt the engagement ring on her hand. The metal was uncomfortably warm. She twisted the ring from her finger and handed it to Anya.

'What are you doing?' said the girl. She slid the ring into a side pocket of the satchel.

'He doesn't think we mean business,' said Dawn. She pulled the parang from its sheath. 'I'm going to show him otherwise.'

She turned to face the lobby again, blade outstretched. It felt heavy, but thankfully no longer a ton weight.

'I said... whoa!'

A single lick of lightning leapt from the bayonet blade and into the hunting knife, zigging and zagging in the air, buzzing and crackling between the two weapons. Instant motivation, if such were needed, for her to keep the parang outstretched. The spectacle would have been beautiful had it not also been deadly.

Dawn composed herself and took a firmer grip of the parang.

'Move away from the knife!' Dawn called to the soldier. 'Do it!'
'He does not speak English,' said Anya.
'Well you fucking tell him then!'
'Otoyti ot nozha!' Anya yelled.

The soldier did no such thing, preferring instead to make another attempt to retrieve his blade, and receiving a painful jolt of electricity for his trouble.

'I get it. It's to do with these knives on the floor, isn't it? They're the same. The *exact* same. It's like when I saw myself, a future me.'

She looked towards the soldier. Both he and the bayonet blade were a short distance from the second elevator.

Close to the void.

'Okay, I've got an idea.'

She looked at the soldier's blade and its double, sparking before her. She shuffled herself slowly around the blade, taking the flow of energy into the parang. She heard an old physics teacher barking instructions in her ear: do this, make sure you don't do that. If only she could remember what "this" and "that" were. Did her shoes have to have rubber soles? Would the parang's handle protect her?

Well, I'm still standing, so I must be doing something right.

Further bolts of electricity shot into the parang blade from each of the swing doors ahead. She edged closer to the doors, arms still outstretched, eventually severing ties with the bayonet blade and leaving it to sputter and spark alone on the floor.

The plasma ball in the lobby continued to crackle and buzz and lash forks of lightning about the place. Some briefly met the hunting knife and then leaped into the strip lights. Cold sparks fell around Dawn as she inched into the large, open space.

The soldier edged away from his weapon as Dawn approached.

'Yeah, you'd better move, shithead,' she said. She kept her focus on him, and held the incredible display of light and energy in her peripheral vision. 'Keep going.'

The parang began to wobble in her hands. Her newfound strength was fading fast. A solid bolt of lightning leapt from the soldier's bayonet blade and into the hunting knife.

Holy shit, this had better work.

The soldier backed into the middle elevator, almost tripping over the metal bar that jutted out from within.

Dawn watched in horror as the man opened the door, jumped inside the elevator and summarily hoofed the metal bar into the lobby. It clattered and clanged over the floor and was immediately struck with fronds of fizzing, white energy.

The elevator door started to close again.

'No you don't!'

She crouched down within arm's length of the soldier's bayonet blade. She could no longer look at the parang. The intensity of the lightning it attracted proved too strong.

Wait a minute.

My belt has got a metal buckle. The sheath has a metal ring.

Fuck.

She dragged the parang across the floor and flicked the bayonet blade towards the gap. It slid and spun over the vinyl, leaving scorch marks in its wake. It struck the edge of the elevator car and teetered agonisingly over the lip of the floor.

She waited for the electricity to find her, to blow her clean across the room. The grey plastic handle felt as if it would melt with the heat of the parang's metal blade.

She watched helplessly as the closing exterior door continued along its path. It sealed the cowering soldier into the elevator car and knocked against the handle of the bayonet, spinning it around once, twice and finally tipping it over the edge and into the void.

The door thunked shut, the elevator inside whirred into life and the ball of energy abruptly disappeared. A number of strip lights flickered back into life. Dawn's hair eased down into place, released from its electrical grip. The intense smell of thunderstorms was immediately replaced with an acrid smell of burning. The metal blade of the parang hissed and smoked.

Dawn hopped over the long, knife-shaped burn mark seared into the vinyl floor. She danced over the fresh scorch marks that lacerated the lobby and returned to Anya.

'That was brilliant!' said the girl, even breaking into applause.

'Yeah, well. The idea just came to me.'

She glanced at the unblemished ground near Anya's feet. The bayonet blade had disappeared.

CHAPTER TWENTY-NINE

Dawn grabbed the metal bar from the lobby floor and felt its pleasing warmth spread into her hands. She approached the middle elevator, holding the bar like a riding crop.

Anya pushed the call button for her. Seconds later the elevator door rumbled aside releasing the upbeat twangs of an Indi-pop tune into the lobby and unveiling the welcome sight of a clean interior. The decorative handrails and opulent panelling inside were a perfect match for the unusual gold foil wrapped around the exterior.

Dawn placed the metal bar onto the threshold and allowed the door to crunch against it. She briefly wondered if the soldier would meet his older self, and cursed him for jumping ship with the few metal bars they had.

'Okay, you take the two elevators on the right,' she said. 'I'll take care of these ones here. The first one to get a service lift wins.'

'Count the number of elevators, please,' said Anya. 'It will help my map.'

'Yeah, I've been thinking about that.' She pressed both her call buttons and waited for the doors to open. 'Your map keeps track of how many elevators service a particular door, yeah?'

'Yes.'

'But we've jammed open this one in the middle.'

Anya nodded. She glanced in through each of the elevator doors on her side of the lobby, coming away dissatisfied.

'We've seen others do the same thing,' said Dawn. 'Oh, yuck!'

A heavily-graffitied elevator which someone had used as a latrine arrived in the first door. In the second, an elevator from an investment bank - judging by the Bloomberg TV channel playing inside. She held in the call buttons until they were gone.

'So, yeah, we've jammed this one in the middle. What's to say I'm going to find all the elevators that come to these doors? One could be stuck somewhere, like this one. Doesn't that mean your map is incomplete?'

'Probably, yes,' said Anya. 'But I have only seen a tiny amount of this place. I hope to find an exit long before we run out of elevators to explore.'

'Knowing my luck, Anya, we've probably already walked past it.'

Another two elevators arrived, both duds. She held in the call buttons to send them away and then staggered backwards, unbalanced. It felt like someone had given her a shove. There were agonised noises of concrete cracking and splitting, and the lobby shook from side to side.

Dawn fell to the floor, jarring her wrist. She watched, helpless and horrified, as Anya toppled over and all the overhead lights cut out.

The lobby was immediately plunged into darkness save for a thin strip of warm light spilling from the open Indi-pop elevator. The light wobbled as the elevator car bobbed around in the oversized shaft, but the metal bar jamming open the door seemed to hold.

The worst of the violence soon eased yet the vibrations did not fully stop. A throbbing sensation rippled across the vinyl floor, rattling her bones. The vibrations were in perfect synch with the heart-stopping racket of clanking and banging and grinding that sounded all around her.

A harsh stink of stale piss still lingered in the air from the first elevator. Something hissed and fell from the low ceiling. Chunks of rubble clattered nearby on what sounded like hollow vinyl flooring. Something huge snapped a short distance away, so abrupt she almost wet herself. Perhaps it was a nearby plastic-covered wall. Perhaps it was the universe. She looked over her shoulder but saw only the swirling colours and patterns of light that swam across the backs of her eyes. Someone could have been readying a razor blade five yards away and she wouldn't have known. She felt her nyctophobia really take hold.

I can't see. I can't see shit!

Her heart rate cranked up another couple of gears and she gasped for air. She heard more hissing from somewhere, distinct from the dulling sounds of grinding concrete and tortured metal.

Sssssss...

The noise came from near the Indi-pop elevator, the only source of light in the room, the only thing she could focus on properly. She watched. And watched.

'So there you are,' she said amidst the clamour.

Four long, bony fingers slowly reached out from the thin strip of light and clamped onto the side of the elevator. The hissing continued.

Esssssssssssss...

I am not afraid of you! I am NOT afraid of you!

'Anya!' yelled Dawn. 'Anya, are you there? Are you okay?'

'Yes. I think so.' It sounded like she was getting to her feet. 'I am just a little shaken.'

The strip lights pinged back into life one by one, bathing the lobby in pale, precious light and stinging Dawn's eyes. Over at the Indi-pop elevator the four bony fingers had vanished.

Spindly inner demons were the least of Dawn's concerns. She found her side of the floor now lay noticeably lower than Anya's. She surveyed the subsidence that ran unhindered from the middle elevator all the way over to the set of swing doors opposite. The crack did not appear to be a fracture in reality, like on deck thirteen. No, this was structural damage, like the lobby was genuinely about to break in two.

She felt an aftershock through her buttocks and up her arms. She braced herself for the worst. Dust fell from the false ceiling and the strip lights flickered but the shaking soon eased again.

Her side of the lobby had lowered some more. The floor continued to vibrate and shudder beneath her. The clanging and clunking of God's own radiators dominated all other sounds around her. It was as if the whole place was unable to settle.

Dawn looked up and met Anya's eyes.

'We need to leave,' said the girl.

'You got that right.'

*****

'This door is spent,' said Dawn. 'Twenty-six elevators in total.'

'Okay.'

'Not that it matters - argh!'

She staggered away from the entrails and small bones that rested in the foot of the elevator. The remains were alive with maggots and flies and reeked worse than the seventh circle of hell. She held a hand to her face and eagerly called for another elevator.

'What happened?' said Anya.

'Guts. Bones. Flies. Maggots. You name it.'

'Oh. Guts too? Sorry, that may have been us,' said Anya. 'It took us some months before we found the ship. We used the elevators for anything we could not flush away in the toilets.' She said this as if she was commenting on the weather.

Dawn popped a couple of glucose tablets into her mouth to ease the taste of death. A little more energy in her muscles wouldn't go amiss either.

'Over here!' yelled Anya. She waved frantically at Dawn. 'I found one!'

'Great! I'm coming.'

She scooped up her plastic bag of goodies and leapt up onto Anya's half of the floor. She ran to the open elevator, relieved to be free of her slow descent into oblivion.

The exterior door rattled shut as she leapt in. The interior doors were little more than rusty retractable lattices that met in the middle. It took a number of attempts to drag the doors into place, as if they hadn't been moved in years. The doors squealed angrily with every inch.

A few greasy fingerprints dotted the buttons of the control panel but there were no handwritten codes anywhere. The same had been true of nearly all the elevators called in the hospital lobby. It made Dawn wonder how close Anya's gang had come to discovering the hospital and its pharmacy. How much of their suffering could have been avoided had they enjoyed a single slice of luck? Maybe Anya was right. Perhaps they were merely all mice in a maze, held captive and ridiculed by cowards unseen.

As the girl examined the controls Dawn felt a new fear taking root, a sickening sense she would someday turn into Anya or, despite her best efforts, Other Dawn. She imagined her humanity being peeled away in long strips, like layers of skin, revealing ever-bloodier depths of her flesh, reminding her of the food that lay beneath, and ultimately leaving in its wake a mind riven with hunger and bent solely on survival.

She looked down at the bag of goodies she had gathered, knowing they would be her last. She'll have wolfed them down within a month, and then she'd once more face the most extreme Atkins Diet imaginable. The thought terrified her to the core.

*****

The first three buttons yielded floors of a like they had already seen numerous times: an office, an apartment block, a hotel, but not a maintenance floor. Not yet. Twenty-two buttons remained, but Dawn doubted they had the will to survive them all.

Each time they had moved on they were forced to cover their ears and clamp shut their eyes, lest the harsh bursts of light from beyond blind them and the immense, throat-rattling buzzing noises destroy their eardrums. The cage-like interior doors offered scant protection from the coldness that flooded in from the pitch-black outdoors. Dawn looked out into the void as the elevator rattled towards the next floor.

I can end it all here. Other Dawn needn't happen. I could just open these doors and jump into the darkness. Let the night consume me.

But then the service elevator started trembling. It soon developed into a steady shake, then a shuddering earthquake. Dawn and Anya fell to the floor to ride it out. The violence felt different to that of the hospital lobby, more pronounced, more localised. It was as if someone was driving them down like a stake through the heart. Fountains of sparks gushed from the sides of the elevator car and out into the void. A thick vein of concrete and metal emerged from out of the darkness, rising up in fits and starts. Anguished squeals of metal on metal set Dawn's teeth on edge, then something snapped.

Dawn rolled away in time to see several jagged fingers of razor-sharp metal burst out from the wall and the floor as something huge, stony and unstoppable ripped its way into the elevator.

Everything came to an abrupt, lop-sided halt. Anya sat up and surveyed the wreckage. She looked like she had seen a ghost.

'That was not good,' she said eventually.

Dawn found her midriff inches from a ragged prong of grey steel, flecked with slivers of gold foil.

'Agreed.'

'At least we have no outer door to worry about.'

This much was true, though the dim light beyond the cage doors made it difficult to see any detail. All Dawn heard was a low, hissing sound set within slow, mechanical thuds.

Thick strata of concrete and metal separated a two-foot gap of maintenance floor at the bottom and a thin strip of black nothingness at the top. A chill descended on Dawn's shoulders and crept down her spine. Her short bursts of breath clouded and dissipated in midair.

The gentle chime of an alarm sounded nearby. She edged further away from the ruptured steel and towards the control panel. She pushed in one of the floor buttons, feeling a satisfying click, but nothing came of it. The panel, like the elevator, was dead.

'We're going to freeze to death if we stay in here,' said Dawn. 'Come on. Help me with these doors.'

*****

Only one of the cage doors would open, and only then by a couple of feet. Dawn knelt and surveyed the gap they had made. There was just enough room for her never-thinner physique. Anya would have to come through feet-first on her back.

Assuming she's really pregnant, of course.

I don't know. The way she blurted it out sounded accidental. It felt real. Maybe.

Dawn threw her bag of pills into the maintenance floor. She lay flat on her belly and popped her feet over the lip of the elevator. She eased herself through the gap, up past her knees, then took a deep breath and went for it. Her stupid, too-big skirt instantly rucked against the rim of the gap, gathered around her waist, and finally pulled itself inside-out as she pushed herself through.

She batted down her skirt and looked around for witnesses, finding none. Dim orange light glistened across the sweaty surfaces of nearby pipes, with nothing but darkness and shadows between them. She caught faint outlines of bulky rubble beneath the elevator where the walls of the shaft had collapsed, further evidence the whole place was falling to bits.

An orchestra of machines hissed and thudded beyond the pipes, out of sight.

Sssssssss.

Now was not the time to listen to the hissing, and yet she found herself drawn into its music. She gazed into the dark mess of pipes and air conditioning ducts. She found nothing but a faint whiff of paraffin in the air.

Anya dangled her satchel from the gap, providing a welcome distraction. Dawn took the bag and carefully placed on the ground.

Despite her best efforts Anya made an equally unladylike entrance to the maintenance floor. She showed off a pair of huge sensible knickers that sagged over her too-thin thighs. Her pregnancy resembled a pot belly, the like of which Dawn had seen fill a hundred and one charity adverts. She took hold of Anya's ankles, then slid her hands up the girl's barely-existent calves to take a firm hold of her bony knees.

'Jesus, your legs are hairy!' she said, unable to stop herself.

Anya delivered the rest of her body through the gap, regained her balance and quickly made herself presentable.

'Sorry,' said Dawn. She rubbed the back of her neck and bit her lip. 'That was a bit harsh.'

Anya retrieved her satchel and looped the strap over her head. 'Maybe I prefer them hairy. You have seen what happens when the men here find a pretty girl.'

Dawn had no response. The girl's words conjured deeply unwelcome recollections of Farkas grabbing her. She could hear his braying shit-for-brains laugh. It made her skin crawl.

She scrabbled for something to quell the memories: Anya calling her "pretty", for example. She hadn't been called that since she left junior school. It wasn't that she was ugly. She scrubbed up fairly well, but "pretty"? That was the kind of thing her Nan used to say. When not pissing her off with "babes" Mike would often call her "hot stuff", due in no small part to her fiery temper. Once they had sunk into comfortable coupledom, however, such compliments became more automatic than heartfelt.

And that only made her think of Mike, lying somewhere three years ago with bullet holes in his body. No, three years hadn't passed. Time had fucked up, that was all. She would get out of here and... and...

You keep believing that, girl.

She let out a long sigh and bent down for the goodie bag. As she stood again she cried out in pain and held her side. It felt as if someone had stabbed her in the hip.

Sssssssssss.

'What is it? Are you hurt?' said Anya.

'I'm fine,' said Dawn. 'It just stung there for a minute. I've probably taken too many of these tablets. I'll walk it off.' She beckoned Anya to follow. 'Let's find the stairwells in this place. It's not as if we have much of a choice now the elevator's buggered.'

Dawn's eyes attuned themselves to the low orange light, lifting the gloom in the near distance and revealing a number of doors along the wall from the elevator: two storage cupboards away to the left, then the door and window of a caretaker's office. After that things became fuzzy. A dense tangle of pipes ran parallel to the wall, forming a wide corridor of sorts. A short gap in the pipes lay ahead, a corner into another pipe-lined passageway.

She found the corner of the maintenance floor close by the elevator, away to the right. The number thirteen had been whitewashed onto the breezeblock wall like an afterthought.

She walked closer to the pipes. She set herself on tiptoes, unable to peer over the top. She looked in the gaps but found only more pipes. She turned to face Anya.

'Ouch!' She lifted the sheath away from her hip, feeling she had been stabbed again. She fixed it with an accusing glare.

Sssssssssss.

'The knife,' said Anya. 'Oh, no!'

Dawn took a tight grip on the handle. She yanked the parang fully from its sheath in one smooth motion. The blade swung close to the pipes. A small, bright flicker of lightning leapt out from the knife, crackled, then disappeared into the dark.

Like the bayonet blades.

They too had sparked, only in the hospital lobby she had found both weapons to be one and the same thing, a paradox lying yards apart, bringing electrical chaos to all between them.

Sssssssssss.

She remembered the same frenzied ganglion of energy ripping through the hotel corridor as she and Joe had fled its fury. She knew now that the screaming man had not come to harm them. He'd come to end his life and that of his other self trapped in the hotel room.

Esssssssssss.

And, of course, she remembered the lightshow that erupted between herself and that nightmarish vision of her future. She knew now the terrible cause of Other Dawn's vanishing. It wasn't due to material things like a change of clothes. No. Someone had simply *prevented* Other Dawn. Whether it was Dawn herself, or Anya, or any one of her fruit-loop cannibal friends, someone had ended her life before Other Dawn happened.

And that meant she was going to die in the maze.

Esssssssss.

She felt faint as her overwrought mind tangled itself into ever tighter knots.

She was going to die here.

Esssssssss.

A shot of adrenaline hit her bloodstream.

She was never going to escape.

Esssssssss.

Her frenzied heartbeat pounded hard against her ear drums. This shithole was her prison for the rest of her life.

Her tomb.

Esssssssss.

She staggered nearer the pipes, feeling nauseous, light-headed.

Another large spark crackled from the large hunting knife and leapt into the metal pipes at her side. She came to a full and terrible understanding of what was happening. The parang sparked and sputtered in the exact same way as the bayonet blades. That meant her knife existed elsewhere. Somewhere close.

And that meant...

[Yesssssssss!]

'Ow! Fuck!' A man's voice. Angry. It came from somewhere in the middle of the floor, in the network of pipes. 'Fucking static!'

'Oh, no!' said Dawn. It came out as a whimper.

The voice that boomed around the floor was one she had long dreaded hearing again; a voice that came from someone she had left for dead; someone she had dared not dwell on lest she conjure him into being again. The moment Anya spoke of meeting people out of order Dawn knew that her nightmare, embodied by The King Of The Castle, the man now standing in the middle, would never end until she was dead. Murdered. Eaten.

'I can fucking hear you!' yelled Clive.

CHAPTER THIRTY

'If you come out quietly I'll make it easier for you. I'll only cut off what I need and then I'll let you go.' Clive dissolved into the giggles of a maniac. A bright flash and a sparking sound sent him into another vitriolic tirade.

Dawn's heart hammered against her ribcage, demanding freedom. She breathed lightly through her mouth as steady as she could, convinced that the slightest noise would give her away. Suddenly keeping a plastic bag of pills seemed like the worst idea in the world. She may as well have had a bell around her neck.

Clive had fallen silent.

Anya readied her scalpel. Both she and Dawn knelt facing each other by the pipes. Anya kept her head bowed to the concrete floor, motionless. For a moment it seemed the girl had shut down. Only the steady pulse in her stringy neck suggested otherwise. But then her eyes flicked up and met Dawn's. Her face was the same cold mask she wore moments before she'd slaughtered Milos. In the gloom the girl's eyes were large, black pits, utterly devoid of emotion.

Dawn looked away but kept Anya's scalpel in sight.

Footsteps sounded in the beyond. The hairs on Dawn's arms lifted. The growing smell of electricity in the air told her everything she needed to know. With a brilliant blue flash, a huge spark bridged the gap between the hunting knife and the pipes.

'Ha! Gotcha!' said Clive. Boot soles scraped against rough concrete. A silvery light developed somewhere above the maze of pipes. It crackled and spat bolts of energy into anything that would receive it. The parangs were closing in on each other.

'Shit!' said Dawn.

A series of large sparks commingled to form a near constant flow of energy between her knife and the pipes nearby. Clive was nearly on top of them.

Dawn and Anya leapt to their feet and gunned it towards the corner of the floor. The harsh *shikka-shikka* of Dawn's pill bottles echoed about the place, keeping beat with the *clip-clopping* of her shoes. She had to get away from that lightning ball. Its very existence threatened the few chances they had of escaping the maintenance floor unnoticed.

They rounded the corner. A long, silvery air-conditioning duct dominated the right-hand side. A further tangle of pipes ran along the left for around twenty yards, then broke for a junction offering left or straight on into darkness.

'DAWN?' yelled Clive.

His voice pinballed throughout the maintenance floor, stopping her a few yards short of the junction. She held the hunting knife close to the pipes and away from her body. It crackled and fizzed and spat sparks onto the floor. She felt the warmth of its energy through the handle.

Anya slowed to a halt close behind her. The girl placed a hand over her belly and winced. She gave a thumbs-up as if to ease Dawn's concerns, an unconvincing show.

'I know it's you, Dawn,' said Clive. 'Oh, I'd know that bitch voice of yours anywhere.' A pause. 'It's not often you hear these Ruskie fuckers say "shit", you know?'

Dawn gasped for breath. She resisted the temptation to lean on something. It seemed too dangerous. She felt her energy draining away, tiredness creeping into her arms and legs. She craved another glucose tablet.

She cast her eyes to the plasma ball that floated in the space between her and Clive. It lashed at the mess of pipes beneath it, again and again, with whip-like cracks of energy. Its position suggested Clive was standing at a similar junction around the corner, yards from where they had just fled. He too was probably keeping his knife, the same knife, close to something metal, discharging it, just as she was. A small spark leapt between a pair of horizontal pipes to Dawn's left.

The metalwork of the whole corner was alive with electricity.

'It's funny, I've just been having a nice chat with you through the elevator,' Clive called out. 'You sounded pretty good for a dead girl.'

Don't rise to the bait, Dawn.

'Did you hear me, you stuck-up bitch?' Clive hollered. 'I said you're dead, and the best thing is I get to kill you again!'

What?

She nearly collapsed against the pipes with shock. Clive had *killed* her? What the hell did *that* mean? Her mind blazed with this new information.

She thought back to Other Dawn, her nightmarish future self, and how someone had prevented her from existing. From the sound of it, the culprit was standing around the corner.

I get to kill you again.

Perhaps her imminent death here in the maintenance floor had caused Other Dawn to vanish. But that didn't quite fit. Other Dawn had vanished before Dawn's very eyes. No, some other *intermediate* Dawn must have died instead; a future self between her and Other Dawn.

Her mind raced further back and hit on the moment she left Other Clive for dead.

Clive kills a future me, I kill a future Clive, and back we go killing each other through time. Jesus, is that *what this place is for? Some kind of arena?*

She sensed a deadly game of temporal tit-for-tat developing, one that would end only when one's future caught up with them.

So maybe this is my time after all.

She felt a cold sensation slowly run from the base of her skull, across her shoulders and down her spine. Her buttocks clenched without invitation.

'I bet you want to know what happened, don't you?' said Clive. 'Rest assured I made you suffer, my sweet little bitch, and when you were dead I made you suffer some more. When I catch hold of you, I'll show you *exactly* how.'

'Fuck you, Clive!' Dawn screamed. She stepped into the junction and looked left, deeper into the maintenance floor. The coast was clear all the way till the darkness set in. The pipeworks formed a crossroad in the middle, just ahead of the dark. She returned her sights to the ball of energy. It had barely moved. She waved for Anya to follow.

A harsh crackling sound raked through the air, immediately followed by a clanging that rang throughout the pipes.

'Ha, so it *is* you, Dawn!' said Clive. 'Oh, we're going to have a lot of fun, you and me. Lotta fun. So much the better with you alive, anyway. And do you know what? I reckon this here knife is hot enough to cauterise the bits I cut off of you while I'm at it.'

'I'm not afraid of you, you sick fuck!' Dawn checked the fizzing orb above them. It still hadn't moved. 'Look at all the sparks flying about the place. It's the knives, dickhead. You can't use your knife any more than I can use mine.'

She caught movement in the corner of her eye. She glanced to the crossroad and saw a dark shape emerge from the corner. There were no bony fingers this time. Nothing that was make-believe. Instead she saw a beard, a pair of gleefully insane eyes and a black overcoat.

'Yeah,' said Clive. He pulled a huge handgun from his coat. 'I know.'

Dawn dropped her bag and grabbed Anya's arm. She pulled the girl into the corridor of pipes, away from the junction, away from Clive.

The savage roar of gunfire boomed around the maintenance floor. Pockets of dust flew up from the concrete. Bullets thunked into the air conditioning duct and sparked and ricocheted wildly against the thick metal pipes, and then all fell silent again.

Dawn felt Anya slip from her grasp. She looked back and saw the girl's face twisted in agony. The girl then collapsed onto the floor, grabbing her leg just below her knee. Blood trickled out from between her fingers.

'No!' said Dawn, but she knew she could not stay to help. 'Oh, God, I'm sorry, Anya!'

She turned and ran deeper into the pipework corridor and a darker patch of the maintenance floor, clattering into a wall of metal. She bounced back and looked at the hunting knife. It popped and sizzled but no longer sparked. She had reached a safe distance from its twin. She heard movement behind her and turned to meet it.

Clive stood over Anya in the light of the junction. He slowly drew his handgun level with the girl's head. He glanced along the corridor towards Dawn. The play of light and shadow against his face turned his shit-eating grin into something hairy and demonic.

The girl covered her eyes behind bloody hands and began to weep. She knew her time had finally come. The scalpel she once carried lay yards away, useless.

Clive dug the hot barrel of the pistol into Anya's brow, causing her to cry out. He stepped back, took a surer aim and squeezed the trigger.

Click!

'You stupid Ruskie bitch,' said Clive. He pulled the weapon away. 'Didn't you hear it run out of bullets?' With that he pulled away the gun and threw it hard into Anya's breastbone. An awful hollow sound rolled up the corridor that Dawn felt deep in her lungs. The gun bounced and spun away under the pipes. Anya cried out in agony and fell onto her side, clutching her chest, struggling to breathe. She coughed and cried openly onto the concrete floor.

Dawn thought back to deck thirteen and felt an immediate rush of guilt for not being able to help. The girl had single-handedly slain two men with nothing more than some quick moves and a scalpel, and what had Dawn done in return? She had gotten the girl shot.

Fucking Clive.

She took a firmer hold of the parang handle and felt her anger bubble like lava deep in her belly. It was a fury she had not felt in a while. It pumped white-hot jet fuel into her withering muscles.

The fucker no longer had his knife, and his gun was spent. It was time for her to kill him again.

But Clive dashed from the junction before she could act.

'Shit!'

She glanced to her right. The metal pipes she had barrelled into ran from floor to ceiling, and not along the wall. She saw another thirteen splashed onto the breezeblocks and then, a short distance ahead, the faint outline of a large doorway.

Yes!

Anya stopped crying and struggled to sit upright. She coughed and winced and held a hand to her chest. She shook away the shoulder strap of her satchel and tried again to stem the flow of blood from her leg.

Dawn set the hunting knife on the floor, close to the metal pipes of the corner. She made for the girl, grabbed her under the armpits and whispered close to her ear.

'There's another elevator here. Come on, we need to move!'

Anya placed the satchel alongside her bleeding leg. She looped the shoulder strap a few times in her hand and nodded.

Dawn hauled her further into the corridor of pipes. The girl was a two-ton weight in Dawn's arms, no matter how skinny she appeared. The exertion quickly burned through Dawn's strength.

She looked to the junction and the plastic bag of drugs she had dropped. What she would give for a Glucozeal now. Then she noticed the sizeable pool of blood and the glistening unbroken trail of dark red that led from it.

Anya cried out and made a grab for her leg.

Clang! Clang! Clang! Clang! Scrrrrraaaaape!

Dead ahead, in the gloom of the corner opposite, Dawn saw him emerge.

Clive held the tip of the hunting knife against a nearby unpainted pipe. He let the blade spark and grind over it as he walked towards the junction. He pointed towards Dawn and began to laugh.

'And where the fuck do you think you're going?' he said. He dragged the blade hard into the rusty metal, making it screech like fingernails down a blackboard. 'Put the stupid bitch down and let's get on with this.' He pulled the blade away in a squealing shower of sparks.

Another fizzing ball of energy formed in the junction as he neared. It zapped the air conditioning duct and the pipes around it.

'Keep moving towards the elevator,' Dawn whispered. 'I'll try to get rid of him.'

Anya nodded. 'Okay. Take care.'

Sparks now sputtered from the blade of the parang by Dawn's feet. She picked it up and held the metal away from her body. She could feel her hair rising again. She looked towards Clive, who stood fully in the junction. The ball of energy above them had intensified. It swirled above the pool of Anya's blood. Any further into the corridor and Anya could attract a stray lick of electricity.

Dawn ran into the dark corridor, past the elevator doors on her right, keeping close to the ranks of pipes to her left.

She heard the soles of Clive's boots grind into the concrete, followed by the sound of quick, hard footfalls from the other side of the pipes.

Between them the swirl of lightning hissed and leapt between the rows of pipes like they were stepping stones.

'Catching you up!' Clive cried, and cackled.

Dawn kept the knife to her left. The sparks from the blade quickly intensified into zigzags of crackling, blinding light.

Clive was closing in on her and fast.

She skidded to a stop and looked to the ceiling for a clue. The ball of energy moved to the left, two ranks back. A fork of lightning slammed into a wall-mounted light behind her. A mass of blinding white sparks burst out onto the floor.

Clive was cutting in through the pipes.

'You're too fucking slow, bitch!'

And you're too fucking obvious.

She turned left at the next junction and sprinted towards the central channel of the maintenance floor. She found it nigh-on impossible to keep the sparking knife away from her body while running so hard.

But then she suddenly remembered her metal belt buckle, the metal ring in the sheath.

Shit.

An enormous pain ripped through her hip and she found herself flying into the clearing ahead. She landed on her side, rolled and flopped to the floor, dazed and facing the corridor of pipes.

Clive stood at the other end of the corridor. He scraped his glowing knife against the rusty metal surfaces, relishing the tortured noise it created.

Above them the blinding whorl of energy continued to strike the pipework along the sides of the corridor, feeding the metal with a million volts of power.

Dawn could barely move her leg. She saw the sparking hunting knife ahead of her. She reached for the handle and missed it by agonising inches.

'Lying down for me, eh?' said Clive. 'That's more like it. Now roll over.'

He walked into the corridor, adjusting himself, taking his time. He scraped the pipes with his white-hot blade with every step.

The plasma ball fizzed and sparked and grew in ferocity as the parangs neared each other.

'Maybe I should cut your hands off first, though,' said Clive. 'I mean, I can't have you fighting back, now, can I?'

He stepped up the pace. He viciously dragged the knife over the pipes, making the metal scream.

The mass of lightning grew, collapsed and instantly hit damn near anything it could. Lightning zigzagged from pipe to pipe and up to the metal supports in the ceiling. Light fittings exploded. The air thinned as the deadly lightshow robbed the area of precious oxygen. The temperature skyrocketed.

And still Clive came forward. He reached the central channel in which Dawn lay and looked down, grinning from ear to ear, as if he cared less of a fuck about anything.

Dawn reached again for her weapon. A crazy display of light and heat spun out from the blade. Licks of volcanic-hot energy tried to find a home. Her fingertips stroked the warm plastic handle and spun the weapon around a little. She felt some life return to her hip and made the most of it. She grabbed hold of the handle and drew the blade into the air the very second Clive brought its twin crashing down on top of her.

The two blades met with a brilliant flash of light and heat. The force of the blow immediately jarred the knife from Dawn's hand. Momentarily blinded, she pulled herself away and cradled her head from the blow that was surely to come.

Instead she heard Clive screaming.

She opened her eyes and let her vision adjust to the newfound gloom. The lightning had died in an instant. Above her Clive stood, his arms outstretched, his face contorted, his hands cut off at the wrists. But there was no blood, just impenetrable darkness, as if he simply ceased to exist beyond a certain point.

'Dawn!' he cried out. 'Fucking help me!'

She got to her knees and slowly stood. She looked about the floor for her knife. It was gone, as was Clive's.

A long gap of nothingness hung suspended in midair, just beneath Clive's lack of hands. Impossible hairline cracks cobwebbed from the parang-shaped hole. The ebony nothingness looked paper-thin, almost two dimensional. She felt it suck the warmth from the air. She leaned in closer and found the hole drawing her in. She struggled away from its grasp.

'Help me, for fuck's sake! I'm...argh!'

She looked up to Clive. An unseen force drew him closer. She watched as the black holes further ate away the ends of his arms. He now no longer existed below the elbows. She looked at the terror etched into his once-mad eyes and felt like ramming her thumbs into them. His yellow teeth were bared to the molars as his agony took full hold. Saliva frothed and flicked from the corners of his mouth. His breath came out in sharp bursts.

She walked around to Clive's side and saw where his hands had gone. Unseen to her from the other side there was another parang-shaped hole in the air into which Clive was fast disappearing.

The man's boots scraped uselessly against the concrete floor as he desperately tried to haul himself away from the hole. He howled, and then that howl became a shriek.

Dawn watched as a steady flow of blood splashed onto Clive's feet, coming from where his elbows used to be. It was as if his arms were too thick for the hole and his flesh was being scraped back along his bones. The hole drew him further inside, deeper and deeper, cracking his arms, popping his shoulders, sucking hard on his ribcage.

'AAARRRGH! HELP ME! HELP ME!'

Clive's ribcage gave way with a horrible ear-splitting crunch, his spine collapsed inwards and he fell silent. He ogled Dawn with dead rolled-up eyes. His body hung in midair, his feet left dangling as the hole continued to draw him in. The flow of his blood onto the floor quickened now with the slops of his insides, and yet Dawn could not withdraw from the sight. To her astonishment what she was witnessing felt *good*.

Within seconds Clive was gone, swallowed whole save for a repugnant pile of his guts that lay steaming beneath the parang-shaped hole.

A sharp bark of a hundred klaxons instantly rang out through the floor - startling, but not enough to cover the huge sound of tearing concrete that soon followed. The entire floor began to tremble. A couple of pipes nearby ruptured, shooting lethal jets of scalding steam into the corridors.

The parang-shaped hole floating in midair developed into an enormous horizontal crack that split everything from wall to wall. The whole world moved. Dawn struggled to keep her feet as the massive black crack in reality splintered and widened.

Then widened.

And widened some more.

CHAPTER THIRTY-ONE

A voice of immense gravity broke through the chorus of klaxons.

'*Vnimaniye! Vnimaniye!*'

Dawn ran for her life through the maze of pipes and ducts. Every step she took felt like it could be her last. A sudden jolt across the floor sent her crashing into the sides.

The voice resumed, this time in English.

'*Warning! Warning!*'

A jet of steam burst out into the aisle ahead of her, scorching the paintwork of the pipes opposite, and only missing her by inches. The scalding steam blocked the path to her bag of goodies lying dead ahead in the junction. She swore and veered to the left, then on towards the breezeblock wall.

The klaxons broke for another foreign announcement.

She slapped into the breezeblocks, looked left and saw the black yawning void quickly dissolve the very fabric of reality ahead of her, so large by now that it resembled less a crack and more an encroaching wall of night. The ranks of pipes each exploded upon contact with the void, shooting rivets and shrapnel through the floor that pinged off metal and bricks like bullets.

'*Structural integrity has been compromised!*'

The words were spoken with a thick Russian accent.

Dawn looked to her right and found Anya lying outside the large elevator. The girl struggled against its cage doors, but at least she was alive.

'Dawn! Help me!' she yelled, her voice enfeebled by the almighty racket of the alarms.

Dawn sprinted towards Anya, vaulted over the girl and slammed her hand into the mesh of the cage, using her momentum to wrench the doors apart. She skidded to a halt and turned. She looked above Anya and towards the black wall that now sped towards them, much too quick for her to fetch the bag of goodies. She slapped the breezeblock wall angrily and dashed into the elevator. Once inside she grabbed Anya by the armpits.

A rivet ricocheted against the cage door and off into the beyond. Dawn dropped the girl and fell back into the elevator. Anya cried out in pain and tried to grasp her wound. Dawn pulled Anya's arms back and dragged the girl over the threshold. She didn't bother slamming the cage doors shut. She stabbed at a random button on the elevator's control panel and let out a primal scream as the whole unit shook into life and began to rise.

'Yes! Yes! Yes!' she yelled, and slapped her palms against the inside of the elevator. '*Move!*'

An enormous sound of creaking, hissing and cracking erupted from the disintegrating floor beneath them.

'*Structural integrity has been-*'

The rest was lost to a huge buzzing noise and a blinding flash of light.

The klaxons continued.

*****

The elevator emerged onto a furnished open-plan floor. The desks were littered with typewriters, telex machines and green-screened computer terminals. It looked like the deserted newsroom of a 1980s tabloid.

Dawn looked out from the cage doors and rubbed the cold from her arms. Here too the klaxons rang out, tickling her eardrums.

Large, dusty windows bordered the floor, beyond them a deep blue sky and the hint of a bustling city far below.

'*Warning! Warning!*'

The voice boomed above the clamour of the alarms in both Russian and English, and was punctuated by distant sounds of metal being torn apart and shredded.

Sickly fluorescent strip lights hung from the ceiling on chains. They flickered and swayed as the floor beneath them gently rocked.

Furniture wobbled from side to side. The outside world, however, kept on ticking as if nothing had happened.

The warnings still sounded, and the ground felt shaky underfoot, but Dawn found no cracks in the floor, the walls or the air. She dragged Anya out onto the dusty, brown carpet.

'Where is your knife?' said the girl. She winced as she came to rest. She cupped the palm of her hand over the wound of her leg.

'It's gone the same route as Clive, my bag of pills and the rest of that maintenance floor. Gone. Swallowed up by... I don't know what it was.'

'What happened?'

'Remember those blades back at the hospital? That's what would have happened if they'd touched.'

'Structural integrity has been compromised!'

'That does not sound good.'

'Yeah,' said Dawn. She listened to the alarms as they continued to echo about the place. She knew, deep down, that the klaxons would be blaring across every single floor. 'I think I've broken their maze.'

'Good,' said Anya. 'Then at least we die taking this godless place with us.'

'Yeah, well, we're not done yet. Keep your hand on that wound. I'll be back in a minute.'

Dawn dashed into the body of the floor. She danced through the wooden-backed swivel chairs and heavy desks. She scanned the area for doors. The ones to the toilets she discounted, same for those to the stairwells. A solid, wooden door fronted a large office sectioned off completely by glass. She spotted another door set into the wall nearby and ran towards it.

The room beyond turned out to be a kitchen-cum-supplies area. She raided the cupboards above and below the washbasin and found each of them empty except for one that contained a white-painted metal box with a peeling red cross sticker on the lid.

It felt like the first bit of good luck she'd had in years.

She grabbed the box and ran back to where Anya sat. She wrenched opened the first aid kit and examined its contents. There were bandages, safety pins, paracetamol, fabric sticking plasters and little else. Life was clearly tougher in the 1980's.

'How's the leg?'

'Bleeding,' said Anya. 'The bullet passed through, I think.'

'Well, that's something,' said Dawn. 'We wouldn't have time to dig it out.'

She unwound a length of bandage and set to work.

*****

'I feel silly walking with this thing,' said Anya. She pushed the back of the wooden swivel chair ahead of her like a Zimmer frame. She dragged her heavily-bandaged leg along. She yelped with every other step. Spots of blood already showed on the white fabric.

'There's only me to see it,' said Dawn. 'We need to conserve our energy, remember? Now so more than ever.' She slid herself under Anya's left arm and helped prop her up. The girl winced. She felt her double over slightly. 'How's the baby?'

'*Warning! Warning!*'

The whole office floor shook with renewed violence, cutting short Anya's reply. There was an unsettling sensation of everything leaning to the left. Dawn looked and saw the outside world abruptly fizzle into darkness. No, not quite darkness. Beyond the glass windows along the left there were barely-noticeable discs of small, unlit blue bulbs, arranged in a honeycomb formation. In the windows opposite she could still see little white clouds floating in a baby-blue sky. It was as if someone had switched off the left side of the office.

One by one, from the far end, the windows cracked and burst inwards. The crashes of glass were drowned in the howl of the alarms and the bilingual warnings.

'*Structural integrity has been compromised!*'

The dirty brown carpet ripped in several places, revealing thick cracks in the concrete beneath. The plaster ceiling crumbled and spilt rubble onto the shaking desks. Tremors pulsed across the floor. The air pressure dipped as if someone had yanked open a huge door somewhere.

'*Warning! Warning!*'

The baby-blue sky in the windows to the right also fizzled away to an odd array of large discs, again filled with dim blue bulbs. A shower of sparks burst out from the array, hitting the glass and cascading down and out of sight.

The floor at the other end of the office buckled upwards, as if disturbed by a gigantic worm, sending chairs and desks and old computers flying left and right.

'Okay, this floor is officially a bust,' said Dawn. 'We need to find a quiet spot somewhere, anywhere, even if it means hanging off a ledge in downtown Beirut for a couple of hours. Get in the chair.'

Anya did as she was told. She placed the satchel at her side.

'Go to the stairs,' said the girl. 'We can work our way through many floors that way.'

'Warning! Warning!'

Dawn pushed Anya over to the heavy, black door and pulled it open. She found the doorway on the opposite side of the landing badly damaged. It was filled from top to bottom with large lumps of concrete rubble, jagged metal and deep darkness in the gaps between. Its broken black door lay across the downward flight of stairs. The landing was intact.

'This'll do,' said Dawn.

She kept the door open and pushed Anya through the way. The moment she crossed the threshold the office behind her shook as if a vanload of C4 had exploded outside. Canyons tore through the floor where only cracks once lay, swallowing desks whole. A crashing howl of tortured metal like the nearby mating call of a planet-sized whale bellowed over the mass of alarms. Dawn turned to find the far end of the office ripped clean away and dragged several yards to the left. When it came to rest she caught sight of another, entirely different, floor adjoining the right.

'Dawn! Close the door! We need to go!'

Dawn pulled on the door, willing it to close faster. An even louder smash rang throughout the office and then, finally, the door closed and all were klaxons and alarms once more.

'Structural integrity has been compromised!'

'Okay, let's find another floor,' said Dawn. She grabbed hold of the metal door handle and stood by the inner jamb. 'Stop me when you see a good one.'

She pushed out the heavy, black door onto a ragged island of charred blue carpet. For the most part there was very little else to the floor. Beyond the island, however, there lay a sight that took Dawn's breath away. It seemed as if a titanic axe had cleaved straight through not only the floor ahead but most of the floors above, below and beside it. In amongst the bent, ruined supports and sparking, mangled machinery she found slices of floors from various buildings: offices; hotels; apartment blocks; even something that looked like a car park. They were all neatly arranged like some intricate block puzzle. Some of the half-floors in the beyond were still lit. On one, Dawn could swear she saw someone running out of sight.

The temperature plummeted. Dawn found herself being sucked into the vacuum ahead as the air behind her decompressed and rushed out from the stairwell. Her ears popped and she instinctively squeezed her eyelids shut. With one hand on the frame and the other on the handle she desperately tried to drag the door back into place. She felt what feeble reserves she had remaining in her muscles drain rapidly as she inched the door closer to home. She could feel the closing mechanism fight with her, helping her, but it was not quite enough. She screamed and swore and hollered with every effort, but the door would come no closer.

Anya launched herself from the office chair and grabbed hold of the handle. She stood on her good leg and leaned back with what weight she could offer. At long last the door sealed shut. The girl collapsed back into the office chair and hissed with agony.

Dawn stood against the wall of the stairwell. The muscles in her arms quivered. She tried to rub some warmth back into her bones. She coughed and cried through chattering fits. Every single square inch of her body hurt as if boiled in tar. It felt like she had torn her biceps and triceps into pieces. Tears ran down her cheeks as she dared to open her eyes. Everything in the stairwell was blurry and swimmy. Her ears were agony. She dared to place a hand to her ear and then examined her fingers. To her intense relief there was no blood. Her vision cleared and she wiped away the thick of her tears. She saw Anya's lips moving, but it was as if the girl was taking through a pillow in the middle of a dubstep all-nighter.

'I can't hear you very well,' said Dawn, the bass of her voice swelling in her ears. She gestured to the racket that was going on all around them.

Anya exaggerated her speech so Dawn could lip-read what she was saying.

'Keep going!'

Keep going? *Keep going?* She knew Anya was probably right, but, there and then, and had she the strength in her arms, Dawn could have quite happily throttled the girl.

'*Wnnn-nng! Wnnn-nng!*'

'Okay', yelled Dawn. 'I'll open the door a crack, but you're going to have to help me if this place turns into a wind tunnel again.' It sounded like muffled nonsense as she spoke.

She saw Anya nod.

Dawn turned to face the door. Wearily, warily, she reached for the handle. The threat of hell that lay beyond sent slithering coils of dread across her insides. Her fingers stroked the freezing cold metal of the door handle, but then the whole thing was suddenly wrenched away from her grasp.

A blood-soaked man stood in the doorway.

CHAPTER THIRTY-TWO

Gregor held open the stairwell door. He breathed hard through his mouth. The frame of his glasses had lost its left lens. His beard suggested he had aged around a month since Dawn had last seen him. Blood dripped from a long strip of raw meat that he held in his other hand. It took a moment for the man to realise exactly who stood opposite him.

He gibbered something that was lost to both Dawn's pillow-hearing and the klaxons that continued to roar around them. His face soured. When he pointed the bloody lump of meat in her direction Dawn knew he was accusing her of something. The raw chunk jiggled and flapped and wobbled as he ranted, and flicked juices in all directions. A single droplet landed on the remaining lens of his glasses and ran down to the frame.

The man took a step forward but still held the door open. Above his hand Dawn caught a glimpse of a lengthy knife as it slipped against the edge of the stairwell door.

Her heart sank. She barely had the strength to reach for a door handle, let alone fend off another lunatic with a knife. The fight left every part of her save for her mind, which raged impotently at how weak she had become.

Gregor stopped shouting when he noticed Anya in the stairwell. She had gathered her satchel from the landing and held it next to her hip like a gun holster. He resumed his rant, only now towards the girl. He threw the chunk of meat in her direction. She managed to get her hand in the way before the thing could hit her in the belly. She let the meat drop into the folds of her skirt.

As he continued his tirade Anya examined the slimy, red flesh with pinched fingers and a distaste that Dawn didn't expect to see. Quite casually, the girl tossed it over the edge of the stairwell. When the meat dropped down from above, smacked off the handrail and landed at her feet she dissolved into madness-tinged giggles that quickly turned into tears.

It appeared that Anya's mind had finally given up. The girl's shoulders dropped. She placed a hand against her brow. She bit against her bottom lip and bawled her eyes out. This much Dawn could hear over the alarms.

Dawn returned her attention to Gregor, catching sight of the space behind him. It was unlike anything she had seen elsewhere in the maze. The floor was little more than a T-junction fully clad in highly-polished metal. At the opposite end, around twenty yards ahead, there stood another black door. A faint rectangular outline midway along the gleaming, blood-streaked wall on the left suggested a simple door to an elevator. A second, wider corridor opposite formed the T-junction. Thin, unbroken strips of light covered the joins between the walls and the ceiling. They bathed the corridor with pleasing, near-natural light. But every couple of seconds they turned red and lit everything the colour of oxygenated blood.

The heavily-mutilated body of a woman rested close to the elevator door. Her clothes lay beside her in a small pile. She had been stripped naked. Her flesh had been ripped open along all of her bony limbs, exposing the raw muscle underneath. Her skinny torso had been mercilessly destroyed by an incredible number of bullets. A thick streak of blood coated the floor from the body to the corner of the T-junction. The blood collected in a dark pool that surrounded the cadaver. Footprints of deep red led to Gregor.

The man swapped the knife into his free hand. It was a long bayonet blade attachment. Fresh blood dripped from the handle.

'Wuhn-nng! Wuhn-nng!'

'Oh, for God's sake!' said Dawn. 'How many of those things are there in here?'

Gregor did not reply. He gestured with the knife for both Dawn and Anya to leave the stairwell. With the doorway behind them blocked by heavy rubble, and with the flights of stairs only ever coming back to this landing, it seemed they had little other option. Dawn staggered around to the back of Anya's chair and pushed, but the castors would not budge.

She was spent.

The man said something and Anya slowly stood. She ducked under the strap of her satchel and let it rest against her right hip. She then placed her left arm over Dawn's shoulder and they hobbled into the corridor: Dawn on the left, Anya on the right. They helped each other along like a pair of wounded soldiers. Gregor let the stairwell door close and followed close behind them.

The intensity of the alarms increased in the confines of the corridor. The maddening clamour cruelly tickled the tender insides of Dawn's ears. The fact that her eardrums had not burst offered scant consolation.

As they approached the corpse Anya looked away and moaned. The body was that of the woman who had tended to Marika; the same woman who then killed her and claimed her body. The woman's face retained the expression of a death she saw coming and felt helpless to avoid, as if she had stepped in front of a speeding truck.

They slowly stepped around the pool of blood. Dawn looked down to the thick, gory streaks on the floor and felt nothing. Her mind had numbed to the sight of death and left her wondering if that was a good thing. She felt a small, stabbing sensation in her left arm. Gregor poked at her again with his knife. The pressure wasn't hard enough to break the skin, but enough to guide her and Anya away from the elevator door and towards the T-junction.

Around the corner they saw what had killed the woman.

'Wuhn-ing! Wuhn-ing!'

A pair of large, ceiling-mounted gun turrets jarred into life and quickly focused beams of thin red light their way. Dawn looked at Anya's chest and saw three red dots slide over the fabric of the girl's blouse. She glanced down and found similar lights trained on her heart.

The wide corridor stretched for some distance beyond the gun turrets. Cyrillic script had been stencilled onto the polished walls in large type, along with the numeral 7. At the end of the corridor there stood a single heavy-duty steel door, akin to that fronting a bank vault. To the right of it there was a large glass window in which Dawn could see the top of a chair's backrest. The chair had been left at a curious angle. The wall behind was a featureless white expanse. The lights in the room pulsed red in tandem with their cousins in the corridor.

A striped line of yellow and black, six inches thick, ran from the floor to the ceiling and back around again, creating an ominous marker in the corridor a few yards ahead. The trails of blood started a couple of feet beyond the line. There were no bullet holes or dents to be seen in the floor or the walls, a chilling clue to the turrets' accuracy.

Above the clamour of klaxons Dawn heard Gregor bark something behind her. Seconds later she felt the point of his blade dig into the right side of her ribs. It was a sensation she remembered from her nightmares and the surprise nearly caused her to drop Anya to the floor. She looked over the girl's arm to launch a volley of abuse Gregor's way and caught sight of a familiar looking pistol in the man's other hand.

She felt Gregor stab his blade into her side once more. He kept it there, pressing harder, until she realised he was trying to prise her from Anya. She released the girl and shuffled, exhausted, to the left side of the corridor. The girl hopped gingerly to the right.

Gregor barked something else. His words were short and repetitive. They sounded like a command of sorts. He jabbed Anya in the back until the girl relented and hopped closer to the yellow and black line.

'Your little decoy plan isn't going to work, dickhead,' said Dawn. 'I bet those guns will still cut you in two before you get to that door.'

Her outburst served only to attract sharp steel to her spine. She resisted the urge to scream, adamant to starve Gregor of the satisfaction. She felt something trickle down her back. Blood or sweat, she didn't know.

The man barked his orders again and forced them closer to the line.

'Wuhn-ing! Wuhn-ing!'

Dawn stared into the barrel of the gun turret. Its red laser beams still targeted her hammering heart. She breathed so hard she felt close to hyperventilating. She recalled the corpse from around the corner. An image of the woman flashed across Dawn's eyes, her chest utterly annihilated with a hundred or more perfectly targeted bullets. She cried out as Gregor jabbed her again in the back.

'*SÉTA!*' he commanded, again and again.

He pressed the tip of the blade into her flesh and this time he kept adding pressure. The pain quickly became too much. Dawn yelped and swore and stepped fully onto the line. She eyeballed the gun turret as a menacing whirring sound underpinned the chaotic noise that echoed all around her. She looked over to Anya and saw that the toes of her shoes rested an inch into the line. The girl winced as she received another stabbing from Gregor.

Dawn stepped back a little in the vain hope that Gregor would not notice. She felt the ground beneath her shake. She watched the gun turrets track her heart as she fought to keep her balance.

'*Structural integrity has been compromised.*'

Gregor shouted something to Dawn and pointed the gun at her. His face was a mask of pure hatred.

'*SÉTA! SÉTA! SÉTA!*'

A shot to the head, a knife in the back, a salvo of gunfire to the chest, or being swallowed up by the ground and cast into the freezing cold darkness: what a choice. Dawn held up her hands in surrender and stepped back onto the line. She returned her attention to the gun turret, listened as it whirred into life again, and weighed up which would be the quicker death.

Her attention was drawn to a flash of white in the corner of her eye. She turned just in time to see Anya pinwheel around and slash Gregor's throat in a single and beautifully fluid motion. The man dropped the gun and the knife to the floor and clutched at the deep wound rent across his neck. Blood gushed out from beneath his hands. It surged in eager squirts and bubbled and ran from the sides of his mouth. His eyes looked ready to pop out from their sockets. He gawped at the scalpel that Anya held in her right hand.

Anya didn't stop there. She hopped forward and continued to attack Gregor's hands and face. She sliced him open in countless places, fuelled by a long-standing, growing hatred of the man, a hatred that clearly dominated any pain she felt. She dislodged his spectacles and went for his eyes. His savaged hands were no match for her fury. As the girl stabbed and stabbed and stabbed again he tried to scream but only hot blood came streaming from his mouth.

And he stumbled blindly towards the line.

Anya let him go and collapsed against the polished wall of the corridor. She kicked out a foot and shuffled herself back along the metal floor.

Dawn turned and fled the scene as fast as she could. The whole place shook once more and then the ear-splitting roar of heavy gunfire boomed around the corridor. She fell to the floor and looked back towards to the carnage. For several seconds, each seeming as long as an hour, she watched Gregor's body dance as a constant barrage of bullets exploded on impact and tore his chest to pieces. His arms flailed uselessly at his sides as wave upon wave of gunfire pushed him back. Eventually his knees gave way and he collapsed into a devastated heap on the yellow and black line.

The gun turrets spun down and refocused their lasers on Dawn and Anya. Smoke spilled from their red hot barrels and up into the polished ceiling. The lights in the corridor continued to pulse red. The alarms continued to ring out and echo around the metal interior. The floor continued to tremble.

'Warning! Warning!'

Anya lay crying in a trail of blood a yard safe of the line. Her scalpel lay nearby. She looked at her quivering hands. Her whole body shook as if she was overdosing on adrenaline.

Another earthquake hit the ground. The sound of agonised metal bled through the endless klaxon call. The pile of meat that had once been Gregor wobbled horribly on the yellow and black line. A noticeable bend formed in the corridor beyond the smoking gun turrets.

'Structural integrity has been compromised!'

'Anya! Anya, come on, we have to run!'

The enormous sound of an old collapsing steelworks rang throughout the corridor. The room at the end shifted another couple of feet to the left. Dawn picked up the gun and realised she had no idea how to tell whether it was loaded. She pointed to the window of the room and pulled the trigger.

Click!

'Fucker!'

She threw the useless weapon into Gregor's carcass and crawled over to where Anya lay, caring nothing for the blood trails she disturbed. She shook the girl by the shoulders.

'Anya! Move it!'

Finally she had her attention. The girl nodded, surprised by the sudden bend that had developed in the corridor. She picked up her scalpel and let Dawn help her stand. Dawn pointed to the heavily bloodstained satchel on the floor but the girl shook her head.

'What use is it now?'

'There is something,' said Dawn.

She knelt by the satchel and opened it, then retrieved her engagement ring from inside. She slid the ring into place and quickly wiped the bloody fingerprints from the white gold. She willed for it to give her strength in this most dire of hours.

Anya pointed to the bayonet blade that lay nearby.

Dawn nodded. She let the girl continue along the blood-streaked wall, picked up the blade and rammed it hard into one of Gregor's eye sockets. She left the knife jutting out from his skull, satisfied with her wasteful act and glad to leave the cursed weapon behind, before helping Anya to the silvery door ahead.

They hit the call button. A panel slid away smoothly, revealing an elevator like neither had ever seen before. It was huge.

CHAPTER THIRTY-THREE

The door slid into place behind them, cutting short the ruthless sound of klaxons from the corridor. A quieter alarm emanated from the ceiling, still warning of structural collapse in Russian and English. Everything inside pulsed in various shades of red.

The capacious interior was clad with handsome polished metal in a similar fashion to the T-junction outside. The elevator could easily accommodate fifty people, and would have been too large to fit through even the most generous of shafts. And yet its size was far from its most unusual feature. There was a hundred-inch touchscreen panel mounted into the wall ahead.

An immensely-detailed metal globe dominated the display, slowly rotating around a central axis. Red lightning forks of various thicknesses flickered and grew across its surface, superimposed onto the image through a secondary membrane of the screen. A small number of noticeable nodules stuck out from the metal planet like spikes on a mine.

A red dot flashed upon one of the nodules. Tendrils of red crept towards it from all sides.

The text across the top of the screen alternated between two words, one of which ominously clear.

EVACUATE!

'I guess this is some kind of master elevator,' said Dawn.

She stroked the screen and watched as the globe gently spun to her touch. She tapped the glassy surface to stop it, then placed the tips of her thumb and forefinger to the screen and drew them apart. The view zoomed in on an intricate mesh of differently sized metallic blocks, like the surface of some immense 3D jigsaw puzzle.

'You know how this television works?' said Anya, her eyes never leaving the screen.

'Ish,' said Dawn. 'Let's just say I've seen this kind of thing before.'

She dragged her thumb and forefinger further apart, zooming in some more. Panels of text and images popped up on the screen. The panels each floated above a single block, and contained dates, locations, brief descriptions, statuses too. Some of the statuses flashed in urgent red text.

INOPERABLE.

'Now this is what I call a map,' said Dawn. She looked to Anya. 'Did you bring a metal bar?'

Anya shook her head.

'Pity. Do you reckon that knife back there will do the trick?'

'I do not think it would be long enough to keep the door open.'

She pinched her fingers until the metal globe had zoomed out into full view again.

The elevator car rocked from side to side. One of the flickering red fractures on the screen had reached the flashing red dot.

'*Structural integrity has been compromised!*'

EVACUATE!

'Seems a moot point, anyway.'

Anya touched the screen and dragged the metal globe around with her fingertip.

'The flashing dot is us?'

'Probably.'

'And the spikes are the exits.'

'I guess.'

'Then we must try them all,' said Anya. 'Some of them may not have guns in the ceiling.'

'I doubt it,' said Dawn. 'But it's as good a plan as any. Pick somewhere that isn't falling to bits so we have a fighting chance.'

Anya slid the metal globe around but found nowhere offering respite from the collapsing structure. The surface was spider-webbed with red fractures. It made the thing look like a newly-formed planet.

The elevator car shook once more. A dull sound of tortured metal seeped in from the outside.

Dawn batted away Anya's hand and zoomed in on one of the nodules. Its panel popped up on the screen covered in writing that made no sense. It looked like "BbIXOA 13", whatever that meant. The text faded smoothly into English.

EXIT 13.

A red haze quickly descended over the display like a diaphanous curtain and Dawn found that the screen no longer responded to her touch. She jabbed her finger at the panel, slapped its glassy surface and finally screamed at it. The thing had locked up.

Stepping back she saw some words flash across the top of the screen, first in Russian, then in English.

OVERRIDE.

The metal globe on the screen zoomed out fully, rolled to an altogether different location and zoomed back in. One of the panels hovering over the surface lit up a pleasing shade of green and the elevator shook into life.

The familiar enormous buzzing sound filled the elevator. Dawn looked anxiously towards their apparent destination on the surface of the globe. It looked perilously close to a long red fissure at least ten floors thick.

*****

The single interior door slid aside to reveal a vast office floor, empty of furniture but featuring a number of slim pillars. The chaotic yammering of a million alarms flooded into the elevator from outside. The large windows of the office floor ahead were all blacked out, as if a starless night had descended outside. Around half of the strip lights above had shorted and a good many tiles had been knocked from the ceiling. They littered an uneven floor of bare concrete that had split and ruptured in several places. Metal rods curled out from the wounds like razor-sharp fragments of bone. The fallen ceiling tiles juddered and slipped across the floor. The place looked ready to collapse in on itself at any second.

She jabbed at the large touchscreen to no avail. The word "OVERRIDE" continued to flash at the top of the display. The elevator door refused to close. For all intents and purposes this was the end of the line. The interior of the car shook independently of the floor outside, as if the elevator was floating on water.

'Fuck it!' Dawn screamed and punched the screen. 'Who are you?' She continued yelling at the corners of the ceiling. 'Who the fuck are you? Show me! We've broken your little maze, now let us out of here!'

But there was nothing except for harsh alarm bells and klaxons. The large touchscreen in the elevator remained static.

'Please!'

'Do not give into them,' said Anya. She placed a comforting hand on Dawn's shoulder. 'We must continue to fight. We are winning.'

'I struggle to call this winning,' said Dawn.

She tore the useless parang sheath from her belt and tossed it into the corner of the elevator car, then wearily helped Anya out into the office floor.

The place turned out to be even bigger than she first imagined. The large central column of the floor played host to an array of storage rooms, toilet facilities, recreational areas, a few small individual offices and - of course - elevators and stairwells. The surrounding floorspace was akin to that of a giant exhibition hall. She could not begin to imagine what kind of building the floor belonged to.

The floor would not stop shaking. Another ceiling tile dropped to the ruptured concrete. It rested against a sheared and lethal-looking metal rod. In the gaps of the ceiling tiles she found only perfect darkness, not even a hint of a proper ceiling above them. The outside world on all four sides of the building had been extinguished, leaving the windows just as dark.

Behind them the elevator door finally closed and a buzzing noise soon boomed around the huge floor.

'Structural integrity has been compromised!'

Dawn released Anya and fell to her knees. The girl hopped around until she regained her balance.

'Shit!' said Dawn. 'Sorry, Anya, I'm exhausted. I need more of those tablets.'

'Keep trying the elevator,' said Anya. 'You might be able to bring back the one we had, or maybe one for another hospital. I will try the door to the stairs.'

'You can barely walk, Anya.'

'I can hop. You can barely stand.'

'I just need a minute.'

But Anya had already reached the stairwell door to the left of the elevator. She stood by the outer jamb, pulled open the door slightly and peered inside.

'Ruined.'

Dawn crawled to the elevator, reached up and held in the call button. Half an elevator car emerged from behind the door. The whole unit had been sheared at a shallow angle. Sparks flew from a tangled array of exposed wires and electrics.

'Same here.'

Anya tugged at the door handle but found it significantly harder to move. After managing little more than an inch she let the door slam shut.

'I think there is no air out there.'

By way of cruel sympathy the elevator opened also onto nothing, only here a black void like the one she had found back at the Atrium. If only she could find the place now. She'd have chanced her arm dropping down to the twelfth floor and catching the handrail if it meant a way out. In fact, anything that led out onto a ledge would do the trick, assuming they could break the windows.

A cold discomforting sensation oozed down the length of her body as she continued to look into the empty beyond; a chill she felt certain had not come from without. She collapsed back onto the floor and gasped.

There, holding the elevator door in place, she found four long, bony fingers.

[Daaaawwwww-nnnnyyyy...]

'Warning! Warning!'

A sudden scream pierced through the klaxons and instantly snapped Dawn free from her daymare.

She found a Soviet soldier holding open the stairwell door. It was the same soldier who had shacked up with Milos and Farkas, one she remembered as Eyepatch, only here the man had twenty-twenty vision and a full complement of arms. He looked like he had just stepped in from a battleground. Ahead of him Anya had fallen onto her backside. The girl was shuffling away to get as many inches as possible between herself and Eyepatch's two comrades.

*****

To Dawn's surprise the soldiers were trying to placate the girl, telling her not to panic, but Anya was having none of it. She brandished her scalpel and waved it menacingly in their direction.

One of the soldiers flapped his hand at her, quite unthreatened, shouldered his rifle and left her to it. He looked around the floor, quite taken by its size. He clocked Dawn but ignored her, preferring instead to continue his reconnaissance.

Eyepatch remained by the door, still holding it open, his rifle also shouldered. The soldier nearest Anya held his rifle in one hand, loose, but keeping his finger near the trigger.

All three rifles sported long bayonet attachments.

Dawn kept a wary eye on the roaming Soviet soldier as he continued to survey the vast office floor. He seemed unfazed by the constant rumble beneath his feet. He batted aside a ceiling tile that dropped on his shoulder.

'Yuri!' bellowed Eyepatch. He gestured with open palms, as if asking whether everything was in order.

Yuri shrugged his shoulders nonchalantly and raised his thumb, as if saying "I guess so".

'Structural integrity has been compromised!'

Eyepatch released the stairwell door, leaving it to close on its own accord. He pulled his comrade away from Anya and gestured towards Yuri.

'Anya!' said Dawn, hoping she could hear over the alarms. 'I think they're looking for an exit too.'

Anya shook her head from side to side. Her face darkened.

Absolutely not, it seemed.

'But, Anya . . .' said Dawn, but saw she was wasting her time. She was about to check on the Soviet soldiers when she noticed the stairwell door had not fully closed. The far edge still jutted out a couple of inches onto the floor, as if a bit of rubble had gotten caught in the way.

She spotted the four bony fingers around the side of the door, long enough to touch the metal handle. She blinked and they were gone.

'Oh, God. Oh, God, no.'

The stairwell door opened and out stepped Clive. His stark eyes seemed incapable of blinking. They took in Anya and then the soldiers ahead of him. His lips hardened somewhere between an angry snarl and a maniacal grin. Drying blood clung to the bristles of his five o'clock shadow. More of the stuff had run down his neck from a head wound. He wore a long, black overcoat that swirled around his calves, and, over his shoulder, there hung the same holdall he'd carried on the morning he snapped.

The man looked like he hadn't aged a second since he chased Dawn and Joe into the maze. In each hand he held a submachine gun. He held them out level to his eye-line. Still refusing to blink, he squeezed hard on the triggers.

CHAPTER THIRTY-FOUR

Clive downed the two soldiers ahead of him with short rapid bursts of gunfire, scoring direct hits across the shoulders and blowing holes through the front of their skulls. They were dead before they hit the ground.

They collapsed a short distance ahead of Dawn. Eyepatch came to rest partly over the lip of a crevasse in the ruptured concrete.

Despite taking hits to the chest the third soldier, Yuri, managed to pull the rifle from his shoulder, but was quickly felled by a shot to the head and another that took away the side of his neck. His lifeless body slumped to the floor, his juices spewing onto the rubble-strewn concrete in diminishing spurts.

The body shook.

Everything shook. Light fittings came loose from the ceiling and dangled in the air. Tiles rained down onto the corrupted concrete and refused to settle. Bullet casings bounced around like jumping beans. Yuri's rifle rattled in a collapsed pocket of the floor. Eyepatch's body jiggled from side to side, then slid into the abyss and was gone.

Dawn looked to the skies and found little there save for a metal grid beneath a black canvas of night and dancing strip lights.

'*Structural integrity has been compromised!*'

Clive crouched onto one knee. He planted his right hand onto the floor for balance. He kept the gun close by on the ground. He dragged his eyes away from his handiwork, then glanced left towards the elevator where he finally discovered who lay there.

'There you are!' he said, and grinned. 'I've been looking all over for you.'

Dawn didn't answer him, preferring instead to stare daggers into his eyes. Clive placed his other gun on the ground. He ran his left hand over the back of his head and examined the blood that clung to his fingers.

'Where's that shit-for-brains, Joe, eh?' he said. 'I've got a bone to pick with him.'

Dawn looked to Anya. Clive followed her eyes.

'I don't think that's him,' he said. 'Her tits aren't big enough.'

He wiped his hand against the leg of his jeans, then picked up the submachine gun and looked out into the buckled floor.

'Joe!' he yelled over the sirens. 'Where are you, you fucking turd?'

'He's dead!' screamed Dawn in return.

The floor jumped suddenly, casting a few more ceiling tiles into the widening ravines. Part of the ceiling collapsed in the distance. The windows shattered in unison across the front of the floor. A bone-shaking screech tore through the alarms, the sound of gigantic cemetery gates opening.

'Warning! Warning!'

'Dead? How can he be dead already? What happened? Did the fat fucker fall down a flight of stairs or something?'

Dawn held back. There was no way on Earth she would give Clive the pleasure of knowing what he had done. Or would do.

Whatever.

She glanced again to Anya.

The girl was creeping towards Clive on his blind side. Another five yards and she would reach him. She dragged herself along the concrete floor with one hand and held her scalpel in the other. She left behind a trail of blood from the soaking wet bandage wrapped around her leg.

'It doesn't matter what happened,' said Dawn. She stared unblinkingly into Clive's eyes, desperate to hold his attention. 'This place is fucked. We're all going to die any minute, anyway.'

'Oh, don't you worry,' said Clive. He took a submachine gun and pressed the barrel into his temple. He flinched, then savoured the burn of hot metal against his skin. 'I'm very prepared for that.'

'Then do it!' yelled Dawn. 'Fucking do it, I double triple fucking dare you. Do it, blow your brains out and do us all a favour.'

Clive drew the gun from his head and aimed for Dawn's torso, his left arm outstretched.

In the corner of Dawn's eye she found Anya closing in on Clive. Only two or three yards remained. The girl was readying her scalpel.

'Yeah, I'll do it. I'll get round to it,' said Clive. He licked the corner of his mouth. 'But not before I've had my fun. You see, you, my dear little cunt, fucked me over big time. Thanks to your little pussy play there's fuck all left for me out there now 'cept a SWAT team. Fuck that. If I'm going to die then I'm going out on my own terms, but not before I've gotten what I'm owed.' He licked the corner of his mouth again and smiled as the warnings sounded again.

'Structural integrity has been compromised!'

'Yeah. I'll have your bitch friend hot for me by the time I'm through with you.' As he spoke he waved the gun over to where Anya once lay.

Shit! Don't look! Don't look!

He then renewed his aim on Dawn, slowly and very deliberately.

'Now take off those fucking panties.'

The floor jolted again, much harder this time. The violence brought down more of the ceiling mesh and flung loose debris high into the air. A momentary sense of weightlessness possessed Dawn, as if the events before her were unfolding in slow motion, leaving her little more than a floating spectator.

She watched, spellbound, as Anya perfectly timed the shockwave's momentum to launch herself towards Clive. The girl reached up a left hand towards his neck.

Yes!

Anya took hold of Clive's collar and dragged herself up the back of his overcoat, her scalpel hand on its way for the kill.

Yes! Do it, Anya!

Dawn followed the trajectory of the scalpel as it headed towards Clive's throat. It seemed to take forever.

Get him! Please!

But then everything started to fall again. Clive released his gun, then twisted himself around, forcing Anya to release her grip.

No!

He knocked away Anya's wrist with his left arm, the sleeve of his overcoat absorbing the bite of her scalpel.

No no no no!
He grabbed hold of Anya's throat with his right hand and managed to get a knee up into the girl's belly before his shoulders hit the concrete floor.
Oh my God, no!
Anya collapsed over his knee. She instinctively thrust her free hand onto Clive's chest to help soften the crush on her belly, but the look on her face spoke volumes for what she feared.
Then Clive pushed up hard into Anya and threw the girl overhead as if she was little more than a limp ragdoll.
NO! PLEASE GOD NO!
Dawn could only watch, mesmerised, horrified, sickened, as the girl was impaled, inch by agonising inch, onto a razor-sharp metal rod jutting from the ruptured concrete floor.
'*ANYA! NO!*'
The girl lay upside down against the raised slab, her rump and bony legs bent over the ragged lip of concrete. Her hands grabbed at the javelin of rusty metal that protruded a few inches from her punctured tummy. Her face was an upended portrait of unspeakable pain. She raised her head, saw her worst fears confirmed and then let loose a gut-wrenching shriek that tore Dawn's heart to pieces.
Dawn sagged to the floor. The air escaped her in one long breath that developed into a deep groan. She lost the will to speak, to react, even to feel. Her head was numb. She felt her insides being slowly pulled out from her. The only thing she could focus on was the bloody tip of the metal spike. Anywhere else and she feared her mind would finally collapse in on itself.
And then the gravity of it all slammed into her. She placed her hands over her mouth, took a huge breath and screamed, screamed at Anya, Clive, the whole fucking world.
Anya gave up struggling to free herself. The girl knew she was dying. Her life ran freely down the raised lump of concrete and pooled in a quaking puddle beneath her. The front of her heavily-stained blouse was wet with fresh blood. It pooled in the deep hollows of her neck and ran down the sides of her face. She grabbed at her belly as if she could still somehow save the life of the child inside her. The girl's anguished cries and agonised shrieks soared above the sound of alarms.

'No! You fucking... you...' Dawn burst into angry tears as she struggled to get to her feet, then stumbled. 'You motherfucker! She's pregnant!'

Clive retrieved his guns, then stood over Anya. He rode the shockwaves of the floor with the deftness of an old sailor. He looked down to the girl who had so very nearly killed him. His face bore the same dispassionate mask Dawn had seen Anya wear, a look that never failed to unsettle. He held the gun out from his right hand, a short distance from Anya's dying body, and aimed the barrel into the girl's face.

He kept the gun there long enough for the grief-ridden girl to see exactly what he was about to do.

He then squeezed the trigger repeatedly until he had emptied the rest of the magazine into her face, into her chest, into her belly, and into every other part of her twitching, blood-soaked body.

He turned to face Dawn, who staggered across the uneven, quaking floor towards him.

'No she isn't,' said Clive. He let the gun swing empty by his side and looked around for his holdall.

'You fucking piece of shit!' screamed Dawn. She tottered after him as he walked away towards his bag. 'Come back here!'

The ruined concrete floor suddenly dropped away as if the Devil had come to drag everything to Hell. For a brief moment everything around her floated as if suspended in water. Tiles slowly drifted upwards. Anya's lifeless arms and legs were drawn to the skies as if played by a puppeteer. Dawn felt the cross of a metallic frame press into her back, then all the strip lights around her shorted and everything came crashing back down.

In the absolute dark there was a faint distant clamour of klaxons. The latest upheaval had succeeded in destroying the alarms of the floor. There were sounds all around of rubble, tiles and bodies settling into place.

The world shook once more. The far reaches of the empty office burst into a thick wall of sparks, behind which lay huge shimmering edges of ripped metal. With a deafening screech the far wall was swiftly torn in its entirety from the rest of the floor. The loose wall then lurched to the right, revealing the edge of another totally different floor in its wake.

The air pressure dropped along with the temperature. A rush of wind ran throughout the office space. The curtain of night that once draped over the ceiling and windows quickly dissolved in random swirling patches, leaving nothing behind other than an awesome sight that pinned Dawn to the floor.

Through the scant remains of the ceiling and walls she looked out onto the immense interior of a hollow metal planet, its inner black atmosphere rapidly dissolving, revealing deep fissures and enormous fault lines across the entire structure. There were ridges all across the surface, a relief of enormous elongated rectangles, each seemingly the edge of a floor. The size of the globe suggested hundreds of thousands of them, possibly millions. Large red lights poked out from each sliver as far as the eye could see. They swirled round and round, becoming twinkling grids of red stars in the far, far beyond.

Something huge moved in the distance. She followed the path of a prominent fissure as it grew and divided, thus loosening a vast section of the globe that easily comprised a thousand floors. She looked up and saw the sky crumbling, slowly falling in from almost every angle.

Where the hell am I?

She stood up on quivering legs and tried to take in more of her surroundings.

Enormous turbine-like cylinders hung from the interior at regular intervals, each trailing a single thick tendril that crackled with bright blue energy. The tendrils were segmented, as thick as ferry boats and as long as minor countries. They crackled and fizzed with the kind of energy that could kick-start dying suns. The tips of the tendrils turned fuzzy and red as they stroked the edges of something Dawn could scarcely comprehend.

At the hollow metal planet's core there was a swirling dark distortion in reality. It seemed like some mighty being had pinched the fabric of the universe and had twisted it around innumerable times.

But the strange beauty of the distortion did little to disguise the enormous damage it was inflicting across the structure. Huge sections of floors, long-weakened by irresolvable paradoxes, had come adrift and now floated gently towards the core. Their turbines exploded in showers of short-lived sparks. Their tendrils shone white with heat and fiery energy, which turned increasingly red as they were inexorably drawn into the void.

THE FLOORS

The side wall, freshly torn from the rest of the floor, hung in jagged sparking tatters. It formed part of a crumbling skyscraper-sized wedge of shredded floors that loomed so high as to follow the curvature of the interior. This vast wedge of floors now also crept towards the centre of the orb, reeled in by its tendrils. Huge fragments of metal, chunks of concrete - even people - spun slowly out from its open sides. With the atmosphere diminishing, the fervour of its whale-like groans lessened as the section of floors continued along its path.

The turbines continued to explode around her like an immense silent fireworks display. Whether they were too far away to be heard or whether she was going deaf again, she had no idea. She could feel the air pressure gradually drawing out her eardrums, but for a wondrous, precious second she didn't care. The slow graceful dance of gigantic metal hulks, some tinged with red, each coursing with electricity and floating into the swirling distortion, was by far and away the most beautiful thing she had ever seen.

For a blissful moment Dawn forgot who she was, where she came from, who she loved, and everything and anything she had ever done, said, or wished for.

She didn't see the butt of the gun until it was much, much too late.

CHAPTER THIRTY-FIVE

When Dawn came to she found a massive spinnaker-shaped chunk of conjoined floors rotating slowly some distance above her. It disgorged itself of assorted detritus from the sheared half-floors along its edges. Drifting amidst the spinning rubble were double beds and wardrobes, office desks and photocopiers, refrigerators and lifeless bodies. As she focussed her blurry eyes on the frozen cadavers they disappeared, each and every one, simultaneously, as if they had never existed. From so far away Dawn only had their clothing to judge by, but a clutch of gowned women convinced her they were all from Anya's old commune, like they had never disbanded.

Her right cheek pulsed with heat and pain. It felt as if someone had sliced her face down to the bone and left a warm, pulsating bag of blood hanging from the wound. She could feel her right eye closing up.

Icy winds continued to blow through the decapitated office floor. Freezing cold squalls pushed through her hair and numbed her scalp. Chilly tongues of air licked the goose-pimpled flesh of her neck and that of her chest. She knew then that her blouse had been torn open and that Clive was all over her.

Waves of hurt, of anger and of shame swept over her. How could she have let Clive down her so easily? Her skin crawled as he pawed and grabbed at her. She raged inside at how weak she had become and wished death on the fiend molesting her. She looked to the heavens again and willed a large chunk of debris to smash down on top of them, but none would come. Even the drifting spinnaker of floors favoured the central distortion over regular gravity.

She felt a sharp pain at her breast and jolted against the concrete. It took her longer to land back on the floor than she'd anticipated.

'Yeah,' said Clive, looking up from her chest and meeting her eyes. 'I thought that would wake you up.'

She raised her hands and clawed at his face, but the man batted her away as if she was only a child. He then pushed his thumb down hard onto Dawn's swelling cheek. Brilliant white light flashed across her eyes. The searing pain that exploded from the wound damn near stopped her heart. She shrieked and reached out blindly for Clive's holsters.

'You're not going to find anything there,' said Clive. 'Now fucking keep still for me!'

He smashed a fist into Dawn's jaw. Her head snapped to the left and she felt one of her back teeth loosen. Through the stars that sparked and twinkled in her vision she found that Anya was no longer impaled on the metal spike. No blood either. She had disappeared without leaving a trace.

An aftershock ripped through the floor and tore a deep canyon into the concrete nearby. Ribs of metal curled up from the wound and steam hissed out from the gaps.

Beyond the floor a corona of red-tinged energy had formed around the swirling distortion. Vast complex forks of electricity crackled over a thousand tendrils and lit the insides of the disintegrating structure from every angle. There was nothing but darkness visible through the vast gaps in the globe.

Dawn felt something warm and hard stroke against the inside of her thigh and the sensation immediately sent electric eels swimming across her shredded nerves. She bucked and thrashed to get away from Clive but the man punched her hard in the gut, winding her. She tried to cover herself as he fought to position himself between her legs. She tried desperately to suck down lungfuls of air from the rushing winds that ran over the floor and out into the void.

Clive grabbed her by the hips and roughly drew her body closer to him. She felt the thick fabric of her skirt slip up her thighs and collect above her groin.

'Oh, God, Mike,' she gasped. She ran her thumb over her engagement ring. 'I'm so sorry.'

'Mike?' said Clive. He leaned over slightly to meet her eyes. 'Old fuckerknuckles over there is the least of your worries.'

He gestured towards his open holdall, and Mike's head that lay inside.

Dawn screamed at the sight of her dead lover, her once future husband. His head had been taken with several swipes of a large heavy hunting knife, a weapon she had once possessed.

Mike's lifeless face looked dispassionately onto the scene of her rape. The right side of his face had been punctured by gunfire. His tongue lolled from the side of his gaping mouth. Vertical streaks of dark, coagulated blood clung to his beautiful skin. Like warpaint.

'I got him pretty good, didn't I?' said Clive. 'He was stood by one of the elevators when I came calling. You should have seen the look on Gil's face when those doors opened.'

For a second Clive looked genuinely pleased. He reached down to his groin and adjusted himself. He returned his attentions to Dawn when she began to struggle again. He took a firm grasp of her knees and drew her legs apart.

'I like to keep my promises, bitch,' he said, and grinned from ear to ear. 'I always said I'd let him watch you bleed out.'

Dawn sobbed helplessly as Clive reached away behind him and produced a blood-stained razor-sharp parang. He leaned closer and rested the chopping edge against the taut tendons of her neck.

In doing so Dawn felt the man's erection throb against her crotch. The sick fucker had already removed her underwear.

'No!' she cried, and then coughed and retched and felt the blade cut into her. Warm blood ran down both sides of her neck. All her insides felt like they were trying to escape through her mouth rather than be subjected to Clive's violation.

'Yeah, that's right,' said Clive. He lovingly stroked Dawn's skin with the slick tip of his blade as he adjusted himself against her.

Dawn clenched as hard as she could but knew she was powerless against him.

Clive leaned in a little closer and whispered some final words for her.

'I want to feel you twitching when I come.'

CHAPTER THIRTY-SIX

The end of a long, thin knife burst out from Clive's throat the moment he sat back. He dropped the parang and instinctively made for the blade, slicing open his hands as he fought for purchase. He gagged, choked and then coughed over Dawn's prone body in red, stringy splatters. He lunged forward in a desperate bid to slide himself free, but then his head snapped back and a harsh force from behind drove him hard into the ground.

Behind the man there stood a furious blonde girl with a Soviet rifle in her hands.

'Anya?' said Dawn, her words stolen by the strengthening wind.

She couldn't believe it. The girl was barely recognisable from the gaunt spindly thing of her most recent days. Only her shoulder-length blonde hair and unusual eyes gave her away. She stood over Dawn, so much younger now, so vital, with her teeth intact and a fuller, curvier figure.

The girl's eyes glowed like amber coals. She growled through gritted teeth as she drove the bayonet into a slim crack of the ruptured floor, not stopping until the crack bit hard onto the metal. She twisted and wrenched the rifle free and left Clive gurgling, flapping and grabbing at the back of his neck.

An old woman loomed into sight, overhead. She had a face lined with the hardships of two World Wars. She helped Dawn to sit and cover herself. She burbled something with great urgency and pointed to the immense swirling distortion ahead.

Anya knelt beside Dawn and helped her to stand.

'Anya! You're alive!' said Dawn, and hugged the girl.

She looked to Dawn as if she had been embraced by a complete stranger. She nodded, embarrassed almost, and spoke something in her native tongue.

'I know you can understand me,' said Dawn, and she hugged the girl again. 'Thank you.'

When Dawn turned from Anya she could scarcely believe her eyes. Massing onto the floor from the stairwell were around forty men and women of varying ages, each struck dumb by the destruction being wrought all around them.

An old man at the side of the gathering seemed to have difficulty breathing. He pulled his eyes from the spectacle and clutched at his heart. An old woman put a hand over his shoulder, evidently concerned for his welfare.

And then something clicked in Dawn's head. She watched the scene unfold and took a step back in her mind's eye. Memories flooded in from all sides. She struggled to process them all.

The old man is having a heart attack.
He will die soon.
The touchscreen of the master elevator said EVACUATE.
The Magyars were carving a path through the maze.
Their path led to this floor.
Someone had overridden the master elevator.
The Magyars found a trick floor.
Someone once occupied the booth at the end of the T-junction.
It was a trick floor decked with white card, or was it thick paper?
A trick floor containing only a microphone and the laughter of the gods.
A trick floor lying only a few stairwells away.
EVACUATE.
OVERRIDE.
The laughing gods want rid of us.
Laughing gods.
A floor made of paper.
A building made of paper?
A building made of paper!

Dawn grabbed Anya by the shoulders.

'Oh my God!' She shook Anya. Nikola stepped behind the girl, a look of concern written across his face. 'Anya, we need to go back to the trick floor.'

The girl shrugged. She spoke words that Dawn could not understand, gestured all around them and pointed towards the stairwell door.

'Damn it, Anya, this isn't the time to play games!'

Dawn released the girl's shoulders. Her mind was alight with ideas. A plan was forming. She looked around and saw what she needed. She bent down and picked up Clive's parang. She ignored the consternation from those around her. She wiped the blade on Clive's overcoat while the man lay twitching inside it. She stood and let the blade hang by her side.

'Listen to me carefully, Anya,' she said, slowly and firmly. 'I know you speak English, okay? We need to go back to that floor, all of us, now!'

The concrete floor began to shudder again. The sound of tearing metal squawked around them all. The wind strengthened. Gravity continued to seep away. A long strip of concrete fell from the floor, creating a steaming chasm of crackling electricity. Their section of the huge metal planet was tearing away. Soon they too would be spun out into oblivion.

Anya shrugged and finally gave up the pretence.

'Everywhere is falling down. Why would we go back?'

'Because that floor is our way out of here!'

*****

The group rushed back through the doorway and into the heavily fractured stairwell. There was no time to waste. The healthy ran with the frail in their arms. Up ahead, Gregor led the charge with the rest of the freedom fighters. Nikola brought up the rear.

Anya ran slightly ahead of him. She urged the group forward and cast concerned glances over her shoulder.

Nikola held Dawn in a fireman's lift. She could see now why Anya had laid with him. He was a handsome brute with broad shoulders, who instantly reminded her of Mike. Her view of the world bobbed up and down with every step Nikola took.

A deep, ripping noise burst through the doorway and into the stairwell. The fractured concrete beyond collapsed completely. The black door closed on the scene and all was klaxons and blaring alarms once more.

'*Warning! Warning!*'

The rest of the stairwell bounced into view around her. The flights of stairs from it had both collapsed, leaving behind a landing that now crumbled beneath Nikola's feet. The wall to her left exploded as if smashed by a giant fist and then the whole structure fell in on itself with an almighty crunching sound.

But Nikola had made it through the doorway and into a floor of howling winds, distressed walls and a buckled, carpeted floor.

Dawn's ears started to hurt. The air grew thin.

To her left she found an entirely different view of the stormy distortion, one from above that afforded a glimpse of the previous floor, now loosening from the superstructure as part of a massive square-shaped lump.

Nikola suddenly checked his run without warning, then picked up the pace.

To her right, she saw the old man fall to the floor, clutching his chest. She heard a cry of despair over the clamouring alarms. The floor gave way beneath the old man, swallowing him whole, and then collapsed outwardly like a grain of salt in a frothy head of beer. Platelets of concrete crumbled and fell away, the hole widening, rapidly eating into the ground, catching up to Nikola.

They were through into another stairwell. Showers of stone and wood and metal cascaded down one side in an endless recurring loop. The air thinned further. Dawn felt herself floating instead of bobbing against Nikola's back.

There were no walls on either side of the landing. Once more she found an entirely new view of the swirling distortion, this time from below. She felt her eyes being sucked out from their sockets. She looked away and squinted towards to the ground.

At Nikola's feet she found the stairwell had reduced to little more than a perilously thin concrete gangplank.

Her surroundings then darkened and Nikola slowed to a trot. The walls around her were smooth and pale white in the gloom. The man stopped and eased Dawn onto the quaking floor. She watched Gregor close the door behind them.

'Structural integrity has been compromised!'

The alarms continued to ring, dampened slightly by the soft papery texture of the floor, walls and ceilings. Dawn turned and saw the others milling around the floor, feeling against the walls, terror etched across their faces.

They ignored the huge microphone that faced the glowing papery wall ahead. She'd reckoned Anya made that part up.

The laughter of the gods rolled like thunder above the sirens.

THE FLOORS

Anya turned to face her. She held Clive's parang in her right hand.

'Okay,' said the girl. 'We are here. What do we do now?'

The floor lurched to the left and everyone panicked.

Dawn grabbed the hunting knife from Anya and staggered towards the long papery wall ahead of the microphone.

She heard the opposite end of the floor crumple and tear.

With the dregs of her strength she swung the hunting knife into the wall and felt it cut through the thick paper. She dragged the parang across the wall, picking up her pace, scoring the surface in her wake. She then grabbed an edge of the rip and tore it downwards, exposing the outside.

The opposite side of the floor tore away. Large gusts of wind blew in from outside, weakening the paper wall, ripping it along the score marks.

The floor lurched to the right. Everywhere around them sounded alive with the sound of crunching metal looming in.

Dawn turned to Anya, to Nikola, to everyone. She waved a hand to the ripped wall and yelled at the top of her voice.

'*JUMP!*'

CHAPTER THIRTY-SEVEN

The man in the pinstripe suit ran a finger beneath his pink bow tie. He wore a shirt that once cost him a hundred thousand forint, but now clung to his skin, heavy with sweat. He shuffled uncomfortably in his shiny black shoes.

He waited for the men and women ahead of him to settle down, beset as they were with hoots of laughter. His presentation hadn't begun quite as well as he had hoped.

It had been his big opportunity: tendering for a new complex to house the Hungarian Special Service for National Security. He so badly needed to land the deal. All the big contracts had suddenly dried up, leaving his firm perilously close to collapse. But he could see his chance float away on the whoops and sighs of his rivals. They sat nearby, ashamed for him.

His heart sank when he saw a couple of the congregation shake their heads in disbelief at his proposal.

As the last of six architects to present his grand vision, the man was sure his design would curry favour with the movers and shakers seated before him. Compared to the dull clumps and cuboids his rivals had cobbled together, his was surely an innovation to win hearts and minds.

He looked back to a large laser-projection of his design. It was a slide from his presentation that showed a building, dull and cuboid in shape, but with a huge bite eaten away to reveal another smaller structure inside.

A building within a building.

To him the idea was unbridled genius. Only the top brass need ever know its true location. Those on the outside need never know of the building on the inside, and vice versa. How could these people not go for such a brilliant idea?

He looked at the collection of scale models that lay on large, sturdy tables around the perimeter of the capacious room. He wished he could disappear somewhere else entirely. Somewhere where he had no wife and kids to support, no employees to keep on his books, no government authorities to wrap him up in red tape, no taxes to pay...

A sudden commotion interrupted his train of thought. He blinked hard and gawped at the sight of umpteen bodies materialising out of thin air. They each fell with a dull thump onto to the plush carpet and rolled away. The momentum they carried made it look as if they had jumped down from the ceiling.

Ten people. Twenty.

By now most of the audience had twisted around in their seats for a better look as more and more people seemed to spill from the hapless architect's scale model. A removable corner fell onto the table, revealing another structure underneath.

Twenty-five people. Thirty. And still they kept coming.

A young woman then fell out onto the floor, her face badly bruised. Her clothes were torn and covered in bloodstains. She landed on the carpet and sprang to her feet. She raged like a madwoman towards the architect's scale model.

As if to deal him one final humiliating blow the woman smashed her hands and elbows into the paper structure. She screamed what sounded like English obscenities and tore the thing apart with her bare hands. Soon his model lay in pieces, strewn around the room.

With the model duly destroyed the woman fell to her knees. She held her ribs, rocked back and forth and shrieked long and loud, far beyond distraught.

The poor young woman's cries reminded him of his mother when dear old Dada passed on.

*****

The large room was alive with foreign chatter and considerable confusion. Ambulance men and women in high-visibility jackets mingled with the gatecrashers. They tended to the frail and the broken bones they had sustained. Around the perimeter a few police officers stood with the unenviable task of taking details from long-vanished individuals and somehow fashioning their accounts into a coherent report.

The congregation of well-dressed, important-looking people had long since been shepherded from the room by their security detail. The seats they once occupied stood largely empty and in some disarray near the lectern and screen. Nearest the front of these and towards the middle sat Dawn, wrapped in a foil blanket. She stared blankly at the white widescreen rectangle ahead. She coughed and shivered and gently wept to herself. She had done little else but cry since escaping the nightmarish maze.

Where the hell am I?

The gabble behind her suggested everybody spoke the same language, which in turn suggested somewhere in Hungary. She glanced to a nearby chair and saw a newspaper resting on the padded seat, but could not muster the strength to lean over and fetch it.

Who cares where I am? I escaped! I'm alive and...

She felt Clive's touch on her skin and shuddered. She remembered the terrible sight of Mike's severed head in Clive's holdall. She gasped, then buried her face into her hands and sobbed loudly. The brilliant brawny lug she was due to marry had been horribly murdered and paraded before her like a trophy.

Fucking Clive.

She looked up to the glowing screen beyond the lectern, and then, above that, a large digital display of the time.

10:45am.

She felt a tapping on her shoulder and found a policewoman offering her a mug of steaming soup. The officer's eyes were dark brown and hard-edged, but tinged with pity. Perhaps it was the look she used for victims of domestic violence.

Dawn took the mug and nodded her thanks. Its volcanic heat suggested the soup had been nuked in a microwave oven somewhere. She swapped the handle from one hand to the other.

Her stomach hurt like hell, but not enough to stop it from growling. She took it to be a good sign. She blew on the steaming broth and found herself staring once more into the shimmering white rectangle behind the lectern.

She felt her gaze being drawn deeper inside the screen until four long, bony fingers emerged from the corner. The fingers were bent as if resting against the other side of the screen. The sight turned Dawn's blood to iced water.

[Daaaaawwwwwnnnnnyyyy...]
Not you. Not now.
'Leave me alone. Please!'
Why are you still here? Why are you still tormenting me?

The shadows of the bony fingers flinched menacingly, sending a cold spear into her heart.

She felt a hand slide onto her shoulder and leapt from the chair. She sent the scalding mug of soup flying into the air and splashing against the lectern. The mug clattered noisily on the floor and settled, unbroken, in the corner of the room.

'Sorry!' whispered Anya. 'I did not mean to startle you.'

Dawn gasped for breath and looked the girl in the eyes. She found herself caught between yelling at the girl, bursting into fresh tears and, oddly, laughing.

The policewoman returned to investigate. The girl apologised and explained what had happened. The woman then went away, presumably to find someone to help clear up the mess. The girl turned to face Dawn. She leaned in as if sharing a conspiracy.

'Sorry,' she said. 'I just wanted to say thank you.'

'That's okay,' said Dawn. 'I never really liked Mulligatawny.'

Dawn's words trailed off. She drank in the scene playing out in the main body of the room. Both the survivors of the maze and the men and women of the emergency services were happy. Even those that had sustained injuries had smiles on their faces. They each looked as if they had just stepped from a long escalator ride into Heaven. Hugs were exchanged for the umpteenth time, while others swapped and recounted stories. The air buzzed with their voices.

And in the oblong glass of the door beyond them all Dawn could see were four bony fingers slide away from view.

[Daaaaawwwwwnnnnnyyyy...]

She looked away and cursed her addled mind. She glanced around for something, anything that could spare her another round of self-torment. She decided to help clean up the mess she had made. She leaned over and grabbed the newspaper, which flopped open in her hand. She caught sight of the date in the banner.

2013. Szeptember 13. Péntek.
The day Clive went nuts.

Dawn looked up at the digital clock. It suddenly felt as if someone had punched a nitro button in the front of her brain.

10:51am.
The shooting started shortly after ten.
It's as if I've never been away.
[Daaaaawwwwwnnnnnyyyy...]
Never been away.
10:52am.
'Anya, where the hell am I?'
'The policemen say we are in Budapest.'
10:52am.
In Hungary.
Isn't Hungary an hour ahead of us?
'Oh my God!'

Dawn threw aside the foil blanket and frantically scanned the room.

'Phone,' she said, then louder, to Anya: 'I need a telephone! Quickly!'

'What has happened?'

'I don't have time! I need a phone!'

She ran to the first police officer she could find and waggled her thumb and little finger to her head, praying for the man to understand her.

'Telephone! Please!' she cried. She then raced to an ambulance man nearby. 'I need to use someone's phone, it's an emergency! Please, somebody help me!'

*****

József slowly approached the badly beaten young woman who sat in the corridor ahead. She was crying into his mobile phone. She struggled to keep her voice down and yet it echoed along the bare walls and shiny floors regardless. Her heavily bloodstained clothes drew looks of curiosity and revulsion from those that walked by.

The young woman had called herself Dawn. He liked the way the word sounded when he whispered it. *Dawn.*

The young woman seemed awfully excited about something. The way she had suddenly gone from near-catatonia to outright hysteria suggested she was close to madness.

He winced as her voice became increasingly loud in the confines of the corridor.

It sounded like she was phoning someone called "Mike". She was pleading with him for something.

He knew better than to interfere, but József sincerely hoped that this Mike hadn't been responsible for the state she was in.

The woman called Dawn looked up and met his eyes.

He smiled and looked away, cursing himself for intruding. He turned on his heels and returned along the corridor.

As he approached the room from whence they came, he heard sounds of laughter ebb through the door. He felt himself smile again. He nodded with satisfaction. It had been a good morning, at least as good as could be expected in the life of a paramedic.

A small clattering noise from somewhere behind him took József from his train of happy thoughts. He turned in time to see a small lump of plastic settle into the hard seat of the chair. It looked familiar.

He stepped towards the chair and was shocked to find his mobile phone resting there face-down.

How on earth has it gotten there?

He found a single fine crack spanning one corner of the touchscreen to the other, which put a dampener on his good morning. He pushed the power button. The phone worked, but it was clear he was going to have to go to the insurance firm for a new one.

He returned the phone to his jacket pocket and wondered how he came to be standing in the corridor.

ACKNOWLEDGEMENTS

This book would never have been written were it not for the tireless support and infinite patience of one's long-suffering better half – the rather splendid and mysterious *She* from the blog – who has somehow endured near enough every day of my all-consuming obsession in getting this story out of my head and onto paper. Thanks, duckie. Sorry it took so long!

My sincere thanks also go to those kind souls who donated their valuable time in reading an early version of *The Floors*, and for the invaluable help they gave me in getting my story ship-shape for the final draft. Squire Boone, Michael Fowler, Robert Krone, Sabrina Morgan and Tom Sanders, I salute you all and your unquenchable thirst for fantastic fiction.

I would also like to thank John Jarrold for putting the story through its paces with a thorough edit, despite *The Floors* being not at all to his taste! Seriously, folks, it felt like I'd hired The A-Team. I still look at the comments he made all throughout my second draft like it's a cheat sheet for future projects.

Thanks also go out to those who lent their support and encouragement for *The Floors* during NaNoWriMo 2012 and beyond. Thanks Kris, Mel, Lena, Leslie and Clive (who in no way, shape or form resembles or represents the Clive you find in this book.) (Sorry, Clive!) I hope to write with you again later this year.

Finally, I would like to thank you – yes you – for taking a chance on an unknown quantity. I hope you found *The Floors* an entertaining read: blood, guts, flies and all. If you borrowed this book from a friend then hello, and good on you! Give your friend a hundred karma points because word-of-mouth recommendations are a godsend for <u>any</u> writer. If you've nicked *The Floors* from the internet, however, then boo-hiss. A review on Goodreads, Amazon or Smashwords in return would be lovely. Unless you thought the story sucked, of course. ;-)

All righty then, onto the next one!

Lucian Poll
September 2013

ABOUT THE AUTHOR

Lucian Poll can be found grumping around Norwich, England, often on weekdays between the hours of 5:30pm and 9am. He will be attending the 2013 World Fantasy Convention in Brighton. If that goes swimmingly then you may well find him at others.

If, in the meantime, you'd like to read more of his stuff then be sure to dip into his assorted witterings every once in a while.

Website: http://lucianpoll.com
Twitter: @LucianPoll
Facebook: http://en-gb.facebook.com/lucian.poll

Lucian Poll will return!